Union Public L
1980 Morris A
Union, N.J. 07
P9-EFI-811

BY TERRY McMILLAN

Mama

Waiting to Exhale

A Day Late and a Dollar Short

How Stella Got Her Groove Back

The Interruption of Everything

Getting to Happy

Disappearing Acts

Who Asked You?

I Almost Forgot About You

It's Not All Downhill From Here

It's Not All Downhill From Here

BALLANTINE BOOKS
NEW YORK

It's Not All Downhill From Here

A NOVEL

Terry McMillan

Union Public Library
1980 Morris Avenue
Union, N.J. 07083

It's Not All Downhill From Here is a work of fiction. Names, characters, places, and incidents are the products of the author's imagination or are used fictitiously. Any resemblance to actual events, locales, or persons, living or dead, is entirely coincidental.

Copyright © 2020 by Terry McMillan

All rights reserved.

Published in the United States by Ballantine Books, an imprint of Random House, a division of Penguin Random House LLC, New York.

BALLANTINE and the HOUSE colophon are registered trademarks of Penguin Random House LLC.

LIBRARY OF CONGRESS CATALOGING-IN-PUBLICATION DATA
Names: McMillan, Terry, author.
Title: It's not all downhill from here: a novel / Terry McMillan.
Description: New York: Ballantine Books, [2020]
Identifiers: LCCN 2019038586 (print) | LCCN 2019038587 (ebook) |
ISBN 9781984823748 (hardcover: acid-free paper) |
ISBN 9781984823762 (ebook)
Classification: LCC PS3563.C3868 I87 2020 (print) |
LCC PS3563.C3868 (ebook) | DDC 813/.54—dc23
LC record available at https://lccn.loc.gov/2019038586
LC ebook record available at https://lccn.loc.gov/2019038587

Printed in the United States of America on acid-free paper

randomhousebooks.com

2 4 6 8 9 7 5 3 1

First Edition

Book design by Andrea Lau

For my mama, again and again

and

In memory of my sister, Rosalyn McMillan

"You cannot go back and change the beginning,
but you can start where you are and change the ending."

It's Not All Downhill From Here

Chapter 1

I don't want another surprise party.

Which is just one reason why a few weeks ago, when my husband, Carl, called while I was walking our dog, B. B. King, to the dog park and asked what I wanted to do for my birthday this year, I politely said, "Baby, let's try to figure out how to get our second wind."

At first Carl high-pitch chuckled like he was a soprano or something, then he said, "Will we need a boat?"

I chuckled right back, even though I was serious as a heart attack.

"Don't you worry, Miss Lo. I've got you covered," he said as he hung up.

I knew he didn't really get my drift. What I meant was, since we both had more days behind us than we have ahead of us, how about we try to figure out what more we can do to pump up the volume? It's not that our life is boring. Well, maybe it is, a little. But even though we don't do very many things that generate excitement, I still love him more than my Twizzlers! Carl is a retired contractor who refuses to retire, and after thirty years of all work and no play selling hair and beauty products in two stores too many, I don't exactly qualify as a thrill a minute either.

I released B. B. King's leash inside the dog park, but he just stood there shivering, as if he were waiting to be invited to participate in some activity that didn't require him to run or jump. In human years, he and I will soon be the same age: sixty-eight. His whiskers and eyebrows are peppered with gray, but unlike me, B.B. doesn't dye his hair. He is our third German shepherd and I don't want to think about how long it will be until he doesn't want to, or can't, hop in the back seat of my Volvo station wagon, which I will drive until, like me, it stops running.

I sat on the green metal bench and watched him sniff a friendly chocolate poodle. I realized I was hoping and praying I wasn't going to have to sit through yet another lackluster party where nobody even thinks about dancing until they hear a song you have to be damn near seventy to remember, which I suppose now includes me. And that's *if* you call doing the cha-cha-cha in flats or espadrilles or two-inch wedges with rubber soles to a beat they all hear differently, dancing. I don't. I watch music videos on YouTube. I find myself rocking my future-size-twelve hips, swinging and swaying my shoulders and popping my fingers to the likes of "Single Ladies" or "Uptown Funk" by that little cutie Bruno Mars until I have to wipe my forehead. *I* have not forgotten how to dance. In fact, sometimes, Carl will sit in his leather recliner, lean way back, and just watch me swirl around in my three-inch heels, which I wear to work every day because I like to appear glamorous. In those moments I feel pretty and sexy and forty. Carl just nods his head like he's agreeing and pops his fingers until the smile on his luscious lips begins to disappear. Then he might hold up his index finger, suggesting that I *give him a minute but don't stop dancing,* slowly push himself up to a standing position, and limp down the hallway to take one of his little blue pills.

Oh, hell. Here I go again. Meandering. I'm just going to have to stop apologizing for it, because from what I've learned reading my AARP newsletter, this is only the beginning. Though, truth be told, forgetting what I was talking about and going off on tangents isn't completely new to me. Back in my twenties, I smoked a lot of reefer with my friends. We'd all sit in a circle on the floor on giant pillows and have deep conversations about the purpose of life or something having to do with God or how we were going to change the world, but then we'd all stop talking because we were suddenly mesmerized by the lava lamp. Then somebody would realize they were one step away from freaking out and would jump to a standing position in order to snap out of it, and then they'd ask: "What the fuck were we just talking about again?" And since not one of us had a clue, we'd just start passing the joint until the next philosophical inquiry overtook our minds.

Thank God I got tired of thinking about things that didn't matter and realized I liked the way I felt when I wasn't under the influence of anything. And when I didn't like how I felt, it was a hell of a lot easier to figure out how to deal with it when my head was clear.

Anyway, now I'm a certified senior citizen, and my mind has earned the right to go wherever it wants, so I decided that when I can't remember something, it must not have been that important anyway. But sometimes, when I do remember, it feels like an accomplishment.

Like right now, I'm remembering last year's dull party. My feelings were hurt because both my twin sister, Odessa, and my one and only daughter, Jalecia, had been no-shows. Now, Odessa is a bitch and proves it on a weekly basis. Like I said, she's my twin. But there are two things about us that make us special. First of all, we were born in different years. I'm December 31 and she's January 1. We are also technically only half sisters, even though we're fraternal twins. Apparently Ma was a hot number back in the day and slept with two different fellas only days apart. This probably explains why we are nothing alike and why we're not as chummy as most twins. Ma didn't bother to tell us this until we were in junior high, but by then we weren't interested in who our daddies were.

It's a fact that Odessa has been jealous of me for years. Jealous I was crowned the first black homecoming queen at our predominantly white high school fifty years ago, even though I wasn't pretty then and I'm not pretty now. Jealous I know how to make myself appear to be more attractive than I am, and occasionally still get honked at. Jealous of my being a successful entrepreneur. She has never once come into my Pasadena store. Never once given me a compliment, no matter how nice I might look. I didn't know our lives were a contest. I love her, but in all honesty, I don't really like her, and if she wasn't my sister I probably wouldn't have anything to do with her.

Right before Odessa took early retirement at fifty from her job as a policewoman for the City of Pasadena, her husband left her for a forty-three-year-old ex–Lakers cheerleader who could still do the splits. Odessa wiped him out and bought a house that seemed purposely much bigger than mine up in the hills of Altadena. Then she started going to church like some people go to AA. Her personality changed after the Holy Ghost struck her, but she doesn't seem to see how unhappy she still is or acknowledge that maybe God intentionally leaves some gaps for us to fill in. She started acting like she would get electrocuted from a mere whiff of alcohol. Before she retired, she lived in bars and just sat around waiting to arrest somebody, but now she won't go inside any establishment where liquor is poured.

My daughter, on the other hand, has the opposite relationship to alcohol. She's had an on-again, off-again love affair with alcohol and lately with some of those designer pain pills for people who aren't in pain. I fired her from my store for stealing from me. Me, her own mother, who gave her a job because she hasn't figured out what to do with her life after forty years. *That* is apparently my fault because I had a job and then a business and then a divorce, so her failure to launch is payback for my not having been present enough or generous enough. But I couldn't be everywhere at once, and I'm tired of being punished for it. She didn't come to my party and hasn't spoken to me in more than a year.

All I can say is thank God for sons, or I should say son, since I only have one. Jackson is Jalecia's younger brother and the product of my second marriage. He wasn't at my party last year either, but he had a good reason. He lives in Tokyo with his wife, Aiko, who had just given birth to premature twin daughters. They still needed a few more months to grow and they needed their daddy there.

My BFFs were there, though. Lucky. Sadie. Korynthia. Even Poochie made the trip from Vegas. I grew up with all of them. Occasionally we all get on one another's nerves. Sometimes to the point that our friendships get temporarily annulled. But we always come running back because we have loved one another longer than some of us have loved the men in our lives.

This morning, right after I felt Carl kissing me on the forehead—and he knew I was awake even though my eyes were closed—he said, "So, we're good then, cutie?"

I smiled, looked up at him, then tugged at the metal button on his coverall pocket and said, "I suppose I'm just going to have to trust you, mister."

"Good. Just wait until you see how much fun you're going to have for finally taking a direct order from your husband!"

I gave him an aww-shucks-but-get-out-of-here-before-I-change-my-mind shove. He stood inside the doorway. His silver Afro almost touched the top of the frame and those broad shoulders reminded me that he was once a wide receiver. I wish I had known him when he was still catching footballs. But all things considered, he caught me at the right time—when my kids were well on their way to being grown and gone. Carl came into the shop one day to buy some horsetail shampoo for himself, and I laughed and he laughed and he told me I smelled like ginger. I couldn't help but notice there was no gold band on his left finger. He told me he owned a construction company and handed me his black business card with smooth white letters and said if I ever needed any improvements I should feel free to call him. And I did. But it was me who got renovated.

"Hold on," he said. "What did you want for your birthday again?"

I let out a long sigh. "Some skinny jeans!"

"You got it, girlie! Now stay put. And I'll see you when I see you." He limped out the door backward.

Carl had pleaded with me to take the weekend off, which was why I'd given in and closed the Pasadena store by putting a sign on the door that said: WATER DAMAGE: WILL REOPEN MONDAY, because you have to have a legitimate-sounding reason to close a beauty supply store. And since I can't really trust the two young ladies who work for me (their days are numbered), I paid them for the missed shifts and told them I was having some plumbing work done. They pretended to care.

I don't like to close except when I get sick, which is not often. I make most of my money on weekends and holidays, which folks use as an excuse to buy more beauty products than they need. It used to be mostly young women who spent a ton of money at the House of Beauty and Glamour, but now it's seasoned women and a lot of men. My goal is to help them look and feel beautiful.

This is precisely why whenever I leave the house (except when I'm walking B. B. King), I try to make sure I look like I'm headed somewhere important. My mother raised me this way. "The only place you should look bad is at home. And if you look good, you will feel good." Folks are always asking me what I used to do for a living (since it's obvious I look like I get social security). I tell them I "sell beauty" (I leave off "products," since it's the truth). Even though I have my share of new wrinkles, which I prefer to call *beauty marks,* they're hard to see since I'm dark brown, and I use a good concealer to smooth them out. I know they're there, though, and that I've earned them. My real hair color is a boring mixed gray, but I dye it what I like to call *sexy silver.* And for the record: I wouldn't be caught dead wearing anything but red lipstick. I make exceptions to this rule depending on my outfit, which might require a hot pink or burnt orange. But that's as far as I go.

The reason Carl left early was to oversee the installation of new cabinets and a kitchen sink in one of our rental apartments. I'm almost ready to give this one away. Rental property is hardly worth the income. All you do is put it back into the property. But Carl likes to stay busy. He will spend most of the day zigzagging back and forth between there and Ma's empty house, the house Carl and I bought her. He is supervising its renovation after she caused it to catch fire. Fortunately, we moved Ma into Valley View, a lovely assisted living residence, but she still thinks she's moving back into the house, which she is not. She has lost her red Corolla in too many parking garages and had one too many fender benders because she was confusing the brake with the gas pedal. She is safe now.

Unlike Ma, Carl has refused to accept the fact that at seventy-three, with both knees full of arthritis, he is handicapped. He won't use his cane, but I know when he's in pain he limps harder, even if he rarely complains.

I feed B. B. King, then pour myself a bowl of granola that tastes like straw and drown it in a cup of tasteless almond milk. I got them both at Whole Foods, where I have recently started shopping sometimes to impress my doctor. After my life-changing breakfast, B. B. King brings me his leash and I decide I can only take him on a short walk because I have a lot of things to do today. As soon as he realizes we're not heading toward the dog park, he tries to pull me in that direction. I suppose he wants to see his new girlfriend, but I don't give in.

When I see a mother coming toward us, taking a video of her little girl in a stroller tugging the strings on a cluster of yellow and white balloons, it dawns on me that Carl filmed my last birthday party. After B.B. and I get home, I sift through a stack of DVDs until I see the one that says: LORETHA'S 67TH BIRTHDAY BASH. Unfortunately, I've forgotten how to work the DVD player because we've hardly used it since we started streaming Netflix. They've become pretty much obsolete—much the way I've started to feel sometimes. As quiet as it's kept, I have finally realized that I will never look like I did last year or the year before that. I'll never be able to do some of the things I once did and I'm still not sure what I was supposed to learn that I haven't.

When I see the title card for my party appear on the TV, I'm grateful I was able to get it to work. I gulp down the rest of my bottled water, kick off my sneakers, flop down on the sofa, and press Play. It starts with the senior citizen version of "*Soul Train* Revisited." When I hear B.B. snoring, I fast-forward to the touching toasts my girlfriends made, and remember they'd sounded more like testimonials from old Oprah Winfrey shows.

"Here's hoping you don't have any reason to be admitted to the hospital or to visit anybody else!"

This is not the kind of shit you say to someone at their sixty-seventh birthday party. But Sadie meant well. She is a semi-attractive spinster who loves visiting sick people, especially if they're still in the hospital. And she doesn't miss a funeral. Even when she doesn't know the deceased! She's a retired librarian, but I think Sadie missed her calling because she acts like she's onstage the way she presses a palm against her flat chest when she reads the names of the "Sick and Shut-In," along with those who recently passed, in the church bulletin. "Why didn't you cry?" she asked me once. I told her, "Because it's hard to cry for a stranger." I have not been back since she went and joined the choir and brags about her solos; I heard they're always off-key and that it's mostly relatives who yell out, "Praise the Lord, Sister Sadie!"

I hate to admit it, but lately, instead of church I've been going to movie matinees, mostly for the senior citizen discount. Carl usually relaxes and watches sports. It's not that we're not religious. I grew up going every Sunday, so I just feel like I've heard it all before. And even though I know I can sometimes be opinionated, every once in a while prone to harmless gossip, and occasionally a flat-out bitch, I do believe in God and I try to live a Christian life. For tune-ups, I watch church on TV, which I can attend in my pj's. Or, sometimes I record it to watch while having dinner with my husband.

As I sit watching my party onscreen, I realize that all of my friends are retired except me. That's probably why most of them are bored. It's like they're sitting around just waiting to die. But I do not subscribe to the belief that it's all downhill from here. Life isn't over at sixty-five. I feel like a car. As long as I change the oil and rotate the tires, I can get plenty more mileage out of it. Easier said than done.

I think Sadie's just lonely. She's never been married and never seemed to care. "Do you think you might be a lesbian?" I asked her about thirty years ago, when she was more attractive. She got mad for my even asking. I told her not to get so worked up. Even back then every lesbian I'd ever met was happy to be a lesbian. What's sad is I don't believe Sadie's ever even had sex. She has no idea how much pleasure she's missed, and she strikes me as the type who would be too scared to even consider pleasuring herself. Not that I ever have.

I push the coffee table a few inches away with my feet, then cross my legs, and lean forward when I see Korynthia's tall, slender frame appear on the TV.

"Here's hoping you'll consider hiring a seasoned woman for your Pasadena shop," she says pointing to herself. "And not the one in L.A. because I am not getting on that 10 freeway for no amount of money: period. Actually, I think you should sell the L.A. store because you're too old to be this busy, and plus you don't need the money. Anyway, where was I? Oh yeah, you should be willing to hire me to work part-time for a few dollars over minimum wage. Because I'm bored, mind you, not because I need the money, unlike those young hoochies who spend more time primping in the countertop mirrors than they do helping a loyal customer find a decent mixed-gray synthetic ponytail or the best scalp treatment for thinning hair. I don't want to waste any more time, but if I did, I'd also add that they don't have a clue about what kind of makeup covers puffiness under your eyes. And that's all I have to say."

Okay. Korynthia can and will talk you to death if you don't cut her off. She is also a beautiful, slender giant. She's six-one and the only one out of all of us who still has her college weight, not that she went to college. She was too impatient. "Four years is too damn long not to make any money." For most of her adult life, Korynthia bartended at clubs and waitressed at twenty-four-hour restaurants. She'd brag, "I get paid in cash and get to keep every dime I make." But Korynthia, who didn't marry any of the three men who fathered her three children, never thought that one day she would get old and need social security and Medicare. And now she wants me to hire her, but her people skills are rough since her customers were almost always drunk or high. I will give her this: she insisted that her kids go to college. They all live in San Diego now. When her parents died, she inherited a few funeral parlors, and unlike Sadie, Korynthia is afraid of the dead so she sold the business. To this day, she has yet to figure out what to do with her free time. Except exercise. She looks so good she pisses us all off.

B. B. King lets out a stinky fart. I start fanning the air with both hands, but it doesn't cut it, so I open the front door and shoo him out so I can go back to the video. Next up is Lucky, whose real name is Elizabeth Taylor. Lucky said her mama was tripping after seeing *National Velvet,* which was why Lucky changed her name to one she liked. Not legally, of course.

"Here's praying you trade in that ugly Volvo station wagon."

Lucky has always been a confused elitist. She thinks the kind of car you drive defines you, along with your zip code. She used to be a costumer for game shows and some TV commercials but now spends her time shopping and cooking—and eating. Lucky, who never had kids because she never wanted any, lives above the Rose Bowl but has never bothered to walk the 3.1 miles around it. When she wakes up she looks straight ahead at the San Gabriel Mountains. I can also see those mountains from my bedroom window, but I have to look up. She drives a nine-year-old gold Lexus that she's had at least six accidents in because Lucky can't navigate turns. Yes, I drive a twelve-year-old white Volvo. It's a safe car and I'm a paranoid driver and have a bad habit of tapping the brakes. Besides, people feel sorry for you driving a Volvo station wagon, especially with an old dog in the back seat who looks like he's being kidnapped. But I know for a fact B. B. King loves it, because once when the Volvo was in the shop and I had a rental car, he refused to get in it.

"Hold on a minute! I forgot! Here's hoping you finally hit your healthy weight goal by this time next year!"

Lucky has a lot of nerve bringing this up. She who still pretends she's a size sixteen. But Lucky takes pills for high cholesterol because she's addicted to fried everything, rocky road ice cream, and any kind of pie. I'm not too far behind her on a scale but I'm not on any diet. I like my curves and so does Carl. Anyway, after forty-five years, Lucky is still happily married to Joe, who is white and a retired architect who now builds miniature houses but rarely comes out of the big one they live in. Us girls all like him but we do think he's a little odd.

I won't lie. The last time I saw Dr. Alexopolous she had the nerve to tell me that I'm heavier than I should be. She also claims I'm borderline diabetic, and that it would be in my best interest if I lost about twenty-five—but preferably thirty-five—pounds, which I think is ridiculous. "I'm big-boned," I've told her. "And I'm black. We have big hips and it's genetic." She doesn't buy it. To be honest, it's hard to change old and especially bad habits. "If you want to prevent future health problems, Mrs. Curry, you need to cut back on fat, carbohydrates, and sugar, and perhaps consider exercising. It's never too late." I don't like anybody telling me what to do. I told her I try to eat light (which was a lie) and that I walk my dog every day (which wasn't). She said at my age walking my dog didn't really qualify as a cardiovascular workout. I've been trying to get up the nerve to fire her, if you can fire a doctor.

I haven't been back to see her since last year and I've been so busy running the House of Beauty and Glamour that I haven't had time to incorporate exercise into my daily routine, although I've been thinking about it. No, I haven't. It hasn't even crossed my mind. I admit it. I don't like gyms because most of the people in them are either young or already in good shape. They make me feel plump. And old. Even if technically I'm both. My doctor told me to consider giving spinning a try and I wanted to tell her she should *consider* getting a makeover. She looks like Grandpa from *The Munsters* with that dirty-blond, see-through hair. But even though I wouldn't admit it to her, I went ahead and pled guilty to being lazy to myself and decided I would start cutting back, one by one, on Twizzlers, Baskin-Robbins Quarterback Crunch ice cream, Roscoe's fried chicken, cheeseburgers, French fries and French bread, gravy, all muffins, and during the holidays I can only have one of either peach cobbler, sweet potato pie, or bread pudding. I even tried saying "eenie meenie miney mo," but have not had as much success as I had hoped for. I have no willpower. My newly revised plan, however, is to try harder. I'm going to think hard about dieting, and make some changes. Starting New Year's. Which is still the day after my birthday.

"Here's hoping you start carrying Vivica Fox's wigs so I don't have to order them online."

Awww. That's my girl Faye, who passed away six months ago from lung cancer. A few weeks after my birthday I had driven out to see her in San Bernardino. She was sitting on her sunporch, behind the screens, smoking a cigarette. She was down to about a hundred pounds and her brown skin was dull, as if someone had sprayed her with dust. I got the first shipment of wigs a week after she died. I miss her something fierce.

I hit Pause, wipe my eyes, and just stare at her face. She was so pretty. Her cheekbones made her face look like a brown heart. She looked like Lena Horne's clone. She tried the patch. Hypnosis. Gum. But she said cigarettes relaxed her and she was willing to take her chances.

"That is the stupidest shit I've ever heard," I'd told her.

"You act like you've never had any bad habits, Lo."

"None that will kill me," was what I remember saying, wanting to believe nothing would ever happen to her, even though she already had that cough.

For the longest time I would dial her number hoping she would answer, but then immediately press End when I realized what I'd done. It takes longer than I ever imagined to accept that someone you've known all your life is not alive anymore. I have not been able to delete her number from my cellphone. I want her to know she still exists for me. Since Faye has been gone, I have often thought about how I'm going to die. But I don't tell anybody. Not even Carl. What I do know is I don't want it to be because of something I did to myself or because of what I neglected to do.

When I hear B. B. King whining, I press Pause before Poochie can start talking and get up to let him in.

"Here's hoping you give our Cruise to Nowhere another chance, Loretha. It's been three years and we want you back, right, ladies?" And the other ladies screamed out a loud "Yes!"

Poochie has been old longer than the rest of us. She could not have kids, which is probably why she became a special-needs nurse, and she mothers anybody who needs mothering. If you're hurt, she will rub your back, rock you back and forth, and squeeze you until you fall asleep. Dennis, her husband of thirty years, died of renal failure almost ten years ago. He was a smart stockbroker and left her sloppy rich, but Poochie just gave up on ever finding love again. "You just make yourself forget how good it felt," she said. But what she does still love is water and big boats, which is why after Dennis's death she became our resident cruise organizer. I don't like floating, and I'm not crazy about the ocean because I almost drowned when I was nine. Poochie begged me to try "just one cruise" and promised I wouldn't even get wet, and since everybody in our "posse" was going, I huffed and puffed and I gave in.

It was one cruise too many. I did not have fun. I didn't understand what there was to like about the entertainment. It was always singers you never heard of who sparkled in sequined evening gowns or shimmied in white fringe or did the Temptation Walk in tight tuxedos with buttons that looked like they were begging for another two inches. And I never heard anybody in the casino shrieking with joy because they'd hit a jackpot. The shrieking was mostly from folks pounding on the slot machines because they hadn't won, including me. What gave me the heebie-jeebies more than anything was that you could only get off the damn ship in Ensenada, Mexico, and I was too scared to eat or drink anything ashore so I stayed onboard. My friends abandoned me for eight long hours and I vowed not to ever cruise anywhere again.

I hate to say it, but I secretly thanked God when Poochie moved to Las Vegas to take care of her ailing mother. So, once every few months we take the midnight casino bus up to visit, and Poochie meets us at the tables or the slots. Each time I've crossed my fingers and prayed she wouldn't bring up a plan for me to try another damn cruise. So far, so good.

After the toasts, which seem less uplifting today than they did at the time, we all lined up at the buffet of fried chicken, BBQ ribs, baked beans, au gratin potatoes, some kind of salad, collard greens, and cornbread. We stuffed ourselves. Carl tied the cluster of yellow balloons to the back of a chair so they wouldn't pop when I blew out the wicks on the thick yellow 6 and 7 candles. I remember how, after the cake, I found a quiet spot to observe all the people I cared about and who cared about me. I know I judge them harshly sometimes and I judge myself, too. I lie to myself about myself. I made a promise that night to be kinder to myself and to my friends because none of us is perfect. I have not been as successful as I had hoped.

As Sadie sliced pieces of the chocolate cake and put them in aluminum foil she had already measured for everybody to take home, I turned to my guests and said, with the utmost sincerity, "Thank you, everybody, for your thoughtfulness and love; now go on back to the senior facility before they send the geriatric police to come get all of your behinds!"

Some laughed. Some didn't. I didn't care because it was my birthday.

Carl gave me pearls and his X-rated toast in private.

When I click off the DVD, B. B. King goes to stand, but he slips on the hardwood floor. I help him up and make a mental note to buy some bigger throw rugs, which is when I feel my cellphone shivering in my jacket pocket. I pull it out and see that I have a text from Cinnamon, my oh-so-cool granddaughter. I hope like hell she isn't about to tell me their rent is going to be late again.

Grandma, I'm so sorry that Jonas and I won't be able to make it to your birthday party tomorrow. We both have to work, but have fun! Oh FYI, I doubt if my mom is going to be there because I know she's still not ready to surrender, but I trust God will bring you two back together when it's time. But happy birthday! Made you something totally groovy!

I text my space cadet granddaughter back: *Not to worry. And thanks for sharing. Don't work too hard.* And I hit Send.

I knew it! I just knew it! When I told Carl I would prefer not to have any more birthday parties until I was in a wheelchair or something, he must've just thought I was joking. But I wasn't. I know he means well, but I'm pissed. I don't feel like celebrating my birthday at the same old restaurant with my same old friends, and it looks like this will be an exact repeat of last year down to the no-shows. Odessa owes me money for two mortgage payments I helped her out with and liquor will of course be served, so she's probably a no. And Cinnamon? She must think I'm already senile or stuck on stupid because the last time I checked, she doesn't have a legitimate job to skip my party for, not one that pays her on top of or under any table, at least not on a regular basis. Her live-in boyfriend, Jonas, also has an ongoing struggle with employment, which is why they are always late with the minor rent we do charge them for their one-bedroom-too-many apartment in a building we own.

No, the real reason they're bowing out is because Carl and I are old, which to them means dull. I don't really blame them, because when I was young, my sister and I dreaded visiting relatives, too, especially the old ones who were at least fifty and the really old ones who were over sixty. I didn't like the way their houses smelled, and I dreaded having to hug them because they were soft and squishy and their eyes looked like they were full of bad memories. They wanted us to do all the talking and I would just watch how slow the hands on the big brown clock moved because I was just waiting to see how much longer it was going to be before we could leave.

So I know why Cinnamon and Jonas are always in a hurry when they stop by to drop off the rent, why they leave their 2006 used-to-be-black-but-is-now-many-different-shades-of-gray Prius running in front of the house, even though it's hard to rush in those Crocs they both wear. It is because they have nothing to say to us. And yet they try.

"B. B. King is looking healthy."

"What a groovy nail color, Grandma."

"It sure smells good in here."

"It's been so hot out, hasn't it?"

Sometimes after they leave, Carl and I just sit there counting how many questions these two didn't ask, and how many times they said *groovy*. I've never known any black people who use this word *groovy*, not even when stoned. These two would've fit right in at Woodstock.

But what I'm really wondering is just how long Jalecia plans on holding a grudge for everything she thinks I owe her. Kids can be cruel and ungrateful, but I'm not going to beg my daughter to forgive me for something I didn't do. And now I'm going to have to pretend I don't know Carl is having another birthday party for me and then act surprised when we get there.

The truth is; I'd much rather spend a quiet night alone with Carl. Maybe find a good movie to watch on television, call one of those new delivery services to order angel hair pasta with prawns, some garlic bread, and a good salad from our favorite Italian restaurant. We could have some raspberry sorbet and not too many glasses of wine so that we still have energy to rendezvous, something we do at least once or twice—and if we're lucky, three times—a month, but definitely on our birthdays and major holidays.

Carl doesn't get home until almost six, tired as a dog. He leaves his dirty work boots by the side door, gives me my regular peck on the cheek since his face is dusty, then takes his usual shower and comes back looking like an old basketball star in one of five or six gray Under Armour sweat suits. He sits down at his end of the maple table.

"You said you didn't want another party so I honored your wishes, but just do me a favor and keep your calendar clear tomorrow evening. Could you do that for me?"

"Yes, I can. What should I wear?"

"Something pretty."

"Any special perfume?"

He winks at me.

"Did everything go okay today? I know that's probably a dumb question based on what time it is."

"You never miss a beat. I have to go back over to the house in the morning, but I'll be back before lunch and in plenty of time to get cleaned up."

"I hope you like this chili," is all I say.

Carl is gone when I wake up, but sitting on the chest of drawers is a giant bouquet of yellow roses with red tips and a giant yellow envelope with a card inside that I decide not to open until tonight. I hope we don't get home too late and I hope he'll take one of his little pills so we can complete the celebration of my being alive 24,820 days. Yes, I did the math.

When I walk into the bathroom, there is another bouquet of white roses on the sink and a Post-it on the mirror that says, *Happy Birthday, You Sweet Young Thang! Be back before lunch!*

I do love this man, even if he sometimes doesn't listen to me.

I'm anxious all morning, watching the sun turn from white to yellow, which is why I've been in the backyard on my knees, digging in dirt, planting a flat of yellow, purple, lime, and white zinnias and painstakingly surrounding them with red petunias, because even though I love to garden, right now I'm really just killing time. I also can't believe I have not gotten a single birthday call from anybody. I keep digging.

"You need any help?"

I look up at Carl, smile, and shake my head no. He bends down and kisses me on both cheeks, then whispers, "Happy birthday, beautiful."

He stands back up. "And that's all you get for now!"

He is silly but it's what I like most about him. He is still handsome. And his skin—unlike mine—is as smooth as satin gloss brown paint. I have to admit Carl is one patient man. I know I am not the easiest person to please, but he doesn't seem to mind.

"Don't wear yourself out, now. You know I've got plans for you this evening, so don't mess up your nails."

He walks over to close the gate to the pool, which neither of us ever gets in. I can't swim and I'm not interested in learning. But I do like to sit on the edge and kick my feet. Every now and then Carl will pretend to do kicking exercises for his arthritis, but mostly he just throws the ball in for B. B. King, who gets more use out of the pool than we do.

I take off my gloves and show him how pretty my pink nails still are, and then I slide the gloves back on like a stripper. "What kind of plans?" I ask just to sound curious.

"Okay. I know you're fully aware that I am having a party for you, so just try to act surprised. Would you do that for me, sugar?"

"What would make you think I already know?"

"Because I know Cinnamon told you."

"How would you know that?"

"Because I told her to keep her big mouth shut, which I knew was impossible."

"It's okay. But, Carl, you promised me no more surprise parties."

"I know. But this one is going to be very special."

"I'll take your word for it, sweetheart."

He winks at me. I yank the hem of his jeans with one of my rawhide gloves, and he jumps up and down as if I just tickled him. Carl still gives me goosebumps. He's been my husband for twenty-four years. I'm not ashamed to admit that I've been married three times. That's how many times it took me to get it right. I've taken to thinking of each one as a vehicle. Antoine was a Ford. Elijah was a Dodge pickup. And Carl is my Mercedes-Benz. He runs really well and he's built to last.

"The reservation is for seven, if you can make it."

"I'll be ready, Carl."

"How ready?"

I toss some peat moss on top of his gray Nikes.

"Well, I've still got a few errands to run so I'll see you later, cutie."

I love it when he calls me that. He rubs the top of my straw hat and I watch him limp away.

I don't hear the doorbell, but B. B. King comes to the back door and barks to let me know someone is at the front. I struggle to get to a standing position, and when I finally make it inside, I'm clearly too late because I don't see a face through the glass. I open the door, and there on the porch, blocking the doorway, is what looks like a nursery of six or seven giant bouquets.

I am ashamed of myself for being such a whining, cranky, judgmental old bitch. My friends do care about me. I decide to read the cards later.

After I pack up my gardening tools and place them inside the adorable shed Carl built for me, B. B. King creeps over to the stairs out of the line of fire, and when I turn on the hose and twist the sprocket to spray a strong mist over the limp zinnias and petunias, I wonder when and why and how I became so damn pessimistic.

I don't like this personality trait. And I hope it's not too late to change it.

It takes all day for seven o'clock to get here. And I can't wait to get this over with.

"You look stunning," Carl says when I walk out of the bedroom in a hot pink skirt suit I bought at Nordstrom Rack last year, and I am just glad I was still able to squeeze into it.

"Thank you, Carl," I say, glad he approves. He looks good in the black suit, black shirt, and light blue tie I got him for his birthday last year. He has been standing out here in the living room waiting for me because he doesn't want to wrinkle his suit before we get to the restaurant. I don't know why he got all dudded up just to go there. It's not like we're going to some swank four-star eatery in Beverly Hills.

"We need to step on it, Lo, because you know there's always traffic."

Traffic? We shouldn't have to get on the freeway to go where I thought we were going: Maybelle's Soul Food Dining Room. Maybe Cinnamon got it wrong. But wait. Did she tell me where my party was going to be? I don't remember. Maybe I made that jump myself. I decide, for once, to keep my big mouth shut. When Carl opens the door for me, I notice luggage on the back seat of his black Explorer.

"Are we staying at a hotel afterward?"

"Why are you so nosy?"

I put my flowered purse on the floor next to my pointy black patent leather pumps and try to cross my legs without success. I turn on the XM soul station, and when I realize we're heading toward the 210 freeway, I turn to Carl and say, "Hold on a minute. When Cinnamon told me about the party I just assumed it was at Maybelle's."

"You assume too much, Lo."

"Well, where are we going, and why'd I get all dressed up?"

"We're on our way to Palm Springs."

"Palm Springs? You mean I'm not having a party?"

"Nope."

"Then, why did you tell Cinnamon, and then me, that I was?"

"Because I wanted to throw you off, because you always think you've got everything figured out, which I love about you, but I'll bet she didn't tell you she's pregnant, now, did she? Don't answer that. Please don't tell her I told you. Anyway, I called all of your girlfriends three weeks ago begging them not to bring up celebrating your birthday this year because I knew you were sick of the same old thing. For once, they listened to me. But it cost me."

"What do you mean it *cost* you?"

"Promise me you won't interrupt me before I finish?"

"I promise."

Carl doesn't say anything. He turns the music down.

Oddly enough, now I'm disappointed I'm not having a party. And I'm furious that my stupid-ass granddaughter is going to be a parent. I wonder if Jalecia knows she's going to be a grandmother or if she even gives a damn. I wonder why Cinnamon told Carl and not me? But I can't worry about any of this tonight. I still have lingering nerves and suspicions because I was all set for the party and now Carl has added a whole new layer of surprise. I kick off the stupid heels that were already starting to hurt and I think how I should've put the hooks on my bra in the first instead of the second row. I do my best to take tiny sips of cool air and try not to ask too many questions.

And then I hear Carl say, "Isn't that sunset gorgeous?"

I turn to look. All sunsets are gorgeous. He's stalling or mad at me now.

"Yes it is, Carl. I'm sorry. I'm all ears."

He turns the radio down even though Tina Turner is just starting to sing what I know are the first few chords of "What's Love Got to Do with It," and I try to be patient by clasping my fingers into a church and then a steeple. Then just when I'm about to open the door and see all the people, I hear him say, "Okay. So your friends were a little sensitive about being left out of your birthday, and I had to promise them a few things to pacify them. You're going to have to go on the Cruise to Nowhere in the fall, which has made Poochie very happy. And you're going to have to sell your Volvo, which, I hate to admit, I agree with Lucky about, Lo. The new Volvo XC90 is pretty snazzy and I'm sure B. B. King would like the smell of new carpet. And don't worry, he still won't have to jump to get in. You're going to have to hire Korynthia at the store and she said she's willing to be trained, but to do what, I do not know. And last but not least, Lucky has signed you both up for Weight Watchers and enrolled you in some SilverSneakers gym so you all can both get fit even though I love the way you look."

"I'm not going on that cruise."

"It's only three days, Lo, and I promised."

I cross my arms.

"Who's going to look after Poochie's mama?"

"She's bringing her, too."

I roll my eyes and press my palm against my forehead.

"Lo, it'll make them happy."

"What about me? This feels more like blackmail."

"It is, but it's also called love."

"Wait. What did Sadie want?"

I roll my eyes at him.

"My bad. But you've got so many friends it's hard to remember them all. Sadie just asked if you would please come to her church just once or three times."

"Oh, hell," I say, and then catch myself. "I suppose it wouldn't hurt for me to get in touch with the Lord this year. But I do not want to sit next to her because she is inclined to get the Holy Ghost. Wait a minute! I forgot! She sits with the choir now! Hallelujah!"

Then we were quiet.

"How much time do I have?" I asked.

"Before your next birthday."

He let out a chuckle and started shaking his head. I watched the orange sun disappearing behind the San Gabriel Mountains, and like magic, snow suddenly started to appear on the peaks. I waited for Carl to tell me he had also spoken to Jalecia and my sister, but he just turned the radio up when "I'll Be Doggone" by Marvin Gaye came on.

When I woke up, Carl was pulling up to the valet stand and my cellphone shivered in my lap. I thought I must've been seeing things.

"Ma?"

"Happy birthday! And happy new year, too, sugar!"

"Thank you," I said slowly.

"I know you thought I forgot but I don't forget important things."

"Why, thank you," I said, pointing to Carl. Then I placed my hand across my heart and pressed it. He put his thumb up.

"Whatcha doing to celebrate?"

"Carl surprised me, and we just drove to Palm Springs."

"Does he golf?"

"He used to."

"Gamble?"

"No."

"Well, you two do not need to work on your tans so what in the hell are you going to do in Palm Springs besides burn up?"

"It's cool here, Ma. Plus, we're staying at a nice resort hotel."

"Well, that's nice. What's the dog's name again?"

"B. B. King."

"I could've sworn it was Otis Redding. Ha! Ha! Anyway, did you bring him?"

"No," I say, shocked she cares, considering he always growled at her and wouldn't let her pet him.

"Did you put him in one of those doggie prisons?"

"No. Apparently Cinnamon's going to feed and walk him."

"I wouldn't trust her with my stuffed animal. Have you heard from her mother who used to be your daughter today?"

"Not yet," I say, which makes some of my joy disappear.

"Don't hold your breath."

"It's my birthday, Ma."

"I doubt she remembered. Something is wrong with that girl. She is troubled, but I don't think she can help it."

Troubled? Yes, from substance abuse. Jalecia could very well be an alcoholic, but we've also caught her pinching Carl's arthritis medication and the Percocet they gave me when I broke my ankle a couple of years ago after falling off a treadmill that I haven't been on since. This was, I'd come to believe, the real reason she'd been visiting more regularly, before our falling out anyway.

"Ma, I'll come visit you on Monday."

"Don't bother. It's boring as hell here. I can't wait to get the hell out of here and go home so I can have two shots of Hennessy. I'm sick of being around all these sick old people."

I just pretend I don't hear her say this.

"Ma! I've gotta go! Carl is waving at me to hurry up. Call you when we get home."

I was not telling the truth. But this was the most effective way to get my eighty-six-year-old mother off the phone.

I don't put my heels back on because my feet have swelled up, so I just carry them over to the seating area outside the registration office and sit down on a lovely green bench that would look great in our backyard. It's new, because I don't recall it from our last visit here. I stand up to find the name of the manufacturer, but don't see one, so I take a picture of it. When we get home, I'll ask Carl if he can google it, and find out where we can buy it. Something tells me it didn't come from Home Depot or Lowe's. I sit back down and cross my arms and legs and just listen to the water running. There are fountains everywhere and hundreds of poinsettias surrounding them. I check my cellphone and there are a ton of text messages, but not one from my daughter. I look around at all the vacationers and obvious honeymooners here to ring in the new year. Everybody looks so happy. Maybe I should reach out to Jalecia. Maybe she is suffering, or struggling with something she can't share. I do know Jalecia is not a real thief. And a year is too long to not speak to your own mother. I start to dial her number, but then I'm offered a glass of water with a slice of cucumber resting between tiny ice cubes. I take it and drink it in one gulp.

"You ready, baby?" Carl asks, as he comes out of the registration office and holds out his hand. I drop my phone inside my purse and slide my fingers between his.

"I've been ready," I say in my sassy tone.

"Happy new year!" the driver of the golf cart says. We say the same to him as we sit in the back. We know this resort like the back of our hand. When we make the first right turn, I know it means Carl has managed to get our favorite room. He puts his arm around my shoulders and rocks me slowly from side to side as we head down the pathway through the white-stucco-and-chocolate-trimmed villas. All five or six swimming pools are quiet, their chlorine gurgling, finally at rest. The palm trees are lit up from their trunks, making their fronds look like giant green dreadlocks. The driver and Carl talk football, but when we reach our building, Carl realizes he forgot something in the car. I ask for the keys, and tell them of course I can let myself in. As they head back, I unlock the gate and saunter up the red clay stairs, which feel nice and cool on my bare feet. I use the same key to unlock the second gate when I reach our private outdoor terrace where the gas logs are already burning in the fireplace. I push open the big wooden door and walk inside our gorgeous room with its domed, beamed ceilings. It smells the way I imagine paradise does: clean and woody and like fresh mint. I drop my heels next to the door, toss my purse on the white-duck-covered chair, take my earrings off, and set them on the table next to a dark green bottle I already know is expensive champagne. I pick up one of the two goblets. Why, I don't know. I set it back down, next to a large plate of figs, squares of dark and white chocolate, green grapes, and four or five different types of cheese. Beige crackers are spread out like cards on a blackjack table. I lay my jacket on the back of a chair. I eat a grape and decide to lie across the four-poster bed until Carl gets back. I press my cheek on the edge of a pillow. It feels nice and cool. I close my eyes and after what feels like only a few minutes, I realize I must have dozed off. But when I look around the room and don't see or hear Carl, I call the front desk and ask if my husband is heading back to the room. They tell me he should've been here by now, so I get up and walk across the patio and open the first gate, and when I look down, there slouched on the stairs on top of our luggage and a yellow gift box, is my husband.

Chapter 2

I don't remember how I got home. I do remember that Carl wasn't able to drive us. I remember being undressed and sponge-bathed. Somebody slipped a nightgown over my head and somebody helped me get in bed and pulled the duvet up under my chin but I still shivered. There were always arms around me but I knew they weren't Carl's arms. I kept wondering what was taking him so long to get home.

I remember people knocking on the front door and pressing the doorbell, and the house phone and cellphones ringing all day and into the middle of the night. I heard Odessa and Sadie and Korynthia and Lucky answering the same questions over and over: "No, he hadn't been sick. It was a heart attack. No, Loretha is not doing well. She thanks you for your prayers. We will let you know about arrangements." Arrangements? I only like arranging flowers for the dining room table. Everything was so loud my ears were ringing. The vacuum. The dishwasher. Running water.

Somebody would sit me up and wipe my face with a moist wash-cloth, rub my hands and feet, and stick a spoon in my mouth. "Eat this, baby," or put a cold glass or a warm cup against my lips and say, "Drink this, sweetheart."

Somebody brushed my hair.

B. B. King refused to leave my side, lying on the throw rug at the foot of the bed except when he heard the side door open, which was when he tried to run to meet Carl. When he realized it wasn't Carl, he just dropped to the floor and whimpered. He perked up when he saw me stand up and try to tighten the sash on my bathrobe, but I couldn't do it yet. My fingers were swollen and numb. Somebody tall put their arms around my back and guided me to the bathroom. I closed my eyes and wished it was my husband. But it was Poochie. "Lean on me," she said, and squeezed my right hand, which I felt tingle.

"Thank you for coming, Poochie."

"Don't you dare," was what she said, as if I had offended her.

It may have been the second or even the third day when I insisted on walking through the house just to see if I could. My friends and family had taken shifts and some slept in Jalecia's old room. She wasn't here. When I walked into the living room, my friends jumped up and parted like the sea and cupped my elbows to make sure I wouldn't crumple. When I made it to the kitchen, which had not been my destination—I just needed to move—I saw all kinds of casseroles and bowls of fried chicken and a honey-baked ham and macaroni and cheese on the table, and all four burners had pots with steam bursting out of the tops of them. I saw squares of yellow cornbread and collard greens and sweet potatoes in chafing dishes. This was what was done, what we always did at wakes, but now I was the beneficiary. I did not have an appetite and didn't really care if I ever ate again. I opened the refrigerator just to see if I could. There were two glass pitchers of lemonade and iced tea. My throat was dry but I was not thirsty. When I looked around, I wished this was my surprise party, and for a minute I wondered why Carl was late.

It was another day or two before I could accept that my husband was not coming home, and that I had to get up, because I had to get up.

I did not wear black to Carl's "Celebration of Life" service. I wore the white dress he'd bought for my sixty-fifth birthday. He always said, "You need to show off those curves," and I thought he would like it. I didn't care if it was inappropriate. When I made it inside that large banquet room it felt like I was sleepwalking. My chest felt like an accordion being pumped, and my palms were sore and chalky from being squeezed so hard. I pretended this was a wedding reception or a large baby shower or a banquet Carl was being honored at, and that he was just late getting here since we had come in separate cars. The scent of all those damn flowers on the twenty-five tables and the pictures of him as a teenager on the football team, of us when we got married, of him when he was in the coast guard, just made me angry. He should've been here by now to see all these people who came to acknowledge how important he was to them. But Carl was not late. He was not coming to this "celebration" of his life. He was in a silver urn at home on our fireplace mantel.

Sadie insisted on handing out the programs. I was grateful, although a lot of people had no idea who she was, so she just pretended to be a family member and introduced herself as such. Even Carl's relatives believed her. I had given her a short Vivica Fox auburn wig she "just had to have" a few months ago, but with her beige skin and faded freckles it made her look like she was on fire. Sadie is afraid of makeup so it's a good thing she's basically pretty. She wore one of the many black suits she owns, but this one still had the tag on it. I managed to pull it off.

There was too much black in this room. Not people but suits and dresses. Carl had friends of every shade and ethnicity, and they were all here. Ma insisted on leaving an empty seat next to me for Carl.

"That seat is taken," Lucky or Korynthia or Poochie would politely say for me.

Odessa helped Ma sit in the chair directly on my left, and then patted my right shoulder and handed me a long white envelope.

"This may be the wrong time, but don't open it until you're calm."

"Why does she need to be calm?" Ma asked.

Odessa raked her fingers through her thick black pageboy and started pulling on the ends. "I just meant when things calm down. This is a lot to handle and I'm sorry I've been so busy I haven't been able to make it over more. It looks like I might be moving, but this is not the time or the place to talk about it. My heart goes out to you. Carl was a good man."

Everybody at the table just nodded.

I rolled the envelope in my hands until it looked like a thick cigarette, knowing there was probably a check inside. Odessa's timing was always bad, and today was no different. I had forgotten that I'd given her that black dress last year because it was too tight on me. I had to admit, she looked good in it.

She sat to Ma's left and kept her white handkerchief balled up in her hand and tried not to notice the liquor that was melting the ice in the light blue goblets at many of the tables, including ours. I was grateful she'd brought our mother, and that Ma'd insisted on coming. Ma said Carl was the only real son-in-law she had. Which was not true; she'd had two others from me and one from Odessa. But according to Odessa, Ma had said, "None of those others amounted to s-h-i-t so they don't count." Odessa, of course, couldn't bring herself to say *shit*.

"Why don't they have valet parking here?" Ma had asked as soon as she sat down. "What kind of golf club is this anyway? Tiger wouldn't play nine holes here, no doubt about it. Are they serving Hennessy at this Repasse?"

"No alcohol for you, Ma," Odessa said. "We're here to say goodbye to Carl."

"A double shot wouldn't stop me," she said, and squeezed my hand. "All I can say is I'll be glad when I die. To be honest, I thought I'd be dead by now but it seems to be taking forever."

I didn't know what to say. And I didn't think she meant it.

I hadn't seen Ma in real clothes in almost a year. She was wearing a navy blue suit with rhinestone buttons that hung off her, along with white gloves, but she also had on gold Nikes because Odessa had forgotten to retrieve her real shoes from the boxes stacked in the garage at Ma's empty house. And even though she was sitting next to me, Ma clutched her silver pocketbook as though somebody might try to rob her.

"Where is my grandson? I don't see him," she asked, looking around as if she was hoping to spot Jackson.

"He's in Japan with his family, Ma. He lives there with his Japanese wife and his daughters," Odessa said.

"Why don't you show some respect, Odessa?" Ma asked, not expecting an answer. "Who cares if his wife is Japanese? Even I know everybody can love who they want to love, my Lord. Could you try not to be a racist today, Odessa? Please?"

This almost made me smile.

Odessa just took a sip of her water.

"I had no idea Carl was friends with so many Mexicans!" Ma blurted out as she looked around the room filled with close to two hundred people. "Who in the heck are all these giant Negroes? Carl's people? Two of them young boys over there definitely got the best of the family genes, because the rest of them are downright homely. Look at how many tables they're taking up!"

She thought this was funny.

The truth was, the "giant Negroes" she was referring to were about twenty of Carl's all-male first, second, and third cousins, and a few of their sons. They had taken a Greyhound from Flint because they were able to get a group rate, even though quite a few of them had never even met Carl. One of them, who looked so much like Carl it was scary, said, "We just wanted to get out of Flint for a quick minute to see what California is all about, and to show our respects, of course." One of the younger ones, who appeared to be a little slow, shocked me when he asked, "Why'd you have to burn him up?" I didn't know how to answer that question in a way he would understand, so I just looked him in the eye and said, "Because it was what Carl wanted."

The entire clan was staying at a Motel 6, but they'd been piling into a single room and sleeping on the floor—including one person in the bathtub. When I realized that, I offered to pay for enough rooms so they could all at least have beds. They accepted my offer. Two of the younger ones said they were not planning to get back on that bus to Flint, and could they move into the newly renovated two-bedroom apartment down the hall from Cinnamon and Jonas? I found myself saying yes, I would give them three months to find a job that paid the rent or back to Flint they'd go.

I was shocked but relieved when I saw Jalecia saunter through the doorway past Sadie without even acknowledging her, looking like she hadn't slept in days. She was wearing a crinkly black gauze dress and black ankle boots I had bought her two years ago from Macy's, and she had that now-dull diamond stud in her left nostril. Looking at her cobalt blue polish, it was obvious she was in need of a fill. She walked over to my table and said, "So sorry for your loss," like people do on a TV series. I almost slapped her. Carl was more a father to her than her biological one. She managed to give me a stiff hug and her mildew-scented dreadlocks scratched my right cheek. It almost felt like she did that on purpose. Her breath smelled like mint, but it didn't cover the stink of what I knew to be eighty proof.

I don't know why I wasn't surprised when her aunt Peggy came sauntering in right behind her with a small package of Kleenex in her hand. She looked unhealthy, too, and her long, thick black braids had lint in them, but then again, it looked more like dandruff, which made her collar look like Swiss dots, even though her black dress was solid. She pretended like she was mourning somebody, but it wasn't Carl. I let her hug me, but I didn't hug her back because I didn't know what made her think I needed her sympathy.

This time last year I was in the backyard gardening when Peggy called and said, "Happy birthday, Loretha."

"Who is this?" I asked, since the number was blocked.

"Peggy."

"Peggy who?"

"Don't try to act like you don't remember me."

Even though I could already tell that Peggy Whoever was a complete bitch, I said, "Refresh my memory."

"I'm your first husband's half sister, which would make me your daughter's step-auntie, or something like that."

"I don't remember meeting you."

I did. But it was years before and I disliked her then, too.

"How'd you get my number, and who told you it was my birthday, and why should it matter to you?"

"Well, that's a mouthful. Jalecia gave it to me a few years ago, right before Antoine died, but I didn't think it was worth telling you then."

I remember shoving my shovel deeper into the soft soil because I was suspicious. I figured Peggy must want something.

"What is it you want?" I heard myself ask.

"Wow. I heard you always had a streak. But to make a long story short, I just saw Jalecia a few days ago, and she told me you were having a birthday party and I would like to come."

"Why?" I asked.

"Just to catch up."

"But what do we have to catch up about?"

"Your daughter."

"Then, another time," I said and hung up. Peggy hadn't come to my sixty-seventh birthday party. But then, neither had Jalecia. I hadn't heard from her again. Until now.

I turned to my daughter.

"So, Cinnamon's going to sing."

"Yes, and maybe the baby she's carrying will be as happy as I am about it."

I smiled at her but she didn't smile back.

"Well, I hope we can catch up soon, Jalecia."

"It's your call," was all she said, and walked away.

They sat two tables over with Cinnamon, who was her daughter, after all, and Jonas, close to the makeshift stage. When Cinnamon begged me to let her sing a song for her grandpa Carl, I told her I wouldn't have it any other way. I also let her know how thrilled I was when her grandpa told me she was pregnant. I did my best to sound convincing.

"I wrote it just for him, Grandma. Because both of you have been so good to Jonas and me. He would love it."

I didn't have the heart to say no.

Korynthia, Lucky, and Poochie filled the seats to my right. They all wore simple black dresses.

Cinnamon gave me a look as her mother sat down beside her. Was it time?

I gave her a look back. *It's okay.*

Cinnamon stepped up to the mic and announced that she'd be singing a song she'd written just for Carl, which everybody thought was touching until she started singing something about him being in "a better place." Everybody was trying to look as if what they were hearing was pleasant, but they kept looking down and turning their heads to the side, and after four-going-on-five minutes, their frozen smiles started to thaw. It wasn't until Cinnamon put the microphone back into the stand and backed away that folks realized she had finished, which was when they started clapping. She didn't sound good, but she didn't sound half as bad as I thought she would. I could tell her mother was pleased as I watched her squeeze her daughter and kiss her on the cheek. Then Jalecia stood up and slung her purse over her shoulder and, as she headed toward the door, Peggy whispered something in Jalecia's ear.

"Well, at least she came," Ma said.

Everybody just hummed.

When I saw Peggy sauntering over to me, I felt myself tensing up.

"Hello, everybody. Loretha, I know this may not be the appropriate time, but do you have a minute?"

"The testimonials are about to start. Is this something that can wait?"

"It'll only take a few minutes."

So I got up and walked to the back of the room. She looked over at the door and I could see Jalecia standing with her back turned, waiting.

"At first Jalecia said she wasn't coming because you two have been on bad terms ever since you fired her from one of your beauty supply stores for something she didn't do. But that's between you two. Anyway, you should know she's been living with people she probably shouldn't be living with, and as you can see she doesn't look so healthy. I just want you to know that I will do all I can to watch over her until you do. Again, I'm sorry for your loss."

And she turned and walked toward the door.

"Who was that?" Ma asked.

"Jalecia's ex-aunt. Antoine's sister or something."

"Is something wrong?" Odessa asked.

"No," I said, and tried to change the worried look on my face back to grief.

"Well, I thought Cinnamon sounded sincere," was the best response I could muster. I waited for one of my friends to say something, but they all just nodded in agreement.

After everyone gave their testimonials about how much Carl

meant to them, Ma turned to me and said, "Remember, Loretha, I don't want to be cremated. I've already got my favorite dress picked out, and by the way I've changed my mind about a wig. I want to show whatever hair I have left but I want to wear my mint green hat over it. They're both in my pink suitcase in the garage at my house. Promise me."

"Okay, Ma. But this isn't the time to talk about it."

"I don't see why not. Try to see if you can get these same caterers when my time comes because this food was delicious and everything was just so classy." She then leaned over and whispered, "I also want you to know I've changed my mind about moving back into my house. I've started to like being around folks my age. I'm leaving it to Odessa, but please don't tell her until after I kick the bucket because I don't trust her. She might try to have me bumped off. But she can't have my Corolla. This is all in my will."

I didn't want to tell her we donated that Corolla right after we found it in the parking lot where she'd lost it, or remind her that Carl and I bought that house for her eighteen years ago, that it was still in our names, and that we had been planning to put it on the market to help defray the costs of her assisted living care.

I did not give a speech at the "celebration" because I couldn't. Besides, Carl knew I had celebrated his life every single day for the twenty-five years he was in mine.

I did not change his pillowcase. I inhaled it for weeks. And when I couldn't smell him anymore, I sprayed it with the cologne he always wore. I turned his pillow sideways and clutched it, hoping I might feel Carl's heart beating again. But my arms went limp each time because he had disappeared and I knew that nothing I did was going to bring him back. I tried anyway. I dreamed more than once that this was all just a big misunderstanding. That he had just taken a vacation without me.

I walked around the house in a daze, stopping to sit down at random. On the couch. In a kitchen chair. It was too quiet. I wanted to rewind this horrible movie. Back to the beginning. I let myself cry quietly and sometimes I'd just wail. I did not know what I was supposed to do without him.

I put a CLOSED UNTIL FURTHER NOTICE sign on the door of the Pasadena House of Beauty and I paid the two girls who'd been working there three months' salary. They didn't know how to run it without me. I did the same for the Los Angeles store even though I had been thinking about selling that one. It was too much work, and besides, I didn't need the money.

Dinnertime was the worst. Eating alone. But I had a hard time at bedtime, too. Sleeping alone made me feel empty. I often fell asleep with the TV on and woke up to shows about glaciers and mountains and the sea and planets and forests on the BBC channel. Their beauty was like a lullaby. I didn't know what to do with Carl's toothbrush. I could not bring myself to throw it away. I hated walking into our walk-in closet and seeing his suits on their hangers. His size-thirteen shoes lined up like they were on a shelf in the Famous Footwear outlet. What to do with his socks? His underwear? I did not want to give up what he'd left behind.

This was just not fair. I wanted to die first! Carl was stronger than me. He knew how to handle loss. When his brother died in a head-on collision ten years ago, Carl ached, but he was more concerned with helping his brother's wife and kids get through it. "You do what needs to be done when people need you to be strong, Lo."

I've been trying to do what needs to be done, but I was not prepared for this hole Carl left in my heart, in my life. How in the world am I going to fill it? And with what? And where on earth do I go from here?

I have no idea.

About five years ago, Carl and I made a little show of "exchanging" our wills. He wanted to have a party to celebrate his life, rather than a depressing service. But his biggest demand was if he should go first, that I not spend the rest of my life mourning him, and that I not give up on finding love again. I had actually cracked up laughing while I was reading it. He didn't think it was one bit funny.

"So, you mean to tell me that if I happen to leave this world first, you would really be thinking about how to find another woman to replace me?"

"Well, I'm not saying I'd be out looking, but I'd imagine it could get lonely, and having a dog around isn't the same thing as having somebody to talk to and have dinner with."

"But where in the world would you look?"

"You're taking this too far, Lo, considering we're both alive and kicking."

"Answer the question, Billy Dee Williams."

We both laughed, and I remember throwing a piece of French bread at him and missing. B. B. King—who still was very quick at the time—grabbed it in his mouth and took off. Carl was lucky I didn't grab a handful of my delicious spaghetti and meatballs, or he'd have been covered in it!

"Not church, I hope. Those old biddies aren't any fun and probably wouldn't even let you kiss 'em," I said.

He laughed. "They have dating sites now for seniors, you know."

My eyes got big, and I was giving tossing that last meatball a lot more consideration.

"You mean you've already put some thought into this?"

"No, sweetie. But they advertise them on TV. I wouldn't want you to sit around here all by yourself. I would like to know you're still having fun."

"Okay. Well, if I should happen to go first, would you please send me a text to let me know when you've found an adequate replacement?"

And then we both started laughing and I ate that meatball. I also asked if we could read mine another day because I didn't want to spend the rest of the night thinking about dying. He agreed, and we downloaded *Coming to America* and watched it in each other's arms.

Truth be told, I'm really pissed at Carl for keeping his high blood pressure a secret, because he lied when he said the pills he was taking were only for his arthritis. I know why he didn't tell me. He didn't want to scare me, or give me cause to worry, but I have since found out from his doctor that he could've and probably should've had surgery to fix the problem in his heart. But Carl was afraid he wouldn't survive. If he was here, I would really like to kick his ass.

But I can't.

Chapter 3

I was pretending to watch *Access Hollywood* when the doorbell rang. B. B. King growled. He's still grieving, too, and hunches down on all fours whenever I take out his leash. I gave up trying. He has put on weight. But he's not the only one.

"Just a minute," I tried to say in a friendly tone. But friendly people call first. When I looked through the glass, I was surprised to see Odessa. But rules of etiquette have never applied to her.

I opened the door and tried not to look suspicious even though I was. Odessa has never subscribed to our mother's advice that "the only place you should look bad is at home." She dresses like a lumberjack, always in plaid shirts and black leggings, no matter how hot it is. She seems to be afraid of lipstick and only wears gloss, but she hadn't even bothered with that today. Her lips were dull.

"Why haven't you deposited that check?"

"What check?" I asked, and then immediately remembered she had given me an envelope at Carl's celebration, which I realized in that moment was now almost two months ago.

"How about a 'Hello, Sis? How are you doing?' And 'Sorry I didn't call first.'"

She stormed right past me, flopped down on the sofa, crossed her legs, and rocked her right foot up and down. She didn't have socks on in those New Balance sneakers.

"I'm sorry. How've you been doing, Lo?"

"Not great."

"Well, it's to be expected. They say grief takes as long as it takes. And I'm sorry to barge in on you like this, but I'm glad you didn't deposit the check yet."

I went into my bedroom and opened both closet doors. When I reached up to a top shelf to grab the black clutch, my elbow accidentally knocked one of Carl's sports jackets off its hanger and onto his black loafers. I looked down at it and then my eyes zigzagged back and forth toward the rows of his other shoes and then back up at all of his dress shirts on the left and then over to his favorite five suits and—

"You can't find it?" a female voice yelled.

Find what? I looked toward the door because for a moment I didn't know who it was or what she was asking me. And then I did.

"I found it," I said.

I picked up Carl's sports jacket and laid it flat across the bed. Then I wrapped my arms around his suits and pulled them out and placed them gently on the bed. When I looked at the shoes and shirts, I realized this was not the time. But it was time for me to pack his personal belongings. He wouldn't need them anymore.

I opened the purse and saw the white envelope Odessa had given me, rolled up like a straw. I took it out and walked back into the living room, where she had helped herself to a Pepsi. "Here it is."

"Why didn't you deposit it? You didn't think it was good?"

"I just forgot. There was a lot going on, if you remember correctly."

"Don't deposit it."

"Why not?"

"Because something else has come up."

"I'm not even going to ask."

"I borrowed against my house a while back and I owe the bank a lot of money. More than I owe you. Anyway, how've you been holding up?"

I'd already told her I was not great, so I didn't bother to respond. But then I heard myself say, "I'm thinking about selling both my stores and retiring."

"To do what?"

"I said I was thinking about it."

"You know, it's not smart to make rash decisions when you're grieving."

"So I've heard."

"They say you should give yourself at least a year."

"Well, I've closed both, at least temporarily, but I'm serious about selling the L.A. one at least."

"Why?"

"Because it doesn't make any sense to keep it. I don't need the money or the hassle and I'm too damn old. And plus, I'm just tired."

"Well, we all grieve our own way."

"I suppose I'll know when the day comes that I'm not consumed by sadness. But right now, it feels like a wound that's never going to heal."

"Come to my church. The Lord can help you mend faster."

"Don't start with me today, Odessa."

"Fine, do it the hard way, then. Not to bring up a sore subject, but how close was Carl to finishing up the renovations on Ma's house?"

"It's not Ma's house. Carl and . . . I own it."

"But she told me I could have it."

"When did she tell you that?"

"At the Repasse!"

"She said she wasn't going to say anything to you! Look, Odessa, can we talk about this another time? I'm not in the mood."

"I want the house."

Just then I heard B. B. King at the back door, whining to be let in. When he saw Odessa, he started growling. He has never cared for her.

"That dog is going to outlive all of us."

"Let me say this clearly. I have tried to be nice to you, Odessa, because you're my sister. I have bailed your ass out every time you get in financial trouble, which seems to be some kind of ongoing illness you have, but I am not the cure. I don't know why you think I owe you something just because you're my sister, but guess what? I'm not your keeper and how I make money is my business. You can't have Ma's house because it's not hers to give."

"Why don't you tell me how you really feel?"

"You drive a 530i BMW and every time I look around you're at Nordstrom or headed to Cabo. You're too old to be living hand to mouth, Odessa, and I'm tired of you thinking me or Ma should fix things for you."

"This is why nobody likes you."

B. B. King growled at her.

"Don't twist this around on me, Odessa. I have a basketball team's worth of close friends who will do anything in the world for me. How about you?"

"I have a lot of friends."

"Then why don't you ever call them to help you out when you mismanage your damn money?"

"I don't mismanage. I can no longer afford my lifestyle. Which happens to a lot of people when they get old. You need to learn how to express yourself without cursing."

"You're a shopaholic. And you're a hoarder. You buy stuff you don't need, don't use, and don't even wear."

And then she started crying, but B. B. King was not moved because he growled at her again.

"Stop it, B.B.," I said, and he dropped to the floor and put his chin on his front paws to watch what I could tell even he knew was a bad soap opera.

"I'm sorry. That was mean," I said. I didn't want to, but I walked over and hugged her. She felt limp, pitiful, so I squeezed her harder.

"I do a lot of things butt-backwards," she said. "But I'm trying to get better. Maybe if you just let me move into Ma's house for a year or two I could pay off my bills and get out of debt. I promise I'll take good care of the house."

"Why do you need a three-bedroom house to live in by yourself, Odessa?"

"I have a lot of furniture."

"That's not a good enough reason."

"We should keep it in the family, Loretha."

"I'll think about it, okay?" I heard myself blurt out, and regretted it right after I said it.

"How long before it's ready?"

"I haven't exactly been focused on finding someone to oversee the rest of the renovations yet, Odessa."

She stared at me blankly.

"Go home, Odessa."

"That's what I'm hoping you can help me do one day soon."

As she headed toward the door, B. B. King growled at her a final time.

"He's probably going to be next to go."

And she walked out the door, proving once again that just because someone is family doesn't mean you have to like them.

Even though it's been three months since Carl has been gone, I have not had the strength to start thinking about doing any of the things he'd promised my girlfriends I would. To their credit, they haven't been harassing me about it.

We're here for you, is what they say in our group text. *Whatever we can do, we'll do. Just let us know when you're ready to let us help you smile.*

I don't know what I'd do without them.

"I'm glad you agreed to walk with me," Korynthia said.

"I need to do something, but you know I cannot walk around the entire Rose Bowl, Korynthia."

"You don't know that, now do you, Lo?"

"No, but cut me some slack. I said yes. My bones are rusty and my muscles have atrophied. Look at you and look at me."

She just shrugged her shoulders.

"I just wanted to get you out of the house, Lo. Away from everything and everybody—including B. B. King."

This of course made me laugh. He wanted to come but I shut him in the backyard on the side of the pool under the one shade tree we have. He looked at me like he was being abandoned. His water bowl was full but when he saw the two small Milk-Bones I had given him since I was now limiting his snacks, I swear he rolled his eyes at me.

"You're more out of shape than me, Mr. King, and we both need to snap out of these blues. Carl would want us to. Now, I'm going to walk at least one-quarter of the Rose Bowl with your aunt Korynthia, who I'm sure sends her love. Bye."

He looked like he wanted to bark at me but changed his mind. Probably because he knew dinner would be more of the same if he dared.

"So," Korynthia said while bending over and stretching those long black legs that do not look like they are sixty-eight years old. "I have some good news."

"I would love to hear some good news, Ko."

"I finally passed the real estate exam."

"Really?" I said, since this made her third or fourth attempt, but then I cleaned it up. "Congratulations! So you're going to be selling houses?"

"I want to fix them up and flip them. C'mon, let's move."

"You know, I'm now the owner of a construction company."

"So, what are you going to do with it?"

"I haven't thought about it. I'm not at all interested in operating a construction company. I really think Carl just wanted to make sure I was financially solvent should something happen to him."

"Carl was not just a good man, but a smart one. I can't even begin to imagine anybody thinking that far ahead about me."

"I think he would want me to sell it so it wouldn't be a burden."

"So sell it."

"I can't walk fast," I warned.

"I'm not expecting you to."

We huffed forward silently for the next five or six minutes.

"So how are you feeling, Lo, even though that's probably a silly question?"

"No, it's not. Like this is all a bad dream and I'm just waiting to wake up."

"That's normal. I felt like that when my mama passed. You remember that. We were in ninth grade."

"Yes, I do."

"I didn't talk for two weeks."

"Because you couldn't?"

"Because I was pissed at her for taking all those pills and leaving us kids to pick up the pieces."

I didn't know what to say, so I just looked up at all the houses peeking out through a forest of all kinds of trees. One of them was where Lucky lived. When Korynthia's mother died, none of us had ever known a black person who had taken their own life. We'd thought only white people committed suicide and that was only because we had seen so much of it on television.

"I don't think your mama did that to hurt you or your brothers, Ko."

"I know that now. But back then I didn't. Aren't you pissed at Carl for dying?"

She stopped and turned to look me in the eye, forcing at least ten people to walk around us.

"Yes, I am. Not deep in my heart. But I wish he hadn't felt the need to keep his health issues a secret."

"What about you, Lo? Have you been taking care of yourself? I know the answer is no, which is why I asked you to come out here and walk with me."

"My heart hurts, Ko, and I wonder: if it stops hurting, will that mean I'm forgetting about Carl?"

"Of course not," she said and grabbed me by the hand and started moving again.

We walked for ten or fifteen minutes without saying a word.

"So. When are you thinking about getting back to your businesses? I still want to work at the shop part-time."

"I've been thinking about retiring."

"Don't. You'll be bored out of your mind, Lo. Plus, it's not good to make big decisions when you're blue. But maybe closing the L.A. store is a good compromise. It makes sense at this stage in your life."

"You mean old."

"We're senior fucking citizens. Forgive me for swearing—no, don't. Lighten your load, girl."

"You must be reading my mind."

"But please sell it to somebody black. Make Madam C. J. Walker proud. You heard from Jalecia lately?"

"No. And I've reached out quite a few times."

"Keep on her, Lo. All of us worry about her. We all agree that she probably needs to go to AA or maybe even one of those rehab places."

"She won't return my calls."

"Like I just said. Bug the shit out of her until she does."

"How's Bird?"

"Well, let me put it this way. He's my oldest son but I don't trust him. He lies about everything, including the variety of drugs he's on.

And he's selfish as hell, a lot like Jalecia, actually. All he cares about is himself."

"How old is he now?"

"He's a year and a half older than Jalecia. He turns forty-two in a couple of months. I swear, Lo, I'm tired of mothering. And I'm not thrilled about grandmothering and especially not about great-grandmothering, though it's less of a commitment since they're all in San Diego."

"You should visit them more often."

"I don't like driving that far."

"Well, why don't they ever come up here to see you?"

"Honestly? My grandkids say they don't like traveling with their little ones and my overeducated daughters are ashamed of me because I don't have a degree, though they don't have any problems asking me for loans they never pay back."

"I wish everything was easier."

"Me, too. Anyway, we can head back to the car if you want to, Lo."

"Wait. This may be completely out of left field, but do you have any regrets about your life, Ko?"

"Hell yes. I should've gone to college. How's that?"

"Did you have dreams you never told anybody about?"

"Yes. But I can't remember them."

"You are so full of shit. Make yourself remember. We're not too old to make changes!"

"Maybe I'll be a senior stripper!"

I pushed her.

"What about you? Did you really grow up wanting to sell beauty products?"

"Of course not. I just wanted to work for myself and I liked helping other women look good."

"You should add a makeup artist to your staff."

"I don't know what I'm going to do. Anyway, let's keep walking."

"I was hoping you'd say that," and she threw her long arm over my shoulders and pulled me against her. I am so grateful she is my friend. I wish Korynthia was my sister. Or that my sister was more like Korynthia.

"What are you going to do with Grandpa's Explorer?" Cinnamon asked, after dropping by with an entire month's rent. But before I had a chance to digest what she'd just asked me, or to give her a definitive *hell to the no,* she blurted out: "Did I tell you we're going to be a family of four in less than six months?"

Did she just say she's having twins? I crossed my arms, leaned all the way forward in my reading chair, and looked her in the eyes. "Lord, Cinnamon, two babies? What are you going to do? They can't live on breast milk forever."

"I know but, well, Jonas just got hired at Whole Foods, and I might have a job, too, Grandma."

"Doing what?"

"It's still up in the air. I don't want to jinx it."

"Well, good luck," I said, even though I was clearly not impressed. I hoped it showed.

I hadn't given one thought to Carl's big black Explorer parked all these months in the garage, but without thinking, I uncrossed my arms, leaned back in my chair, and heard myself say, "You can have it."

I immediately wished I hadn't said it. But, of course, I couldn't take it back. Seeing the small globe forming under the waistband of her orange paisley skirt with the straggly hem made me feel sorry for her stupid ass. Pregnant with twins, no less. Neither she nor Jonas has a clue about what to do with their own lives, let alone the lives of two babies. And I would not be able to sleep at night knowing they were riding around in a 2006 Prius with no working reverse.

I don't remember being this clueless when I was her age, although I probably was.

B. B. King barked when Cinnamon started screaming "thank you" over and over. She ran to me and kissed the top of my silver head. She even smelled like cinnamon, and her belly was warm and soft, and I realized that this was the first time I'd felt an ounce of gladness since Carl had been gone.

When Cinnamon left, I dialed Jalecia's number but got her voicemail. I hadn't thought about what I would say, so I just dove in: "*Hi, Jay, this is Mom calling again. I wish there was a way we could see each other soon. Could you please call me? I'm worried about you, and I would like us to act more like mother and daughter again, if you'll let us. Anyway, I love you, Jalecia. Please reach out. I promise not to bite. Oh, and congratulations on becoming a grandmother! Bye-bye.*"

As soon as I hung up I wished I could've hit Rewind and deleted that bite business.

Two weeks later I was sitting at the kitchen table, thumbing through the mail, when B. B. King started barking. I knew it couldn't be the pizza delivery because I'd only placed my online order ten minutes ago, so I rushed to the front door thinking maybe it was Jalecia, even though I hadn't heard a peep from her. But it was not my daughter. It was one of Carl's nephews, one of the two who'd decided not to go back to Flint, and who was currently living rent-free in one of my apartments until he could find a job. I opened the door.

"Hello, Miss Loretha. I'm sorry for just dropping by like this, but I was wondering if I might speak to you about something."

"Sure, come on in, Kwame," I said, although I was thinking, *Please don't ask to borrow some money because I'm tired of being a lending tree.*

"Thank you," he said, and ducked so his head wouldn't hit the doorframe.

"Is something wrong?" I asked.

B. B. King, who usually growls at strangers, didn't. In fact, he strutted over to where Kwame had sat down, and rolled over so his nose rested on the young man's humongous sneaker. Kwame bent over and rubbed B. B. King's head.

"Thank you, ma'am. No, nothing is wrong. At least I hope not. I've been wanting to talk to you about something ever since I got to California."

"Is it good or bad news? Because I can't handle any more bad news."

"I guess it depends on how you look at it."

I eased down in the recliner, realizing that this was the first time I'd sat in Carl's chair since he's been gone. I did not lean back.

"Well, first off, Boone—you know the cousin who's been sharing the place with me? He took a bus back home yesterday."

"Why?"

"He said he didn't like it here."

"What didn't he like?"

"Well, he said California is just different."

"In what sense?"

"Too many weird folks, and he didn't feel like he fit in here. Truthfully, I think he really just missed his girlfriend."

"What about you?"

"I don't have a girlfriend. And I like it here. So far. It's just been kind of hard finding a decent job, since I don't have a college degree."

"It sounds like you've been to college."

"Really? Well, I'm about ten credits shy of getting my associate's degree from the junior college in Flint."

"What happened?"

"I just got bored. I played basketball in high school and everybody thought I was going to get a scholarship to a D1 school."

"So why didn't you?"

He started rubbing B. B. King's head again. "I wasn't that good, plus I really didn't like playing. Just because I'm tall everybody thought I should play."

"How tall are you?"

"I'm only six-six."

Only?

"You ever think about going back to school?"

He nodded.

"What interests you?"

"A lot of things, but nothing in particular."

I decided not to press the issue, because for some reason I didn't think this was why he had come over here.

"Can I get you anything to drink?"

"No, ma'am."

"Well, I'm just waiting on a pizza, but it seems like something else is on your mind. Talk to me."

He stopped rubbing B. B. King and sat up straight.

"Well, this is kinda hard for me to say, but . . . I thought you might want to know that I'm not Carl's nephew. I'm his son."

I don't know why, but I wasn't surprised to hear this. He looked just like Carl. But what I also knew was Carl obviously hadn't known about him. Because he would've told me if he had.

"Thank you for telling me, Kwame. And I don't want you to think for a minute that hearing this has upset me."

He looked stunned, and who could blame him?

"I don't want anything from you, ma'am. I just thought it was important that you know."

"How old are you?"

"I just turned twenty-five."

"Where's your mother?"

"She's still in Flint."

"What does she do?"

"She drinks, mostly. And does a few drugs."

This made me lean back in Carl's chair. I did my best to soften my tone.

"How long have you known Carl was your father, Kwame?"

"I only found out when he passed away."

"Really?"

"Ma never told me."

"Why not?"

He looked down at the floor and then wiped his long fingers back and forth across his chin.

"Because she didn't want me to know."

"Why not?"

"I think because she was ashamed."

"Ashamed of what?"

"Herself. And plus, I think she was worried that if I knew I had a father out in California, I'd leave."

"Who was it who told you?"

"Everybody seemed to know but me. But a couple of my cousins finally told me on the bus to Carl's celebration."

When the delivery guy rang the doorbell, B. B. King didn't jump up. He just gazed up at me, his eyes full of what looked like empathy, as if even he was certain that Carl had had no idea he'd made a child before I'd met him and that right here was a young man who needed some mothering. I got up and paid for the pizza, and then I heard myself ask Kwame if he would like to stay—and not just for dinner—and he said, "Yes, ma'am."

Chapter 4

"I hope you got a DNA test," Lucky said, as she jabbed her fork into my last candied yam. We were having dinner at one of our favorite restaurants, Roscoe's House of Chicken and Waffles, because Lucky wanted to get out of the house and away from her husband, Joe. Truth be told, we both needed some fried chicken and collard greens. Lucky *also* had macaroni and cheese, which I passed on.

"No, I have not, Lucky," I said defensively. "It happened before Carl and I met. In Flint, when he was home visiting. Anyway, Kwame is a nice young man. He's twenty-five. And FYI, he didn't ask to move in. It was my suggestion."

"How long is he staying?"

"Why?"

"I just want to know."

"But why?"

"Because I want to make sure he doesn't turn out to be another burden."

"Maybe if you'd had children you'd know that they're not a burden."

"You can't tell me Jalecia isn't a burden. And Kwame isn't even your child, Loretha."

She never calls me Loretha unless she's trying to act superior.

"He's got my husband's blood, Lucky. I don't need to explain it any more than I already have. But suffice it to say he can stay until he gets on his feet."

"You've already got a daughter who needs help getting back on her feet."

"Come on, Lucky. I have bent over backward to help her. I gave her a job. Bought her a car. Paid her rent. Her cellphone bill. I've done far too much for her, and what have I gotten? She steals from me and can't even be bothered to call me on my birthday or say more than two words to me at my husband's memorial? She's forty frigging years old, Lucky. I cannot save her from herself."

She took a long sip of her iced tea and almost slammed the glass on the Formica table.

"But you're probably going to have to if she hits rock bottom."

We were both quiet for a minute. Lucky looked as if she wished she could take that thought back. I just shoved my fork into her macaroni and cheese. But I couldn't taste it.

"Does this boy do any drugs? Has he been to college? Does he have a job?"

"I got him a spot working with Carl's construction crew. And he's a few credits shy of an associate's degree, and no, he doesn't do drugs."

"And you trust him?"

"Yes. Waitress?"

"We haven't even eaten what's on our plates, Lo, what is it you could possibly want?"

"Water."

"This is your third glass. What's up with that?"

"I'm thirsty."

"You should tell your doctor. It's a sign of something."

The waitress appeared. A young Hershey-brown girl with thick, kinky tendrils that looked like a halo and round breasts like I used to have. She reminded me of that girl who used to sing with the Fugees, but I could not for the life of me think of her name.

"Sweetheart, could I please have another glass of water?"

"Yes, ma'am."

When she turned to leave I realized I also used to have a waistline and a behind that didn't jiggle, just like hers.

"What's that pretty young girl's name who used to sing with the Fugees?"

"Lauryn Hill. Why?"

"Dang, I forget a lot of shit. The waitress reminds me of her."

"So how does Odessa feel about Carl's kid moving in?"

"She doesn't know because I haven't told her. It's my house and she'll find out when she finds out. Anyway, enough about my life, Lucky. Let's talk about your world for a change."

"Nothing to talk about. Joe's still living in the guesthouse and if I wasn't so old I'd divorce him. He feels more like a pet than a husband at this point."

"Shut up, Lucky. I like Joe. We all like Joe. Sometimes more than we like your ass. And we almost don't blame him for moving into the guesthouse. You should try a little tenderness because all you do is complain."

She knows this is true, which is why she didn't or couldn't say anything.

The waitress brought my water and smiled at me. I wished she could be my daughter just for today.

"Are you going to eat that cornbread?" Lucky asked.

"No, and you can't have it. I am going to take it home for Kwame, along with a breast and thigh and a wing for me for later."

"I talked to Poochie today. She said she has to get a hip replacement."

"She's been putting that off for too long. I'll bet she doesn't have any problems sitting in front of those slots. How's her mama?"

"Her days are numbered. Poochie's going to need help, but the rest of her family is on her last nerve."

We both just nodded at that.

"You know what," I said. "I think I'll forget about the wing and get two pieces of sweet potato pie instead. One for me and one for Kwame."

"Aren't you cutting back on sweets?"

"I am. I'm eliminating things one by one."

She looked at my plate and knew I was lying. I haven't figured out how to make any changes yet. I've only just started getting used to being without my husband. Hell, you can't change everything at once.

"It looks like you've put on a few yourself, Lucky. And from what you wolfed down this evening, it doesn't seem as if you're really all that interested in losing any weight either."

"I have no willpower. I admit it. But my pressure is up, so I'm considering getting that gastric bypass surgery."

"Really?"

"My doctor told me I need to lose at least a hundred pounds or I could be in trouble, and I can't see any other way to lose that much. I'm already taking blood pressure and cholesterol medication."

"Since when?"

"What difference does it make?"

She then bit off a big piece of honey cornbread.

"Neither one of us should even be in here," I said as I looked down at my plate. The chicken was fried. I could see the ham in the collard greens. The candied yams had brown sugar and butter oozing out of them. And then there was my beautiful cornbread. Did I really need to eat all this?

"Let me say this, Lo. I know Carl kind of forced you to make some promises to us as part of his grand birthday bargain, but even though I know you're still grieving, I think the sooner you start making good on them, the better."

"I know. I'm almost ready."

"When are you going to trade in that ugly Volvo?"

"None of your business."

When she whipped out her gold American Express card, I realized it had been four months since the five of us had had a group dinner. We try to get our whole crew together for dinner once a month, so we can catch up and bitch and pretty much have our own version of female church. It's a thing we've done for decades, through multiple kids and multiple husbands and good and bad. But we hadn't had one since before Carl died.

"Lucky, I was just thinking, it's your turn to host a group dinner."

She looked at me like I'd said something wrong. "You sure you're ready?"

I nodded my head. The truth was I was lonely, and I missed us spilling our guts and being silly all together. My friends are the sisters I wish I had, even when they do get on my nerves and call me out on my BS. But we've been doing this for one another all our lives. We grew up in the same neighborhood, went to middle and high school together. Some of us went away to college or didn't go far, and one not at all. We know one another's secrets, the ones we're brave enough to share, which is why kids and husbands and divorces have not been able to loosen our ties. Of course, we occasionally divorce one another but we always find ways to annul it.

"But I can't have the dinner at my house," Lucky blurted out.

"Why not?"

"Because I'm doing some renovating."

Now she was the one lying. Her house is beautiful and completely up to date, like a small castle on a hill above the Rose Bowl. Rather than question her, I gave her a chance to improve the lie. I just looked at her. And waited.

"The hardwood floors are being redone. I can do next month or the one after."

She tried to push her chair back but it wouldn't move. So she gave it a harder shove.

"I need to get some peach cobbler to take home to Joe. Speaking of which, please don't tell the girls he's still living in the guesthouse."

"Why would I?"

Of course I'd tell all of them, including Poochie, who'd say she didn't blame him.

When I got home, Kwame wasn't there. B. B. King was asleep in Kwame's room. Traitor. I took a hot shower, put on one of the old-lady nightgowns I got from Macy's during one of their Buy One Get One Free sales, got a bottle of water from the fridge, fell across my bed, and turned on the OWN channel. I closed my eyes for a minute.

"Do you like spicy food?"

"I like spicy everything," I say. I don't know why I'm trying to be so cute when I haven't even been out with Carl but twice.

"So, can I ask you a very personal question?"

Butterflies start flying around inside my belly. I take a sip of my margarita.

"How personal?"

"No no no. Not that personal. I was just wondering how old you are."

I am thinking about lying, subtracting a few years, but then I think I shouldn't since, after we get married, he will find out the truth anyway.

"I'm forty-three. And you don't have to tell me I look younger than that, because young men hit on me all the time."

I start laughing to let him know I am just kidding.

"I believe it. You look about thirty-six. I'm forty-eight."

"I already knew that. You look good for being so old."

"I like you."

"I think I might like you, too."

It is hard for me to eat but I force myself to, trying my best not to eat too much salsa, which always gives me gas. When we finish, we step outside and, of course, the moon is spying on us. Then he takes me by the hand and says, "You feel like walking off some of those enchiladas?"

And so we walk all the way to a park where he asks me to sit in a swing and he sits in the one next to me. We tell each other where we've been and what we've done and who we have spent our time with in all the years up until now.

"So," he says, squeezing my hand gently as we head back to our cars, "you might as well get used to me because I'm pretty sure we're going to spend the rest of our lives together."

I melt. He opens my door for me, bends down, and kisses me on both cheeks.

"I don't want a big wedding," I hear myself say.

"You can have whatever you want."

I sprang up in bed. My nightgown was drenched. I looked at Carl's pillow and touched it. It was cold and smooth. I pressed my hand to my forehead and felt a smile emerge on my face.

"I still miss you, baby," I said aloud. "I'm trying to learn how to live without you. It's not been easy. I've met your son. But you probably know that, and that he's living here with me. He looks like I imagine you did at twenty-five. I'm going to do all I can to help him find his way. And my daughter, too, because she's still lost, Carl."

I turned the television off and drank the rest of my water in one gulp, then closed my eyes again, but this time I whispered, "My love still runs deep. Good night, sweetheart."

"I thought I was borderline," I said to Dr. Alexopolous. "Are you sure?"

She looked like she was about to roll her eyes at me but then changed her mind. "Numbers tell us everything."

"Well, I don't want to take any pills."

"You don't necessarily have to take medication. There are injections you can give yourself."

Was she nuts? I'm scared as hell of needles. Ma said she had to hold me down with her knee pressed against my chest to make me stay still for my shots when I was a kid—and that I kicked a few doctors in the process.

"You have to do one or the other. Either will help you lose weight."

"I believe I have lost about eight or nine pounds."

"You have not. In fact, you've gained twelve."

I so do not like this bitch.

"Well, my husband of twenty-four years passed away five months ago. I made some good changes before that but got derailed."

So I lied. Because she didn't look like she would respect the truth. I hoped if Carl was listening that he would forgive me.

"I understand. And I'm very sorry for your loss. The receptionist told me it was the reason you canceled your last two appointments. But you need to focus on your health now."

Since I was now sitting on the edge of the examination table, I started pulling on the tissue-paper cover, tearing off the corners, then I jumped off and stood upright. She moved to the side as if I were going to harm her.

"Look," I said. "I don't mean to sound so combative, but I've heard of people reversing type 2 diabetes if they change their diet and exercise."

"Well, Mrs. Curry, for the past year and a half I've been encouraging you to change your lifestyle, but you have not. And diabetes is the result of your not taking my advice."

"I have tried," I lied. "But it's hard to break old habits."

The truth is I don't like exercising. I don't like to sweat and I like being lazy. But I suppose it really was time to make a change. "It's not too late, though, is it, Dr. Alexopolous?"

"It depends. Your age might make it a little tougher."

I could've cut her the way I looked at her. "What's my age got to do with anything? It's not like I've got stage three cancer or something."

"That's true. I didn't mean to frighten you."

"Well, you did. I'm a little pissed, to be honest with you."

A burst of cool air from the vent made the thin blond nest on her little head waft to the side. I could see her pink scalp.

"I apologize," she said, with a half ounce of sincerity.

"It's okay, Dr. Alexopolous. I have never really trusted you, if you want to know the truth. You doctors are all alike. You aren't encouraging. You like to scare the hell out of people. You write prescriptions that don't cure the problem, just postpone it. Well, I'm going to find a doctor who has a better attitude about how a person can improve their health regardless of how old they are."

She said nothing as I opened the door and walked out.

I'll show her ass. And I'll come back when my numbers prove her wrong. But not starting today, because what I needed before making this transition was a double cheeseburger, some soft fries, a diet Coke, and three farewell Twizzlers. After all, I needed to process the promise I'd just made to myself.

I was surprised when I saw Kwame's car parked in the driveway, in my spot, so I parked on the street instead and grabbed yesterday's mail. When I walked inside the house I heard what sounded like rap music coming from the backyard. I put my purse on the table and walked through the living room. When I opened the back door, B. B. King was lying on the top step, wet.

At first I heard water splashing, but then it stopped. When I opened the gate, there, in the pool, was Kwame with his arms around a tall, blond young man.

He looked over at me and his brown skin seemed to turn red.

B. B. King barked.

"Go lie down, B.B."

"I'm so sorry, Mama-Lo," Kwame said.

Even though this is what we'd agreed that he could call me, it had sounded more endearing up until now.

"What's your friend's name?"

"Parker, ma'am."

"Well, hello, Parker," I said, acknowledging Kwame's embarrassed companion. And then my eyes turned back to Kwame. "What I really want to know is what are you doing at home this time of day, Kwame?"

He looked surprised at my question. I'm sure because the tone of my voice did not indicate outrage or anger.

"I got fired."

"Who fired you?"

"The supervisor."

"You mean Marquez?"

"Yes, ma'am."

"How many times have I had to tell you not to call me that, Kwame?"

"Yes, Mama-Lo. I'm sorry."

"Sorry about what?"

"This," he said, pointing to Parker in the pool.

"What's to be sorry about?"

They both looked shocked.

"You have a right to like who you like. I'm old but I'm not that old. So why did Marquez fire you?"

"Because he found out I . . . like guys."

"What's that got to do with the quality of your work?"

"Nothing."

"Did he bust you doing something like this on the job?"

"No."

"Then, what?"

"He saw us holding hands after work."

"That's it?"

He nodded.

"That is none of his damn business. Look, I will talk to him. It's your father's company. I'm sure we can get your job back."

"But I don't want it back."

"What?"

"I don't like doing that kind of work, but I wanted to have an income after you were kind enough to let me move in with you."

"And so, now what? Are you rich, Parker?"

"No, ma'am."

"Are you two going to live together?"

"No," Kwame said. "Are you going to kick me out?"

"No. But you can't just do nothing."

"I was hoping to go back to school, but I don't know what I want to study. I thought I could work part-time until I figure it out, if that's okay."

"Doing what?"

"Do you need any help at the House of Beauty?"

Shit. At this rate, I'm going to need to get a bigger place just to staff all the people I hire as personal favors.

"Possibly," was all I said. "Look, I'm going inside. Have fun but not the kind of fun you would have if I wasn't here," and then I closed the gate and B. B. King followed me back to the house.

I wish he had just told me he was gay. He was probably scared and thought I wouldn't be able to handle it, but he was wrong. Nobody should have to hide who they are inside to please people on the outside.

Chapter 5

"Can you please bring me some stamps?" Ma had asked when I called to tell her I'd be over later today.

"Who are you going to write?"

"None of your business. I'll tell you when you get here."

"Do you need envelopes?"

"I suppose they would help. But not those long ones. I don't have that much to say."

When I pulled into the parking lot at Valley View Assisted Living, which looks more like a four-star resort than a care facility, I recalled the first visit after we'd "suggested" Ma would be safer here. That was two years ago. When she was a young eighty-four.

An attendant had pushed a wheelchair over to help us.

"That better not be for me. As you can see, I can walk. I'm not disabled, and to my knowledge, not even close to being senile."

"This is just for your safety and to make you feel comfortable," the attendant said.

"Are you blind? I only need help when I say I need it. My daughter here—what's your name again?" she asked and started laughing. "Just kidding! My daughter here says the food is good. I hope I don't have to have her sneak in some Old Bay because you know you white folks don't know how to season food."

"Ma, stop it!" I whispered loudly and pulled her plaid suitcase down the hall.

Ma looked suspicious when the attendant opened her room door, but when she saw how bright and spacious the room was, that the bathroom had a tub and a shower (with grab bars in both), and that the TV was mounted on the wall, she actually seemed excited. She ran her hand across the chenille bedspread, which happened to be her favorite color: powder blue.

"I hope you like it," I said.

She looked at me like I had just said the dumbest thing in the world.

"Okay! I'm all checked in so you can leave now! Gimme a kiss right here," she said, pointing to her cheek. So I did.

Today, when I knocked on her door, she said, "Whatever you're selling, I don't want any."

"It's me, Ma, and I'm not selling anything, but I brought stamps and envelopes like I was ordered!"

"Come on in, Loretha, but you can't stay long."

I opened the door and put the plastic bag on her dresser.

"Why not?" I asked, not taking her seriously. She was sitting in the pink-and-white pinstriped gliding chair I'd bought her from a baby store because she didn't like to rock, wearing her pink jogging sweats, with one of her paisley-covered scrapbooks open in her lap. Her hair, white as a snowflake, was pulled into a soft knot. She was a sight to see.

"Because I'm in the middle of reminiscing."

"About what?"

"I don't remember."

I sat down at the foot of her bed and I could smell that sweet lily of the valley lotion that always made me nauseous. I slipped my sneakers off so they fell and thought about lying down and putting her white throw blanket over me, but I didn't. I wondered if one day I'd be living in a place like this. Would my daughter and son visit me?

"You cold?" she asked, looking over at me. I could see the veins in her glassy eyes from behind her glasses.

"A little."

"You shouldn't be, chile. You are much thicker than you should be. Are you trying to eat away your grief? It won't work."

"Ma, I have only put on about ten pounds."

"That's fifteen pounds you don't need. Don't go getting fat, Loretha, because then it'll just be downhill from there. One illness snowballs into another. Just look at how sexy and lean I am in comparison."

She had the nerve to stand up. Her light pink jogging suit was hanging off her.

"Are you still eating those cheeseburgers and French fries every other meal?"

"No."

"You can lie to me but lying to yourself is a whole lot worse. Go pull that throw over your shoulders."

She slowly turned a few pages in her book and I could hear the plastic cracking. And then she just stopped and looked at me.

"Don't hold grudges, Loretha. Even when somebody does something you find unforgivable."

"What are you talking about, Ma?"

"Don't play dumb."

"I don't hold anything against anybody."

"For starters, you've got a grudge against your sister. I know this for a fact. I know she owes you a lot of money, and she owes me a lot, too. But I never expected her to pay me back. You shouldn't have either."

"She takes advantage of me and I don't like it."

"Not everybody knows how to manage money, Loretha, and not everybody has good judgment. Odessa was a smart cop but dumb as hell when she punched out. You can't change people by punishing them for being who they are. So just accept them."

"So, what's on that page, Ma?" I asked, because I didn't want to talk about Odessa anymore. "I can't stay long."

"And I don't want you to. It's *Wheel of Fortune* night."

I stood up and tried looking over her shoulder.

"I have no idea who most of these folks are. None whatsoever." And she started laughing. "But hold on. I think that might be me!" she said, pointing at a young girl who looked like me about fifty years ago. "Hey, so how's your memory coming along, Loretha?"

"I miss a word or two here and there, or forget what I was thinking or saying or what I was about to do every once in a while. But other than that, my memory is good!"

"Well, get used to it, because before you know it you'll be looking in your old scrapbook and won't be able to recognize folks you know meant something to you, or they wouldn't be in here."

"I don't have a scrapbook."

"I know it's all google-able, but one day Google will be obsolete, too, mark my words. So make sure you print out pictures of every place, everything, and everybody you don't want to forget."

"I will."

"So, are you and Odessa speaking these days?"

"I don't know."

"What about your daughter? What's her name again?"

"Very funny, Ma. No, she won't return my phone calls."

"Seems like you're on the outs with quite a few members of your family."

"I didn't do anything to them, though, Ma."

"That's how you see it."

"No, that's how it is."

"You need to lighten up because some of the things you think weigh a lot, don't."

"So, who is it you're going to write to?" I asked, trying to change the subject again.

"You."

"Me? You're gonna write me? About what? Just tell me whatever it is you want to say."

"I can't always say what I'm really thinking to you. You make me nervous."

"What? How do I make you nervous, Ma?"

"You don't listen. You think you've got all the answers. You worry about the wrong things. I still have wisdom to give you before I kick the bucket."

Then she started laughing.

"What's so funny about dying, Ma?"

"It's not funny, but it happens to everybody and sometimes when we least expect it. I'm getting a little bored being alive to be honest. I've done enough, and had enough fun to last. But you, baby girl, you still have miles to go."

"Ma, I don't need to be preached to. Odessa does a good enough job of that."

"See, there you go. Judging her simply for who she is."

"Maybe I can be a little harsh, but I feel like I've been on *E* since Carl has been gone."

"I know, baby. But you've gotta decide if you want to keep the engine in Neutral or shift gears and put it in Drive."

I just squeezed her hand.

"Anyway, look, baby. I'm not trying to be Ann Landers but I know you're suffering from loneliness and I still remember what that feels like. This is why I read things that lift me up. I read my horoscope every day. Actually I read all twelve of them and write down any encouraging things I can use. But I also read O and *AARP* and that *Real*

Simple because they always have some feel-good stuff in them. I just thought it would be nice to send you a line or two when I find something worth sharing. Would you mind?"

"No. But do I have to write you back?" I laughed.

"No. But I hope you do that more often."

"What?"

"Laugh."

"Are you sending notes to Odessa, too?"

"No."

"Why not?"

"Because she already thinks she's got all the answers. She took getting the Holy Ghost way too far. God can't solve all of our problems. He gives us the tools but some of us are too lazy to use them. Anyway, here's a picture of both of your fathers," she said, and handed me two black-and-white Polaroids that made both men look gray and dull. "There's something I've been meaning to tell you. Well, two things."

"Is this going to be depressing?" I asked, handing the pictures back to her.

"No."

"What's the first thing?"

"I want you to understand what made me have sex with two different men in two days."

"Ma, I don't want to hear this."

"I need you to."

"I haven't even spent much time thinking about it, Ma."

She just looked at both pictures and shook her head.

"I was not a whore. It was about power. My power. I was the one who decided I wanted to be with both of them. I even told each one about the other, just to piss them off." She laughed like she had just heard a good joke.

"Really?"

She nodded. Then her eyes became glazed like she was looking out a window. I couldn't believe she was telling me this and I didn't know if I wanted to hear it. It just felt wrong. I didn't want to know her secrets.

"Men have always slept with as many women as they wanted to and nobody ever thought anything of it. Like they had a right to as much as they could get. I wanted that same power. And I got it. But I also got you and Odessa out of the deal. Who knew twins could have different fathers?"

I couldn't say a word.

"Anyway, I've been wanting to get that off my chest for years."

"Okay. What's the second thing you wanted to talk about?"

"Odessa has always been selfish and I'll just say it: she can be a bitch, but I want her to have my house. She's got no other options."

"What do you mean?"

"She was about to lose that ridiculous house of hers because she just kept borrowing against it. And she's been renting the little guesthouse from the people who bought it, but now they want to move into the guesthouse while they do some renovating. She didn't tell you? I guess she didn't want you to know."

Why do people keep secrets like this?

"Anyway, let her play house so she can stop worrying. Can you do that for me?"

"I did tell her I'd give it some thought, but why does she need a three-bedroom house with a yard just for herself? I own an apartment building. A two-bedroom should be enough for her, maybe I can arrange that."

She closed her eyes.

"Ma?"

And then they opened.

"Can't you see me sitting right here in my candy-striped chair? I'm not deaf, Loretha."

"What would you like to do for your birthday?"

"I'm having another one? I just had one a few months ago!"

I nodded and smiled. "The big eighty-seven."

"You have got to be kidding! I thought I was turning ninety on the next one, if you want to know the truth. I do not want a gift and I do not want to celebrate. Unless you want to sneak me in a pint of Hennessy!"

"No, I do not. It's next month. Odessa and I will take you to P.F. Chang's."

"I'll check my calendar. But tell me this: Did you bring the stamps?"

I looked at her and could tell she didn't remember. "Of course I did. They're on your dresser."

Just then, Marvin Gaye singing "Ain't No Mountain High Enough" rang out from my purse and I reached inside to get my cellphone.

"I used to love that song, Loretha. Can you put Otis Redding's 'Sitting on the Dock of the Bay' on mine one day?"

I nodded and pressed my finger in the air to shush her when I saw it was Jalecia.

"Hello."

"Ma?"

"Jalecia? Is something wrong?"

"Why does something have to be wrong?"

"Well, it's usually the only time you call."

"I need to know if you can pick me up in the morning."

"Where are you?"

"Jail."

"For what?"

"A DUI."

"Is she in jail again?" Ma asked loud enough for Jalecia to hear.

"Is that Grandma? Please don't tell her where I am."

"What is it you need me to do?"

"First let me say this: I was not drunk, Ma. I passed a car too fast without putting on my blinker so a cop pulled me over and made me take a Breathalyzer and it was only .10. Okay, the legal limit is .08, but

I am here because of my priors. Plus, they towed my car so it's impounded."

"I haven't heard from you since Carl died. Should I take a wild guess why you're calling?"

"It's five thousand dollars bail. I got very lucky. This is only my third DUI so it's still just a misdemeanor. The bail bondsman told me all you need to put up is five hundred."

If I hadn't been in the room with my mother staring me down, I'd have screamed, "I'm not fucking doing this again, Jalecia." But I was, so I tried to remain calm.

"Where are you?"

"In Palmdale."

"Palmdale? What the hell were you doing way out there? Never mind. What time tomorrow?"

"Noon. If possible. I have to stay here overnight. Until I'm sober."

"Anything else?" I asked, not wanting an answer.

"Thank you," she said. "Give Grandma a hug and tell her I'll be up to visit her soon."

She hung up.

"I'd leave her ass in there if I were you, Loretha. What'd she do this time?"

"An outstanding warrant for a moving violation."

"I'm old but I'm not stupid. That chile has got a drinking problem. Even Helen Keller could see that. And Lord only knows what else. Did you bring the stamps?"

This caught me completely off guard, but when I looked in her eyes, I could tell that Ma had forgotten. The caregiver had warned me that this was how dementia worked, but I had not seen it come on this clearly.

"Yes," I said.

I took the book of stamps out of the plastic bag and handed them to her.

"What about envelopes?"

I was already pulling them out.

"Wait a minute! What day is it again?"

"Saturday."

"Oh heck! I'm saved from arts and crafts because tonight is *Wheel of Fortune* night!"

"You told me. I didn't think you liked group activities."

"I don't know. I like being entertained. And the popcorn is good." I bent down and gave her a kiss on both cheeks. She patted them both and tried to smile.

"Know when to say no," she said. "And check your mail next week, but don't expect something from me every week. I've got a busy life, you know."

As soon as I got home, I saw Kwame's car in the driveway. I wasn't in the mood to talk to him this evening, so when I heard B. B. King bark, I was surprised. He hardly ever barks when Kwame's home.

B.B. licked my hand when I walked in.

"Hey, handsome," I said, and rubbed his head.

"Kwame?"

There was no answer. And then I saw a text on my phone. *Mama-Lo, I went to Las Vegas with a friend. Be back on Sunday. I fed B. B. King and took him for a walk. He wanted to go to Vegas, too, but he's broke! Love, Kwame*

The next morning I spent over an hour on the phone with the bail bondsman to figure out how best to pay Jalecia's bond. I went ahead and put the entire five thousand on my credit card. She was right, it would've only been five hundred if I had been willing to use my house as collateral, but if she failed to show up in court in thirty days they could've put a lien on my house. I did not trust her.

It took an hour to drive all the way out to Palmdale, and the mountains kept me company. The yucca trees on the side of the freeway reminded me that I was in the desert. I was trying not to grind my teeth or grip the steering wheel too tight and I tried to think of what Ma had said about accepting people for who they are. My daughter is not a criminal. She's an alcoholic and this is the result. But I can't make her stop drinking. I can't make her see where she's headed. It's this feeling of helplessness that's making me lose faith. Even though I have never stopped praying for her.

When I saw Avenue Q, I wanted to just keep driving, but I exited and immediately saw the sheriff's department, a beige stucco building that looked just like a lot of the tract houses I passed on the way here. But this was a jail. I turned in to the entrance and there was my daughter, sitting on a bench smoking a cigarette. She didn't look like she had just gotten out of jail. She looked like she was waiting for a bus. I was her bus.

I got as close as I could, but had to turn in to the parking lot. She walked over before I had a chance to park.

She had on the same dress she'd worn to Carl's Repasse. I was trying to process the reality that I had driven more than sixty miles to get my daughter out of jail for drunk driving, that this is what her life had come to at forty years old. I wondered if it was my fault that she was lost. I thought about asking her. But when I unlocked the passenger door and she dropped down hard on the seat, she said, "Thank you for picking me up, but please don't ask me any questions, Ma. It was all a big mix-up."

"What exactly were you doing all the way out here?"

She sighed and took a red scrunchie out of her purse. She grabbed a handful of dreadlocks and pulled and twisted as many of them as she could on top of her head, forming a spray that looked just like those yucca trees.

"I have friends out here. They were having a birthday party. I got pulled over. End of story, Ma."

"No, it's not the end of the story, Jalecia."

"I'm grateful, but don't worry, I won't miss my court date so you'll get most of your money back."

"Where's your car?"

"In impound."

"And how much is that?"

"Well, that's kind of another problem."

I pressed the brakes a little too hard and gripped the steering wheel too tight. The car screeched to a halt.

"Take it easy, Ma. Okay. So, the towing company is charging me a hundred-eighty dollars and impound fees, but I have to have proof of insurance before they'll release the car."

"Which means you don't have proof of insurance."

"It lapsed because I didn't have the money."

"You have to stop this shit, Jalecia."

"Ma, I'm not in any mood for a lecture right now. Please."

"I don't care what you're not in the mood for, Jalecia. I wasn't in the mood to drive all the way the hell out here to get you out of jail, but I did because you're my daughter. But pay attention. You have a drinking problem. And Lord only knows what else. But this is just one reason why your father left this world too soon: doing too much of the wrong things with the wrong people. Look at yourself, Jalecia. You're forty. There's still time to turn your life around, you just have to make smarter choices."

"Thanks for the pep talk. Look, I know I messed up and I'm sorry I had to call you, but my boyfriend . . ."

"What boyfriend?"

"Forget it, Ma. I'll pay you back, every dime."

"I suppose you already know the closest place to get instant car insurance, then?"

"Yes, it's less than five minutes from here."

"Let me ask you a really personal question."

"I've already been interrogated enough in there, Ma. Could you cut me just a little slack? I f'd up. I'm working on getting my life together."

"Really? And tell me, just how are you doing that?"

"Is *that* your personal question?"

"Where are you living these days?"

"In Compton."

"And just who's in Compton?"

"I've got family there."

"Peggy?"

"Yes."

"Then why didn't you call her to bail you out?"

"Because she's not in a position to help me."

"Tell me something, Jalecia. What would you have done if I had refused to pay your bail?"

"I'd be in that cell for thirty days, until my hearing."

"Remember that the next time this happens."

"There won't be a next time," she said.

It took two hours and $336 more to get the insurance and the 2008 Hyundai out of impound. Jalecia gave me an impatient hug and followed me out of the lot. But I got on the freeway heading home. She took the streets. Maybe the party she missed was still going on.

Chapter 6

I walked into the grocery store and stared. I looked to the left at the apples and pears and oranges stacked like pyramids and then straight down the aisle at the detergent and paper towels and all the other household items, which was when I felt someone tap me on the shoulder.

"Hello there, Mrs. Curry. You look lost. May I help you find something?"

I just started laughing because it was Joe, Lucky's giant husband, whose once-blond hair was now silver. He was still a good-looking man. He always reminded me of a country singer whose name I couldn't remember.

"Yes, Joe. Could you please tell me what the hell I came in here for?"

He gave me a bear hug. His stomach was now a soft globe and the lower buttons on his gray plaid shirt looked ready to pop off.

"Welcome to the club. Apparently, I came in here for these, which it took me a minute to recall." He held up two small boxes of figs, one purple and one green, then lowered them for me to try, but as soon as

I reached for a purple one I remembered reading somewhere that figs were full of sugar. And for once, my conscience won.

I waved my hand back and forth.

"So how are the floors coming along?"

"What's wrong with the floors?" Joe asked. I knew it! Redoing her floors, my ass. Lucky likes to lie about things that aren't worth lying about. She's always been like that, and I don't know why.

"Oh, my mistake," I said, and gave him another hug. I have always liked Joe, and actually feel sorry for him, because he has worshipped Lucky for almost half a century, and back then white men didn't marry black women. Lucky was half her size then, sexy as hell and quite the flirt. And him being her boss at the studio where they worked didn't hurt him any. None of us ever understood what else he saw in her besides her body because Lucky is so unforgiving and always complains about everything and everybody. When she told him she did not want children, he agreed. Like I said, he'd do anything for her.

I decided not to call Lucky out on her lie about the floors, which was why we all reported to Korynthia's house for our first group dinner since Carl's passing. Lucky, Korynthia, and I were sitting at Korynthia's dining room table, wondering where Sadie was.

Out of all of us, Korynthia has the best taste. Her home and everything in it is modern, and looks like something you used to see in *House Beautiful*.

"Sadie just texted. She said she might not be able to make it," Lucky said.

"Why?" I asked.

"I'll bet I know why," Korynthia said. She leaned forward in her chair and put one elbow on the table next to the straw basket of sliced French bread. She had just gotten her hair braided neon silver. Against her root-beer skin tone and fit body, she looked like a sixty-eight-year-old fashion model.

"Tell us!" Lucky yelled.

"I saw her in the church parking lot an hour ago, but she didn't see me. The parking lot was full, must have been a big funeral."

Skipping out on the first meeting of our posse since Carl passed to go to yet another funeral for somebody she probably didn't know? As Ma used to say, Sadie is "as full of shit as a Christmas turkey."

"If there's something to tell, tell it!" I said.

We all slid our glasses down to the bridges of our noses in an attempt to see Korynthia over them. I wondered when we all started wearing them. All of our glasses were ugly and it was obvious none of us put much thought into the styles we'd picked. We really looked like old ladies. I made a note to buy two new pairs with colorful frames.

"Okay. I was driving by her church and like I said, I saw Sadie in the parking lot. She was with a woman. A white woman with short silver hair, who kissed her on the lips."

"What kind of kiss?" Lucky asked.

"What difference does it make?" I asked.

"Did she see you?" Lucky asked, hoping she had.

"Maybe?"

"This is not news. To be honest, we've always thought this about Sadie and none of us has ever really cared except you, Lucky," I said. "If it's true, and she's happy, then I'm happy for her."

"Me, too," Korynthia said. "The woman was cute."

"Don't make me throw up," Lucky said.

"You need to get a grip, Lucky, and stop being so damn judgmental," I said. "Everybody should be whoever they are and there's no shame in it, so shut the hell up!"

"I agree," Korynthia said. "But Sadie doesn't strike me as being cool enough to be a lesbian. She's just so lackluster."

We all just nodded in agreement.

"So, what are we having tonight?" I asked even though I could smell the cheese on top of the tomato sauce. "I can't stay late."

"Why not?" Korynthia asked. "Are you finally going to reopen the shop?"

"I've been mulling everything over, Ko. Believe me, I'll let you know as soon as I decide what I'm doing."

"Well, hurry up. I need something to do all day because I'm not selling any mansions and I'm also tired of driving back and forth to San Diego to babysit my great-grandkids, or doing it when they drop the little suckers off here."

"Hold on!" I said. "We're supposed to wait until after we have a drink and the food is on the table and Poochie is on the line before we start spilling our guts."

"Then where's the beef?" Lucky asked, thinking we'd laugh, but neither of us did.

"I made lasagna and a salad and as you can see, French bread and steamed asparagus."

We all looked at one another with a smile of relief and poured ourselves glasses of red wine. Korynthia then set her cellphone in the middle of the table and punched in Poochie's cell number. Her big brown face popped on the screen. The only other time I do this FaceTime is with Jackson, and even then Cinnamon usually has to help me.

"Hi, everybody," Poochie said. She looked older than all of us and she was wearing a curly black wig, clearly a cheap one and she should know better. Even though we're all friends, I thought she could've put on some kind of powder and any kind of lip gloss just to look more presentable. I suppose she didn't feel like she needed to impress us. "I miss y'all." And we knew she meant it.

Just then, the door opened and in walked Sadie, dressed in yet another ugly church dress. This one was a sad shade of gray I wouldn't be caught dead in. And if I were a lesbian I would not be attracted to her.

"We miss you, too, girl," Sadie said for everybody. "I'm sorry I'm late. Choir practice went on a little longer than I expected, and we had to get the church ready for a funeral service tomorrow morning but I'm here now. Hey, Poochie!"

"Hey, Church Lady. I hope you've been praying for my mama."

"Chile, my prayer list is long and Mama Kay is on it."

"How is your mama doing, Poochie?" Korynthia asked for all of us.

"Not good, but I'm making sure she stays comfortable. So, how is everybody there? Wait! Before we get started on the usual, I want to say something to Lo. Lo?"

I almost jumped out of my chair wondering why she was singling me out.

"Yes, Poochie?"

"How are you?"

"Fair to middling."

"Look, I know you're probably still grieving hard and I just have to say it took me almost a year to get used to my sweet Donald being gone. I just want you to know that you can only do what you can do."

Everyone nodded around me, but Sadie said, "We all agree."

"Anyway, you've been through a lot these past months and I wanted to say that I think we're all overdue for some fun so I propose it's time all of you got on the casino bus and came on up here to Vegas. I could use some company and we can gamble and go to an outlet and maybe see a show. Sadie, we already know you're afraid of sinning, but don't veto the plan, just stay home."

"I'll go," she said without hesitating.

Everybody's mouths dropped open.

"I don't have to gamble. I can't stand the cigarette smoke, but I'll sit in front of the water show. Plus, I like to people watch."

"Promise us you won't preach on the bus," Lucky said.

"I promise."

"I wouldn't have any objections to seeing O again," Korynthia said.

"Is Celine Dion still at Caesars?" Sadie asked.

We all just looked at her.

"I don't like her," Lucky said.

"Just because she's white," Korynthia said.

"What a stupid thing to say. My husband's white, although I guess I don't like him anymore, but being white has nothing to do with it."

All of us just looked at one another.

"Well, I've always liked her," I said. "I don't care what color she is."

"I don't like her voice. And she's homely and too skinny."

"Get over it, Lucky," Poochie said.

"I like her," Sadie said. "I'd go see her."

We all looked at Poochie on the screen and then at one another again and nodded. Sadie gave me a high five and I gave one to Korynthia.

"Seems that's a yes from everybody," Lucky said.

"Okay," Korynthia said. "Now shut up, Poochie, so we can eat and then do our roundtable catch-up because I have to throw you out by ten. My granddaughter needs me in San Diego in the morning to watch her kids for four days. Again. Pray for me. Three under the age of seven."

"Wait a minute," Poochie said. "How many great-grandkids do you have now?"

"Eight. Maybe nine. Who the hell can keep up?"

"We'll call you back when we finish eating and before we have a few nightcaps," Korynthia said.

"I'll go check on Mama, but my phone is plugged in so just let the FaceTime run and don't worry about my battery."

She disappeared.

And we ate. The lasagna was delicious, and Lucky and I almost fought over the last piece of bread. I let her win because I thought I saw Dr. Alexopolous's face looking up at me from the basket and then I heard myself say: "I am not having dessert tonight."

"Since when?" Lucky just had to ask.

"Since right now."

"Good for you," Poochie said, scaring the hell out of all of us because we didn't realize she had picked us back up.

"Can I please start the roundtable?" she said. "I have to give Mama a bath tonight and my back is killing me."

We all looked at one another.

"I just had my colonoscopy."

All of us just slapped our foreheads with our palms and pushed the remaining dishes away.

"Anyway, I've got some polyps. Let me ask you all, how long has it been since you had your colonoscopies? And please don't let me hear anybody say never."

"Poochie, c'mon. This is the worst shit, no pun intended. I mean, just bad timing to bring this mess up knowing we're all sitting here at the damn dinner table. But anyway, I had one five years ago so I'm good for another five," Korynthia said.

"I had mine last year so I have nine more to go," I said.

"I've been putting it off. Please don't lecture me. I'll schedule one tomorrow," Lucky said.

"That's really stupid, Lucky," Sadie said. "I have one every two years because my father had colon cancer. So far, I'm good. If I have a polyp, they take it out. Anyone want more wine?"

Everybody held up their glasses.

"Wait! I forgot! Get your bone density, and have your eyes and hearing checked and . . ."

"Would you repeat that?" Lucky asked. "I didn't hear you!"

I moved my fingers in the air like I was signing.

We all laughed.

"And get a complete physical every damn year. It's important."

We laughed again.

"Come on, you guys. This is not funny. We're all pushing seventy and this is when all of our shit starts falling apart. What about mammograms?"

Everybody raised their hands.

"Glucose levels?" Poochie asked.

Everybody looked at me.

"Diabetes is no joke, Lo. Have you been checking your numbers?"

"I've been on her about this for the past three or four years. But everybody thinks I just like to preach," Sadie said.

"You do," Lucky said.

"Yes, I check my numbers," I said as seriously as I could, even though I was lying. I was too embarrassed to tell the truth.

"Well, I just take the medication because I can't exercise because of my sciatic nerve, and I'm probably going to have my hip and maybe both knees replaced, but you don't have any excuses, Lo," Poochie said. "Have you been exercising?"

"Yes."

"She's lying," Lucky said. "She walks to her car and into the grocery store. Tell the truth, Lo."

"I've been walking some of the Rose Bowl."

"We've been walking it together," Korynthia said. "So shut the hell up, Lucky. What about your limp?"

"It's my hip, I'll have you know. But I probably am going to do the gastric bypass surgery so I can kill two birds with one stone," Lucky said.

"Then just do it!" I yelled.

"I go to the gym because I have a SilverSneakers membership," Sadie said.

"I don't want to work out with a bunch of old people," I said.

"This is the most stimulating conversation I've had at the dinner table in frigging years," Korynthia said, rolling her eyes.

In our younger days, our once-a-month catch-up dinners usually meant complaining about ex-husbands or current husbands (even though I rarely had any complaints about Carl), and whining about our kids or grandkids, or pets for Sadie who didn't have either. But the last few years, it has gotten to the point where new health problems or old ones take up the majority of the time. At least once a week one of us seems to have a date with some kind of doctor and the scale of the problems seems to escalate by the month. I'd been avoiding doctors before Carl passed because I didn't want to know if something was wrong with me.

"Get your blood pressure checked regularly," Poochie shouted from the phone.

"Okay, Poochie, there's nothing left inside or outside our bodies to check, so bye! We love you!" Korynthia said.

"And we'll see you soon," I said.

And the screen went blank.

We all just sat there for a few minutes.

"You go next, Lo," Korynthia said.

"I'd rather go last this evening," I said.

"Well, since the real estate market is slow, if you don't let me work in the store soon, I might just put my house on the market and move on down to San Diego," Korynthia said.

"Why would you want to do that?" Lucky asked.

"My kids asked me to."

"There's nothing but a lot of rich boring white folks in San Diego," Lucky said.

"I'm probably not going. But I'll tell you something I *am* thinking about doing, since I don't have anything holding my interest at the moment."

"What's that?" I asked.

"Going on a senior dating site."

"I've heard a lot of people have found love on those things," Sadie said, shocking the hell out of us.

"How would you know, Sadie?" Lucky asked.

"Because I know people who've met folks."

"I do, too," Ko said. "This getting old shit is getting a little boring. I'm lonely as hell and if I meet somebody maybe I'll have a reason to stay put."

Sadie took a loud, deep breath, which caused everybody to look at her.

"I've been sinning," Sadie said.

"It's about damn time!" I said.

"With my minister."

"Your minister? I thought you were a lesbian?" Korynthia said.

"What would make you think that?" she asked.

"I saw a woman kiss you on the lips in the parking lot at your church."

"That's how we all say good night. Anyway, as soon as he gets the nerve to tell his wife, we're going to get married."

"So you're both sinning," I said, and shook my head.

"I thought you were too smart to do some stupid shit like this," Lucky said.

"Me, too," I said. "How in the hell did this happen, Sadie?"

"By accident. After choir practice one night. His wife is not very comforting and he wants a divorce but he's afraid how it might look."

"So, how does Mr. Preacher Man think God feels about him committing adultery?"

"You sound like a damn fool, Sadie," Ko said.

"I love him."

"That's so sweet," Lucky said. "Just don't go picking out a white dress."

Silence.

Then all eyes were on me.

"I want to start with the good news."

They crossed their arms and leaned back in their chairs.

"My granddaughter Cinnamon called me today to tell me she's having a boy and a girl and you won't believe this: she's naming them Pretty and Handsome."

Everybody downed their drinks.

"Also, Carl's partner bought out his share of the construction company from me. I'm going to use some of the proceeds to take a trip to Tokyo. I need to see my son and his wife and finally meet my twin granddaughters."

"When?" Sadie asked. "I'd go with you if you wanted someone to travel with."

Everybody, including me, rolled their eyes at her.

"I don't know exactly when yet, but I'm a big girl and don't really need an escort."

"Do twins run in your family?" Lucky asked.

"I suppose they do."

"What about Kwame? How's he doing?" Korynthia asked.

"He's fine. He's moving back into the two-bedroom he'd been in and I bought him a used Prius."

Lucky just rolled her eyes.

"Why?" Korynthia asked.

"He needed a better one so he could drive with Uber. Plus, he didn't like construction."

"So, tell us what's going on with Jalecia," Sadie said. "I've been praying for her."

"Well. It's been over three weeks since I bailed her out and I haven't heard a word from her."

"Sadie, maybe you can offer up an extra prayer to ensure she makes that court appearance," Lucky said.

"I will," Sadie said, rather convincingly.

"You didn't use your house for collateral, I hope?"

"I'm not stupid, Lucky. But at least I now know where she's living."

"Where?" Sadie asked.

"Compton."

"You're shitting us?" Korynthia asked.

"She's been living with her aunt Peggy."

"Peggy looked a little rough around the edges her damn self at the Repasse," Lucky said.

"Can you contact Peggy?"

"I don't have her number."

"Have you reached out to Jalecia?" Korynthia asked.

"She won't answer my calls. I'm worried about her, but I don't know what else I can do right now."

"Would you like to pray?" Sadie asked.

She reached over Lucky and squeezed my hand.

Then it got quiet. Korynthia crossed her arms. Lucky leaned on her elbows.

Everybody took a sip of something and then started to help clear the table.

"Hold on a second," Korynthia said, and pressed her palms on the edge of the table. "I would just like to say this about Jalecia: Lo, you may be pissed at me for saying it, but I think you just need to be patient and wait to see what she does. You can't make Jalecia do anything. And if she's lost, she'll reach out when she wants to be found."

Chapter 7

I was sitting in the dog park, watching B. B. King pretending to enjoy himself but failing. He was walking along the fence, like he was in prison wishing he could escape, but it had more to do with the fact that he knew he couldn't run as fast as the other dogs. He looked lonely, especially since his girlfriend had apparently moved out of the neighborhood. But then a black Lab walked over to him and dropped his red ball. B. B. King looked him in the eye as if to ask: *You mean you want to play?* The Lab gave him a look: *Pick the ball up, dummy!* Which is exactly what B. B. King did, and then dropped it so it rolled. The Lab went after it, and B. B. King slowly galloped after him.

I checked my phone. I had a missed call from Dr. Alexopolous's office. What could she possibly want? And even though it was starting to rain, which is something it rarely does in Pasadena, I decided to call her back since I was sitting under a tree filled with a flock of green birds.

The receptionist advised me that she had called because they had not yet received a request for my medical records from my new endocrinologist. I forgot they had told me I needed to start seeing an endocrinologist in addition to Dr. Alexopolous. I was too embarrassed to tell her I hadn't gotten one yet. So, I lied.

"I'm surprised to hear this," I said.

"Well, if you could give me his or her name, I'd be happy to forward the records."

"No! Don't! To be honest, I haven't actually decided on one."

"Just a second, Mrs. Curry, the doctor's just here at the desk."

Before I could say, "I don't want to speak to her," I heard her say, "Well, hello, Mrs. Curry. I've been worried about you and hope you're doing well."

"Thank you, Dr. Alexopolous. I've just been so busy I haven't managed to find an endocrinologist yet."

"Are you still angry at me?"

"No," I said.

"I'm so glad to hear that. I just wanted you to know that I only have your best interests at heart."

"I know."

"So have you been testing yourself?"

"Yes," I lied.

"How are your numbers?"

"Good. Wait. No, that's not completely true. I haven't been checking them on a regular basis."

"I appreciate your honesty. How about you go have your blood work done? Let's see how you're doing, and then we can sit down and discuss a realistic plan; and I'll do my best not to chastise you. Please know that it's your health that's important to me, even though it would be nice if you liked me a little."

That made me feel bad.

"Okay, I can do that. I'm only just finally getting used to the idea that my husband is not ever coming home."

"You don't have to explain. I lost my husband a year ago, which is one reason I probably come across as a bit harsh in trying to convince my patients to take better care of their health."

"I'm glad you understand, and I'm sorry for your loss. I'll go down to Quest Diagnostics as soon as you send them the request."

"The request I sent after you came in is still there. Nothing to eat or drink . . ."

"I remember."

I was there when the doors opened the next morning.

When my phone rang at five forty-five in the morning, I answered assuming and hoping it was Jalecia, since I still hadn't heard a peep from her.

"Grandma, Jonas and I wanted you to know we are the proud parents of Pretty and Handsome, and as soon as they put on a few more pounds we will be welcoming them home to our new apartment with their very own bedroom. We really can't thank you enough for asking Uncle Kwame to move into our one-bedroom instead of his two-bedroom!"

"Congratulations, Cinna! To you and Jonas! How much did they weigh?"

"Handsome weighed in at four pounds and Ms. Pretty at the bantam weight of three pounds eight ounces. But they're both otherwise pretty healthy. We could not be happier. How are you?"

"Good. Better now that I've got this good news. Let me know when I can come see them."

"Not sure just when they'll be home, although I come home tomorrow. But I'll be living in this hospital. I am not leaving our babies longer than I have to."

"Have you told your mom?"

"Yes. She looked and sounded better than I've seen her in years."

"You mean you actually saw her?"

"Yes. She came to the hospital, which made me feel so good. I almost didn't recognize her because she cut her dreads off, if you can believe it. The court ordered her to go to AA at her appearance and she's actually been going. Hallelujah. Anyway, I have to run. Love you. And tell all of my great-aunties the good news! Can't wait for you to meet your great-grands!"

I hung up, and realized my feelings were hurt that Jalecia hadn't bothered to reach out to me, especially since she'd been doing so well. I would just keep praying for her, especially that her sobriety lasts. I'm not sure how powerful my prayers have been lately, though. I'd also prayed that maybe Cinnamon and Jonas would come to their senses and give those babies human names instead of adjectives. Oy vey, as Lucky likes to say even though she's not Jewish.

Later that day, my phone screen lit up with a man who looked just like my second husband the day I married him.

"Hi, Mom!" Jackson said. His skin was the color of Lipton tea and the glint in his eyes made it clear that he was happy.

"Hello there, Jackson. What a nice surprise. I look a mess! You should call first to let me know you're going to FaceTime so I can at least put some makeup on! How are you, son?"

"You look fine, Ma! I'm fine! How are you? I feel like I can never catch you."

"I'm better."

"That's great. I don't want to pressure you, but you mentioned you were thinking about visiting last time we talked, and I wanted to call to say Aiko and I really hope you decide to come over here to spend some quality time with us and the girls. Maybe you could take ten days off of your busy schedule? I've been working like a slave. Wait—bad analogy. Anyway, I've been operating at an extremely high stress level because I just got a new gig at a major tech company here and I'm doing all of their photography, but anyway that's neither here nor there. Aiko wants to finally meet you in person, Ma."

"That makes two of us, Jackson."

Carl and I were all set to attend their wedding, but Ma fell and broke her hip and had to be hospitalized so we couldn't go.

"Well, we'd really love for you to visit. How are you for real, Ma?"

"I'm adjusting. And I'm now a great-grandmother."

"Cinnamon?"

"She had twins, too. A boy and a girl. Please don't ask me their names. How are your daughters? And Aiko?"

"They're all fine. But I so want Akina and Akari to meet their grandma before they start to think Aiko's mom is their only one. And I want to see you, too! It's been over a year since I've been home. It's too much to leave Aiko alone with the babies and it's too hard to travel with them. I'm still sorry I couldn't make it for Carl's service."

"I know. But you're on the other side of the world. Is it tomorrow over there?"

"Yes, or I could say it's yesterday where you are. How is my sister?"

"She's fine. I haven't seen her in a few weeks."

"Really? Why not?"

"Because she's been working on making some major changes in her life."

"What kind of changes?"

Why does he have to ask so many questions? I wish I could tell him the truth, but I didn't feel like ruining the tone of our conversation.

"Positive ones. But look, sweetie, I have to be at the hairdresser in fifteen minutes. I was just heading out the door when you called."

"Oh. Okay, then. But let's start comparing calendars and see when we can get you over here. Do you think you could find time in the next couple of months? At least by your birthday?"

"I'll do my best."

"Great, tell all of my pretend aunties I said hello, and I'll send you the latest pictures of my beautiful girls as soon as I sign off. Love you, Mom."

"I love you more."

And the screen went blank.

Japan will be nice. I'll make myself make the time.

And did he say birthday? I just had a birthday a few months ago, didn't I?

Just then two little brown faces popped onto my screen. Their hair is black and curly, and they look more mixed up than mixed. I always hope they'll be a lot cuter, but maybe they will be by the time I get there.

I was running late and decided to take the freeway three exits to get to my hair appointment.

When I heard a police siren and then saw red flashing lights behind me, I was just about to move to the side so they could go around me, but I realized it was me they were after. What did I do? I pulled over and stopped. I looked at my watch. I was now fifteen minutes late but Xenobia is usually late, too. I was texting her to let her know what happened when I heard a tapping on the window. I rolled it down.

"License and registration, please."

"Officer, why did you pull me over?"

"Because you were swerving."

"No, I wasn't."

He glared at me. Tall. Pale. Blue eyes, freckles, and bright red hair. All the signs of a redneck.

"You were swerving, ma'am. Please, let me have your license and registration, and keep your hands where I can see them."

"Oh, you think I might have a gun or something?" I should not have said that, but it should be obvious that I'm an innocent senior citizen he knew was not swerving. And what I am and always will be is black. But I reached inside the glove compartment and got the registration, then plopped my red Dooney & Bourke vinyl handbag in my lap, took my driver's license out of my wallet, and handed them both to him.

"Are you the owner of this vehicle?"

"Yes."

He looked at my registration, then at my license, then at me, and then at my license again.

"Who is this?"

"It's me, officer. My name is on it, isn't it?"

"This does not look like you."

"Let me see that."

"Keep your hands on the steering wheel, please."

He lowered my license so I could see my picture. Damn. I have not bothered to get my picture changed in ten years. I looked good! And young! But I still looked like myself.

"That is me. A few years ago."

"It's been longer than a few years. I suggest you update this photo and use your blinker when you're changing lanes."

"I always do," I said.

He handed me back my documents and I snatched them.

"Have a good day," he said without a drop of sincerity and strutted back to his ugly police car just like they do on TV shows.

"Go fuck yourself," I said after I rolled up the window. When I went to put my registration back inside the glove compartment, staring at me was a brand-new package of Twizzlers. Without even thinking, I pulled them out, ripped them open, and bit off two or three inches of two stems at the same time. Then I dropped the entire package into my purse and pulled onto the freeway a little faster than I should have.

After I had my hair rinsed a brighter metallic silver, trimmed, and conditioned, I called Kwame to tell him I wasn't in the mood to have the lunch we'd scheduled to talk about his next steps in life. He pretended to understand. When I got home, I walked straight into my bathroom, stood in front of the mirror, and just looked at my face. It was a sad-looking face. I smiled at myself and I looked worse. The spiderwebs at the corners of my eyes were now creases. Underneath them were brown and puffy half-moons. There were brown freckles on my cheeks and the ridges on both sides of my nose. Did I now have a moustache? I pushed the light on my vanity mirror and turned it around to the magnifying side, which was a huge mistake. I stepped away and took off my running suit: first the jacket, then the top, and then the sweats and even my bra and panties. I stood in front of the floor-length mirror and could not believe my eyes. Who in the hell was that? I did not recognize this body because it wasn't mine. I couldn't remember the last time I actually looked at myself naked, but all I could say was, "Who would want to fuck her?" I looked around, embarrassed, as if someone might have heard me. I know I'm not supposed to be thinking about sex or using the word *fuck,* but what the fuck? It also dawned on me that I hadn't had sex in more than six months. Young folks don't think they'll have these desires when they get old, but we do.

I remember once when I was staying with Ma after a divorce, I'd hear her, making the sounds I had come to know as sounds of pleasure, and I'd know she had male company. My room, unfortunately, wasn't far from hers. She was fifty-five then and I thought there was no way she should still be having, or even thinking about, sex. I was embarrassed for her. One night, after the man left, I came right out and asked her, "Ma, what were you doing in there?"

She rolled her eyes at me. "What do you think I was doing in there?"

"But why?"

She looked at me as if I had asked her the stupidest question in the world.

"Hold on a minute, Loretha. Let me ask you a question. Do you have sexual intercourse?"

I thought I would die hearing her say "sexual intercourse" but I said, "Yes."

"And do you enjoy it?"

"Of course I do, Ma."

"Well, so do I. There's no age limit on it. And FYI, fifty-five is not old, just so you know."

"It just seems creepy."

"My body is the same as yours, just older. I feel the same pleasure you do, hallelujah. You better hope somebody still wants to touch you when you're in your fifties and sixties, or even seventies. Now beat it."

Now I was forced to admit she was right.

Carl made me feel sexy and forty for twenty-five years. But since he's been gone, I hadn't thought about sex until standing in front of this mirror. But I really didn't care if I ever had sex again.

So, I stared at myself and realized I was almost unrecognizable. I was wondering when and how this happened to me, or when did I do this to myself? I know better. And I sell beauty. I was never a ten, but I was definitely a seven-and-a-half and some weekends an eight. Even in my early sixties I was still somewhat attractive, a size twelve or occasionally a fourteen, but now I'm five minutes away from a 2X. I certainly didn't have these damn mountains and valleys masquerading as skin all over my body. Even my breasts look like brown water balloons someone had squeezed too much of the water out of.

And my hands: they were starting to look like brown spiderwebs with freeways of green veins leading nowhere. I looked down at my legs. Thank God something on me hadn't changed in all these years. They still looked good. Still smooth and strong and shaped like I'd been swimming all my life, even though I can't swim.

I did not put my clothes back on. For some reason I did not understand, I walked through the house butt naked. When B. B. King looked up at me, I heard myself say, "What? You haven't seen an overweight, naked old woman before?"

He looked at me as if to say, *Not this old and not this overweight.*

"Not to worry, B.B. Pretty soon there is going to be less of me to see."

I walked out the side door and down the steps, grateful my neighbors couldn't see into the backyard. I opened the gate to the pool and closed it behind me. Then, without even testing the water, I put one foot on the top step and it felt like peppermint on my toes, then I put the other foot in and walked through the turquoise water until I got to five feet. I took a deep breath, went under, and then opened my eyes.

After my dip I decided to bring in the mail since it was one of the things I'd been ignoring after Kwame moved out. The basket by the front door was full. Not of bills, because Carl had set it up so they're paid automatically from our checking account, but with what mostly looked like junk.

I pulled the basket over to Carl's chair, which I have only sat in once since he died. There, I finally said it. He did die. And if he weren't dead, he would be here. It is hard to stop hoping that one day the person you lost will just show up and say this was just a big mistake. I know I couldn't possibly be the only one who thinks this.

I sat down slowly, and the cushion felt warm.

"Hi, baby," I whispered, then smiled as I bent over to start going through what looked like months of mail. There were my favorite magazines: *AARP,* which seems to come almost daily; *Real Simple,* which I look at just for the pictures and never do any of the things they say would make my life, well, simpler; mileage magazines from different airlines, which made me think I could use miles to go to Japan even though I didn't need to.

Underneath all of this were two envelopes with Ma's handwriting on the front. God bless her. I picked up the piles of coupons and the you've-been-preapproved-for-a-million-dollar-line-of-credit envelopes and walked slowly toward the kitchen and tossed them all into the recycling bin. Then I poured myself a cold glass of orange juice, which I know I have to stop drinking in the near future because it's one of a million things diabetics shouldn't even think about consuming. But hell, I can't just give up everything at once, even though I haven't given up much of anything yet.

I took a quick, delicious sip and opened the first envelope from Ma. I assumed my horoscope or a magazine article would fall out, but inside there were two large, bright pink Post-its. On the first, she had printed: *Sell your house. Buy a condo. No, rent an apartment. Travel. See the world while you're still able.*

On the second: *Even though you sell all those beauty products, you know damn well they don't work. The only thing that will make you look younger is surgery. But who really wants to look younger? Ha ha ha.*

Do I even sell beauty products anymore? I guess I do. I had listed the L.A. store, but took it off the market because I just didn't have the energy or the time to deal with it. But I will.

In the other envelope was a yellow Post-it: *If and when you cough or sneeze or laugh too hard you wet yourself a little bit, get some of those crinkly underpants and you won't have to be embarrassed.*

I started laughing so hard and when I felt something trickle inside my undies, it only made me laugh harder.

Chapter 8

"I think I want to be a producer," Kwame said.

"Why?" I asked. I was playing devil's advocate because ever since he stopped working construction, he has come up with about five or six different professions, some of which he doesn't seem to understand. I'm sure this is another one that can be added to that list, but he's young and it takes as long as it takes to find your true path. I'm not real sure if I ever really found mine.

"Because I like movies."

"So do I, but I've never wanted to make one, Kwame."

I let out a little chuckle to lighten up.

"It just sounds exciting," he said.

I could've said, "A lot of things that sound exciting aren't," but I didn't want to ruin his enthusiasm.

So I said, "You're young, Kwame, and chances are you're going to change your mind several more times. Eventually, you'll land where you need to be."

"It's nice to know someone understands," he said.

"Are there people who don't?"

"Folks at home. And my moms."

"Well, I'm sure they mean well. Speaking of which, how is your mother?"

He shrugged his shoulders.

"What do you mean, you don't know?"

"I ain't—I mean, I haven't—talked to her in almost two months now."

"Why not?"

"Because her cellphone is disconnected."

"What about your cousin? Boone? Is he in touch with her?"

"He thinks my moms might be going through a rough patch."

"Write her," I said, which sounded more like a command than a suggestion. "I'm sure she'd like to hear from you."

"She knows my number."

He sounded like Jalecia, which was why I said, "Send her a card or something. Mothers need to know their kids care about them."

We were having Mexican food at one of my favorite spots, even though I had completely forgotten that Kwame wasn't crazy about Mexican food.

"It's too much stuff going on in a taco," he had said the first time I brought him there. "I grew up eating pinto beans in a pot with juice and I don't understand why they have to smush them all up. And rice should be white, not orange."

The young waitress with flowers in her hair and a floral dress stood there patiently as Kwame's eyes scrolled up and down the menu. Finally he said, "I'll have the pizza with ground beef, but with no beans, no sour cream, and no avocado."

"Anything else?"

"I would like to try the fried ice cream."

"To drink?"

"I'll have a virgin margarita."

"What kind, sir?"

"A normal one."

I winked at her, so she knew I wanted my regular: combination chicken tacos and chicken enchiladas with sour cream. All the combos come with beans and rice and I almost always end up taking something home.

I ate guacamole and chips and Kwame drank what was really just lemonade, then asked for another one as if he liked the buzz he'd gotten. The more I looked at him, the more he started looking like Carl, or the way I imagine Carl looked all those years ago, long before I met him. He never had any photographs of himself as a kid because their house caught on fire and although the scrapbooks were saved, the firemen hosed them and everybody's faces had stuck to the clear lining.

"So," I said now. "What else besides liking movies excites you about producing, Kwame?"

"It seems like it could be interesting, and you can also make a lot of money and get to travel and meet movie stars."

"That's true."

"You don't sound that enthused, Mama-Lo."

"I think everybody should do what fascinates them, and what they enjoy. I like helping people look beautiful. In fact, I'm thinking about looking for a bigger shop, maybe even adding some services."

This was news to me, but it just rolled off my tongue.

"Really? I think it's so cool that even though you're old and all—no disrespect, Mama-Lo—you're still doing stuff like that. Don't you ever think about retiring?"

"And do what?"

"I don't know. But don't people your age retire?"

"A lot of them do. But not if they're healthy and still able to do what they love, especially if they're good at it."

"This is why I have so much respect for you. Your attitude is so cool."

"Well, thank you. But back to you. You don't strike me as having the Hollywood DNA."

"What do you mean by that?"

"What I can't tell is if you're only interested in producing because you think it's glamorous."

"That's it exactly."

"But is that enough?"

He hunched his shoulders.

"Maybe you should explore other possibilities. Maybe go online and check out Pasadena City College or UCLA or the state universities and see what kind of programs they offer. Maybe one of them might appeal to you."

"That's a good idea. I never thought of that. Well, until then, promise me you'll call me if you need me to help do anything around the house, including walking B. B. King."

"I will."

I folded my hands and leaned back in my chair. "So tell me the truth, what's the real reason you're not talking to your mama?"

He looked down at his empty plate as if it wasn't empty. "She refused to talk to me when I didn't come back to Flint with Boone."

"Does she live alone?"

"I don't know from one week to the next, but probably not. With all those cousins, somebody always manages to sleep on the couch or on the floor in my room, which is one of the reasons why I didn't want to go back. They're always just drinking and smoking and sitting around watching sports or Netflix or BET."

"Well, people usually have reasons."

"I know that. They're bored, but living like that was very boring to me and it didn't get them anywhere. I don't want to end up like them. I want to do something with my life. This is one reason why I'm scared to drink. My moms always made it seem like once you start you can't stop."

"You should reach out to her."

"I will. Soon."

"Send her a gift card. I know they have Target and Walmart there."

He nodded.

"You can buy a card and put any amount you want on it. Even twenty dollars, but probably fifty would be more helpful. I'll pay for it the first time."

"She'll probably just sell it."

"So what? She'll still know you were thinking about her."

"That's true. I could do a few more Uber shifts."

I reached inside my purse and handed him two fifty-dollar gift cards from each store, which I had planned to give to Cinnamon and Jonas for the babies.

He looked at me and smiled. "You are a thoughtful and caring person, Mama-Lo, and I see why my father loved you. Thank you."

This made my heart feel like a warm wet sponge being squeezed, as corny as that sounds. It also made me think that his mother did something right.

"So, are you going to eat the last of those chips?"

"No," I said. "How is Parker doing?"

"I couldn't tell you."

"You mean you guys broke up?"

"Yes, we did. He wasn't looking for anything serious. I guess you could call him—what do they say here in California? A free spirit."

"Well, there are plenty of young men out here to choose from."

He just smiled and insisted on paying the check.

"You're going to like my church," Sadie said, when I called to tell her I wanted to come. I decided it might be time to keep at least one of my promises, and Sadie had been the most diligent about reminding me.

"It's been seven months since Carl passed and you have not set foot in my church once. Shame on you! What would Carl think?"

I wanted to say, "Oh shut the hell up, Sadie! You adulterer!"

But I didn't. I'm waiting for the right time, though. I'm just glad to know she's not the saint she wanted us all to believe, even though I never quite bought into it. Sadie was sneaky as hell in high school, but she put on a goody-two-shoes front until even she started believing it.

"I'll be there on Sunday," I said, even though I really wanted to tell her to stop fucking with me! But I've been trying not to swear so much, especially when it's directed at someone I love.

The truth is, I have lost a lot of respect for Sadie because not only is she an adulterer, she's also a hypocrite. The day after she realizes this minister was not heaven-sent but just a man who cheated on his wife and stood on the pulpit under a robe every Sunday, lying to—and in front of—God and all of his parishioners, I'm going to call her ass out for being so damn stupid and selfish. We all will. But we have to plan it. We don't want to lose Sadie as a friend because we still love her. What I really want to know is: What does she pray for? And, does she lie to God, too? Has she even bothered to imagine how she'd feel if *she* was the minister's wife? Does she think about what this affair says about the minister? That son-of-a-bitch's feet should catch fire every time he walks inside the church.

"And we have a really good choir," she said.

"Nothing like a good hymn to lift you up," was the best I could do, because Sadie's in the choir and had recently been promoted to choir director, which I'm sure was one of the perks of her relationship with the unhappy minister, especially since we all knew Sadie could not carry a note with a single melody inside it.

I begged Korynthia to come with me.

"I pray all day every day, but Sadie's church is too much for me."

And Lucky: "I'm not an atheist, but I don't like going to church because I don't like being preached to. And plus, you know I have never been all that crazy about Sadie."

Once a bitch, was all I was thinking.

When I called to tell Poochie my dilemma, she said, "Girl, just go and pray like you mean it, and stop being so wishy-washy. Sadie knows she's doing wrong. But she needed to get it out of her system.

This thing with the minister won't last, but our friendship will. By the way, I'm working on our cruise and we're all going to be on it, and I think we should go to Mexico. Bye now."

Lord, why did she have to mention that cruise? It made me seasick just thinking about walking up that ramp or whatever it's called.

Sadie asked if I wanted to ride with her.

"No," I said. "Because I might be babysitting the twins." Of course I was lying. I didn't want to be in a car with Sadie because I wasn't prepared to talk about her situation all by myself. It wasn't a very good lie, though, because I wouldn't know what to do with two babies at once, and Sadie probably knew that. They are very nice babies, though. The last few times I saw them I think I only heard them cry twice. They looked like they were already trying to roll over, or at least Handsome did. Pretty just waved her arms.

"Well, please find me after the service, because I would like to introduce you to the minister. His wife will be standing by his side, so please don't act like I am anything but a close parishioner, okay?"

"I won't. But you are a close parishioner," I said and laughed a phony laugh. Sadie didn't.

When Sunday came, I had to admit, love and sex were doing wonders for Sadie. Even the adulterous minister, Reverend George Washington (did his name have something to do with his arrogance?), who was not attractive, looked a little spry. He looked like a bird—a hawk, actually. I could tell he dyed his hair black because it was too black, and he was short and pudgy. I also don't know why he wore a white suit. I could not tell what any woman might see in him.

But some people see what you don't see.

This was a nondenominational church, which has become quite the ticket to getting more folks to come out to worship. I was baptized Methodist though I never went to a Methodist church because my cousin Josette was Pentecostal, and her church was livelier. It was like going to a play, with lots of shouting and people running up and down the aisles and praising God, even though it wasn't clear if that would help God hear them better. I always tapped my feet and secretly popped my fingers under my dress, which I'd spread out like a fan on the seat if Josette wasn't sitting next to her latest boyfriend.

I noticed there were a lot of white people in Sadie's church and it was very modern. I think the only cross I saw was outside on the side of the railing. Where was Jesus? He wasn't hanging anywhere here.

I sat at the end of a row that looked more like the United Nations, with more ethnicities and colors and hues than I was used to. It made me happy that I had sat there. My black pantsuit was too tight, though, so I couldn't cross my legs.

The minister was not that good at preaching. In fact, his sermon was all over the place. I thought they were supposed to have a topic or a theme or at least a point, but not Reverend Washington. I guess he really did believe in free will.

When it was time for the choir, Sadie stood up, proud, in her red robe and she motioned the twenty members to stand. They stood, except for one woman in a wheelchair. I opened my eyes wider as they started, because they sounded quite good. That is, until Sadie turned to the congregation, lowered both palms to belt out a verse, and her voice was so rough it scratched *my* throat. It was obvious she loved her singing more than everybody else did because when I turned to look at the folks in my row, they all had kind of a stoic look on their faces. It was a long verse and when Sadie finally finished, the congregation was so quiet you could have heard a fan drop. Sadie stood there a second too long, as if she was waiting for applause. She didn't even get an "Amen."

Chapter 9

I decided to stop by the Pasadena shop since it had been months since I had even stepped foot inside it. I had driven by just to make sure the sign was still on the door. The window behind the bars was dirty. I had to push the door open with my hip and I inhaled so much dust I started to sneeze. Boxes were everywhere. It looked more like a warehouse instead of a beauty supply. This place was ugly and old now, the way I'd been feeling lately.

I did wonder if my customers had gotten impatient and sought out my competitors. I didn't care. But I did. I was also wondering if grief could last forever. And if I ever stopped thinking about Carl, would that mean I didn't miss him anymore? What I've also been wondering: What if I'm just bored selling beauty products?

When I heard the bell on the door, I jumped off the stool I'd been sitting on behind the counter and put my hand on my pepper spray because sometimes transients come in not realizing what kind of store this is, although most of them are harmless.

"Someone here to train me?" I heard a familiar voice ask.

"Korynthia, what are you doing here?"

"Out of habit I drive by here when I go to my boring real estate office—and before you ask, no, I have not even sold a condo. I think I really just wanted to prove I could pass the damn test. Anyway, I saw your sexy Volvo parked out front, so I made an illegal U-turn and beelined it in here to see why you didn't bother to call me to help you get this shit organized. But it looks like what you could really use is a moving truck."

"I don't even know where to start," I said and moved a box of eyebrow pencils and horsetail shampoo out of the way so we could hug.

"You need to move this store. It's too small and it's old. And I have never liked this street or this neighborhood."

"Well, like us, it wasn't always old."

"Speak for yourself, huzzie. I went on a date."

"A what?"

"You heard me. A date."

I pulled out two Twizzlers from my secret drawer by the register and tried to bite off about three inches, but they were so hard I instantly regretted it.

Korynthia snatched them out of my hand and threw them on the floor. "You know damn well you're not supposed to be eating these nasty things, Lo. Hand me the rest of them."

I whipped out the clear package. "They're stale," I said with remorse.

"Have you been checking your levels?"

"Sometimes."

"So, that's a no. I'm not stupid, Lo. You need to take this more seriously."

"I know. I've cut back on a lot of stuff."

"When were you last tested?"

"About a month ago."

"And what was your level?"

"I don't know."

"What do you mean you don't know?"

"I haven't heard back from my doctor."

"Then call the bitch! Look. I'm only asking because too many people in my family had diabetes—and yes, I said *had,* since they're gone now because they didn't take it seriously. You can't do that."

"I'm going to call her tomorrow."

"What's wrong with today?"

"Just tell me about the date, Ko."

"I've actually had three dates. I was gonna wait until our next dinner to tell you, but anyway, the first two were scary old men who had so many wrinkles it looked like they had been in the pool all day. The third one was round and had droopy eyes, which he had photoshopped out of his photo. Scared the hell out of me when I saw him sitting in the window at the Cheesecake Factory, but I didn't want to be rude so I texted him and told him I broke my leg. He looked disappointed but then he looked a little wacko."

"Aren't you afraid? I mean, these men are strangers."

"These old fuckers are harmless. They're not serial killers or rapists. Plus, I tweaked my profile."

"You mean your age?"

"You damn straight. I want to date somebody who has at least ten years left to live. Anyway, I have a date tomorrow night with a fella who looks like he's still alive."

"What did you change your age to?"

"What difference does it make?"

"Sixty?"

She threw a bag of pink cotton balls at me. "Fifty-five. I thought that was an exciting number."

"What do you expect to get out of this, Ko?"

"That is a dumbass question, Loretha."

"Well, I know you're not interested in having sex."

"What is wrong with you? Of course I want to have sex."

"But you don't know these guys."

"I will after we have sex."

"Well, good luck, you old ho," I said.

And at that we both started laughing even though I found this to be quite scary. I had no idea Korynthia was really serious about going on a dating site. What's the point at our age?

"Hey, I can't breathe in here with all this dust. Can we go outside?" she asked.

"I suppose so."

"Anyway, Lo, do me a favor. Don't tell the girls about any of this, please."

"I won't. They'd only be jealous. Well, not Sadie, since she's got a married lover."

"I still find that hard to believe. Sadie was never smart, but I didn't know she was stupid."

I crossed my arms and looked at my sad building, which you wouldn't even know was here unless you knew it was here. And just as I had done when Kwame asked, I heard myself say, "I'm going to look for a nicer, bigger place. It's time to make a change."

Korynthia gave me a high five. "Hey, have you had any offers on the L.A. store?"

"I had taken it off the market for a minute because I started getting queries and was not prepared to deal with all the energy and time it took. But I just put it back on."

"Well, let me know if you need some help or company when you start looking for a better location for this ugly place. Remember, I do have a real estate license, so I have access to all listings. But I will only be available afternoons."

"Why is that?"

"I couldn't wait around for you to hire me, so I got a part-time job."

"Doing what?" I asked.

"I teach a cardio and strength-training class for seniors at my gym."

"What, you mean like that SilverSneakers business?"

"Yes, and even though I know you probably won't come and work out with your own kind, you need to think about doing some kind of exercise on a regular basis, Lo."

"Please cut me some slack, Korynthia. This is my second lecture from you in an hour."

"It's called love, huzzie."

And she walked over and bent her six-one body down and gave me the biggest squeeze, then kissed me on my forehead.

"And I don't like that shade of silver you got. It looks too much like Cruella de Vil."

I gave her the finger.

Right after she left, I dialed Dr. Alexopolous's office. It was Saturday, but I decided to leave a message anyway.

"Hello, this is Loretha Curry calling to find out if Dr. Alexopolous received my test results. Since I haven't heard back, I'm hoping it's good news. I've been doing my very best to cut down on sweets and carbs, and I recently joined a gym and have been exercising with SilverSneakers. It's so refreshing to work out with people my age. Anyway, I've already lost about four pounds and am hoping to lose about thirty more by my birthday, which gives me about five months. I look forward to hearing from you soon. Again, this is Loretha Curry."

I don't know why I lied.

Yes, I do. Because I want it to be true.

The next day I was in the Petco parking lot, having just bought B. B. King some new rawhide bones and a thirty-pound bag of his anti-arthritis food. I was loading the giant bag into the back of the Volvo when it slipped out of my hands, splattering brown kernels all over the asphalt. I just stood there and watched them roll. I was on the verge of crying as I thought about how Carl and then Kwame always did this for me.

"Just leave that, ma'am," I heard a young male voice say. "I'll run and get you another bag."

When I turned around, he looked like he didn't weigh more than a hundred pounds, but I just said, "Thank you, young man."

"Next time, ask for help. That's what we're here for. I'll be right back."

And off he went.

I felt my cellphone shiver, and I was surprised to see a text from Odessa.

I need to talk to you about something important. Can you meet me at Carroll's Diner if you're not too busy? It's VERY important.

I texted her back. *Give me about ten minutes.*

Of course, I was wondering what could be so important and I was just praying she didn't need to borrow any more money. I was tired of saying yes and felt it was time for me to start saying no. I was already coating myself with some invisible armor to prepare for her latest sob story.

"Here you go, ma'am."

He slid the bag in the back of the wagon and lowered the door. I tried to hand him a ten-dollar bill and he waved his hand no. I stuffed it in his shirt pocket anyway.

"Never turn down a tip," I said. "And thank you."

Odessa waved to me from the window. She was sitting in a booth. As usual, there was a worried look on her face. I wish she would wear makeup and stop frowning so much. I can't remember the last time I saw my sister smile.

I waved back.

When I got inside she jumped up to give me a hug. Her breasts felt larger than they used to, and she was squishy. I wondered if I felt the same to her? She was wearing baggy blue jeans and a purple sweatshirt even though it was eighty degrees outside.

I sat down.

"So," I said. "What's going on?"

"I have to move out of the guesthouse."

"Why?"

"Because the new owners have evicted me. They've given me twenty-four hours."

"Can they do that?"

"Yes."

"But why did they just decide?"

"I knew they wanted me out because they were going to start renovating, but they hadn't given me a timeline. We don't really get along, after all they're living in what used to be my house and have made me feel like a squatter. I guess they're just fed up with dealing with me."

"I'm sorry, Odessa."

"Do you have any vacancies at the apartment?"

"I think I have a one-bedroom."

"I would really prefer two. Doesn't that Kwame live in a two-bedroom?"

"He did, yes."

"Can't he move into the one-bedroom?"

She has so much nerve I almost can't stand it.

"No, he cannot. He swapped with Cinnamon and Jonas when they had the babies. I do have a two-bedroom coming up, but it won't be ready for a couple of weeks."

"I have to be out by tomorrow."

"Goddamnit, Odessa! And I meant *goddamnit*, so don't even think about correcting me."

"Can I stay with you for two weeks?"

"No."

"Why not?"

"Because it just won't work and because B. B. King doesn't like you."

"Well, the feeling is mutual. Anyway, what am I supposed to do?"

I just looked at her. I cannot believe we're twins.

"You can stay at one of those long-term-stay places. Oakwood Apartments, I think they're called. They're clean."

"You need a credit card to stay there and mine is maxed out."

"What about your social security, Odessa?"

"I only get about seventeen hundred a month and I have a lot of bills."

I didn't even feel like asking what kinds of bills, so I just said, "I'll put it on one of my cards."

"Thank you, Sis. But let me ask you this, what floor is the two-bedroom on? Is the kitchen updated?"

Three weeks later she moved in.

She called me once she was settled. "I can't wait for you to see how I've decorated the apartment!"

"Have you seen Cinnamon and Jonas and the twins yet?"

"No."

"Have you bothered to say hi?"

"No."

"Why not?"

"Well, I'm not crazy about babies and I'm not crazy about Jonas and Cinnamon either. They're such hippies. It's like they're stuck in a time warp and think it's the seventies."

"Well, I love them."

"I'll be cordial when I do see them, I promise," she said. "But guess what? I got a job. I'm working as an attendant at a senior facility: the one Ma's in."

"What? Why?"

"Take a wild guess, Loretha."

"You don't work with Ma, I hope."

"Why in God's name would you say it like that?"

"It just doesn't seem like that would be healthy for her."

"Really? And why not?"

"Because you make her too emotional."

"Like you don't? Anyway, I work in a completely different wing, with patients who have more problems than Ma."

"Ma doesn't have *problems,* Odessa. She's just old and occasionally has a hard time remembering things."

"Anyway, I have to go. I need my rest to deal with those old folks. I work the evening shift."

And she hung up.

The following morning, I woke up and reached for my cellphone, but it wasn't there. I bolted straight up because I always put it on the nightstand. But then I remembered I had taken my shower, put on my pajamas and bathrobe, sat in Carl's chair, and taken one of Ma's newest envelopes out of the basket, which was full again. Reading Ma's letter was the last thing I remembered doing. I looked in my purse but the phone wasn't in there. I was trying to remember the last time I used it, but I couldn't. I put my robe on and walked into the kitchen to look, but decided I would eat something first because I knew the only other place it could be was the car and my stomach was growling. I grabbed the tasteless granola, some raspberries, and low-fat milk and sat down at the kitchen table to pretend I was enjoying it.

B. B. King started whining to go out and when I reached for the doorknob, I thought I was seeing things, because there in the driveway was Jalecia's car and she was slumped against the steering wheel inside it.

I flung the door open so fast it forced B. B. King to jump off the small landing. I reached into the pocket of my robe for my phone to dial 911 but, of course, it wasn't in there. I tried to open the car door but it was locked. I yelled as loud as I could and banged on the window, "Jalecia!" She leaned back slowly, rolled the window down, looked at me, smiled, and in a slurred voice said, "I just stopped by for a quick visit. I was on my way home."

She was still drunk.

But I didn't care. I was just relieved she was breathing.

I reached into the window, opened the car door, wrapped my arms around her waist, squeezed her as tight as I could, and helped her inside. She smelled like alcohol, which I was almost grateful for, given the alternatives. When we got inside the kitchen, I rubbed my hand up and down her back and looked at her glazed eyes, her balmy skin, her short Afro, and her chapped lips. This woman who is my only daughter suddenly looked just like me when I was her age, and I kissed her forehead and her cheeks and I said, "You are home."

"That's good to know. I just need to lie down for a minute," Jalecia said, as I helped her walk up the steps like she was handicapped. She looked like she hadn't slept in days. I led her to the guest bedroom, which was right down the short hallway from Carl's and mine.

When I opened the door, I was glad Kwame had moved out. Even though there's another bedroom down the hall, she would be close enough to hear in this one. She pushed her sneakers off, then pulled up the throw at the foot of the bed. She fell on one side so her head landed on a pillow and within seconds she was snoring. I backed out of the room slowly and closed the door as gently as I could.

Once in the living room, I walked in circles trying to decide what I should do. Ma's envelope was still open on the table from the night before. Inside it was a smaller pink envelope with a flimsy, yellowed piece of notebook paper in it and a Post-it stuck to the front.

"Found this in my scrapbook. I wrote this to you, the future you, when you left for college. Anyway I'm sending it now." I decided to read the letter again.

"Dear Loretha. I have a lot of regrets and I'm not even forty yet. But I don't regret having you and Odessa. Well, that's not all the way true. What I regret is having you when I had you. I wish I had waited. I wish I had had a husband to help me raise you both. But just make sure you don't give yourself away to the highest bidder. And don't be a

cheap date, as the saying goes. If you're reading this and you're over forty, I hope you are doing what you want with your life. I hope you are more patient than I was because none of us are perfect. You will stumble but figure out how to get back up. Ask for help if you can't and if someone else needs it, give it to them. I hope you understand what I mean. Love, Mom. P.S. And have some fun! Get on as many airplanes as possible! The only reason I've ever been to the airport was to pick somebody up."

As I folded the notebook paper and put it back in the pink envelope, which was inside the white one I had bought her, I wondered if Ma had written more of these letters. But this one was what I needed today.

I got up and walked down the hall to check on Jalecia, who I knew was still sleeping because I could hear her snoring. I decided it was safe for me to take a shower. But by the time I got dressed and walked out into the hallway, I saw her bedroom door was open, and the bed was empty. I rushed to the kitchen and, through the window, I saw that the only car in the driveway was mine.

I sat down at the table, folded my arms, and lowered my forehead on top of them. I didn't know what to do. I didn't know how to help my daughter because she didn't seem like she wanted help or knew she needed it. But I couldn't just abandon her. I didn't want to just sit by and watch her fall and not be able to get back up.

I took B. B. King on a short walk to the corner and back, then put him in the backyard by the pool. He had a spot he liked under the tree, and a bone. He liked to watch squirrels and birds from there, and every once in a while he would capture a snake.

I got inside the Volvo and I almost lost it when I heard my phone ringing under the front seat. There it was! I reached down and pulled it out, answering louder than I should have.

"Hello?"

"Good morning, Mrs. Curry. This is Shana calling from Dr. Alexopolous's office. Are you okay?"

"Hello, Shana. Yes, I'm okay, I suppose. I've been waiting to hear back from Dr. Alexopolous about my test results. And because I haven't, I assumed no news meant good news."

"I've left three messages for you at your work number."

"Work?"

"The last receptionist accidentally deleted the files for patient home and cell numbers from the computer, which is why she's no longer working here, so all we had was your work number. I see from your file that you left us a message about a month ago but you didn't leave a contact number. We mailed you your results and a letter instructing you to contact us. When we didn't hear back, we finally called the pharmacist to get your cell number, which is why I'm calling you now."

"So, where's the doctor?"

"Dr. Alexopolous is at a medical conference in New York, where her daughter also goes to college."

I wanted to yell: *Am I going to live or what?* but instead I said, "So were you calling about my results?"

"You should have a message from the doctor on your work voicemail, but your A1C was eight-point-three, which is much too high. The doctor called in a prescription with two refills to CVS to get you started on medication to bring it down, but she'll want to see you as soon as she's back to discuss a treatment and lifestyle plan."

"What did you say?"

"I said—"

"Never mind, I heard you. So what should my A1C be?"

"I don't want to alarm you, but the doctor said it would be much healthier if you could get it down closer to the seven range, although six-point-anything would be ideal. You can google the table and see for yourself."

"Please have the scheduler call me with her next available appointment. Thank you," I said, and hung up.

I was pissed. At the old receptionist. At this new receptionist. At the doctor. At my daughter. And at myself for being so stupid. So weak. We both have a damn disease. I started crying because I felt helpless and I wondered if Jalecia felt the same way.

I picked up the prescription.

I called Jalecia but of course it went straight to voicemail. I texted her every day for five straight days.

I know you've got a drinking problem, Jalecia, and it is nothing to be ashamed of. I hope you go back to AA.

I was glad you came home, even under the circumstances, because it told me you knew you would be safe here.

Please don't shut me out, Jalecia. I'm on your side.

I have diabetes.

Please call me or Cinnamon to let us know you're okay. I love you. Mom.

Chapter 10

"Can you babysit the twins, Grandma?"

Oh, Lord.

I was just dropping B. B. King off at the groom shop when Cinnamon called. He got some kind of prickly thing stuck in his fur and it had matted. He hates the groom shop but I love how good he smells and how shiny his coat is when I pick him up. "When?"

"Today! About one! No, noon would be better, Grandma!"

"You mean you trust me with two babies?"

"Of course I do. They're good babies. They won't give you any trouble."

"What time do you want to drop them off?"

"Oh. I need you to come here. It's too much to pack them up. Besides, it would be nice for you to see what Jonas and I have done to the apartment. And we will even be able to pay rent soon because Jonas has been promoted to manager in seafood at Whole Foods. He's thrilled, even though he always smells like fish. And I'm going on a job interview today for a production assistant job on *The Voice*! That's why I need you to babysit."

"But don't you have to have experience?"

"Not for this. But that saying 'it's who you know' is so true. One of the executives from the show shops at Whole Foods and Jonas told her about me, including that I sing!"

Oh, Lord, again.

"That's great, Cinnamon. I'll cross my fingers for you, sweetie. So tell me, what can they do since the last time I saw these little cuties?"

"Giggle. And gurgle. They think they're talking. Follow you with their eyes. Kick their feet up and down. And sleep and sleep and sleep. So you might be bored."

"Well, I can't wait to hug them. So, noon at your apartment?"

"How about eleven, because there's always traffic and I do not want to be late."

"And what time do you think you might be back?"

"Not sure. I have no idea how long the interview will last. I've never been on a real one. I'll call to give you a heads-up. It shouldn't be much more than three hours. You think you can handle that?"

"Would you mind if I asked your aunt Odessa to help me?"

"Actually, yes, I would mind. I love Great-aunt Odessa but I'm not sure I trust her around my babies. She's rather . . . impatient. Plus, I think she got a job."

"Okay, I'll ask one of your pretend aunties. Unless you have objections to any of them?"

"No. As long as they don't wear any perfume. And I would prefer if they had their natural nails rather than acrylic because of the chemicals."

"Not a problem."

Oh, but it was. I have acrylic nails, but I certainly wasn't going to mention it. Out of all the chemicals out there that could actually harm a child, what was under my nail polish was not one of them. These holistic folks sometimes just go too far.

"Just a minute! Has your mother seen the babies since the hospital?"

"No. And I would prefer that you not mention her to me right now, Grandma."

"Why?"

"Because she had Aunt Peggy call me to ask if she could borrow two hundred dollars to help her with rent because she was a little short."

"Are you serious? Did you happen to get Peggy's number?"

"No. It's a blocked number, which was why I answered it. No one calls us with a blocked number so I thought it was important. Anyway, I asked if I could speak to my mom and she said she was indisposed, so I said, 'So am I' and hung up."

"If she calls back, would you get her number? Tell her it's because you might be coming in to some money soon. Maybe it'll be the truth. I don't want you to worry about this right now, Cinna. Just think about getting that job."

"Pretty! No no no! . . . Anyway, Grandma, I'll see you soon and thank you!"

Jalecia has *my* number. Why didn't she have Peggy call me?

It felt like it'd been a century since I'd watched one baby let alone two of them. They say you don't forget, but I thought I'd feel safer if I had some help. So I dialed Korynthia. I know she likes children of all ages. She's got eight or nine great-grandkids in San Diego that she visits on a regular basis and occasionally they spend weekends with her. She complains about it, but she loves it.

Before I could even say hello, she said, "Hey girl! Please tell me you're calling to tell me you're ready to start working out!"

"Soon. I'm gearing up, Ko. Actually, I was wondering if you might have time today to help me watch my great-grandkids. At Cinnamon's from about eleven to three and, no, I'm not offering to pay you."

"Girl, I wish I could but I can't! I'm on my way to San Diego right now. My son is having issues with those damn pills again, and he did some stupid shit so I'm going there to kick his ass. But I've also paid for him to go to one of those twenty-eight-day programs where they wean him off the drugs and give him some kind of psychological assessment. The only thing that's wrong with Bird is he likes getting high. But he's going, even if I have to beat his six-foot-four ass."

"I'm really sorry to hear that, Ko. Know that he's in my prayers. And keep me posted on how it goes."

"I will. Have you asked Sadie?"

"No, and I'm not going to. She doesn't know anything about children. I'll just do it myself. After all, I've got two arms. Good luck with Bird, Ko. And please, only do the speed limit. Love you, girl."

I've been too scared to take the diabetes medication. I picked it up at CVS, but so far I have only looked at the orange bottle with my name on it. I did decide to get one of those little gadgets to prick my finger so I can keep track of my glucose levels. I also discovered that granola, which I thought was healthy, actually has a lot of sugar in it and, to my surprise, was not meant to be eaten on a daily basis. In fact, when I googled "stuff diabetics shouldn't eat," it didn't seem as if there was much left I should eat. At least not what I liked or what I was used to. If Carl were here, he would make sure I did this right. But then again, he kept his health problems a secret.

At least I have company in my misery, even if B. B. King doesn't know it. He's on a diet now, too, because his last trip to the vet was disappointing. He needs to lose ten pounds and the doctor upped the steroid medication for his arthritis, which has flared up due to his weight gain.

The doctor blamed me.

I left the house at ten thirty, even though it only takes fifteen minutes to get to Cinnamon's apartment. I knew I was going to need at least a fifteen-minute tutorial and I wanted the little ones to feel comfortable with me before Cinnamon walked out that door.

The seven-story brick apartment building is nice. Carl renovated each apartment one at a time and put good lighting in the hallways and good outdoor carpet in front. We put in brand-new appliances and each unit has a washer and dryer. The bathrooms used to be depressing but we uplifted them, too. We also haven't jacked up the rent every year, because we didn't think our tenants should be penalized for us choosing to make their building a classy place to live.

Cinnamon buzzed me up. I walked through two doors and took the elevator (which is still old but beautiful) up to the third floor. I could hear baby laughter when I rang their bell.

I admit, I was shocked when I saw Cinnamon wearing a real dress that came to her knees in a solid color, burnt orange. And on her feet was a pair of black patent-leather three-inch pumps. She wore a bracelet that was not made of string or beads, her hair was pulled up in a ponytail, and, Lord have mercy, the chile was wearing makeup! I knew God had stepped in if the possibility of getting a legitimate job had made her do all this. Hallelujah.

"Hi, Grandma! Come on in! They've been waiting for you!"

And there in two swings, side by side, smiling at me, were two brown babies with clusters of black curls on their little heads, who were so perfect they almost didn't look real. I walked over to them, not sure which one to pick up first. But I took them both by the hands and said, "Hi there, remember me? I'm your great-grandmama."

They bounced up and down, as if they already knew it.

"They are so happy to see you again. But let me just give you a few tips, and don't worry, I'm not going to ask you to do all the things Jonas and I do, just as long as they're still alive when I come back. The long and short of it is their bottles are in the fridge. They'll be ready to go down for a nap in about an hour and when they wake up they'll be ready to eat. Their diapers are in their room. You still know how to change a baby, right?"

"Let me think." And then I laughed.

"They love music. Especially if you sing to them. That big alphabet pad over there is where you can lay them on their tummies. They enjoy playing with each other and with their toys, especially the ones that make noise. Any questions, Grandma?"

"Not that I can think of. Wait. What do I do if they cry at the same time?"

"I usually just sit on the floor and put one on each side and sing. They always stop. Unless there's something in their diaper."

She bent down and kissed me.

"Wish me luck! We need this. I need this. I'm ready to join the real world, Grandma. Not just because of them," she said, pointing to the twins. "But because of me," and she pointed to her heart.

"It's called growing up, Cinnamon. And I'm very proud of you and Jonas. If it's meant to be, the job will be yours. Good luck, sweetie."

She gave her babies one more kiss without messing up her lipstick and went out the door.

I turned around slowly to look at these little humans and they started rocking in their swings as if begging me to pick them up, which I did. I laid them on their bellies on that spongy alphabet carpet. At first they looked at me and then started gurgling and entertaining each other. I felt a little obsolete. So I got down on my hands and knees and rolled over on my back and I pulled them up on top of me and I did not remember feeling this much joy since my husband told me we were spending my birthday in Palm Springs.

I fed them. I checked their diapers every fifteen minutes, praying they were only wet, which they were, hallelujah. They had apparently learned patience by being twins, because one waited for me to change the other. I gave them bottles, and as I sat there and watched them on their alphabet mat, I started singing some song I didn't even know I still knew the words to. They seemed to like it because they started singing along with me in their language. Try as they might, their tones began to get lower and then, almost in slow motion, they stopped moving and their eyes started blinking more slowly until they stayed shut. I got blankets from their bedroom and gently placed them over them and after an hour I dropped down on my knees to make sure they were still alive. When they both started snoring, I just sat there waiting for them to cry but they didn't. They stayed in that same spot for another hour until their mother walked in the door. When they heard her voice, they stirred and smiled and after she kicked off those pumps, Cinnamon told me she got the job and I started clapping and Pretty and Handsome looked like they were trying to.

I finally took a pill, even though I didn't want to.

I was afraid that if I started taking them, I would always have to take them. But that little needle on my new glucose monitor hurt like hell when it pierced my skin and watching those numbers go up was downright terrifying. Was I going to live or die today? I decided I would take the medication and check my numbers once every week, or two. But starting next week.

I also planned to go see Ma, because I hadn't seen her since Odessa started working there, but she called to tell me she had a cold and also not to expect any of her written insights until she could think of some.

I wish I could write to Jalecia. I'd tell her how important she always was to me, and still is. I'd tell her that her brother, Jackson, was an addition to our family, not her competitor. I'd tell her how much energy I spent trying to make her feel important.

I think my daughter might just be angry at herself for not making smarter decisions and being unwilling to accept any responsibility for them. I can't fix that. I just pray she doesn't give up on herself.

"So," Korynthia said to everybody as we assembled for our group dinner at her house again because they still didn't think I was ready even though I felt like I might be; Lucky pretended Joe was sick; and Sadie had just moved into a tiny apartment, didn't even have a table yet, and was too cheap to have her turn at a restaurant. "This is the deal. I did not cook and you should all be wondering why."

"I'm not. But I would like to pay for whatever it is you ordered since it is my turn and I don't smell any recognizable aroma coming from your kitchen," Lucky said.

"How thoughtful, Miss Thang. You can pay me later. I ordered from Grubhub. You will hear about it after we imbibe. And yes, that's a new word I've added to my vocabulary. Get used to it."

The adulteress, who was not looking so blissful, simply said, "I hope it's something light because I feel heavy. Don't ask. What did you order, Ko?"

"Chinese. And you will eat it."

"How soon before it gets here?" Lucky asked.

"Slow your roll, Lucky. How about asking if I need any help?"

"Do you need any help with anything, Ko?"

"Yes. You could help us all by keeping your negative thoughts to yourself this evening."

We all laughed. Except Lucky. In fact, since Sadie was distracted checking her cellphone for messages, Lucky gave Ko the finger. Then I gave the finger to Lucky, and we all started laughing. Except Sadie.

"So what dishes did you order?" Lucky asked. "I hope not those string beans and that stuff with the scrambled eggs in it again?"

"I ordered pot stickers and various types of chow fun and a lot of other shit you will eat."

"Where's the wine?" I asked.

"Where it always is," Ko said. "According to Grubhub, the food should be here in five minutes."

Just then the doorbell rang and scared the hell out of all of us.

We headed to Ko's cool dining room. She likes glass so the table was burgundy glass and the chairs were deep pink silk. One wall was filled with photos of her grandkids, at all ages. I've always thought they should be on the wall heading up the stairwell, but I keep my thoughts to myself.

"Sadie and Lucky, pay attention," Korynthia said as she handed the delivery guy a ten-dollar bill. "This is called a tip. Thank you." The delivery guy had a wide grin on his face.

"How much change?" he asked.

"No change," Ko said, and he almost skipped off her beloved front porch. Ko has rocking chairs out there and since she's lived in this house almost thirty years, I can't count how many times we've sat out there and just rocked, sometimes without saying a word.

We went into the kitchen and washed our hands, then sat down as Ko started pulling out all of the round containers with plastic lids, the white boxes that we knew were pot stickers and brown and white rice, and the fortune cookies, at least ten of them. I was praying I'd pick a good one.

"Is Poochie joining us this evening?" I asked.

"No, but she called. She didn't want me to tell you, but I'm telling you anyway: she might have to have her hip replacement surgery sooner than she thought."

"We're all falling apart," Lucky said.

"No, we are not, Lucky. And no negativity tonight, got it?"

"I'm sorry," she said.

"Okay. This is the deal. I've finally got some good news to share so . . . shall we eat first?" Ko said.

"Even though I would like to eat right now, I'm all ears," Lucky said, shocking the hell out of all of us.

"Just don't mention anything about love," Sadie said.

"I agree with you, Sadie," Lucky said.

We all looked at Sadie, wondering what had gotten into her. Although we assumed her honeymoon was probably over, we were not about to ask.

"Then let's eat," I said.

And we did. And when we finished everybody except Sadie had another glass of wine.

"So," Korynthia said, "my good news is that Bird has been in a twenty-eight-day program now for almost two weeks and even though he's been going through hell withdrawing from those dreadful pills so many folks are addicted to, he's almost over the hump and told me he's going to stick it out!"

Everybody, including Lucky, made one hard clap, then threw fist pumps in the air. Sadie followed up by bowing her head so we let her pray like she always does and waited for her to open her eyes. When she did, we saw tears rolling down her cheeks and I knew they probably weren't for Bird.

Ko continued: "Thank you all. Now, I'm going to shift gears here by asking a very personal question, since we've all known each other since high school and it pertains to my current life."

We all looked somewhere between curious and suspicious.

"What's the most orgasms you've ever had in one session?"

This caught us all off guard.

"Why would that be any of your business?" Lucky asked.

"That probably means you've never had one," I heard myself say and then wished I could take it back.

"Three," Sadie blurted out.

"So, that's what made you fall in love with that minister then, huh?" Lucky asked.

Sadie just put her chin in her palm and stared Lucky in the eye.

"Four," I said. "Back in the good old days. Carl knew how to please and please and please and . . ."

Everybody laughed except Lucky.

"What about you, Ko?" I asked.

"We're tied, Lo."

"I don't think I've ever had one," Lucky said. "There, the truth is out. But to be honest, I don't care. You can't miss what you've never had."

"It's because you're mean and your karma is bad," Sadie said.

"Okay, let's stop! Enough! I was just curious," Ko said.

"Wait, you said the personal question pertained to your current situation. What? How?" I asked.

"Okay," Korynthia said with a smirk on her face. "So, you guys already know I've been on a senior dating site and met a few old farts. Well the last one, Lloyd, I went out with four times and finally decided to have sex with him."

Everybody leaned forward.

"So anyway, we were at his house—the one his wife died in, I might add, which did not make for great foreplay. It's a very nice house over by the Langham hotel. Anyway, we were getting touchy and I realized he was already very excited, if you get my drift, and when I took off my clothes and he saw how fit I was he looked like he wanted to get a plate and fork or something. But to make a long story short, Lloyd had taken a pill while we were at dinner, and Lord, I cannot even tell you how long that man's miniature erection lasted. I was just watching the clock, getting pissed off because he kept asking me to turn this way and that way. And after what felt like years had passed, I finally pretended I needed to go to the bathroom because I was trying to figure out how I was going to get the hell out of there. He was still at attention when I got back and then he wanted to get on the couch. We tried up there for about ten painstaking minutes, but then he pulled me down on the carpet and he was moving like a jackhammer. I felt sorry for him but when he started yelling 'Ride it, girl!' I heard myself yell: 'Give me something to ride!' Apparently that hurt his feelings, but I didn't care, and I sat up and said, 'How many of those pills did you take?' He said two and that's when I jumped the fuck up, put my clothes on, and told him to go find a prostitute and do not call me anymore."

We were in tears by the time she finished.

"Well, there is no way I can top that," Lucky said. "But my news is that I am going to do the gastric bypass because I realize I have no self-control and I just keep getting bigger and bigger and I don't want to die this size."

"Don't think like that, Lucky!" Ko said.

"Yeah, please don't," I said. "But it's not a bad idea."

"I should've done it a long time ago."

"How soon?"

"I won't know until I get a physical to make sure I won't die on the table."

"How does Joe feel about this?"

"I haven't told him."

"That's ridiculous, Lucky, he's your husband," Korynthia said. "I do not for the life of me understand why he has tolerated your mean ass all these years."

I needed to lighten up the conversation a little. No, a lot, so I said, "Well, I've decided to ask my real estate tycoon friend Korynthia to help me start looking for a new space for the House of Beauty. And I finally started taking diabetes medication because I don't have enough willpower to do what it takes on my own, but one day soon I will change the way I eat and make exercise part of my life."

"Taking diabetes meds is nothing to be ashamed of. And Carl hasn't even been gone a year. So cut yourself some slack," Sadie said, then she cast her eyes down and I knew I'd been right that those tears hadn't been for Bird.

"I'm being punished for what I've been doing," Sadie whispered. "George told me his wife found out about us. He is leaving our church because he violated the rules of marriage in the eyes of God. He said he was sorry for giving the devil the power and that he was sorry if he broke my heart."

"What did you say?" I asked.

"I said, 'Fuck you' and 'Good luck finding a new church.'"

"You swore?" Korynthia asked.

"It's about damn time, and isn't it ironic it took a preacher to get you to do it!" I said.

"Are you leaving the church, too?" Lucky asked.

"Yes. But I don't know where I'm going to start worshipping."

Even though she'd been stupid, I could tell her heart was broken, which was why I reached under the table and took her hand and squeezed it.

"Pray on it," Korynthia said.

Lucky stopped herself in the middle of rolling her eyes and turned to me. "So, Lo, now that you seem to have gotten used to Carl being on permanent vacation in heaven, we think he's probably wondering when you're going to get around to fulfilling some of those promises he made you make?"

"I went to Sadie's church. That's one down. I'll get to the other ones in due time."

"Well, the clock is ticking. You're going to have another birthday in about four months, so get on it."

I gave her a thumbs-up with a smirk.

Korynthia grabbed a fortune cookie. "Okay, since I'm hosting, I'll read mine first: *A good way to keep healthy is to eat more Chinese food.*"

Korynthia tossed that one in the air and grabbed another one.

"*You will marry your lover.* Oh hell to the no, I won't! Read yours, Lo! And if it's better than mine I want to trade!"

We all started laughing.

I opened my cookie and read: "*Be able to recognize your prime at whatever time of your life it may occur.*"

I gave my cookie a thumbs-up then devoured it.

Lucky snatched hers: "*A conclusion is simply the place where you got tired of thinking.*"

"No shit," she said to the fortune cookie, and then plopped it in her mouth.

Sadie read hers: *"Do not mistake temptation for opportunity."*

We all shook our heads and muttered, "Ya think?"

"Okeydokey, then," Korynthia said. "Now that we all know where we're headed, when do we start?"

Chapter 11

I was checking my glucose when my cellphone rang in my bathrobe pocket. It was six thirty in the morning and no one calls me at this hour unless it's an emergency. Even B. B. King knows this, so he crawled across the floor as if he was trying to protect me. I was hoping it wasn't Jalecia and when I looked at the number it was the security guard who monitored the House of Beauty.

"Good morning, Mrs. Curry. I'm afraid I've got some bad news."

"I suppose I've been robbed."

"I'm sorry to report it, but yes, you were."

"How much damage?"

"A lot. The place has been ransacked and I doubt if there's anything salvageable, ma'am."

"What happened to the alarm, Officer Clark?"

"Well, these new thieves are pretty sophisticated. They know how to disarm them. They also know when we're making our rounds from one facility to the next, and I admit, I stopped at Dunkin' and got to talking about the Lakers with a buddy. I'm so sorry. All these years, we've never had any problems in this part of town. The police just got here."

"I'm on my way."

I didn't bother to look at my monitor. I slipped on a pair of sweats, a sweatshirt, and sneakers, took B.B. outside near his doghouse, poured some dry food and fresh water into his bowls, and ignored his *please take me with you* stare. I stopped at the drive-through window at Starbucks to get a latte and was surprised that they already had my favorite: Pumpkin Spice. But I ordered a low-fat mocha latte with no sugar instead. I didn't like it.

On the fifteen-minute drive to the shop I felt tears rolling down my eyes. Not because the shop had been robbed, but because this was the kind of situation Carl would've handled. Since he's been gone, I have had to make every decision myself. I have not been able to ask him for advice, or weigh his unsolicited suggestions, or know that when something was too hard for me to handle he would comfort me until I was able to put things in perspective.

When I pulled into the parking lot, police cars took up all of the parking spaces and they didn't want to let me through until I identified myself as the owner. I did not even go inside. I could see how much was missing through the broken glass and I had no interest in trying to figure out what was still in there. This was a sign: it was time to move the store. Because unlike my husband, everything in here could be replaced.

Instead of going home, the Volvo steered itself to the Rose Bowl. I considered walking off some of this stress, even if it was only for fifteen minutes. While looking for a parking spot, I glanced up at Lucky's house and decided I would drop by, hoping maybe I might get her to take a few baby steps with me. But I immediately changed my mind. Lucky doesn't like being surprised. So I called her.

"Put your behind in something comfortable. I'm on my way up the hill to drag you down here to walk just a quarter of a mile with me. My shop got robbed and I'm feeling antsy."

"Wait, have you heard from Korynthia this morning?"

"No, why?"

"Bird left that rehab place before his treatment ended. She's on her way down to San Diego. I'm so glad I never had any goddamn kids."

"Shit! Does she know where he is, Lucky?"

"Apparently he went home. I've been calling her since I got her message but she's not picking up."

"Shit."

"Come up, Lo. Forget about walking. We can call Ko together and figure out what we can do to help her. And don't tell me my being nice is out of character because I do love all you bitches."

"I'm on my way up now," I said, wondering what made her say that.

"But don't say anything about how this house looks. The housekeepers quit a month ago and I just haven't been in the mood to find new ones. Anyway, I just made a strong pot of Peet's Sumatra and I baked a delicious apple pie for Joe."

I went to dial Ko but realized I had a voicemail from her.

"Hey, Lo. Bird walked out of rehab yesterday but he's at home now. He's okay, but he's not okay. He went straight to buy more of those goddamn pills. I'm not leaving here until I can get to the bottom of this because he's going back to rehab and I will stay here until he finishes the program, even if he has to stay another twenty-eight days. If he doesn't, I might kill him myself. Anyway, I'll be in touch, so don't worry. But do this for me, Lo. Call Jalecia and show her all the love you can. Something makes them do this shit to themselves and we need to help them figure out what it is so they can stop. Love you."

I had to wipe my eyes as I drove up the hill. I pulled over and looked down at the Rose Bowl. The last time I walked it was with Ko. The people looked so much smaller. But at least they were trying to be stronger, healthier, and sounder. As I watched, I was wondering how many of them were suffering from something, trying to recover from something. How many of them had lost a loved one or were suffering from a broken heart? How many of them were worried about a loved one? A child. A parent. A friend.

A few minutes later I pulled into Lucky and Joe's driveway. Their house is a stucco mansion. If it weren't white, it would be scary. The guesthouse is practically the same size as my house. I can't believe that's where her husband lives. Well, yes, I can.

I didn't ring the doorbell because Lucky's door is always unlocked. I walked in.

"Lucky? Where the hell are you?"

She came from around the kitchen corner in an orange-and-green-flowered muumuu. When she threw her arms around me she was too soft. Her hair looked like she had two or three different styles going on at the same time, which meant no style at all. And she smelled weird. In fact, it smelled weird in here. Not like apple pie.

"What's that I smell, Lucky?"

"Marijuana."

"What?"

She grabbed me by the hand as we walked through the living room, which looked like it hadn't been cleaned in months. Newspapers were strewn on both ends of the long brocade sofa. Empty cups and wineglasses filled the cocktail table in front of it. It also smelled like the windows hadn't been opened for years.

"Wait a minute," I said and walked over and pushed open the wide French doors that led out to a beautiful backyard.

"What is your problem?" she asked me.

"It stinks in here and I don't want to inhale that nasty smoke. What is wrong with you, Lucky? When did you start smoking marijuana?"

"Slow your roll," she said like the young people.

"No! What in the hell is going on?"

I walked past her into the kitchen, which was an even worse mess. Flour was all over the counter and the sink was full of dishes that were not from her pie making. The Spanish floor tiles were sticky. I couldn't believe what was going on inside this beautiful house. It looked like someone had a party in here and didn't bother to clean up afterward.

"Sit," she said. "You want a piece of my delicious apple pie?"

"No, I do not. And you don't need any either."

"I enjoy my own baking."

I realized Lucky was high as hell. So this is what prompted the friendly call and her change in attitude. She must have been smoking when she got Ko's message and something inside her hard heart cracked.

"Lucky, what's wrong with you?"

"Why does something have to be wrong with me? I'm up here in my house minding my own business and just enjoying life."

"Who do you think you're talking to, huh? That is total bullshit. You're in here smoking reefer and your house is a fucking mess. Now I know why you didn't want us to have dinner here. What in the hell is going on?"

She turned so I couldn't see her face.

"I have made a mess of my life."

"That's not true," I said. "What happened to your damn housekeepers?"

"They quit. They didn't like the smell of this," she said and pulled a joint from the pocket of her muumuu.

I walked over and snatched it, moved some of the dishes out of the sink, dropped it down the garbage disposal, and turned it on.

"I dare you to say something. Now, where's the rest of it?"

"That's it."

"Go get it, Lucky. You are scaring the hell out of me. Is this what you do all day? Can't you see what you're doing to yourself?"

She shook her head no.

"Well, I can."

I grabbed her by the arm and dragged her into the living room in front of the biggest, ugliest, floor-length mirror she had.

"Who in the hell is that?" I asked.

She wouldn't look up.

I slapped her behind.

She lifted her head up slowly until she was looking at herself and then her head dropped until she was looking at the floor.

"Let's rewind the videotape. Whose bright idea was it that we both lose weight and start exercising?"

She pointed to her chest.

"You said you want to get bypass surgery, but have you even tried to lose any weight?"

"No."

"Why not?"

"Why haven't you?"

"Don't turn this around on me."

"I . . . I don't think I love my husband anymore, and I don't think he loves me."

"Joe does love you."

"No, he doesn't."

"Well, you're not all that loveable, Lucky. You're mean and all you do is complain about everything and everybody."

I was surprised when I saw tears rolling down her cheeks and even more surprised when I felt them falling from my eyes, too. I wiped mine dry because I didn't want there to be two people falling apart, which wouldn't solve anything. Somebody needed to be strong.

"Why did you tell me to come over here if you knew your house looked like a pigsty? We were supposed to be worrying about Korynthia and her son, but now you've got me worrying about you."

"I know that, Lo. I just felt so overwhelmed that I wanted you here. I'm also ashamed and bored with my life, and I feel old and I don't know what to do with so much free time on my hands. I even stopped shopping because I have too much of everything but not enough of something."

I grabbed her by the hand, walked her back to the kitchen, and pulled a chair out from the table in the nook and made her sit. I picked up that big-ass apple pie and started shoveling it out with my hands and pushing it down the garbage disposal until the glass pan was clear. Then I opened the dishwasher and started emptying it but realized the dishes weren't clean and there was hard dishwashing detergent caked inside it, so I shut the door and turned it on. I then grabbed some rubber gloves and washed every dish, every pot, and every surface as Lucky sat in that chair and watched me until she fell asleep, head down on her folded arms. By the time she woke up I had vacuumed the entire living room, cleaned the kitchen and all four bathrooms, and shaken the dust out of the goddamn rugs. When I finished, I went outside and sat on the patio and looked down at the Rose Bowl.

"Thank you, Lo," I heard her say from behind me. She squeezed my shoulders and sat in a chair next to mine.

She looked over at me. "I'm worried about all of us. You. Korynthia. Sadie. Poochie. Bird. Jalecia. And me."

Odessa called the other day to ask if I wanted to see what she'd done to the apartment, so I was back in the building waiting for the elevator. I really wanted to stop on the third floor to hold the babies, but I'd probably never leave, which was why I pressed 7 instead of 3.

She was standing outside her doorway with her arms crossed as I walked down the long hallway. She should consider wearing something besides earth tones. Today was tobacco. She's already mocha. But as I got closer, I couldn't believe she was wearing lipstick. Maroon lipstick. She looked like fall, which I suppose it was.

"Hi, Sis," she said and gave me a bear hug. "I have to warn you that it's a little tight in here. I'm doing the best I can with the space I have," and she moved out of the doorway to let me in.

Even though it wasn't yet dark outside, it was dark in here. It looked like a museum or a funeral parlor from a previous century. The first thing staring at me was Jesus.

In fact, the dining room table looked like the Last Supper except there were only two placemats, two plates, and two glasses at opposite ends. Ma used to have a table similar to this but hers was real mahogany. This looked like walnut veneer. The legs curved out at the top and then curled back in and had little claws on the bottom. Odessa had dismantled the cream-colored drum shade we'd installed and replaced it with a chandelier. A grandfather clock scared the hell out of me when it dinged. Odessa had also chosen to paint this room a mustard yellow. I thought I could almost smell it, but it turned out to be beef stroganoff, which I knew she was going to force me to eat.

"You want to see my bedroom?" Odessa asked.

"That's okay," I said. "I remember the brocade from your house."

"The second bedroom is filled to the brim, so if I had a guest they would have to sleep on the couch."

"You've downsized from a house, Odessa, when are you going to get rid of some of that stuff?"

"It's not *stuff,* Loretha. It's my personal belongings. Things I cherish. Let's eat. Are you in a hurry?" she said and stormed out into the living room.

"Actually, I'm supposed to be meeting Kwame at my house because he said he has some good news to tell me."

"You really like that kid, don't you?"

"Yes, I do."

"And it doesn't bother you that he's a homosexual?"

"No, it doesn't."

"Too many of them out here for my taste."

"Somebody recently asked me if you were a lesbian because you haven't been with a man since your husband left you."

"That is the most disgusting thing you could say to me, Loretha. I have given my heart and soul to the Lord Jesus Christ our Savior, which is all the love I need. I hope you came to my defense."

"Of course I did," I lied.

She moved toward the modern kitchen that I could see she'd stuffed with knickknacks from the same era everything else in here was from. It was all just creepy.

I would normally ask if I could help, but I decided not to.

"Can we open the drapes?" I asked, and then wished I hadn't.

"I don't like to have to look at the streetlight changing every so many minutes. I do not like this neighborhood and will be glad when I can move into Ma's house. How long before it'll be ready?"

"I told you I wasn't sure."

"Yes, you are."

"Odessa, I told you I do not want you to live in Ma's house. It's too big. I might just sell it."

"I don't believe you." She bowed her head.

"Lord, please bless this meal," she said and let it go at that.

We did not say a word during the meal. I could hardly eat the stroganoff, which was terrible, and also because I had snuck a hamburger (not cheeseburger) with small fries before I came over, just in case I didn't like what Odessa was serving. After we finished, I offered to help clean up.

"Don't bother," she said, and led me toward the door. "If you try to sell Ma's house, I might sue you."

I didn't bother to respond but I was sure thinking about a church sign I passed on the way here that said: A GRUDGE IS A HEAVY THING TO CARRY.

She slammed the door before I could even think about hugging her.

Chapter 12

"Mama-Lo! Guess who's going to be a college student?"

B. B. King howled as if he knew this was good news and then started jumping up and down a few inches like it was a happy dance.

I stood on my tiptoes and squeezed Kwame as hard as I could. I was close to tears but I didn't want to confuse B. B. King because he has only seen me cry when I was sad.

"I told you I had good news to celebrate. I even brought food, which I know is going to shock you. It's Italian!"

"Congratulations, Kwame! I'm so freaking proud of you, son! Give me those bags before Mr. King nabs them!"

I didn't want to seem ungrateful so I didn't mention the pre-dinner burger and fries or the stroganoff I'd eaten at Odessa's. Kwame set the food on the kitchen counter and shook his index finger at B. B. King: *Wait until we're finished and you'll have a gourmet meal, too.* He looked so handsome, his dreadlocks had grown and were shiny and smelled like mint.

"So, where?"

"Los Angeles City College. They have a whole television and film department!"

"Well, that's wonderful!"

"Anyway, classes start in January and I can still drive with Uber so I'll still be able to pay my bills."

"It's all good news, Kwame. So, what's in these bags?"

"I got lasagna and sourdough bread, and a Caesar salad and asparagus for you. No dessert. Have you been watching your numbers?"

"Yes, I have."

"You don't sound all that convincing, Mama-Lo. Are you taking that medication they gave you?"

"Most days."

"Most isn't gonna cut it, Mama-Lo. Seriously. And when was the last time you saw your doctor?"

"Let's eat. You sound like my mother!"

"Your son, you mean?" he said. "I want you to live a long life, long enough to come to my first movie premiere!"

"You'll have to fly your mom out here for it!"

"No doubt. And I'll pick her up at the airport in my Range Rover. The big one. But for now, I'll set the table."

"Speaking of sons, did I tell you I'm planning to go to Tokyo to spend some time with Jackson and meet his twin little girls?"

"That sounds cool. Y'all can make some twins in this family! Wow. How long is that flight?"

"About twelve hours."

He started shaking his head. "No way could I be on a plane that long."

"What's the longest flight you've been on?"

"Zero hours. I've never had a reason to fly anyplace. You remember we took the Greyhound for my dad's service."

"Well, maybe when I go you'd like to housesit and dogsit. If your schedule permits, that is."

I didn't have a date nailed down yet. I just wanted to know if Kwame was willing because my friends had too many things on their plates, especially when it came to walking B. B. King.

"You can count on me. I can only afford two classes for now because I'm not a California resident yet. Which is cool because I don't know how many of my units from Flint can be transferred. How's the search for the new shop going?"

"So, you heard the House was burglarized?"

"Cinnamon told me. Good thing you had insurance."

"Of course I did, Kwame."

"Well, I had a little fender bender last week."

"And? Don't tell me the other driver didn't have insurance?"

"He did not."

"Whose fault was it?"

"His."

"But *you* have insurance. It usually covers uninsured drivers."

"It had lapsed two days before."

"What did you just say?"

"Don't worry, I paid it this morning because you have to have proof of insurance when you drive with Uber."

"What will you do about the car?"

"The driver promised to pay me."

"And you believed him?"

"Yeah. I mean, yes. His grandma and auntie were in the back seat and he was more worried about them than anything. Anyway, he gave me his work number and I got the estimate and sent it to him yesterday morning."

"And have you heard back from him?"

"Right before I got here I got the notice from Western Union that the payment was there."

"So are you going to get the car fixed?"

"No. I've got a few other bills I need to pay since I couldn't drive until I got reinstated with Uber."

"So how do you plan on paying for the car repairs?"

"Dancing."

"What kind of dancing?"

"Don't ask."

"I won't."

"It's legal."

"Just don't end up dead. Because I like you."

"I love you," he said.

"Good. You might end up in my will. One day."

"Don't talk like that, Mama-Lo, please."

"Speaking of mamas, how is yours doing?"

"I don't really know."

"Why don't you know?"

"Because she never answered my card."

"Call your cousin who stayed with you out here. Boone."

"Right now?"

"Yes."

"But it's eleven o'clock in Michigan."

"Call him."

He dialed the number and looked at me with those big brown eyes. Just like Carl's.

"Yo, punk. What up? You heard from my moms?"

Listening.

"Has your dad spoken to her?"

Listening.

"What do you mean I sound white?"

Listening.

"Can somebody go over there and check on her? Her phone is still disconnected."

Listening.

"Ask somebody for a goddamn ride, man. And call me right back."

"Can't you call another relative?" I asked.

"I can't think of anybody else. Sorry for swearing."

"No apology necessary under these circumstances, Kwame."

We tried to eat. Kwame lifted the wide lasagna noodles and let them fall back on top of the red meat sauce. Then he pulled on the cheese to form a string, wrapped it around the fork, and rested it on the edge of the plate.

Five minutes went by. Then ten. Then twenty.

"Call him back," I said.

And he did.

"She's not?"

Listening.

"It is? Then go look through the side window."

Waiting.

I watched Kwame's face; his eyes opened wide and I could see he was terrified.

"What did you just say? Call 911! Right fucking now!"

He put down the phone and the phone rang again and he jumped up from the table. Walked back and forth from the kitchen to the living room, then opened the front door and came back in and started walking in circles. B. B. King followed him until Kwame dropped down on the couch.

"Kick the fucking door in," he said.

He held his head down and covered his eyes. I went and sat next to him, rubbed his hand. I already knew what had happened.

I could hear someone yelling something through Kwame's phone and then he said, "Call some-damn-body!"

And he jumped up.

"I have to go! I knew I should never have left her there by herself!"

"Did he say she wasn't breathing?"

He stopped cold. "Boone, is she breathing? Please tell me she's breathing, man?"

He started walking in circles. "She is? Thank you, Jesus. You already called 911? Can she talk?"

He turned and started jumping up and down. "How soon before the ambulance gets there?"

He grabbed my hand and squeezed it. B. B. King hunched down on all fours because he could sense something was wrong.

"You hear 'em now? Call me when you know she's going to be all right. Please. And tell her I love her and I'll be there as soon as I can."

And then he slumped down on the sofa. And immediately jumped back up.

"Kwame, baby. Slow down. Let's figure out how to do this. She's breathing. That's a good thing. Now maybe you might want to go pray. Any way you want to. Go sit on the front porch. I'll call to see how fast we can get you to Flint."

I gave him a hard hug.

"Thank you, Mama-Lo."

I called American Airlines and explained that I was trying to get a flight out tonight from Los Angeles to Flint, Michigan. They asked me if it was round trip and I said yes, then no, and then if it was economy. I asked if they had that extra legroom fare in economy. Then I asked what the difference in price was between that one and business class. I thought that because of his frame of mind he was going to need all the comfort he could get, so I said make it business class and she said he would have to change planes in Chicago and would be in Flint by ten thirty tomorrow morning. I gave her his name, my credit card, and his cell number and it was done.

I heard him walk back inside and B. B. King was with him. Kwame looked calmer.

"They said she might have had a stroke, and she's at the hospital now. They can't say for sure until she sees a doctor. But she's breathing."

"See how fast God works. Check your phone. There's a flight in three hours. You can be sitting by your mama's side right after breakfast."

"This says business class. I know that costs more money. Please call back and change it. I'll get there the same time in coach."

"But your legs won't. This way you might be able to get some sleep. Do you need to go home to get anything?"

"No."

"Do you have any money in your checking account?"

"Sixty-three dollars."

"Text me the account number and I'll transfer enough to get you through this. And if by chance you end up staying, know you'll always have a home here."

He bent down and gave me a hug. Then he pulled up the app for Uber and within seconds he raised his head.

"Three minutes," he said. "I'll be back as soon as I know she's okay, definitely in time to housesit and watch B. B. King."

"Don't even worry about that, Kwame. Besides, I've got enough friends and family here in Pasadena to watch the house if you aren't back. And B. B. King loves those doggie hotels." That got a chuckle out of him. We walked to the door.

"Call me as soon as you land and then after you see your mama. And do give her a hug for me."

"I will," he said. "I definitely will."

And there was Uber.

The Italian food was cold and stiff and still sitting on the table. I put most of it in the refrigerator. I ate a piece of hard bread. Got a cold glass of water. Took my pill. And fell across the bed with my clothes on. When I felt my cellphone shivering in my palm, it was morning. I read the text from Kwame that he had landed, that his mother was going to need him, and he could not leave her until he knew she was going to be okay.

Chapter 13

"Did you bring the Bengay?" Ma asked.

"Of course I did," I said. "Don't they have it here?"

"I want my own."

"For what?"

"Why are you so nosy? I'm old and old people ache and Bengay helps."

"I'm sorry, Ma."

"You don't have anything to be sorry about. Anyway, it's for my wrists. They get a little stiff sometimes, especially when I'm doing my push-ups," she said, and then started laughing.

I tried to laugh but couldn't, so I just said, "Funny Fanny."

"When you get old you better hope you have your sense of humor. Laughing keeps you young."

"I am old, Ma, in case you didn't know."

"You're old when you think you're old."

"Okay, Ma. I get it."

"What's that tone I hear in your voice? You don't sound like yourself. Is it Jalecia?"

"No. I haven't heard from her in months. Kwame had to go back to Flint. His mother had a stroke."

"Awww. I'm so sorry to hear that. He's such a nice homosexual."

"Who told you he was gay?"

"Odessa, who else? She's homophobic, you know."

"I didn't know you knew that word, Ma."

"I watch TV, Loretha. Everybody's gay now. I don't mind. I can think of at least three boys and one girl in my gym class who were probably like that, but back then everybody just used to say, 'You know he funny.' Or 'You know she a butch.' Even then, we just figured they were born that way."

"I hope he comes back soon. He was going to be starting college right after the new year."

"Which reminds me. You're having another birthday soon, huh?"

"I suppose so."

"Whatcha gonna do this time? And please don't say nothing."

"The girls want to take a casino bus to Vegas. We promised Poochie we'd do it, but I don't know if I'm up for celebrating my birthday this year, Ma."

"That's stupid. You need to celebrate every single one of them while you still can. Carl would want you to, I'm sure of it."

I wish she hadn't said that because it was just a reminder that my birthday would always mark the anniversary of him being gone.

"Ma, your hair is a mess. You want me to brush it?"

"You must be reading my mind," she said. "Grab the brush off my nightstand over there. And thank you for the geraniums you sent, although I thought they might be from a new boyfriend!"

And she started laughing. Her silver hair was iridescent and thin, so I was gentle. As I stood behind her, I remembered how hard she used to pull when she brushed my hair, because it was "thicker than thick," as she used to say.

"That feels so good. You know Odessa works here at the facility now. I'm glad she doesn't work in my wing."

"I heard. I would think it might be nice, though, Ma."

From her dresser mirror I saw her eyes move from east to west.

"I don't want her knowing all my business. Odessa acts like she's older than I am, you know."

"I think I do."

"No, you don't. It's because she hasn't had sex in twenty years. Maybe thirty. Anyway, she is nosy as hell, and I don't want to have to answer personal questions when she's not a doctor."

"Well, like you said, she's not in your wing, so not to worry."

"It's a good thing she works nights, because I'll be honest: I can fake being asleep when she taps on my door. I know the night nurse's tap."

"So, Ma, I was wondering if you might want to come visit me at my house."

"No."

"Why not?"

"Because I just feel more comfortable right here. Carl's service was the end of my being sociable. I don't like to travel any farther than I need to. That's when you know you're old. You haven't been feeling that way, I hope."

"No, I haven't."

"Don't lie."

"I'd tell you, Ma."

"Odessa told me you were diagnosed with diabetes. Do you check your numbers regularly?"

"Yes," I lied.

"Every day?"

"Almost."

"Don't be stupid, Loretha. You've gotta check them every single day. I've been diabetic for more than thirty years."

"What? Why didn't you tell us?"

"It just didn't cross my mind."

"Everything crosses your mind, Ma."

"Because I didn't want you girls to worry. Besides, I take my medication and my numbers are good. They test us here."

"Well, that's good to know."

"Are you getting any exercise?"

"I just started," I say.

"Stop lying. You're thicker than I've ever seen you."

"Okay! But I am about to start. And that's the truth, Ma."

"I'll tell you something. Back when I was young, only athletes exercised. We played dodgeball in gym class and did some other silly shit—but if we had known back then that we needed to exercise on a regular basis our entire lives, a whole lot of my friends would probably still be here."

"So, are you telling me you exercise, Ma?"

"Of course I do. We have great classes here."

"And you go?"

"I'm in better shape than you and Odessa."

I could see that this was true, which was embarrassing.

"What do you do?"

"Water aerobics. Sit-ups. We have dance class. Sometimes I have been known to jump rope."

She started laughing.

"Thank you, Jane Fonda! But seriously, Ma, I do know all this stuff."

"Diabetes is no joke, baby. Half the people on your daddy's side had it, though they were also alcoholics."

I have never heard her mention my father's family. I wanted to ask her about Odessa's father's side, but I didn't think it was appropriate. Both men passed away years ago.

"Anyway, you need to stop acting like you live twice. So, have you been reading the little tidbits I've sent?" Ma asked.

"I have. Especially my horoscopes and the *AARP* articles. They're encouraging and inspiring and usually find me in the right moments."

"I like mailing them. I like putting the stamp on the envelope and addressing it. And I like imagining you opening them and sitting there in Carl's chair reading them with B. B. King at your feet. Now, put my hair in a ponytail and get out of here. *The Voice* is coming on."

I was dozing off watching reruns of *Scandal* when I heard my phone ring. I looked over at the clock and it was two twenty in the morning. I knew when a phone rings at this time of night it almost always means somebody is in the hospital or dead. My caller ID said BLOCKED. I knew instantly who it was and I put my hand over my heart, which I suddenly felt thumping so loudly I could hear it.

"Peggy?"

"How'd you know it was me?"

"Cinnamon told me you called her from a blocked number. Please tell me Jalecia is okay."

"Your guess is as good as mine. I haven't seen her in a week, but she owes me some money for letting her stay here. I'm doing all I can to keep her out of trouble, but she is eating me out of house and home, and she drinks too much and I'm worried about her safety. I could use three hundred dollars unless you want her to come live with you."

I sat up to turn on the light, but moonlight was already making my room glow.

"If she wants to come live with me, she can."

"She doesn't want to. That much I do know. We can talk about that another time. I want you to know that she's safe here with me, but sometimes she disappears and binges. And I just hope she's not in jail again. It would be a felony this time and she couldn't just come home. She might be with her lowlife boyfriend, but she's not answering her cell. Wait. Hold on a minute, Loretha, maybe that's her trying to get through."

I heard a click as she put me on hold.

I sat there staring at the moon, hating the fact that my daughter was calling her trifling aunt instead of me.

"She's downstairs. I was right. She's been holed up with her loser boyfriend who's got three kids and no job. I don't know from one day to the next what she's going to do or not do, but can you Western Union me some money before we're both standing on your doorstep because we don't have a roof over our heads? My social security check won't be here for another two weeks and I'd really appreciate it, Loretha."

"Okay! But please, would you ask her to call me?"

"Thank you. But I wouldn't count on it. She's scared of you. But I'm working on her. Just give me some time. Sorry for waking you up."

Click.

I just looked at the phone. Scared of me? She's working on her? Who did this bitch think she was? For a minute, I thought maybe I had dreamed this, but the moon was still there and when I heard B. B. King walk into my bedroom—something he rarely does—I was pretty sure it was because he also knew something wasn't right.

In the morning I drove to a drugstore where I always see people in line for Western Union. When it was finally my turn, I picked up the phone and waited for all the prompts that asked me the amount I wanted to send, the name of the person I was sending it to, and their email address or phone number, but I realized I still didn't have Peggy's number. She hadn't given it to me.

I was sure she'd call back.

"I've been approved for the surgery," Lucky told me after we agreed to meet for dinner.

It had been two whole days and I hadn't heard back from Peggy. I hadn't bothered to share any of what happened with anybody, especially Lucky, but we hadn't seen each other since that day at her house. I figured they'd all find out eventually so what was the difference?

"But now I'm scared," she said.

For once, we had decided to eat at a healthy, cafeteria-style restaurant called Lemonade and from about eight different salads, we chose four and a bowl of chunky homemade vegetable soup. That is, until we slid our trays a little farther down and spotted those pots of red miso short ribs, Thai chicken meatballs, and shredded jerk chicken floating in thick golden sauce, which was when we just looked at each other as if to say, *Fuck it, let's splurge before we both start our disappearing diets.* We had to order the seasoned rice and bread. At checkout, we decided to get the salad and soup to go and bought two of those little round macaroon cookies that come from France. I ordered watermelon mint lemonade and Lucky decided to be adventurous and got the same.

We did not say a solitary word until our bowls and plates were clean, and then Lucky said, "Joe wants a divorce."

And I said, "I don't blame him."

And she said, "I don't want a divorce."

And I said, "I don't blame you."

And she said, "What should I do?"

And I said, "Fight for him."

And she said, "Why?"

And I said, "Because he still loves you."

And she said, "How do you know that?"

And I said, "Because I just know."

And she said, "Are you going to eat that cookie?"

And I said, "No."

And she said, "Me either."

But when we stood up, we both picked up our plastic bags and I saw Lucky drop the cookie inside her purse.

As I crossed the street to a valet stand, my phone rang and of course it was Peggy.

"I thought you cared about your daughter, Loretha?"

"You might want to watch your tone, Peggy. I don't need your judgment on how much I care about my daughter. I don't know if you're drinking with my daughter or not, but you do realize your phone number is blocked, right? Does it now make more sense to you why I wasn't able to wire the money?"

"My bad," she said. "FYI, I have been drug and alcohol free for over twenty years. I'm also disabled and living off social security, and I have no children of my own. For some unknown reason, *your* daughter has attached herself to *me*. I'm just trying to help her get her life back on track, so give me some damn credit."

And then she gave me her number.

"How soon can you send it?"

"Is Jalecia there?"

"No. But she'll be back. This is the way she rolls. I would certainly appreciate it if, in the future, you could show me a little more respect for caring about your daughter's welfare."

"I do respect you, Peggy."

"Then make it five hundred."

And she hung up.

Chapter 14

"Bird is doing great," Korynthia said. "And I'm on my way home, so please tell everybody I'll be at Sadie's."

"Are you sure?" I asked. I was walking around the empty warehouse she had arranged for me to look at.

"Yes, I am. He agreed to start another twenty-eight-day treatment session."

"I'm so glad to hear it, Ko. I'm starting to wonder if one of those places would be good for Jalecia. She can't seem to stick to AA meetings. She's giving their coins back faster than she gets them."

"I think they have to hit bottom before they realize they need help getting back up."

"But I don't want her to fall that hard."

"Well, I think we just have to be patient and do what we can. Pray. Anyway, so, were you able to take a look at that facility I sent you the link to? It might be too big."

"Believe it or not, I'm in here now! Can you hear my echo?"

"No. But yell."

And I did.

"Dang. Sounds like you could roller-skate in there. But all of these kinds of spaces look bigger empty. Do me a favor. Don't rule it out yet. Let's go look at it together once I get back."

"Will do, although I can picture it."

"By the way, I'm thinking of selling my house for real this time."

"Why?"

"Because I could use the money."

"But you own that house, don't you?"

"No, I've borrowed against it over the years to help my kids and their kids and blah blah blah. But I had it appraised last year and it's gone way up. Anyway, I'm pulling into a gas station right now. Please don't mention any of this to the girls since I haven't figured out what I'm going to do yet."

"You're serious this time?"

"I don't know. Maybe. But I don't need to live in a big-ass house by myself. And it might be nice to be closer to Bird and my daughters, and my grandkids and those bad-ass great-grandkids."

"Don't be ridiculous! You're only two hours away as it is and they don't exactly go out of their way to come up here unless they need something from you. All of us have been wondering why they can't get in their damn cars for your birthday or during Christmas—you're always running down there and always bailing their broke asses out."

"Well, why don't you tell me how you really feel, Lo?"

"Look. Why don't you get a second and third and fourth opinion and let us vote on it?"

"Vote? You can't vote on my life."

"We're your longest friends, which makes us family, don't you think?"

"That's a stupid-ass question, Lo."

"Don't our opinions count?"

"Not Lucky's and not Sadie's, which leaves Poochie, who isn't even there. Whatever, it was just a thought I was having on this long boring-ass drive back to Pasadena."

"Which is your home. See you tomorrow, huzzie. And I'm glad to hear Bird is back on track. Bye."

As soon as I hung up, I pulled a folding chair across the concrete floor and sat down. I didn't want Ko to leave me here to deal with Sadie and Lucky and Poochie by myself. Ko would not like living in San Diego or being around all those damn kids, who would just get on her nerves and make her wish she had us there. Plus, I would miss her. I moaned a sigh of relief, as if I had willed her not to move.

I finally looked around the place. There were a lot of huge windows, almost floor to ceiling, which made me somewhat uncomfortable. This wasn't exactly a busy street, and what if I was in here alone at night?

"Hello, anybody, can you hear me?" I yelled.

The young Asian agent who had brought me opened the back door, stuck her head inside, and said, "I can!"

We both laughed.

This was not a good space to sell beauty products. And you really could roller-skate in here. Or, more appropriately for us senior citizens, ballroom dance. I decided to keep looking.

When Cinnamon called and said, "Grandma! I might get to try out," I felt obligated to go over for dinner to hear all about it. She was talking about *The Voice,* of course. I was wondering if maybe they'd given her a few free singing lessons as a perk, because I still didn't think she'd hit very many pleasant notes at Carl's Repasse. I also hadn't seen the twins in two months. Cinnamon had also told me the apartment felt like it was getting smaller and smaller, almost to the point where it felt like it was closing in on them because of all the gadgets and toys and strollers and what have you, so I was eager to see if I could help them arrange it better. But before I rang the doorbell, it dawned on me that they were the ones who should live in my mother's house. After all, they were young, struggling, and on the right track. They'd also shown how much they'd matured and they deserved a break much more than my ungrateful sister.

They buzzed me in, and I could not believe it when the elevator in the lobby opened and there was Odessa, looking better than I'd seen her look in years. Her hair was styled like she had finally put some thought into it, twisted like rope and the strands of gray almost sparkling. And was that a tangerine dress? I have never seen her in a bright color.

"Well, hello there, Sister," she said, and gave me a bear hug. "What a nice surprise! I know you weren't coming to see me. How are you?"

I couldn't believe the upbeat tone of her voice, especially after her parting words after dinner in her dungeon upstairs. I also hadn't heard her sound like this in almost twenty years. I was wondering if she'd finally rediscovered sex because the only other thing I could think of that would make her voice go up a few octaves was money.

"I'm good, Odessa. My oh my, don't you look pretty! How are you?"

When the doors of the elevator started jerking, begging to close, I dropped my hand and let them.

"I've been well, thank you. You don't look so bad yourself, Sister."

Sister?

"What's going on with you, Odessa? You look and sound different."

"Well," she said, and slid her very nice black-leather-that-looked-new purse over her shoulder, "I've recently gotten some good news."

"I love good news. What kind?"

"Well, first of all, my attorneys sent me a letter advising me that I, along with hundreds of other innocent and honest senior citizens, was the victim of some kind of scam when I took out those loans that caused me to lose my home. And we're all going to get some kind of settlement."

"That's so good to hear, Odessa!"

"I won't see the money anytime soon but at least I know it's coming. I can't wait to move out of here."

All I was thinking was: *You ungrateful bitch!* But I just said, "I know you're used to more space."

"A lot more space. But I'm not one to complain. I'm glad you and Carl had enough sense to buy this building, but I don't like knowing people are walking above and below me and on both sides. But at least I know I won't have to live here forever."

"I certainly wouldn't want you to be inconvenienced."

"Don't go there, Loretha. I didn't mean it the way it came out. I'm grateful. And I apologize for what I said about suing you. I was angry. You're my sister. Anyway, I know you're headed up to see those spoiled rotten twins, so get to it."

"Where are you headed looking so nice?"

"I'd rather not tell you. Yet."

"Well, have a good time, whatever and wherever it is."

She waved and headed out the front door. I sure wished I knew where she was going.

Through the door, I could hear the babies' cooing, which sounded like they were being tickled. I stood there for a few minutes before deciding against the buzzer, and I tapped on the door. As soon as I did, the cooing stopped. For some reason, this made me remember when I had to put a sock around the doorknob to keep Jackson from turning the lock. I'd found him outside on the front steps in a onesie, apparently trying to decide where he wanted to go. Which reminded me: I needed to firm up the dates for my visit to Tokyo.

When the door opened, there they were, sitting in their automatic swings rocking back and forth, but I was able to bend down and kiss them on their cheeks, then took them by their little hands and they squeezed. I felt like mush.

"Hi there, Ms. Pretty and Mr. Handsome!"

They looked at my face as if to ask: *How do you know our names?*

They looked at me even harder, like they were trying to remember me but didn't, and just started kicking their feet anyway.

Cinnamon, in paisley leggings, gave me a fast kiss on the cheek and Jonas, who was busy setting the table, stopped to pick up Handsome and gave me a hug while holding him. It felt so good.

I realized I smelled some kind of seafood cooking when Jonas said, "Grandma, I have prepared the finest halibut for you along with baked sweet potatoes and a salad and brown rice. I hope it satisfies your palate."

I ate every piece of the flaky fish and everything else until my plate was clean. The creamy little-people formula that the twins had been served had apparently gone right through them, so Cinnamon had taken them one by one to clean them up, before telling me it was time for their bath because she had to get up early to go to work.

I wondered who babysat, but I didn't feel it was appropriate to ask. They had worked it out.

"So, Grandma," she yelled even though the bathroom was so close she didn't need to. "Did you hear the shocking news about Aunt Odessa?"

"I don't think so, but I'm all ears."

"You tell it, Jonas."

"Okay. So, we were in the lobby bringing in groceries and she was getting out of the elevator. . . ."

And then he just stopped.

"And?"

"She was not alone, Grandma."

"Was she with a woman?"

"No. A man!" Cinnamon shouted from the bathroom.

"What did you just say?"

"You heard me right, Grandma. She was all dudded up and I didn't know she even wore makeup, but she looked like she had been busted and then she said, 'Hello, Cinnamon and Jonas and you little cutie pies! This is my friend Derrick. He's my handyman.' And I slipped and said, 'So nice to meet you, Derrick. Is something broken in the apartment?'"

"No, you didn't!" I said. This was better than an episode of *Empire*.

"And she said, 'He's just making some improvements. But I would really appreciate it if you wouldn't mention any of this to Loretha.' And I said, 'Not to worry. Have a nice evening.'"

A date? And what kind of improvements? Oh my. Odessa with a real man. That explained where she was going this evening looking so nice. I decided right then and there that I was going to pretend like I hadn't heard any of this. I would wait for Odessa to bring it up.

And out came Handsome in a gray onesie. He looked up and then put his head back down.

"Don't mind him, he's an old soul. He'll be snoring in a minute. So anyway, did you want to hear the latest about my mom?"

"Is it good news?"

"Well, it's an improvement. She moved to Las Vegas."

"What?"

"She moved to Las Vegas last month with her boyfriend and she's going to school to learn how to be a blackjack dealer."

"You have got to be fucking kidding me? Oh, shit, I'm sorry for swearing."

"It's okay. They don't know what you're saying."

"When did she tell you this?"

"Actually it was Aunt Peggy that told me. She said she was glad to get her out of the house, and if Mom managed to finish the eight-week course, she could come back down here and get hired at one of the local casinos. Isn't that cool?"

"Only if she doesn't drink."

I couldn't wait until I got home to call Peggy, so I pulled into a parking space at a KFC and left her a voice message.

"Peggy, this is Loretha. I just heard that Jalecia moved to Vegas last month and I want to know what kind of game you're playing asking me for money when you knew damn well she wasn't there. I knew I never liked your ass."

I hung up.

I called Jalecia and, to my surprise, she answered.

"Hi, Ma. You found me! I take it you've heard that me and Jerome are living here in Vegas? I'm learning to be a blackjack dealer. What do you think?"

"Honestly?"

"No, lie to me."

Which is exactly what I did.

"I think this is a very smart move, Jalecia. So, tell me, is there a reason you couldn't let me know you were moving?"

"I wasn't comfortable with you knowing yet."

"That is so nice to hear. So what does Jerome do for a living?"

"He's between jobs right now."

"Of course he is."

"Ma! See how negative you are? I'm going to hang up now. Things have really turned around for me and I don't think I want to talk to you until you change your attitude. Bye."

And she hung up.

Was I being too negative? Should I try to be more supportive? After all, even though I think moving to Vegas to become a blackjack dealer is ridiculous, she thinks she's making progress. But I'm not buying this. I worry about her. I also don't know who she is anymore. Or where in the world she's headed. She is scaring the hell out of me, that much I do know.

I could smell the fried chicken coming through my vents and I figured it wouldn't hurt to have a drumstick and a wing on hand for a late-night snack. I wasn't hungry but I knew I would be in about an hour after the fish wore off. I had already planned to watch another episode of *Empire,* just to stop thinking about how much I'd really like to kick Jalecia's and Peggy's asses.

I pulled up to the drive-through window and ordered. Then while I waited for my chicken, my cellphone rang and, without even looking at it, I yelled into it: "Peggy, if you have something nasty to say to me keep it to your damn self. I sent you five hundred dollars and my daughter wasn't even there. What kind of fucking scam is this?"

"Mama-Lo? This is Kwame. Did I catch you at a bad time?"

"Oh my Lord, I'm so sorry, Kwame, but someone has made me very angry. I don't normally use that kind of language. Anyway, please tell me, how is your mama doing? I've been waiting to hear from you."

"Well, I was calling to tell you that I won't be coming back to Pasadena until I know my mom is healthy again. Strokes make it hard to move and even talk so she needs my help here."

"I totally understand that, Kwame. You know I do."

"Thank you. So, would it be okay to keep my car in the garage?"

"Of course. Is your mom home yet?"

"Yes, she is. She's glad I'm here. And guess what, Mama-Lo?"

"What?"

"I'm still going to be able to drive with Uber, even though I have to rent a car to do it. Boone said he'd stay at my mom's during the hours I'm driving. We need some money around here."

"Do you need me to send you some?"

"No! Absolutely not. You've done enough. We'll be fine. But I want you to know that as soon as it feels like she's doing good, I'm going to come back to Pasadena. I still intend to go to LACC. You have been very encouraging and I want to make you, my mom, and my dad proud."

"We're already proud of you, Kwame. You take good care of your mom and give her my best, even if she doesn't know who I am."

"Oh, she does."

"Really?"

"Yes. She's known who you were for a long time."

"Maybe I'll meet her one day."

"Maybe. Anyway, I need to go brush her teeth. I miss you, Mama-Lo. And tell B. B. King I said to behave!"

When I got home I shared some of my chicken and a few potato wedges with B. B. King. But not the biscuit.

Kwame is a wonderful son.

Which was just one reason why, in the morning, I wired him two thousand dollars from my favorite Western Union at the drugstore, but this time I was first in line.

Chapter 15

I was listening to Kwame's voicemail thanking me for sending him the money and saying what a lifesaver I was, when B.B. started barking at the front door. Kwame had just said that his mother's recovery was going to be slow, but she was improving a little bit every day, when I heard the knocking. I hit End.

I was surprised to see Sadie standing there when I opened the door. Her short platinum hair on her tiny head looked like a French poodle, and she was wearing a lavender dress with puffy sleeves, which was so out of character it was almost funny.

"What's wrong, Sadie?"

"I have to cancel dinner tonight," she said, and stormed right past me and sat in Carl's chair, which I didn't really like. No one sits in that chair but me.

"What's wrong?"

"It's him. Again."

"Not the preacher?"

"He's back. He left his wife."

"What's that got to do with dinner tonight?"

"Do you remember how you felt when you fell in love with Carl, Loretha?"

"Of course I do. But Carl didn't have a wife and I also wasn't a sanctimonious hypocrite."

"He left his wife for me."

"You know what? I wish you had been a lesbian."

"What's that supposed to mean?"

"We always thought you were. Well, I did. And Korynthia did."

"What would make you think that?"

"Because we never once heard you talk about any guy you were with and we never saw you with one."

"I was saving myself."

"For who?"

"For the Lord."

"Well, you sure found him, didn't you? But why do you have to cancel dinner?"

"Because he has no place to stay."

"Are you standing here telling me you let that son-of-a-bitch move in with you? Please don't tell me that, Sadie."

"I did."

"Well, I'll tell you what. Why don't you tell him to go find a church that's open late and stay there while we have dinner at your apartment. And while he's there, he can beg his Lord and Savior to forgive him for his sins and for being unworthy of your love and his wife's love."

"I don't know if he'll understand."

"You are making me want to slap some sense into your ass, you know that? Have you told anybody else your good news?"

"No."

"Why not?"

"Because I'm afraid of what they might say."

"Oh, so you came to see me thinking I was going to get all

Oprah on you or something? Tell you to live your best life with this man?"

"Can you just tell them I'm sick?"

"No. Hell to the no! We are coming over to your apartment for dinner because you promised us you wouldn't back out this time, so it better be ready when we show up at seven o'clock. And he better not be there when we get there or we will sprinkle his ass with the kind of water that burns."

"Lo, please?"

"No. In fact, hell no!"

"Okay! I'll tell him to just stay in the bedroom."

"No. That's too close. He needs to be gone."

She just stood there, looking stupid in all that lavender.

"And we've got a lot of other things we need to talk about."

"Like what?"

"Should I go down the list?"

"Yes."

"Korynthia's thinking about selling her house and moving to San Diego, and she's serious this time. My alcoholic daughter has moved to Vegas with her unemployed boyfriend to become a blackjack dealer."

"Really?"

"Yes, should I keep going? Lucky might be getting a divorce. Oh shit, wait: I didn't mean to say that."

"You mean she wants a divorce?"

"No, Joe does."

"Who can blame him? She's mean-spirited and judgmental, and my prayers for her to change her heart have not been answered."

"Keep that to yourself, Sadie. And maybe pray a little harder for yourself while you're on your knees."

She got up from the chair and moved over to the sofa. I didn't feel any more comfortable.

"Would you like some coffee?"

"No," she said, sinking against the back cushion.

"Good, because I don't have any. And even if I did I wouldn't make you a cup because right now, Sadie, I am so pissed at you I would like to slap you into next week. No, I'm not pissed. I'm embarrassed for you. That you would stoop this low over a man, and a married one at that!"

"You've already made your feelings clear, Loretha."

"Wait until everybody else hears this shit."

"That's why I came over. I don't want you to tell them."

"What? You can't be serious."

"Not yet. Please?"

"I thought you had integrity, Sadie. I thought you were a woman of God. You are a fucking hypocrite. And don't act like your heart doesn't know it."

"Look. You've made your point about a million times. Haven't you ever done anything stupid?"

"Of course. But I have never slept with a married man. Let me ask you this: If he'd cheat on his wife of twenty-five years, what would make you think he won't cheat on you?"

"There are no guarantees in life."

"Fine, I'll tell everyone we're having dinner here at my house. You can stay home with your man."

"No, I'd still like to come if you don't mind, Lo. I'm confused and I just need a little time to figure out what I'm going to do."

"Well, I guess you better pray on it. Now get out of here and I'll see you tonight. And if you're not here at seven we're all going to storm your apartment and break down your door and drag your ass back over here."

"Do you have to swear so much, Loretha?"

"I guess the hell so," I said.

She pushed herself up to a standing position and walked in slow motion to the front door. And for the first time ever, I let her show herself out.

As soon as she left I called Korynthia, Poochie, and Lucky and told them everything.

It had been so long since I had cooked, I was afraid I'd forgotten how. I wasn't sure what would be easy and tasty and something that everybody would like, and I wasn't in any mood to go to the grocery store. Then I remembered that Korynthia had used that Grubhub app so I sat down at my laptop and signed myself up. I could not believe all the restaurants there were to choose from. I knew everybody loved Mexican food, but the thought of beans made my stomach turn. Shit. We just had Chinese at Ko's last time and I didn't want to repeat it, so I decided it wouldn't kill me to cook.

But as I was staring at all of the beautifully staged fish behind glass at Whole Foods, my cellphone rang. It was Korynthia.

"Lo, I'm on my way back down to San Diego. Bird is on the way to the ER. He left the treatment center a few days after I got home and went straight to his dealer's, but he may have taken too many. I'm going to strangle his stupid ass as soon as I see him. So, I'm not going to make it tonight. Are you there?"

"I'm here, Ko. And I'm so sorry to hear this. He's going to be all right, isn't he?"

"I don't know yet. I'll call you later. I'm an hour out."

And she hung up.

"Hi, Grandma." Jonas came out from behind the counter with a wide I'm-so-happy-to-be-working smile. "Are you looking for some of our super-fresh seafood?"

"What?"

"Wait. Is something wrong? You look worried. It's not Jalecia, is it?"

"No," I said.

"Are you all right?"

"It's my friend Korynthia's son. He's just been taken to the hospital in San Diego. He may have taken too many pills."

He went to give me a hug but had on a green rubber apron, so he took off his rubber glove and squeezed my hand.

"I will pray for him," he said. "And I'll tell Cinna and she'll pray for him, too. You want to go upstairs and sit down for a few minutes, Grandma?"

"I just might. I need to make a few calls."

I took the escalator up to the second floor and walked over to the tables where people ate. I wasn't sure who to call first, but then my phone rang again and Lucky's name appeared.

"Did you talk to Korynthia, Lo?"

"Yes."

"This is fucked up. What should we do?"

"Let's wait to hear back from her."

"I don't like this," she said.

"I'm scared for Bird. And for Ko. I'm canceling dinner tonight."

"Fuck dinner, Lo."

"Who can eat?"

"I'm coming over to your house. And I'm going to call Sadie and tell her to come over, too. If that's all right?"

"Come."

I left whatever I had put in my cart. I walked out of the store and wanted to keep walking all the way to San Diego to hug my friend, to give her some strength.

When I got home, my driveway was full of cars so I had to park in front of my house. All my friends know where I keep the key and when I walked in the side door, Sadie and Lucky were sitting at the kitchen table. B. B. King was waiting in front of the sink. He knew something was wrong, which was why he put his snout on his front paws and closed his eyes.

"Has anybody heard from Korynthia?"

They both looked down and folded their hands. That's when I saw the tears falling.

I covered my mouth.

"Bird overdosed," Sadie said.

"What did you just say?"

"You heard right." Lucky sighed.

I couldn't say what I wanted to because I couldn't stop my teeth from chattering.

Then there was nothing but silence. I took a deep breath.

"But he made it to the hospital? Somebody please tell me he's in the hospital."

"Yes. But he's in the morgue," Sadie said.

I stomped my left foot and then my right one and then I jumped up and down because it just felt like too much death and pain and suffering was happening all around me, when something could've and should've been done to prevent it.

B. B. King whimpered.

"How did it happen?"

"He took more than half a bottle of pain medication," Lucky said.

"Percocet?"

"No, OxyContin. The one they do documentaries about. But what difference does it make now? What can we do to help Ko?" Sadie asked.

"What would make him take so many?" I asked.

"I don't know. Some people are troubled. I don't think they all get high just to get high," Sadie said, with a sigh.

"Maybe he was in pain," I heard myself say.

"You're probably right," Lucky said. "But not the kind a pill can stop. And he's only forty-one."

"Isn't Jalecia around the same age as Bird?" Sadie asked.

It felt like a dart had just been jabbed in my heart.

"She'll be forty-one on her next birthday," I said. "Goddamnit!

Where's my phone? We need to call Ko, right now. Can somebody call her? Please?"

"She's not taking calls," Lucky said. "She asked me to tell everybody to please wait until tomorrow morning to call. She's with her kids."

"I hope she'll come back to church. He will hear her," Sadie said.

"God can only do so much," Lucky moaned.

"Let's just pray for Bird and Korynthia," Sadie said. "She's going to need our strength and support to help her get through this."

"Oh, just shut up, would you, Sadie?"

"Loretha, are you okay?" Lucky asked.

"No, I'm not okay!" I said in what I knew was a cracked voice. "I wish we could put our arms around Korynthia right now. And even though she's there with her daughters, we're her family, too."

"Yes, we are," Lucky said at the same time as Sadie nodded her head.

Then we all just sat there and watched the clock move from one minute to the next. My shoulders felt like they weighed a ton. I thought about picking up the phone to send Korynthia a text but my fingers wouldn't let me. I knew what it felt like to hear "I'm so sorry for your loss" over and over and over. I'm tired of death.

I'm tired of illness.

I'm just tired.

When I saw daylight sneaking through the blinds, I sat up and picked up the phone, which had been on my stomach all night. I dialed Korynthia's number, but she didn't answer. All I could manage to say was, "Ko, I'm so sorry for your loss."

I took B. B. King for a walk and when we got home I had a voicemail from Korynthia. "*Hi, Lo. Thank you for your call. This is probably the hardest thing I've ever had to go through. I don't know if losing a child feels anything like losing a husband, but I know you know what loss feels like. I've decided to stay here in San Diego to be close to my other kids but will let you know when I come to clear out my house. It'll be a minute. We are not having a big service so please don't come. Just do everything you can for your daughter while you still can. Love you."*

I decided not to call her back. Instead, I called Sadie and Lucky and simply said, "Get dressed. Meet me at my house in an hour. We're driving to San Diego."

I put B. B. King in one of those doggie hotels and told them I wasn't sure if I'd be gone for two or three days.

None of us uttered a single solitary word until we saw the sign that said San Diego in 23 miles, which was when we realized we didn't know exactly where we were going.

Finally, Lucky said, "This isn't like a surprise party. Let's just text her and tell her we'll be there in a half hour and to let us know where she's staying. By the way, where are we staying?"

"I don't care," Sadie said.

"I need room," Lucky said. "And a big bed since I'm big. But not for long."

I was driving, but I didn't bother to look at Lucky through the rearview mirror.

"Did anybody call Poochie?"

Everybody had a *not me* look on their face.

"Who wants to call her?" I asked.

"Let's wait until we talk to Korynthia and find out if she called her," Sadie said.

"Somebody text Korynthia, please," I said.

"I will," Lucky said, and did, and we waited.

Five minutes passed.

Then ten.

"Nothing yet?" I asked.

"Wait," Lucky said, pointing. "Get off at that exit."

I pulled off the freeway and into a Starbucks parking lot, put the car in park, and put my hands in my lap.

"Why'd we get off?" Sadie asked.

"Because this is what she just texted: *As grateful and thankful as I am for all your love and support, please turn around and head home. I am planning to stay here for however long I'm needed. I love all of you and thank you for your prayers. I'll keep you posted about when I'll be back. No need to send flowers or anything. My son is at peace.*"

We sat there motionless and in silence for what felt like an hour. I rested my head on the steering wheel and tried to imagine what Ko might be going through. What I would be feeling if this was my daughter. A cold chill made me shiver at the thought and I leaned over and snatched a handful of Starbucks napkins out of the glove compartment and just held them up for everybody until they were gone.

"I'll drive if you want me to," Sadie said.

"It's okay," I said and backed up and drove to the entrance that would take us back to Pasadena.

Chapter 16

For the next two months we didn't meet to have dinner because we didn't have anything new to talk about except how worried we were that Korynthia was always too busy to talk to us. Besides, Poochie and Lucky would have had to pretend they didn't know about Sadie and her on-again relationship with the man of God.

Poochie told me she was gearing up for hip and knee surgery, but I didn't know if she'd decided which should come first. She also complained about a sciatic nerve she had to have shots for. I thought all of her ailments were somehow connected. Like me, Poochie is too thick. She rocks when she walks and can't go more than a few steps without a cane, which she always keeps in her purse. She scared the hell out of me once when she slung it like a whip and it unfolded like magic. It also sounds like her mama has pretty much been hoping death will hurry up because she has gotten bored as hell waiting for it.

Lucky postponed her gastric bypass surgery because she said she was too depressed to start losing weight so rapidly and because she has not been able to stop smoking marijuana, which makes her hungry. She claims her husband wants to start divorce proceedings, and she's waiting to see if they're going to quibble over the house. Lucky is so full of shit. Joe would stop all of this if she'd just tell him she still loves him, but she's too damn stubborn to admit it.

Sadie is still a fool in love but she hasn't given me much confidence that Mr. Minister is ever really going to file for divorce. I really don't care one way or the other. I feel that maybe once he fucks her over the way he fucked over his wife and her heart cracks into a lot of pieces that she has to glue back together all by herself, then maybe there's a chance we'll get her back. We pray for her stupid ass.

And me? I have not been taking my diabetes medication, even though Dr. Alexopolous called in a new three-month refill and ordered another lab test to see if my numbers looked better. I've had so much on my mind I didn't even realize I was eating even more of all the things I shouldn't be eating and I have actually put on ten (but probably fifteen) new pounds. I'm taking naps off and on throughout the day even though I haven't done much to make me tired, and I've started feeling thirsty all the time but, in all honesty, I really haven't cared, especially after I found out from Cinnamon that Jalecia did not finish her blackjack-dealer training. She and her boyfriend got into a fight right out there on the Strip with a crowd watching them and she took a Greyhound back to L.A. She is back living with Peggy and neither one of them has bothered to call me. But I know it's just a matter of time.

Finally, last week, instead of having our regular dinner at someone's house, we all agreed to just meet at Roscoe's House of Chicken and Waffles for old times' sake. Poochie and Korynthia decided to join us via FaceTime.

"First I have an announcement to make," Korynthia said. She looked tired, and like she had also put on a few, too. Her face was puffy and the bags under her eyes were sunken. This meant she had been doing too much. Probably crying. I was dreading hearing the inevitable news that she'd sold her house.

"I can't live down here. My kids have been treating me like I'm their slave and my grandkids and my great-grands are needy and unappreciative. I don't like feeling this way. I'll be back next week, so let's go to Vegas for Lo's birthday!"

"Ko, I am so happy you're coming back here I could cry! But I don't want to go to Vegas for my birthday," I said to all of them. Of course my birthday just had to come up. As if mine was so important. I really wanted to skip celebrating it this year.

"You're going," Korynthia said. "I need to throw some dice, I need to hear the sound of slot machines paying, and I need to hear people screaming with joy at the top of their fucking lungs and I don't want to have to hear little voices saying, 'Grandma, can you do this, can you do that?' So, we're going."

"And I need to see you guys in person," Poochie said.

I looked at Sadie. "Will you be able to get away?"

"I'll ask."

"Don't ask," Poochie said to Sadie, which made Sadie realize I had opened my big mouth. "I've got discount coupons for you to stay at the Venetian and I'll get two double rooms so you all will be close. Please don't take one of those casino buses again because a lot of folks will be drunk and loud; and if you take the one for seniors they're even worse because they'll most likely be filled with church members who put God on hold until the morning. Although, Sadie, word on the street is that you've been sinning again, so you'll fit right in."

Sadie rolled her eyes at me and I rolled mine right back. She should know by now it's impossible to keep secrets in this group.

"I'll get tickets for the male strippers," Korynthia said and rubbed her palms together.

"I'm not going to a strip club," Sadie said.

"Yes, you are," Lucky said. "Pray on it."

"I'll get the tickets to Celine at Caesars because we agreed on that already and to Cirque du Soleil as a birthday gift to myself from you ladies," I said.

"That doesn't make any sense. Wait, which one?" Lucky asked.

"O."

Everybody clapped.

"Then it's settled," Lucky said. "We can hire one of those fancy black vans with black windows to drive us there. We all have credit cards that work, don't we?"

We all laughed.

Although Sadie looked like she had to do the math.

I decided to skip Christmas entirely, but then changed my mind a little bit. Instead of getting a tree, I bought seven beautiful perforated stars with lights inside and put them in my windows. Carl would've loved them. I didn't send cards like I've done the past thirty or forty years. But I couldn't resist giving Cinnamon and Jonas gift cards to Target for the twins. And I thought it only fair to give them something just for the two of them: gift cards to my favorite movie theater with the promise to babysit, should they ever have a desire to tear themselves away.

I let B. B. King eat the last two kosher hot dogs and a few French fries and a half hour later, I scraped the vanilla out of the ice cream sandwich and put it on a saucer, which he licked so clean I had to take it from him.

"You're going to get diabetes, too, B.B."

When I sat down for a minute, it hit me that I had not been kissed or hugged or had sex in almost a year. It's the longest I'd ever gone since I was in my thirties. And here I was trying to figure out how to celebrate Christmas without my husband. I decided that if I couldn't have sex, I would bake. I called everybody and told them I would have my usual sweet potato pies, peach cobbler, bread pudding, and apple pies—and they could fight over them.

I rolled crust. I sliced apples. I opened ten cans of peaches. I boiled sweet potatoes and mashed them with cinnamon, nutmeg, sugar, eggs, vanilla flavor, and a drop of bourbon. I made bread pudding that was so fluffy it almost floated out of the little baking dishes I bought. The peach juice boiled onto the aluminum foil I knew to put under the cobbler because it happens every year.

I was too tired to drive so Jonas stopped by and picked up each Christmas box and delivered them to all three of my homegirls. He only wanted a sweet potato pie since he and Cinnamon try not to eat much sugar, though they always made an exception for the pie.

And then I slept.

I knew I was trying to fill up the day.

And because Carl and I always ate lobster tails with butter and baked potatoes with chives, sour cream, and butter and a salad and sourdough bread on Christmas, I had a lobster dinner for one delivered. After I ate some of it, I had two glasses of wine and lit the two lemon-lavender candles he always loved, and later took a hot bath and hoped Carl knew this was my way of saying Merry Christmas and how much I wished he was still here.

I realized I really didn't want to be celebrating my December 31 birthday in Las Vegas with half a million people, so I convinced my friends we should wait until the following week. Plus, Poochie called to let us know that her discount coupons weren't valid on New Year's Eve and, besides, the Venetian and every major hotel on the Strip had been booked up for months. None of us had made the reservations for our chosen activities yet, so we booked them for the following weekend.

When they all asked, I told them I did not want a pre-birthday celebration. I did not want to go out for cake and ice cream. I did not want to have drinks at the Langham hotel. I didn't want to see a movie at that theater with the reclining suede chairs like they have in first class, where they had a real menu with real food and served you drinks, and only about thirty or so folks even fit inside each of the seven theaters. And no, I did not want to have a deep-tissue massage and an age-defying facial at Burke Williams. I wanted to stay home and be quiet and remember how Carl surprised me last year. I wanted to remember that that was the last time I saw my husband. I wanted to remember that it was the last time I'd been kissed. Hugged. I wanted to remember how he smelled. I also wanted to think about how I might spend the next year and maybe the rest of my life without longing for the past or worrying too much about my future.

They didn't fight me.

I got cards. But not from my daughter. Ma sent me the same one she sent me last year, which made me smile.

I got calls. But not from my daughter. Jackson FaceTimed me and I was thrilled that those twins were getting cuter. He was hoping I'd make it there for my birthday but knew this one might be hard. I told him I'd be there by spring. He understood.

I got flowers from all my girlfriends and Jackson, and Odessa, and Cinnamon and Jonas and Handsome and Pretty, but not from my daughter.

My feelings were hurt, but I tried to pretend like they weren't. I went to Macy's and bought myself a pair of yellow pajamas that were 40 percent off. Later I took a bubble bath and turned on the Spotify playlist of some of my favorite songs from the seventies through the nineties, which Jonas had made for me. I put on my new pj's and poured myself a glass of medium-priced champagne. I was wide-awake so I started watching *Dick Clark's Rockin' New Year's Eve* special and loved watching the young kids party like they had everything to live for. And when the ball dropped, I realized I still did, too.

The black limo-van picked me up last. The driver looked like Billy Dee Williams forty years ago, which made all of us nostalgic, and I for one immediately thought of him in *Lady Sings the Blues* and only snapped back to the here and now when I heard a not-so-deep voice say, "So, who's the birthday girl?"

I raised my hand.

"Happy birthday, Miss Loretha. My sister's name is Loretha. A pretty name for a pretty lady. So, is this your fiftieth?"

I said, "Of course. It's my second time," and then we all laughed. We were all wearing some kind of colorful but not too bright sweatsuit since we wanted to be comfortable for the drive. Lucky was sitting right behind Billy Dee because she said she needed more legroom even through Korynthia, who sat right across from her, was taller. Korynthia didn't say a word, but Lucky just had to add, "Is your mirror fogged, young man? She's sixty-nine and her birthday was last week, so really she's almost seventy now!"

Nobody laughed.

"Well, ladies, you all look great. I just want you to know that the seats recline and if you're uncomfortable at all, just press the call button and I'll do everything I can to make this six-hour drive as pleasant as possible. The TVs have headphones so you don't have to disturb your neighbor, and refreshments are available. Are we okay?"

Everybody said we were.

"And I can change the lighting to suit your mood. Whatever you like: blue, pink, purple, yellow, and red, which I don't recommend."

"Purple," I said, and I had no idea why.

"Well, since this is for your birthday I'll just keep my mouth shut, but I hope I can sleep," Lucky said.

I gave her the finger and just missed touching the back of her head. Korynthia cracked up. Sadie must not have seen me do it.

"What's that?" Sadie asked after we pulled up in front of the Venetian and saw Poochie gripping both hands on a walker as if she couldn't stand without it. Tending to her mama had obviously taken a toll on her because Poochie now looked about eighty. Her breasts sloped like two eggplants under that ugly grandma floral dress and she had a beige shawl wrapped around her neck. We didn't know what to say to one another but were glad the windows in the van were black so she couldn't see us staring at her.

Before Billy Dee Williams opened the door, he said, "Happy birthday, Miss Loretha. It has been my pleasure to drive you young ladies. Harold will be your return driver and you will like him, but not as much as me! Don't pick up any strange men, I hope you all win lots of money, and thank you for your very generous tip. Much appreciated. And much needed."

He gave us each a hug after helping us disembark.

Poochie was waving at us like we had just gotten off the *Titanic*.

"I'm so happy to see you girls in the flesh, and please don't say anything about this," she said as she pointed to her walker. "It's necessary. But anyway, give me a hug!"

And we took turns hugging her.

"Your rooms are ready and I typed up our itinerary so we know where we're supposed to be because we have a lot to cover in forty-eight hours."

The Venetian never makes me feel like I'm in Venice because Carl and I went to the real Venice. This is an over-the-top imitation, but I'm not going to complain. I do love coming to Las Vegas because people come from all over the world to witness this spectacle. Carl and I used to drive here three or four times a year and pretend like we were eloping.

"So, who's sharing a suite?" Poochie asked.

"Me and Korynthia," I said.

Lucky tried not to but failed and gave an *Oh, hell* look at Sadie.

"And you better not preach or I'll cut you," Lucky said.

We had to cover our mouths to stop ourselves from laughing out loud.

As we followed the bellman toward the elevators to head up to our rooms, we oohed and aahed over the gigantic floral arrangements, and after we walked by millionaire-shops row, there on our left was the first set of slot machines and the casino alive behind it. When I heard people jumping up and down screaming and saw red lights flashing, I heard myself say, "I want to play the slots."

"Nobody's going to stop you," Korynthia said.

"Right now," I said.

"Can't you wait until we get settled?" Sadie asked.

"No. Isn't this my birthday celebration?"

"You old bitch!" Korynthia said. "I'm down with you! I need some excitement, too!"

And we both started laughing.

"Well, here are your keys, ladies," Poochie said. "Do this: go over our itinerary before you go to sleep, if you sleep that is, and let me know if you're too rich or too hungover to have breakfast in the morning."

"Then, I'll see you all in the morning," Lucky said, holding on to the luggage cart. I knew Sadie would follow her up. We all gave Poochie a peck on both cheeks and I gave Sadie mine and Korynthia's key to put our luggage in. Korynthia and I spent the next four hours winning and losing hundreds of dollars until we realized it was almost four A.M. and we decided to call it a night.

I didn't know where I was when I woke up and whoever it was banging on the damn door didn't help. Korynthia wasn't in her bed, which scared me. I got up and looked through the peephole. It was Sadie, in her thick white bathrobe.

"I cannot sleep in that room with Lucky. She snores like a pig. Where's Ko?" she asked when she saw her bed was empty.

"I don't know. Wait." And I picked up the white notepad at the foot of my bed that read: *Went to the gym. I need to start my day off right. See you before breakfast.*

"Good for her. Good for her. So, I'll just take her blanket and lie down there on the sofa."

Which she did.

When I felt Korynthia shaking me, she said, "Get your lazy asses up. And, Sadie, I can only imagine why you left Lucky in there. Anyway, according to Poochie's itinerary, we've got a long, fun day ahead of us and we should be at breakfast in twenty-four minutes. I have already showered. Try it. You'll like it. Leave now, Sadie."

And she did.

Poochie was waiting for us in the restaurant. As was Lucky, who seemed to have an attitude for having been abandoned. We pretended not to notice.

"I want to go to the mall," Korynthia said. "I need to shop."

"I don't feel like shopping," Sadie said.

"Me either," Lucky said.

"Well, I do," I said to Ko. "Wait," I said looking at the itinerary. "So, O is at seven, but I don't see the strip club on here."

"Good," Sadie said.

"I didn't know you were serious," Poochie said.

"Oh, hell yeah, I was!" Korynthia said. "Look, I paid to see penises and bare-chested young men and it's at ten o'clock so after we leave O we will drink a double-double latte and have our asses in seats four rows from the front. I need this."

"I don't know what I need," I said. "But I'm due for some excitement and I haven't seen a penis in over a year."

Sadie and Lucky said nothing.

As we stood outside the Bellagio and watched the spectacular water show along with hundreds of other people while Michael Jackson sang "Billie Jean," I found myself thinking about my daughter as I watched the spray of water do its final dance, skipping across the pond until it came to a halt and the music stopped. I felt a sigh of relief knowing she was safe.

Even though we'd all seen it before, O was, of course, spectacular. It was a real wet dream. I still don't understand how you can walk on water and have flickering circles of flames on it, but the costumes combined with acrobatics were what always took my breath away.

"They're mostly ex-Olympians," Sadie said.

"And French Canadians," Lucky said. Both were not true but Ko and I just bumped elbows rather than correct them.

Only forty minutes into the ninety-minute show we heard Poochie and Lucky snoring. I nudged Korynthia, who nudged Lucky, who nudged Sadie, but Poochie, who was right behind us in the handicapped section, didn't budge until Lucky shook her walker.

When the show was over, we waited for Lucky and Poochie at the bar and were able to have two drinks before they sauntered over to us.

"I'm too tired to go to any strip club," Lucky said.

"I'm staying at the hotel tonight," Poochie said. "And I don't want to look at any penises."

"When was the last time you saw one?" Korynthia, who had had two Rusty Nails, asked.

"Take a wild guess," Poochie said.

"So, who's with your mama?" Lucky asked.

"Her caregiver is staying over. You want to watch a movie in my room, Lucky?"

"Sure. As long as there's no blood in it."

Ko and I peered at Sadie as if we dared her to back out.

She stomped her rubber sole. "I'm going even though it's against my better judgment," she said. "But mostly to shut you two up."

"Then we will see you ladies tomorrow for more shopping and an early dinner and then I will bid you all farewell before Celine," Poochie said. "You pack your bags and send them down and your driver will be waiting for you with them outside the lobby entrance after the show."

"What?" I asked.

"I'm not going to see her," Poochie said.

"Why not?" Lucky asked.

"Because I've seen her too many times."

"Well, I don't like her voice, but I didn't want to be a party pooper," Lucky said.

We all looked at one another and laughed.

I hadn't been inside any kind of strip club in at least forty years. I was tired but not too tired for this. Carl was the last shirtless man in briefs I'd seen.

Sadie looked scared.

The place was full of women of all ages and quite a few men. When the music started, the dancers came out strutting to the beat, wearing gold neckties, showing off those shimmering chests and strong quads in satin G-strings. By the time they lined up and started swirling and dipping, we could hardly hear the music because everybody was screaming and standing up. When one of them bent down and grabbed Sadie's hand, she looked like she was about to have a heart attack. At first. And then a smile appeared on what had been an annoyed face and the next thing we knew Sadie was moving to a beat in her seat and we cracked up when we saw her pop her fingers and then slip a twenty inside a fine Asian guy's G-string. By the time we left, Ko and I were exhausted, but Sadie seemed to still be a little wired. Thank you, Jesus.

We slept in, spent two hours at an amazing outlet, and I did not buy anything because I didn't need anything. Korynthia bought yet another sexy workout outfit. Lucky had a vanilla shake. Sadie bought a dress on sale that was just like the one she had on but a different color. To kill time, we decided to play a little blackjack and some slots. None of us knew how to play craps, so we just stood there and watched for about twenty minutes until I decided to take a chance and put some chips on a bunch of numbers like everybody else had been doing. When it was my turn to roll the dice I threw them so hard they went over the rim. They let me roll again and this time I rolled an eleven and everybody jumped for joy and so did I when they handed me two hundred dollars' worth of chips. I rolled again, a wrong number this time, so I cashed in my chips. I did not want to gamble anymore because I couldn't tell if it was easier to lose or to win.

Poochie just had to bring a cake. I had pleaded with her not to pick a fancy restaurant and she still insisted on four stars.

"Okay, first of all, I just want to say what a good time I've had celebrating my birthday with you all. I would really appreciate it if we could just pretend this is one of our regular catch-up dinners, except I'd like to go around and hear each of you say one thing you are grateful for and, since it's still New Year's, one thing you resolve to do to improve the quality of your life so that we can still be doing this for the next fifteen years."

"Then, why don't you start since it's your birthday," Poochie said.

"Well, I'm grateful we're still friends after more than fifty years. I intend to start taking my diabetes more seriously and I'm going to try to be nicer to my sister and listen to everything my mother has to say. And I'm going to go to Tokyo in June to see my son and grandkids. I know that's about four or five things, but this is my damn birthday party!"

I got applause.

Poochie went next: "First, I just want to say how grateful I am that you all understood why this wasn't a good time to see my mom. But I'm also pleased to announce I've booked our cruise for late May, so schedule everything around that time since I know your social lives are so busy. My biggest goal to improve my life is to have one or both orthopedic surgeries so I'll be healthy by then."

We all nodded.

Korynthia said: "I'll be grateful when this grief I've been feeling will begin to ease. And I hope to learn how to have fun again, like we've had here in Vegas."

She got fist pumps.

"I just want to stop being so goddamn mean and lose some of this fucking weight." Classic Lucky. "What am I grateful for? This will surprise you, but I am grateful for my husband, who I want to spend the rest of my life with, and I hope he still loves me."

We were not surprised, which was why she got fist pumps, nods, and tears.

Sadie said, "I'm grateful for a loving God, who I hope will forgive me for sleeping with someone else's husband. I've also been thinking about going back to work at the library. But this time I don't want to be paid for it."

And then Poochie lit the candles and I blew them out.

And I did not eat any of the cake.

We hugged and kissed Poochie goodbye then thanked her for all that she'd done to arrange the weekend and told her we would pray that her mama's suffering eased soon.

In the sold-out Colosseum at Caesars Palace, our seats were so close we were able to see the perspiration on Celine's forehead. She was still as skinny now as she was before she had those kids. And she sounded as good in person as she did on her CDs, even though Lucky said she was probably lip-synching. Celine sang every song I ever loved and Lucky sat there like she was watching the hands on a clock move, but when Celine belted out "My Heart Will Go On" and everybody gave her a standing ovation, Lucky didn't get up because she was sitting there crying like a baby.

Chapter 17

Anyone watching would've sworn I'd been gone for years by the way B. B. King jumped a whopping six or seven inches off the ground when I went to pick him up at the doggie hotel. But apparently, he hadn't been all that lonely. The attendant introduced me to his new friend Molly, a much younger schnauzer who wore a yellow bow in her black Jheri curl. She wagged her tail at about 45 rpms and when the attendant handed me B.B.'s leash and we headed toward the exit, he acted like he didn't want to leave. When I opened the door, he actually turned around to blow Molly what appeared to be a kiss and the look in his eyes made it clear he was telling her he couldn't wait to see her again.

"You should've gotten her number," I said after Mr. King took his sweet time getting in the back seat. I could tell he hadn't heard a word I said because he was too busy looking out the back window! And then I heard him flop down on the seat and moan. It was then that I realized B. B. King had fallen in love. Lucky for him.

Before we got inside the door my cellphone rang and when I saw the blocked call I just said, "Yes, Peggy."

"Have you seen or heard from Jalecia in the past forty-eight hours?"

"No, I haven't. Why, what's going on?"

"If I knew that, I wouldn't be calling you."

I thought about hanging up on her right then.

"Well, I'm not high on her call list, as you very well know."

"You don't even sound like you're concerned."

"You've got a lot of nerve saying that to me, Peggy."

"I apologize. She usually checks in, that's all. And I'm worried. But she's not back with Loser #10 and she's not in jail, so I'm just stressing that she might be on a binge."

Just then, a call came in on the other line. I saw Jalecia's name appear and I just said, "That's her calling me now. I'll call you back."

And I clicked over.

My heart was beating so hard I could almost hear it.

"Jalecia? Hello?" I said.

"Hi, Ma. How are you?"

"I'm doing okay, I guess."

"Sorry I missed your birthday."

"It's okay. How are you doing? Peggy just called asking if I'd seen you."

"I'm not surprised."

"Are you on something? Your voice sounds sluggish."

"I've been in a very bad way, which is why Aunt Peggy kicked me out."

"What do you mean she kicked you out?"

"She asked me to leave until I sobered up."

"Well, where are you?"

"You don't want to know."

"Yes, I do."

"I'm in line to register at a shelter."

I wanted to scream out: *A shelter? Are you crazy?* But I didn't. Instead I composed myself and said, "Would you like me to come get you?"

"Would you?"

"Give me the address and I'll get there as fast as I can."

"I don't know the address."

"Please ask somebody, Jalecia."

"Hold on. A lot of these people in here are stoned out of their minds."

I waited.

And I waited some more.

And then she came back on and told me the address.

"I'll be there in fifteen minutes. Don't go anywhere, Jalecia."

"I'll be standing outside," she said, slurring.

I was there in ten minutes.

But she wasn't there.

The attendant had no record of her checking in.

I was angry but mostly scared.

I dialed her back but it went straight to voicemail. On my third call I left a message.

"Hi, Jalecia. This is Mom. I'm at the shelter but you aren't standing outside like you said you'd be. I even went inside and they didn't have a record of your being there but I'll just wait here a little longer because maybe you'll be here soon. I'm praying you're okay. Please call me. I'm worried about you. Love you."

And then I just sat there for ten or fifteen or twenty minutes hoping she would call me and that maybe she was just around the corner, or upstairs asleep and had used a fake name. Maybe she was in the ER, but if so, which one? And what would her emergency be? I called the closest ER but they weren't allowed to give out that information, so I just sat there and worried and waited.

Then I called Peggy.

"I haven't heard from her. She's probably somewhere trying to sober up. Just wait a little longer."

"She said you kicked her out."

"It wasn't the first time. When she gets out of control she has to go."

"Are you trying to help her or not, Peggy?"

"Look, I'm her aunt and she can trust me, but she's got issues and I've got rules. I'm doing all I can to keep her healthy but I'm no psychiatrist."

"What's that supposed to mean?"

"I think there might be more to her drinking than she lets on. Jalecia is smarter than you might realize, but something is making her crave self-destruction."

I didn't know what she was talking about, but rather than piss her off I just said, "When and if she decides to stop drinking, maybe she'll be her smart, witty self again."

"If only," she said. "God, she reminds me so much of Antoine, and myself of course. I've been where she's headed and I've just been trying to stop her from going there."

And she hung up.

I still wasn't ready to leave. I believed Jalecia might be in there or on her way. So I decided to wait.

I didn't realize how hard I had been gripping the steering wheel until I let go of it. I was trying to figure out what to do. I was also trying not to cry, but then I cried. Where could she possibly be? And did she lie? I wondered if I should call the police. But what would I tell them? That my forty-one-year-old daughter is missing? I was starting to wonder if she'd done this on purpose, just to upset me. I never knew what I did that made her think I was her enemy instead of her advocate. Except say no to her. But I said no to Jackson, too, and he respected my authority. Jalecia resented it.

I looked around and there were homeless people asleep in a park across the street, some lying on the grass, some on top of a royal blue tarp, and some rolled up in dirty blankets. Quite a few had dogs with them. I watched cigarette smoke swirl into the air and disappear. Grocery carts overflowed with possessions. I pretended I wasn't looking for my daughter, even though that was exactly what I was doing. But I didn't see anyone who looked like her.

I wondered if her being so lost in life was my fault. I had tried to be a good mother to her and Jackson. All I ever wanted to do was make them both proud that *I* was their mother. I always wanted to make everybody proud. That was why I spent four years in college, and that was fifty years ago, when black girls weren't getting degrees in business. But I wanted to work for myself. I wanted to be a modern Madam C. J. Walker. But being ambitious can backfire when you're black, a woman, and a mother.

Maybe I should've been there more. Maybe I shouldn't have used the money my absent father had left me to open my beauty supply store. And maybe I shouldn't have married Jalecia's father because he was in love with drugs and alcohol. And maybe I shouldn't have married Jackson's father who turned out not to be crazy about the truth. I can't even remember why I said yes, except that I was pregnant and he wanted to marry me. Maybe I shouldn't have let Jalecia quit singing or stop playing the piano, even though she lost interest when she got pregnant in her senior year. Her brother went to art school and she resented him for loving what he did and being good at it. Maybe I should have been a better referee. I always felt split because I loved them both.

The parking meter clicked Expired but I did not get out of the car to add more money even though I didn't want to go home yet.

I called Cinnamon.

"Have you heard from your mom?"

"Yes. She was drunk but she said she loved me and the twins and you and that she was sorry for always disappointing us. She said she is tired of not being a good mother and daughter and that she is going to clean up her act, and not to worry if we don't hear from her for a while because she's going somewhere safe to dry out."

I pressed the palm of my hand against my chest because this was the first time I'd ever known Jalecia to admit that she cared about my feelings. It didn't matter that I had to hear it secondhand. Some emotions are hard to express, and maybe my daughter had to go through hell to get to higher ground. I just wished I knew what demon she was struggling with. But maybe she didn't know yet either.

"Do you really think she's somewhere safe drying out, Cinna?"

"I hope so, Grandma. I give her credit for reaching out and for saying what she did. I'm going to try not to worry. Even though she was drunk, she seemed steely. Love you."

I said the same and hit End.

I sat there until a police officer pulled up beside me. Before he could write me a ticket, I started the car and pulled out of the parking space.

I didn't want to go home.

I turned the headlights on and drove straight to Sadie's new church because I knew it was Tuesday and she had choir practice.

I felt like praying.

Her new church was old. It used to be a movie theater. The front had dull blue-green columns and the windows needed to be washed. It was another nondenominational church. When I pulled into the parking lot, I wondered how I would explain what I was doing there. I would tell Sadie the truth. She liked honesty, except when it came to herself.

But as soon as I put my Volvo in Park, I changed my mind because Sadie was not the one I needed to talk to, which was why I closed my eyes, bowed my head, and wove my fingers together.

"Dear God, first of all, please forgive me for not going to church on a regular basis, well, for years, even though you already know that. But I also hope you know how much respect I have for you and all that you've done for me, especially helping me learn how to live without my husband. It has not been easy. I still believe in your power and, right now, I'm just asking if you would give some relief and strength and courage to my daughter. I'm not asking you to fix her problems because I know you're not a magician, but it would be our little secret and I promise to do my best to be a better mother. My daughter needs more than my help. She needs yours, too. Thank you. And Amen."

As I slowly lifted my head I heard a tapping on the window. Wow! That was quick!

"Girl, what are you doing here? Why are you sitting in your car in the dark with the lights off? You okay? Roll the window down!"

And I did. At first I was embarrassed and then I wasn't.

"I was coming to see you, Sadie."

"I find that hard to believe. This is about Jalecia, isn't it? I can just tell."

I nodded my head slowly.

"Well, God will hear you. You feel like stopping by my apartment? I'll make you some hot tea."

"Is the minister there?"

"No, he is not."

"Where is he?"

"I evicted him."

"You did? For real? Why the sudden change of heart?"

"I busted him talking to his wife and I told him he should go back to her."

"Good for you, Sadie. Really, I mean it. So, did he go back?"

"Nope. She didn't want him back. She changed the locks and filed for divorce."

"How do you know?"

"Because I called her to apologize for what I had done, and she told me I wasn't the first but I was the last. She said as women we need to stop blaming each other when it's really men who are weak."

"And you thought she was your enemy," I said.

"The problem was I never thought about her at all, enemy or otherwise."

"Well, Sadie, I just have to say how proud I am that you finally showed some self-respect. Where'd you get the courage?"

"Honestly?"

"Honestly."

"What all of us committed to in Las Vegas was just what I needed to hear. You said what I already knew to be true. That it is still important to keep improving our lives, even at our age, and we should treat ourselves better and stop acting like our best years are behind us."

"Amen," was all I could say to that.

Chapter 18

"What are you doing, Lo?" Korynthia asked after I picked up the phone.

"Watching TV."

"What are you watching?"

"How to lift saggy skin."

"What channel is it on?"

"I don't know."

I pulled the covers off and pressed Pause on a woman who had wings.

"What's wrong, Ko?"

"Poochie didn't call you yet?"

"No, why? Is it her mother? She's gone, isn't she?"

"Yes. Her message said she passed yesterday evening."

"Yesterday? Did you speak to her?"

"Of course I did. She sounded okay but still, it's her mama. Doesn't matter how old she was."

I lifted the comforter up with both feet and swirled it to the side.

"I think mentally she was prepared, but it's still devastating when it happens."

"Because we only get one mother."

"What can we do?"

"Poochie's already done it."

"What does that mean?"

"She already had her cremated and is going to spread her ashes out in the desert."

"What? No service?"

"Poochie respected her wishes."

"So, what's Poochie going to do now?"

"I don't know. Before we left she told me she didn't want to stay in Las Vegas after her mama passed but, you know, she's got her surgeries to schedule, so we'll see."

"She hasn't scheduled them yet?"

"I don't know if she ever really intends to do them. The recovery time is supposed to be six to eight weeks for each one and she already booked the cruise for May and that money is nonrefundable unless one of us dies, so we have to go. That being said, Poochie doesn't want to be there all by herself."

"You think she could come here to have her surgeries? I don't know how this stuff works, Ko. Her doctors are there, but she could find new ones, right? We're her family. We could take care of her."

"I'll call her as soon as I hang up. In fact, I think I'll just drive back up there to see her. No, I won't. I'll fly. That way I can be there in two hours. You want to come?"

"No, I can't."

"Why?"

"Because Jalecia is missing."

"Since when?"

"Since Tuesday."

"Is Peggy sleeping on her responsibilities?"

"She's not responsible for Jalecia, Ko. But she's been acting as her caregiver. She said she'd let me know as soon as she heard from her."

"Do you really trust that bitch?"

"I'll put it this way: technically, she's the only lifeline besides Cinnamon that I have to my daughter, and I believe Jalecia's well-being and safety are Peggy's primary concerns."

"I don't trust her ass. I mean, the first time we saw her in years was at Carl's Repasse. Where the hell has she been all these years?"

"How should I know? But until I can figure out how to get Jalecia to trust me enough to get her some help, I just have to deal with Peggy."

"I think Jalecia needs to see a shrink. I wish Bird had been able to talk to one. Maybe he could've gotten help sooner."

"Black folks don't go to shrinks," I heard myself say.

"That's such an outdated stereotype, Loretha. How else are you supposed to figure out the shit that confuses you?"

"Pray," I surprised myself by saying.

"Well, God is not a doctor."

I didn't know what to say to that.

"I'm not going to bother calling Poochie back. I'm just going to get on the plane first thing in the morning. Oh, by the way, I think I may have found the perfect spot for the House. There might be a snag or two, but location and square footage are perfect and it's a steal. I'll send you the link and you can tell me what you think. You might have to use a little imagination. I'll let you know when I land."

I texted Poochie my condolences and turned off the TV. I didn't want to watch any more about other women's sagging skin. I had my own to pull at, and it covered almost every inch of my body.

In the morning I left Poochie a message, but when she didn't return my call, I sent her a longer text and told her that if there was anything I, or any of us, could do to help her get through this, to just let us know. I also told her that Korynthia should be landing by the time she read this. Within minutes she texted me back and said she was grateful to hear from me, and Ko had just reached out. She said she would call me as soon as she figured out what to do next.

I thought the address the agent gave me had sounded familiar, so when I drove down Fair Oaks Avenue I knew exactly what building I was going to see. It used to be a boutique I shopped at back in the day, but five or six years ago the owner just up and moved to Lake Tahoe. It's been empty ever since. No one else in our posse ever shopped there because the clothing and jewelry and even the shoes were too funky for them, but I never wanted to look like what I was wearing came from a department store, so it suited me just fine.

Pasadena is old. And a lot of the shops and storefronts—especially in Old Town—have been restored to preserve the art deco charm from the early 1900s. This building was three miles from there but had the same charm. The shop was foam green stucco, and pale pink bald eagles with gold heads were perched on both sides. The doorframe was dark oak and the beveled glass was so thick I wouldn't have to worry it would break if someone slammed it.

I cupped my palms on the sides of my eyes to block out the glare and saw what was missing. Everything. I remembered the long wooden case with the glass fronts where all the imported and handmade jewelry had been displayed. The owner was a beautiful woman with thick silver braids that went down to the middle of her back and the most sincere smile ever. She would hang all of my must-have items on a rack to give me time to change my mind. She didn't push. To the immediate right had been a wall of shoes and boots and sandals that looked like an art installation by designers you would never find in Macy's. And farther in, one step up, was another large room where they'd sold gorgeous velvet and silk nightgowns and pajamas that would make you feel like a movie star from the thirties and forties. Carl loved seeing me in everything I bought from here. "Try it on for me, baby," he would always say. And I would. And I'd feel sexy and glamorous and beautiful.

As it turned out, the building was not for lease. It was for sale, which was probably why it had been on the market for so long. That beautiful owner had passed away not long after she had moved to Lake Tahoe and apparently her children had fought over the building all these years and then finally decided to sell it.

With no racks of clothes to hide the cracks in the plaster and parts of the ceiling, floors, and walls, I realized this place would need to be restored. I didn't know whether it would be worth it.

I would wait until Ko got back. Maybe she could help me decide what I knew I had already decided. *Spend the money,* she'd say. *Take the time to turn this into the coolest beauty supply in town.* I'd find someone who knew how to design the store specifically for beauty products, so it would be more interesting than a generic Sephora, and because it was three times the size of the old House, I could also hire legitimate makeup artists who could do before-and-afters and styling appointments for graduations or weddings or any special occasion like they did at Nordstrom. The difference is, we would offer hand and foot massages, good wine, espresso, and sparkling water, and if Kwame was back by the opening, maybe he could make me some new playlists.

"I'm probably next," Ma said. "Death can sneak up on you. Sometimes you don't know you're sick until you just die."

"Come on, Ma, don't say that."

She was sitting there in her gliding chair with knitting needles and orange yarn, but it didn't look like she was having much success.

"What is that you're making, Ma?"

She just looked at me. "What does it look like I'm making?"

"I couldn't say. Maybe it's too early to tell."

"I have no idea what it is. I just started taking a knitting class."

"Is this why I haven't gotten any notes or anything from you in a minute?"

"I suppose. I got bored doing it and, plus, I made a big mistake and lent my friend some of my stamps, but she passed before she could pay me back."

"Well, I do miss them. And, look," I said, and pulled out two sheets of stamps.

She dropped her needles in her lap. She was wearing the exact same outfit she had on the last two times I was here. Pink sweats. Pink sneakers.

She snatched the sheets from me and looked at one and then the other.

"I don't like these birds," she said, and handed that sheet back to me. "But I do like these mountains and fields and clouds and that rainbow. Thank you. I'll try to figure out if I have anything else to say or something I read that's worth sending."

"I appreciate everything you have to say and the meaningful and funny clippings, too," I said.

"That's good. But not everything is as important as we think it is, and some things aren't worth remembering."

This woman never ceased to amaze me.

"Are you feeling okay, Ma? You sound kind of blue."

"No. I've just been a little lonely. When you live in a place like this, it's not smart to get too close to folks. You don't see someone at breakfast or dinner and you ask where they are and you find out they passed the day before. I've lost four friends since I've been here, so I've just decided to stop making them."

"I'm sorry, Ma."

"Me, too. But anyway, how've you been?"

I did not want to tell her more about Korynthia's son or Poochie's mother. I wanted to try to lift her spirits.

"I'm good. Spent my birthday in Las Vegas with my girlfriends and we had a blast."

"That's good to hear. Do you think you ever might want to entertain the company of the male sex again?"

That caught me completely off guard.

"What would make you ask me that, Ma?"

"Don't you get lonely?"

"Of course I do."

"What do you do about it?"

"I wait until it passes."

"Carl died. You didn't. And after a year of mourning, I think you might want to think about doing something besides spending time with your old-ass girlfriends. Do any of them have a love interest?"

"Well, Korynthia has been on a dating site."

"That sounds like fun. Do you just click on a fella and, if you don't like him, just send his butt back? Has she met anybody nice?"

"Not yet."

"You should try it. At least go have some coffee with someone. Just to get out of the house and away from B. B. King. Wait, he's still alive, right?"

"Yes, he is, Ma. In fact, B.B. is in love."

"See there. Even old B.B.'s hormones still work! Anyway, Carl wouldn't want you sitting around watching TV all night, I'm sure of it. You can't grieve forever."

"So, Ma, do you think one day I can pick you up and take you somewhere?"

"How many times are you going to ask me? No. I'm fine right here. Odessa still wants to move into my house, but I think I changed my mind. I don't think she needs to live in that big house by herself. She claims she's getting some kind of lawsuit money. Always waiting on a settlement, that one. And already spending the money."

"What do you mean?"

"She went and bought herself a new car."

"What kind of car?"

"I don't know. Not a Kia."

"I've been thinking about giving the house to Cinnamon and Jonas and their twins."

"Well, that'll surely piss her off, but I think that would be a very nice thing to do. Anyway, I will keep my mouth shut when and if Odessa mentions it."

I stood up.

Ma had her knitting needles in her hands again and was trying to mimic a picture on the table that illustrated how to hold them.

"I don't think I'm going to be knitting you any socks," she said. "Now bend down here and give me a kiss."

And I did.

And she squeezed my hand.

And I squeezed hers back.

I was starving and decided I was overdue for a cheeseburger and fries. I had been good. I could count how many I'd had since I got back from Las Vegas, which was almost two months ago: five. I could also count how many times I went to Carol's and had their French toast with bacon: three. I had not been in Roscoe's at all. Lucky was finally scheduled to have her gastric bypass surgery and once she had it, she would have to pretend fried chicken and candied yams and honey cornbread would kill her. I thought that was a little dramatic, but it wouldn't hurt me to think that way, too, and it was the first time I had ever known Lucky to say no to herself.

"What can I get for you today?" the voice coming out of the speaker said. I was thinking B.B. might want a hot dog to celebrate his birthday—he was now ten in human years, so I ordered him one with nothing on it and I would not let him eat the bun.

"Ma'am, will there be anything else besides the hot dog?"

"Yes, I would like to have a double cheeseburger with a purple onion and a small order of fries."

"What kind of cheese would you like on that burger?" the voice said.

"Cheddar. Oh, and can you also put pickles on it?"

"You got it. Any of our delicious desserts strike your eye? Our apple pie is killer and our ice cream sundaes are made with the best chocolate syrup. And there's a new flavor of ice cream to choose: strawberry cheesecake."

I thought about that, but then heard myself say, "I'll pass on the dessert, but thank you for asking."

"My pleasure, ma'am. So that'll be fourteen dollars and nine cents. Just pull up to the drive-through window. My name's Casper."

Like the friendly ghost?

Casper was a sexy twenty-year-old kid with the most perfectly white teeth I'd ever seen. His eyes were shiny black and his lips . . .

"Your food will be right up."

I handed him a twenty.

"Keep the change, young man."

He looked down at the twenty.

"Are you sure about that?"

"Absolutely. You've been very polite and patient with me."

"Thank you so much, ma'am. I'll be right back with your food."

And he was. I put the big bag on the passenger seat and just when I was about to put the car in Drive, I heard Casper say, "Wait a second, ma'am."

And he handed me what I could see through the clear round top was a gigantic strawberry cheesecake sundae.

"For being so generous. You have no idea what this means to me today. Thank you."

"You're quite welcome, young man." I set the sundae in the cup holder, and because no one was watching me drive, I kept sticking my index finger inside the little opening and pushing it into the cheesecake ice cream and strawberry jelly, so by the time I got home there was nothing left of it.

I pulled into the driveway and I hit the brakes too hard when I saw Kwame's name pop up on my cellphone. The empty sundae fell out of the cup holder onto the carpet, and I felt grateful. The reward I get for not practicing self-restraint.

"Mama-Lo, are you there?"

He sounded so upbeat.

"Yes, I am, Kwame! How are you? How's your mama doing?"

"Moms is doing much better. She's walking, with a cane, but she can move her arms and turn her head and she's talking great! How are you doing, Mama-Lo? I miss you! And B. B. King!"

"I'm so glad to hear that. Your four-legged friend and I are doing fine. We miss you, too."

"Well, I'm moving back to Pasadena. And I'm bringing my moms with me."

"That is just wonderful, Kwame. Will she need any kind of medical attention, though?"

"She's been going to the rehabilitation facility here, but the house she lives in is being torn down to make room for some condos and I don't want to leave her here, so she's coming. We'll find her a place to continue her therapy. She's got Medicare and social security, even though it's not much."

"Well, I'm going to have a vacancy in the building—it's a one-bedroom, and not for another two months, but it's something. Were you trying to come sooner than that?"

"I'm not sure. Don't you worry about any of this. I just wanted you to know I was heading back. Is my car still in the garage?"

"It is and I start it up whenever I remember. B. B. King always barks when I do because he wants to know where you've been and when you are coming back."

He laughed.

"It sure is good to hear your voice, Mama-Lo. And you've been doing okay, right?"

"I have."

"How about your diabetes?"

"Under control."

"For real, Mama-Lo?"

"I wouldn't lie about something this serious."

"I know. But I'm just checking."

I thought about the sundae I had just devoured and my insides churned at my lie.

"And is Jalecia back on track?"

"I wish I knew."

"Don't give up on her, Mama-Lo. She'll thank you one day."

"I'm trying my hardest but when you hold out a branch to someone and they don't grab it, it makes you wonder if they really want help at all."

"You *have* to get on her nerves. And *piss* her off—that's really how she'll know you love her. Well, look, I have Moms calling me, so look to hear from me in the next few weeks or so. By then our plans will be firm. Oh! Please tell Cinnamon and Jonas and the little ones I'm looking forward to seeing them and that as soon as I get my moms settled, I'll be available to babysit free of charge! Love you."

And I love him.

Chapter 19

I signed up for SilverSneakers.

Which was a baby step.

But I didn't tell anyone in case things didn't work out.

I also didn't want to start at the gym Ko teaches at. I wanted to get into shape a little bit so I wouldn't look like I hadn't worked out in years. I don't like to sweat. The only time I really work up a sweat is in the summer when I walk B. B. King to the dog park and, even then, I carry my little battery-operated fan.

I decided to start out easy by taking a Zumba Gold class. It was a modified version for old folks. This way I could have a little fun and just get some of my unused muscles moving.

I bought a new workout outfit. It was black because I didn't want to draw attention to myself. I also had every intention of standing in the back. But it turned out there was no "back" because there were only ten or twelve of us in the small studio with mirrored walls and blond wooden floors. The instructor was old, fit, sexy, and gorgeous. She had on a tight purple sleeveless top and her stomach was so flat it looked like she had had liposuction. But I knew she had earned it. I couldn't tell what nationality she was, until she started showing us how to move our hips. Brazilian. After she told me not to feel intimidated, as a first-timer, by how smoothly other people moved because most of them had been in her class for over a year, she said, "Just watch me, but slow it down to thirty-three-and-a-third or forty-five rpms if I'm moving at seventy-eight." I was happy as hell to hear her say "rpms" because it was from a time when we listened to music on vinyl and called them records and they came in three speeds.

But when she pressed a button on her iPad and the salsa music came blasting out, it scared the hell out of me. She started out by taking a slow step to the left and a slow step to the right and when she moved forward she swirled her hips so smoothly, as if they had a brain of their own, and then she did the same thing when she stepped backward. When I tried to imitate her, my stomach got in the way, and then she had us shake our booties and mine just kept jiggling, and finally she had us speed up all these moves. When it felt like I was going to pass out, I just stopped, caught my breath, waved thank-you and goodbye to her, and left.

I was never going to be Shakira.

I decided I should go with a boring aerobics class, but I would come back to Zumba one day and shake my booty as smoothly as the rest of those silver-haired huzzies *and* the two fine gay men who moved like Ricky Martin.

I did not mention any of this to Ko, of course, because I knew for a fact that she now taught a hip-hop class. I decided when I felt I was in good enough shape not to pass out in the first ten minutes, I would walk into her class and strut my stuff.

Poochie finally moved back to Pasadena.

Her new local orthopedist suggested she have both knees replaced, but wait on the hip. She had lost a lot of weight since we saw her in Vegas—too much, we all agreed—except in her stomach, which was still bloated probably because she couldn't really exercise for the past five or six years since caring for her mother had been her whole life.

"When will you do the hip?" I asked.

"Next year."

"But how will you walk if your hip's still bad, Poochie?"

"The way I've been walking. With a walker."

"What about the cruise?"

"It's still three months from now. I should be good to go by then. Even if I have to use a wheelchair."

We were all surprised that she hadn't gotten herself a fancy apartment. Poochie had always lived large. Instead, she was living at a senior facility a lot like Ma's, except hers was newer.

She was also bored, so when she asked if she could see where the new House was going to be, I happily agreed to meet her there.

"So, this is going to be the spot, huh?" she asked as she pushed her walker with the tennis balls on the front through the space.

"This is it," I said. "Lots of renovation to be done. But I finally signed all the paperwork, and thanks to my husband, the bank won't have to be my friend."

Poochie smiled as if she was remembering Carl.

"I can see the potential, although it seems too big just to sell beauty products."

"I've got plans, Poochie, but let's go across the street and have a coffee because the dust in here is getting to me. It's not bothering you?"

"No. I don't smell it, but I do need to use the bathroom. I can't stay long anyway because I've got a doctor's appointment."

"It feels like we're always going to the doctor these days, huh?"

"Yes, it does."

"To be honest, Poochie, you look a little weird. How much weight have you lost?"

She shrugged her shoulders. "About fifteen or twenty pounds since you were in Vegas. It's the grief, but it'll help with my recovery after the surgery."

It looked more like twenty-five. Poor Poochie. As she rolled her walker toward the room on the left, it hit me that her real name is Pearlene. She never liked it. Her grandmother always called her Poochie. It stuck. In high school, some of us didn't know what her real name was.

I always wondered why black folks liked to nickname their kids. Although I admit, I never liked Loretha either. It sounded like a name for an old lady, which of course suited me now. I don't mind being called Lo, although sometimes it does get on my nerves, especially when people used to say, "How low can you go, Lo?" I never thought it was funny, which was why I never laughed. When my second husband's sister, who I didn't like, said that to me at a barbecue, I said, "Let's see how low you can go, ho." And I pushed her onto the table where the hot dog buns were and they flew all over the grass and into the pool like little submarines. There were other reasons I couldn't stand her, of course. She once accused me of being high-and-mighty because I went to college and got one of those things called "a bachelor's degree."

"College don't make you better than everybody who didn't go," she said at a family reunion, right after I'd had Jackson.

"Not better," I said, cutting my eyes at her. "Just smarter." And I stormed off, wondering how I had managed to marry into this family of misfits. But then I banished that thought because it would prove her right.

"Poochie," I said, as I watched her push her walker across the concrete floor, leaving her size-eleven footprints in the dust, "what's really on your mind?"

"I'm scared," she said.

"Oh, come on now. A lot of folks have knee replacements, and as long as you do what the doctor tells you to, you'll have a good recovery."

"That's what they say."

"Well, at least it's not something life-threatening, Poochie."

"I know. But just pick a joint or body part and it feels like I have to replace it."

"Do you really think it's smart to have both knees replaced at the same time?"

"The jury is out on it. My doctor says yes, kill two birds with one procedure. I can't stand this arthritis pain."

"Everybody has arthritis," I said just to make her feel better.

"Where's yours? I've never heard you complain."

"In my ankle. I twisted it getting off that van when we came back from Vegas and it feels like it's taking forever to heal."

This was a lie. And I prayed I wasn't jinxing myself.

"Have you gone to Korynthia's hip-hop class yet?"

"Well, I wanted to start, but the doctor told me to take some yoga classes first, which would help me stretch better."

Of course, this was another lie.

"Wow! And that doesn't hurt?"

I shook my head no. I didn't know why I was lying. But once you tell one . . .

"Is yoga hard?"

"Not really."

"What kind of yoga is it?"

Why does she have to be so damn nosy?

"Siddhartha."

"I heard that one's really rough. But good for you, Lo!"

"So when is your surgery?"

"Two weeks from tomorrow."

"Well, we'll make sure to be there to cheer when they push you out of recovery."

"No. I don't want you all to come."

"Why not?"

"Because I just don't. I'll only be in the hospital for two or three days and then I'll do rehab for two or three weeks. I don't want you to see me until I'm strong."

"This is the stupidest idea I've heard come out of your mouth since that cruise to no-damn-where. We're your friends, Poochie."

"I know. And speaking of cruises, everything has been finalized, so don't say shit, but you huzzies do not owe me a dime because I've already paid for the whole thing. Including a guest for each of you because this is the last time I think I'm going to be able to do this dog-gone cruise."

"Have you lost your frigging mind?"

"Yes."

"But why, Poochie?"

"Because I think it's time for us to figure out somewhere we can go on dry land."

"I've got some good news and some bad news," Ko said as we finished walking around part of the Rose Bowl. This time I'd brought B. B. King. I could tell he was skeptical and jealous of how perky some of the other dogs were. He'd tried to trot like some of them who passed him, but he just ended up limping, then groaning, and then finally just dropped down. I bent down and rubbed his head and said, "It's okay, B.B."

I then shook my head as I looked up at Korynthia.

"Give me the bad news first, as long as it's not something that will take me a long time to get over."

"I don't think I want to work at the House of Beauty when you have it back up and running."

"This is the *bad* news?"

She looked disappointed that I wasn't disappointed.

"Well, yeah. Don't you want to know why?"

"I'm sure you have a good reason but okay, why?"

"Because I don't know a damn thing about hair and makeup and beauty products. And with all the new services you want to offer, I just think it makes more sense for you to hire some foxy young girls instead of my old ass."

"I agree."

"You bitch!" she said and then we both started laughing.

"So, tell me the good news. Wait, don't. I'll take B.B. home and you keep running and meet me at my house when you're done."

"To be honest, I don't really feel like running because I'm too excited about what I have to tell you. So, I'll meet you at your crib in ten minutes."

When I pulled into my driveway, I didn't recognize the black Kia parked out front, but I did recognize Peggy. What in the world did this woman want and why didn't she call me first?

I got out of my car and let B. B. King in the side door, then turned around and headed for her car. She was getting out of hers, too, and walking toward me like she was going to shoot me or something.

"What are you doing here?" I asked.

"Well, hello to you, too, Loretha."

"Did you forget how to call?"

"No, I did not."

"Did something happen to my daughter?"

"No, she's fine."

I felt relieved, although I didn't quite believe her and I knew she was up to something.

"Where is she?"

"At my house."

"Speaking of which, could you please give me your address since you obviously have mine? And also, I have a friend on her way over here and we have something important to discuss, so could you please let me call you a little later?"

"Jalecia is pregnant."

"Did you just say pregnant?"

"And she cannot and should not and does not want to keep it."

"Why not?"

"Because she doesn't know whose it is. She can't remember."

I saw Ko turn the corner, but when she saw the look on my face she just kept driving.

"So, what do you want me to do about it?"

"It's about four hundred dollars plus add two or three hundred for rent."

"Are you serious, Peggy?"

"Google it."

"How many months is she?"

"She claims two, so probably three."

"You drove all the way over here to tell me this?"

"I was in the neighborhood."

I crossed my arms and put all my weight on one foot.

"Your daughter needs help, you know."

"I thought she was going someplace to get clean. That's what she told Cinnamon."

"She goes to AA when she feels like it. But I'm not talking about that kind of help, Loretha."

"Drugs?"

"I'm sure she does some of that, too, but I believe she's suffering from depression. I just don't know what kind. She doesn't like to talk about how she feels. If you could get her some good health insurance, and she could talk to a doctor about *this* problem, it might help her get the other ones under control."

I looked at her hard and I could tell she was not trying to bullshit me, that she really was concerned about my daughter.

"Thank you, Peggy. I want to help her, but I don't know what kind of help she needs. And I still don't. But maybe a doctor does."

"Look, Loretha, I know you don't like me, and you think I'm just pimping you for money. I've got a good pension, but it's only enough for me. My niece has been costing me extra and I can't afford to take care of her grown ass by myself. You feel me?"

"I feel you. You want to come in?"

"No."

"So how do you want it?"

"You can use Western Union."

"I would also appreciate if you would give me your address."

"I thought I gave it to you before."

"No, you didn't."

"I'll text it to you right now."

And she did.

"Can you send it today?"

"I suppose I can."

"But get on top of the insurance, Loretha, because it might help you save your daughter's life."

And she got in her black Kia and sped off.

Pregnant.

And.

Depressed.

I just stood there and felt tears rolling down my face and then I heard myself yell after her: "I've been trying to help my daughter save her own life, but first she needs to know it's worth saving! Bitch."

Chapter 20

When my doorbell rang later, I thought it was Korynthia returning but it was Cinnamon.

"Wave!" she turned and said to the babies who were in the back seat waving like windshield wipers on high. They were even cuter and fatter than the last time I saw them, and when they started laughing, if I wasn't mistaken, those little white things pushing out on top of their gums looked like teeth.

"Hi, Grandma, we were just coming from Whole Foods and I thought I'd take a chance on dropping by. And guess what?" she asked, and then kissed me on both cheeks and gave me a squeeze.

"I can't begin to guess, sweetie," I said as I waved to the twins.

"A few weeks ago one of the producers at *The Voice* heard me singing and thinks I might have potential!"

"I've always felt this way, Cinna."

"Well, I won't be auditioning on camera anytime soon, but it was really nice to hear that."

"Hey, I've been wanting to ask you: Who's been watching Pretty and Handsome while you're at work?"

"Aunt Odessa!"

"What did you just say?"

"Only for a few hours. Until Jonas gets home."

"That's nice," I said, lying. Why didn't they ask me? It's not like my schedule was full. "It's awfully kind of her considering she's never been around babies."

"They like her! And I didn't know Aunt Odessa could sing!"

"She can?"

"She's got a great voice! Maybe I got my talent from her! Can you sing, Grandma?"

"No."

"Anyway, keep your fingers crossed for me and invite us over soon because Pretty and Handsome would love to crawl around your hardwood floors and climb in your bathtub, but I have to put them down for their nap, and mine too!"

This made me laugh.

"Hey, Cinna? I have a surprise for you."

"Can you give me a hint, Grandma?"

"Well, you know how Ma's house is pretty much finished except for the crack in the pool? Well, once it's fixed, I am also having a safety fence installed and I was thinking maybe you and Jonas and Pretty and Handsome might want to live there."

She covered her mouth.

And then I saw tears falling from her eyes.

And then she hugged me.

And then she started jumping up and down and clapping.

And the twins started jumping up and down in their car seats and clapping, too.

"We've already been inside and we love the renovations!" she said.

"Who let you in?"

"Aunt Odessa. She still has a key. It's our dream house, Grandma, and we don't know what you would want us to pay each month but—"

"Nothing."

And then she hugged me so hard my breasts flattened.

"You have a kind heart and soul to match, Grandma. *Thank you thank you thank you* and I can't wait to tell Jonas!"

"I'll let you know when everything is finished. But how soon do you think you would want to move in?"

"Would yesterday be too soon?"

And then she kissed me on both cheeks and my nose, and right after she left I went straight to Western Union.

"Is the coast clear?" Korynthia asked when I answered the phone.

"Yes and no," I said. I was just lying across the bed and apparently had dozed off.

"Peggy wore you out, again, huh? What did she have to say?"

"Jalecia is pregnant."

"No. Please don't tell me she's having a baby at forty-one years old?"

"She's not. Can we talk later, Ko?"

"How much later?"

"You wanna come over and watch Netflix? We can order something from Grubhub and then you can tell me your good news."

"I can't. I have a date. Or, I should say, another date. With the same man. And this will make our fifth date and this is my good frigging news. I think I might be falling in love, Lo!"

I sat straight up. "Did I just hear you right, Ko?"

"Girl, yes you did. His name is Henry, but he doesn't look like a Henry."

"Is he black?"

"Yes."

"How'd you meet him?"

"On my dating site, chile. Lo, whenever you feel like you're ready to put yourself out there, you let me know. I will tell you how to find a date on this great senior site. No riffraff. Interesting older men who are still very much alive. Oh, I mean . . . I'm sorry for saying that."

"No apologies necessary, Ko. I get it."

"And he knows how to take just the right amount of Viagra, not like Mr. Roto-Rooter."

"I can't even believe this. But congratulations. So, when's the wedding?"

"We haven't decided yet."

I jumped off the bed, then flopped back down. B. B. King sauntered in the room and looked at me as if to ask what all the excitement was about.

"What? I was just kidding. This is a lot for me to take in right now, Ko. So let me just digest it and then tell me again tomorrow so I can make sure it's true."

"Oh, it's truer than true. And you know why? Because we don't get a do-over and I have never been married and WTF, I'm going to do it. And if it lasts three weeks or three years what do I have to lose?"

"Does Henry have his own money?"

"Lots of it."

"Good. That's something. How old is he?"

"Sixty-five but he looks fifty-six!"

"Have you told the girls?"

"No. I don't know if I want to yet. Poochie's focusing on her surgery, and plus, she doesn't understand anything about passion. I think Sadie is now celibate to make up for being a whore. And Lucky, well, she's just too opinionated, which reminds me: Lucky has guaranteed that she's finally having us for dinner at her house next week. And she's cooking, hallelujah! Anyway, I'll tell them about Henry once I know we've crossed the finish line. I know I can trust you to keep your mouth shut, can't I?"

"I'm not even going to answer that. But this is exciting. I can't even imagine having sex with anybody except Carl and I don't care if I ever do."

"He would want you to and one day you might want to, honey. You're not dead down there, are you?"

"There are occasional stirrings."

"Well, let me tell you: ain't nothing like some warm arms around you and something warm and stiff inside you."

"I think I still remember, Ko. But I'm good right now."

"Can you let Poochie know about dinner?"

"I'll text her. Her surgery isn't until the week after next. She said she doesn't want us to come to the hospital, so obviously we will be waiting for her in the recovery room."

"And don't worry, Lo. We'll help you help Jalecia. She is going to be okay as long as you don't give up on her."

"I can't. And I won't. And I love you, Ko."

"And I love you, too, huzzie. But I'm still only giving you a few more weeks to get your black behind in one of my hip-hop classes before I drag you myself."

In the morning I called Dr. Alexopolous's office.

"Hello, this is Loretha Curry."

"I know, I can see your name on caller ID. What can I do for you, Mrs. Curry?"

"Are you new?"

"Yes, my name is Cecilia. Is there something I can help you with?"

"Well, it's been a while since I've seen Dr. Alexopolous, and—"

"Actually, you're due for your physical. Did you get our reminder by mail?"

"No, I didn't."

"I sent it over a week ago. Do you check your mail on a regular basis, Mrs. Curry?"

"Most of the time."

She was getting on my nerves. And this felt more like an interrogation. She was not friendly enough to be a receptionist, but then, Dr. Alexopolous wasn't friendly enough to be a doctor either. I'd just been too lazy to find another one. But soon.

"Well," Cecilia said, and then I heard her say, "just fill that out and please don't forget to turn it over."

"Hello?" I said just for the hell of it.

"I'm so sorry, Mrs. Curry. I'm here alone. Anyway, we can schedule it now if you'd like. Are you having any medical issues the doctor should be aware of?"

"No."

"Was there a reason for your call besides scheduling your checkup?"

"Now that you mention it, I was calling to ask about getting an order to take the A1C test."

"No problem. I can see it's been four months and the doctor suggests you have one every three months. Have you been feeling drowsy? Tired? Thirsty?"

"Sometimes, but not all the time."

"That's not good, Mrs. Curry. But I can send over a request for you right now."

"Thank you."

"Consider it done! And as soon as the doctor gets your results she'll call if she's concerned about anything."

"Thank you."

I made an appointment and as soon as I hung up made one for the A1C test. I could not believe I was able to get one for the next morning at six. I admit I was nervous because I had not been doing everything I should have been doing to deal with my disease, which is what it is. Truth be told, I hadn't changed much of anything. I still ate the same foods, just not as often. I had not been exercising although I had been meaning to. I supposed that new number was going to tell me the truth. I knew I'd been bullshitting myself, but because being diabetic doesn't hurt every day, it didn't feel like I really had it.

But I promised myself I was going to do better.

Starting tonight.

Because right before I called the doctor's office, I had had two thick pieces of French toast with butter, drenched with maple syrup, two strips of bacon, a glass of orange juice, and a cup of coffee. With two packets of Splenda.

I bought Jalecia the best insurance possible, but I used my address instead of Peggy's. Jalecia still hasn't wanted to see or talk to me. It's been almost a week since Peggy came by. I was sitting on the front porch throwing a ball to B. B. King—who walked to get it—when Peggy called.

"First of all, Jalecia is not pregnant anymore."

"Hello to you, too, Peggy."

"Secondly, thank you for getting her insurance so fast. This is really good coverage. I've already been doing some research and, with this kind of plan, I'll be able to find her a good psychologist or a psychiatrist. She's probably going to need both."

"How can you say that, Peggy?"

"Because they do two different things. . . ."

"Wait a minute. You don't know my daughter. You think you do. But you're seeing her at her worst. And since you're not a doctor, I would appreciate it if you would stop trying to diagnose her."

"Okay. But when was the last time you spent any time around her, tell me that?"

"She has distanced herself from the entire family, including *her* daughter."

"Don't you think there's a reason for it?"

"Of course there is, but I don't think you're qualified to diagnose her. That's all I'm saying."

"You're right."

"I need to see my daughter, Peggy."

"She's not quite ready to see you because she knows it's going to be a confrontation. Just do this, Loretha. Give her a minute to get her head on straight. Now that she's got insurance, I can try to coax her into talking to somebody. Would you just let me try?"

"Okay. But, Peggy, promise me you'll let me know what she decides?"

"Of course I will. She's in good hands. I promise you that."

I believed her.

Because I had to.

"You know, she's also got other needs that I don't have the financial means to see to, so, if you could put another couple hundred dollars into my account, I would really appreciate it. Jalecia may be suffering but not when it comes to her appetite."

They've started to recognize me at Western Union.

"Did you finally get a housekeeper?" I yelled to Lucky because I thought I was in the wrong house. It was spotless. As usual, I was the first to arrive, but it was because I wanted to be helpful. Not really, I was just being nosy and wanted to see what mood Lucky was in. When she heard me, she came from down the hall in a pretty purple paisley muumuu. I couldn't believe she had on makeup and somebody had improved her perm. She also wore orange earrings that dangled and matched some of the orange swirls in her dress. If I wasn't mistaken, Lucky even had on some kind of perfume.

"Hey, you," she said in a tone I hadn't heard in years. It was nice. "No, I didn't get a housekeeper. I got three. They come in here and in one hour they're out the front door. It took me long enough."

"So, what brought this on, Lucky? You couldn't come up with yet another lame-ass excuse as to why we couldn't have dinner here?"

"Yes and no. I was just tired of living in a pigpen. And Joe said something to me about it one night."

"What?"

"Honestly, he said he didn't understand what was happening to me. No. What *has* happened to me. He said I used to care how I looked. I used to be sweet. Do you remember when I was ever sweet, Lo?"

"No, but I wasn't having sex with you."

"Oh, shut up and let me finish because I don't want to talk about this at dinner. Anyway, so then he said that both of us needed to lose weight because we shouldn't be the cause of our own deaths, and then he said he really didn't want a divorce. He just wanted us to be nice to each other again and he was lonely sleeping in the guesthouse."

"I love hearing this, Lucky! I love Joe. We all love Joe. Why wouldn't you want to share this with everybody?"

"Because instead of talking about what I want to do, I want to do it first and then you all will respect me more. I have been a mean bitch for too long and I don't even like myself. I don't know how you guys have tolerated me all these years."

"Because we love you, that's why. We know you don't mean to be a bitch, but you're our bitch. Did you go to Sadie's new church or something?"

"No. Do you remember that TV show called *Scared Straight!*?"

"Carl used to watch it."

"Well, my weight and losing a man I've loved for more than forty-five years has scared the hell out of me. I'm going to be seventy fucking years old this year, Lo."

"Well, that makes two of us," Korynthia said.

"Three," Sadie said.

"How much did you guys hear?" Lucky asked.

"Everything we needed to."

And they rushed over and hugged Lucky.

"So, did you guys carpool?"

"No," Korynthia said. "We Ubered. Poochie should probably be here soon, too. She used to be the first one here, back in the day."

"So," Sadie said, walking over to the picture windows and looking at all the lit-up homes sprinkled throughout the hills. It was truly magical to see, especially now that Lucky actually had the shades up. "What are we having that smells so good, and are there any appetizers?"

"I'm keeping it simple. We're having marinated rib-eyes, steamed brown rice, no bread, a salad with oil and vinegar, and sparkling water for me and Loretha, right, Lo?"

"Hell yeah!"

"And for dessert?" Sadie asked suspiciously.

"Fruit salad. Take it or leave it."

"Did you have a few hits before we got here?" Korynthia asked.

"No. I'm tired of living in a goddamn fog. I want to know how to think on my own again. I want to feel whatever I feel and see what I see clearly. Plus, I'm tired of it stinking up the entire fucking house. I want Joe to move back in and we want to get a dog and I just want to live better."

"I concur," Sadie said. "But can we try for a change to start cutting back on the profanity, just a little bit?"

"No," Lucky said. "Sometimes there's no other fucking word that will do."

And we all laughed.

"Okay, so go wash your hands and everybody grab a plate, dish out whatever you want, and take a seat."

"Aren't we going to wait for Poochie?"

"She should be here in a minute. Poochie's never late."

"Then let's wait for her," I said.

"Yeah, let's," Ko said.

"You're right," Lucky said.

Sadie nodded in agreement.

Five minutes passed.

Then ten.

Then fifteen.

"Call her," Lucky said.

And we all grabbed our cellphones.

"I'll call," I said. It went straight to voicemail.

We dropped our plates on the counter and when we heard one fall on the floor and crack, nobody cared.

We piled into my car and drove straight to Poochie's senior apartment and when we saw her car in her parking space we took two elevators up to her floor and ran to her door. We pounded on it and yelled her name over and over and over, but we did not get an answer.

Chapter 21

She was in her bedroom, under the covers, fully dressed, her arms crossed. She looked so peaceful. As if she was having a good dream.

After we stopped howling and stomping our feet in disbelief, each one of us bent down and kissed her on both cheeks and backed out of the room in slow motion. It hit us that our best friend was in that bed and she was not going to wake up. We sank back into the sofa as if we'd been pushed, which was when we saw two envelopes on the coffee table. One had all of our names on it and was propped against what we realized was not a silver vase but an urn. The other one was lying flat and faceup, and on the front Poochie had written: *Open Immediately.*

I got up and sleepwalked back into her bedroom. "Poochie," I whispered, and touched her hand, which was not soft or warm. "I wish you had told us how bad it was, sweetheart. We would've helped you take baby steps. You didn't have to go through this by yourself. We are your sisters, Pooch. We will always be your sisters."

"Come on back out here with us," Sadie said, and I felt her wrap her arms around my waist, then she took me by the hand and walked me back out to the living room.

She closed the door behind her.

"Leave it open," I said. "She needs to know we're out here."

Sadie did and then she went out into the hallway and called for help. The rest of us were staring at the envelopes.

"I think we should open that one now," Lucky said, pointing to the one lying flat. "Because whatever is in it is important."

And she picked it up and opened it.

"Don't read it out loud," Ko said. "Please."

I was shaking my head in agreement.

Lucky read it to herself, then slowly and methodically folded the paper and slid it back inside the envelope.

"She wants to be cremated. Tomorrow. She has already made arrangements. And she does not want a memorial service."

We were quiet, trying to process what we had just heard, wishing we could go in that bedroom and ask Poochie if she was sure about this.

"Did it say where she wants her ashes?" Sadie asked. She was standing in the doorway, which none of us heard open or close. She was used to being around the dead from all of her hospital visiting, but Poochie was her friend and I resented the matter-of-fact way she was handling this. At first. But the reality was that Sadie was the only one who could think and move, so I—we—were grateful she was able to do what we couldn't. We looked at Lucky.

"She didn't say," Lucky said.

"I know where," was all I said.

None of us wanted to open the other envelope. And it took us two days to get the courage and another two to gather our bearings. Sadie had agreed to keep Poochie's ashes at her place until we went on the cruise and none of us had any objections. I couldn't do it. I just couldn't.

We met at my house because we didn't know when we'd ever be able to go back up to Lucky's house again. No one was really hungry but I ordered Chinese anyway.

"I'm not hungry," Lucky said, which was the first time I'd ever heard her say that. "But you all go ahead. I'll wait."

And then one after the other we shook our heads because we couldn't swallow our grief.

I got up and threw the entire bag in the trash.

We just sat at the dining room table and folded our hands in our laps.

Lucky opened the envelope and unfolded the single piece of paper. We could all see Poochie had typed this on the computer. Just like her: so efficient. We all took a deep breath and made ourselves blow it out slowly.

I'm sorry, Lo, Ko, Sadie, and Lucky, and I hope you know I didn't do this to hurt any of you. I have not been honest about a lot of things. I have been battling colon cancer for quite some time. Remember our first dinner after Carl passed, when I lectured you huzzies about taking care of yourselves? I knew then. But I didn't want to scare you all and I didn't want you to feel sorry for me. I invited you all to Las Vegas, sort of as our last hurrah. When I learned I was going to have to have both knees replaced, and then my hip went out, too, I knew I was not going to be able to withstand all of it. And I couldn't. But know this: I am at peace now and I don't feel any pain. But you huzzies are still very much alive and I am begging each of you to please please please give everything you've got to taking the best care possible of yourselves and of each other for the rest of your lives. It does not have to be all downhill from here. So put it in fourth gear and floor it! Love, Poochie. P.S. Check your cruise tickets. Bring a friend.

We did not, could not, move.

We swallowed her words.

And we all had smiles on our faces.

When I stood up, I felt lighter. Much lighter. And from the look on everybody's faces, I was not alone.

"You will never in a million years guess who came to see me," Ma said.

"I can't," I said as I held her hand and we slowly walked down the wide hallway to the visiting room.

"Jalecia!"

I stopped in my tracks. "Jalecia?"

"Two or three days ago. I almost didn't recognize her. She looked a little wild even without those dreadlocks and she was talking a mile a minute, but she brought me some flowers."

"How did she get here?"

"She said she took a bus because there's something wrong with her car."

We turned into the crowded room where everybody's hair was white or silver. Even the frail ones were wearing smiles.

"Where should we sit, Ma?"

"See that old lady over there who has the nerve to wear red?"

"You can't miss her."

"I don't want to sit anywhere near her because her ears are too big and she can hear clear across the room. So just keep walking."

The woman waved to Ma and Ma threw a wave back.

"Why be so mean, Ma?"

"She's putting on an act. Nobody likes Millie. She likes to swear for no reason and she's senile as hell. See that table back there by the window? Let's sit there. I like looking at the parking lot."

So we sat. And she crossed her legs and then pulled her beige shawl so it covered her bare arms, which I hadn't seen in years. They were golden and the wrinkles looked like soft spiderwebs.

"Anyway, how've you been?"

"I've been better," I said. "I lost one of my best friends a few weeks ago. Poochie."

"I heard. Odessa told me."

"Who told her?"

"Cinnamon."

"It doesn't matter."

"It's not easy losing a good friend. I've lost quite a few over the years. Makes you wonder if you're next."

I didn't need to hear that.

"I heard she took her own life."

"She was terminally ill and decided she couldn't take the pain anymore."

"I want to say I understand but I don't. I'm in pain, too, with arthritis running wild, but I'll take as many pills as they'll give me just to be able to look out a window. Anyway, I'm sorry you lost your friend, Loretha."

"I am, too."

"I'd send you a sympathy card but the ones in the gift shop are ugly and depressing, and I don't want to depress you."

"Thank you, Ma. So what did Jalecia have to say?"

"She said you're mad at her."

"I'm not mad at her. I haven't heard a word from her in a couple of months."

"She was pregnant, you know."

"I know."

"But now she's not. She said with all the drinking she'd been doing she didn't want to take a chance that something might be wrong with the baby."

"She said that?"

"Anyway, she didn't stay long. But she said she was coming to see you soon."

"Really?"

"That's what she said."

"Did she say how she was doing?"

"No. But I know something big is wrong because she has never just come here to see me. She was a little fidgety."

"I've called and called but she doesn't return my calls, Ma."

"Is she still living with that Peggy?"

"Yes, the last I heard."

"Then go see *her*."

"I think I will."

"So, nothing in your pocketbook for me?"

She started laughing.

"As a matter of fact, here you go," I said and whipped out the latest issue of O magazine.

"I do still love Oprah."

I left it on the table.

"One day I hope you will be thoughtful enough to sneak a half-pint of Hennessy in here."

"One day I just might."

"You know good and well I'm just kidding. Are we through visiting?"

She pushed the chair back and stood up slowly.

"I suppose we are, Ma."

"Good, because Bingo is starting in ten minutes and I'm feeling lucky. Give me some sugar."

I bent over and kissed her.

"And go see Jalecia. I think she wants to be found."

As soon as I left, I put Peggy's address into Waze and drove straight to Compton. It took an hour and ten minutes. I was afraid but mentally prepared, knowing I was entering a gang-filled war zone. But when I turned on to Peggy's street I saw her black car parked on a spotless tree-lined street with small but well-maintained houses, manicured lawns, trimmed shrubs, and flowers of every color. Happy children played on the clean sidewalk and waved to me as if they knew me. I was ashamed of myself for believing what I now knew was a stereotype.

I didn't see Jalecia's car.

I dialed Peggy's number.

She answered on the first ring.

"If you're looking for your daughter, she's in the hospital. Right there in Pasadena. I thought you would know, since you're her next of kin."

"What's she doing in the hospital, Peggy? Is she okay? Why didn't you call me? What's wrong with her?"

"She's depressed, Loretha. Clinically depressed. It's a good thing you got her that insurance."

"What hospital?"

"Huntington. You can be there in ten minutes."

"No, I can't."

"Why not? Where are you?"

"I'm outside your apartment building."

"Took you long enough to finally get out here. Come on up the stairs. I'm in apartment C. I look a mess because I wasn't expecting company, so please don't judge. I'm retired."

"Did Jalecia call you?"

"The hospital did."

"Why didn't they call me? I'm her fucking mother, Peggy."

"I guess she gave them my number. Don't start tripping over that right now. Would you, please?"

This hurt. I'm her mother. Not this bitch.

"Then why didn't you call to tell me, Peggy?"

"Slow your roll, Loretha. Maybe check your messages."

She hung up. I looked down at my phone.

I had two missed blocked calls and voicemails. Sometimes I forget to check them regularly. I listened to her messages. Peggy hadn't made it sound like it was life threatening. In fact, she made it sound like Jalecia had been checked in to a hotel for the last three days.

I called Peggy back.

"I apologize. I do see that you called. I'm going to head over there right now."

"She's going to be okay."

"How do you know that?"

"Because I spoke to the doctor and he told me so. They are treating her for catatonic depression."

"What is *that,* Peggy?"

That's when I saw her running down the outside stairwell and heading toward my Volvo. I rolled the windows down.

"Can you please open the door, Loretha?"

I did and she got in and flopped down hard in the passenger seat, then crossed her arms.

"You mind if I smoke?"

"Yes. No. Go ahead, I don't care. First, tell me what catatonic depression is and what does it mean?"

She then reached down inside her sweatshirt, pulled out a pack of Marlboro Lights and a lighter, and lit a cigarette, inhaling like it was the last puff she'd ever have.

"It's a kind of depression that can make it so you can't move or talk, and you can just sit and stare at nothing for hours."

"What? Then how did she get to the hospital?"

"A thoughtful McDonald's employee had seen her sitting at a table for over an hour. Apparently she wasn't eating anything and she hadn't moved and she was just staring at nothing. When they asked her if she was okay and she didn't answer, they knew something was wrong and they called an ambulance."

"And this was three days ago?"

"Yes, and she might be there at least three more. She's being treated. She'll be okay once the meds kick in."

"And you're sure she's not on drugs?"

"No, but she probably needs some. I have a pretty good idea what she's going through."

"And how is that, Peggy?"

"Because she's suffering from the same thing her daddy suffered with. Depression. You didn't know that's what was wrong with Antoine?"

"No. I just thought he was moody and he drank too much and liked drugs. But when he was sober he was upbeat, which was when I liked him."

"Well, he didn't drink and do that other mess just to get high, Loretha."

"How do you know that?"

"He was self-medicating. It runs in our family but, back in the day, there was no name for it. I did the same. But I got tired of feeling purple inside and drugs didn't help, so I checked myself into a place with a ghetto plan just for folks like me. I was a mess. Jalecia reminds me so much of myself back then."

I was shocked to hear this. But I was also grateful for her honesty. "Well, I just want to make sure my daughter gets the help she needs."

"Well, let me say this, Loretha. She doesn't realize she's treating you badly because she's *sick*. I didn't speak to our parents for over a year. They pissed me off, but I couldn't tell you why. I would disappear and they couldn't find me. And back then we didn't have cellphones. I liked knowing they were worried about me. But Jalecia's not doing this intentionally to hurt you."

"Right now I'm not worried about me; it's my daughter I want to help."

"Then wait until after she comes home."

"I want her to come live with me after she's released."

"I don't know if that would be such a good idea."

"How can you say that?"

"Because Jalecia is up and down. Angry. And I don't know why, but I know she seems to like taking it out on you. She needs a psychiatrist to prescribe the right medication to help her think clearly and not feel hopeless, and a psychologist that will help her talk about her feelings. Her thoughts."

"She can talk to me. I'll listen."

"You might judge."

"No, I won't."

"Loved ones always say that. Take it from someone who knows. I know you didn't do anything to abuse her, but she might *think* you did. I know she believes you favored her brother."

"Maybe I did, but Jackson never gave me any trouble."

I was surprised to hear myself say that because I'd never really admitted it. In fact, I'd always denied it.

"I'll find her both types of doctors," I said. "But what if she doesn't want my help, Peggy?"

"Well, she can stay here with me until you can find doctors who can see her regularly. I'll convince her it's what she needs to do if she really wants to feel better. She'll listen to me. Only because she knows I don't want anything from her."

"I want to go see her."

"I would wait another day or two for the medication to kick in. Seriously."

"Then, I'll just try to be patient."

"I know I've said this before, but even though I know you're not that crazy about me, please, please trust me. And it would sure help if you could send me a few more dollars to cover food and gas. And Jalecia's car has been in the shop. Could you do that for us?"

"Yes."

"How soon?"

"Tomorrow."

"Good. Three or four hundred would surely help and I'll text you my account number so you won't have to keep going to Western Union."

I drove straight to Huntington Hospital, gave the attendant Jalecia's name and then my name and told her I was Jalecia's mother. I said I was here to see her and the attendant asked me for my ID. I gave it to her and she looked at her computer screen. I listened to her clicking the keys and scrolling down and then, when she stopped, she said, "I'm sorry but you're not on her visitation list."

"But I just found out she was admitted and I'm her mother."

"I understand. You might want to call her later to see if she can add your name to the list."

"Who *is* on the list?"

"I'm sorry, ma'am, but that information is confidential. You should call or come back tomorrow during visiting hours."

"I'll do that," I said, and stormed out.

Chapter 22

Because I had canceled two follow-up appointments with Dr. Alexopolous, I decided to keep the appointment I had scheduled with her for nine A.M. I figured I would have plenty of time since Jalecia's visiting hours didn't start until eleven A.M. I was not really in the mood to see the doctor since her new receptionist and then the doctor herself had left messages reminding me how important it was that I not miss my next appointment and also chastising me for not taking my health seriously. They said they needed to see me as soon as possible to go over the results of all my tests. But the doctor was late. And I'd been sitting in this waiting room for forty-five minutes. It was probably to punish me. In addition to worrying about my daughter, I was also a nervous wreck thinking about my A1C, which I knew without a doubt was higher than it was when I last saw her. Because no, I had not changed my diet or eating habits, and no, I had yet to incorporate regular and rigorous exercise into my life.

"Mrs. Curry, the doctor is running behind schedule and wants to know if you could possibly give her fifteen more minutes. She apologizes for the inconvenience."

"Is she here?"

"No, but she's on her way. She just left the emergency room at Huntington, so she'll be here straightaway. May I get you a bottle of water?"

"That would be nice," I said because I had forgotten my bottle in the car, rushing so I wouldn't be late.

"What's your name?" I asked.

"Jalecia," she said, and I almost lost it. She was of Spanish descent, that much I could see, and her straight black hair was down to her waist.

"Are you okay?" she asked, apparently noticing my expression.

"I'm fine. That's my daughter's name," I said.

"I love my name," she said. "Is she okay? Your face looks worried, Mrs. Curry."

"She's been struggling with depression."

I couldn't believe I just said that.

"Aren't we all?"

"You, too?"

"Oh, yes. But I got help. I'm not ashamed to admit it. It's just like any other illness. Believe me, working for a doctor helped me understand the stigma. So many people suffer from it but just think it's the way they are. I learned the hard way that it's not."

Then the phone rang and she had to answer it. Dr. Alexopolous came storming through the door, her thin hair still sticking up like a rooster, and when she saw me she said, "Hello, Mrs. Curry! I apologize for being late. I had a patient break her ankle and I had to see how much damage she'd done. Rollerblading. So good to see you after all these months! Come! Follow me back to my office. Our appointment won't take long."

My heart was pounding so loud I thought she might hear it. I was tempted to turn around and run out the door because I didn't want to hear that I might be terminally ill.

I followed Dr. Alexopolous, who was wearing a mint green

smock, and it looked like she had dyed her hair a shade darker so I couldn't see her scalp. She was now a brunette.

"Have a seat," she said.

And I did. Her office was colorful. The wall had little photos of Greece and Greek artifacts.

Dr. Alexopolous sat behind her wide oak desk and crossed her palms. "So, your tests indicate you're having second thoughts about the medication?"

"I don't know. And I owe you an apology, Doctor."

She started shaking her head.

"No, you don't. I get patients all the time who don't like my diagnoses or my prescriptions for medication that I know for a fact will help them. And like you, they lash out at me, but they often do return because I am a good doctor."

And still a bitch.

"So, how've you been feeling?"

"So-so."

"That doesn't surprise me."

"Just tell me this, Dr. Alexopolous: Am I dying?"

She looked shocked to hear these words come out of my mouth.

"What on earth would make you think that, Mrs. Curry?"

"Because I know I haven't been eating right and I haven't been taking my medication and I haven't started exercising. I know my colon is okay and my bone density and my ears are okay but . . . I'm just worried."

She pushed her chair back and walked around her desk and put her hands on my shoulders. I didn't realize I was crying and she just said, "You're not dying. But I would like to thrash you for not taking your medication because your A1C is pretty close to eight-point-five, which is too high. I don't know why it's so hard for you to take diabetes seriously. You're a smart woman, so I'm sure you did your research."

I shook my head to say, *No you're wrong,* and then nodded to say, *Right, I have done the research*. I hope she knew which was which.

"Relax, Mrs. Curry. We can get it under control if you take the suggestions I have given you a number of times over this past year."

She patted my shoulders, then gave them both a big squeeze and walked back behind her desk and sat down. She handed me a tissue.

"Are you okay now that you know you will probably live to see ninety?"

"Yes."

"Can you hear me?"

"Of course I can."

And then she laughed.

"Good, that means your hearing is good."

And I let out a chuckle.

"Is something else going on in your life?"

I folded my hands and told her about Poochie and my daughter.

"Now I understand," she said. "And if it's any consolation, depression is very common and so many people don't know they're suffering from it. What are you doing to help your daughter?"

"Nothing yet. She's been estranged from me for quite a long time. She's over at Huntington Hospital right now."

"Does she live alone?"

"No, she lives with her aunt in Compton."

"Don't say it like I should be alarmed. My husband grew up there. And don't be shocked by that either. We were married thirty-six years. How old is your daughter?"

"Forty-one," I said.

"So, is she catatonic?"

"What would make you ask that?"

"That's usually how people suffering from untreated forms of depression end up in the ER."

I nodded my head.

"Does she have any children?"

"She has a daughter. She's in her twenties."

"Is she in her daughter's life?"

"Every now and then."

"Drugs?"

"She drinks more than anything, but I really don't know what all she does. All I know is I want to help her, but I don't know if she'll accept my help."

"She will. It still might take a while, but just try to be patient. They're going to treat her and give her antidepressants, but if she doesn't take them or keeps drinking they're not going to help her. Have you been to see her yet?"

"I tried. But my name wasn't on the visitors' list."

"Try not to take that personally. Her thinking is just skewed. How many days has she been there?"

"Four, I believe."

"Then the medication has probably brought her out of catatonia, so she'll be able to talk."

"I would really like to find her a good black psychologist and psychiatrist. Preferably female. Would you happen to know of any reputable ones?"

"I do. And do this: Check your text messages in about an hour because I'd like to call them both to give them a heads-up about your daughter's situation."

Then she came around the desk again and patted me on the shoulder. "It's good that you're trying to help your daughter. Don't be discouraged if she refuses at first."

"Thank you, Dr. Alexopolous."

"But you. You have to start taking better care of yourself. Will you promise me?"

"Yes. So, that's it for me?"

"That's it. I'll see you in three months and your numbers better be good. And I want to see at least twenty pounds less of you, but preferably closer to thirty. There are some really good cookbooks for diabetics and, just so you know, you're also looking at a reformed diabetic. Am I a sixty-two-year-old sex symbol, or what?"

When I walked into the hospital, I was excited to tell Jalecia about the two reputable doctors I found for her. But she wasn't there.

"What do you mean she's not here? I was here last night and you told me to come back this morning to get added to her visitors' list."

"Well, she was picked up by a relative this morning."

"What relative?"

"I can't release that information."

"But I'm her mother."

"I'm sorry but there's nothing I can do."

As I turned to leave, I stopped dead in my tracks and turned back. "If something happens to her, I'll be back to sue you for negligence. She's not well."

I walked down to the cafeteria that looked more like a good deli and bought a slice of pepperoni pizza, a salad, a Diet Coke, and a chocolate chip cookie. Then after I slid my tray down to the cashier, I sat at an empty table and just looked at what was on it. I stood back up, picked the tray up, walked over to the trash, and dumped everything except the salad in it. Then I took my cell out and called Peggy.

"Is Jalecia with you?"

"Yes, she is."

"Why?"

"Because she asked me to pick her up."

"How?"

"She wasn't in prison, Loretha. It was a hospital. She was able to call me and she said she wanted to come back to my apartment."

"I don't believe you. Is she there? I want to speak to her."

"Just a minute."

I started tapping my right foot.

"Hi there, Ma!" she said as if she was happy to hear from me.

"Jalecia, why did you leave the hospital?"

"Because I was feeling much better. So, no need for you to be worried."

"I found two good doctors for you, Jalecia."

"For what?"

"I think it would be good if you saw a good psychologist and a psychiatrist. They're both black."

"That's nice. But I don't need to talk to any shrinks. I know why I feel the way I do."

"Really, could you please tell me?"

"Not today. I'm tired."

"I was hoping you might want to come stay with me for a while."

"I'm too old to be living with my mama. I'm comfortable here. Plus, I'm thinking of going back to school and looking for a job and I have access to the Metro here."

"Is your car still in the shop?"

"Not anymore. Aunt Peggy had my extra key and she went and got it. But her car isn't running so well."

"Well, all this sounds great. Just great. Give Peggy my best regards and I hope you two will be very fucking happy."

And I hung up.

Chapter 23

I was grateful and surprised when both doctors that Dr. Alexopolous had referred me to returned my calls. She had reached out to them and it was obvious they knew and respected each other personally and professionally. I explained my daughter's history. At least what I thought I knew. That she has had an alcohol problem. That she has been distant for years and only recently came back into my life, but even that has been from a distance. I told them she was forty-one years old. Both doctors made it clear that it could take some time before Jalecia might be willing to talk to anybody. And until then, no determination about appropriate treatment could be made. They suggested I communicate with her either by text or email and give Jalecia their numbers. And should Jalecia call either one of them, they wouldn't be able to tell me anything they discussed with her. It would be strictly confidential. I told them I understood.

I texted photos of their websites to Jalecia. And then, when I thought about it, to Peggy. I explained the who, what, and why. And I said something about hope.

A month inched by.

I did not hear a word from Jalecia or Peggy. But I continued to make deposits into Peggy's bank account.

I stayed busy overseeing the renovations of the new store, which was coming along nicely and would be finished before we left for the cruise. It was still a month away, but we had decided not to tell one another who we were bringing, mostly because some of us either didn't know or didn't want it to be known. Except, of course, Lucky. She was bringing Joe.

"Don't embarrass me when I walk into class," I said to Korynthia. "In fact don't even act like we know each other, please."

We were at the dog park watching B. B. King party with his new and old friends like he was a rock star. His new arthritis medication was starting to work.

"Maybe we don't know each other," she said, then chuckled. It was good to hear her joke. Although I was serious.

"I'm going to pretend like exercising is fun because I've been warned that if I don't start soon, one morning I'm going to have a hard time getting out of bed."

"It shouldn't take a doctor to tell you that when you've got common sense. The truth is, you're lazy as hell, Lo. But you've got a lot of company."

"I get it, sweetheart. I'll just be glad when Lucky starts losing weight, then maybe she'll bring her behind in there, too."

"You need to adjust your attitude and worry about what *you're* not doing or you're going to be spending the rest of your life alone."

"What are you talking about?"

"You've got all the symptoms of a lonely old lady and you aren't even old yet. You complain about everybody except yourself. Anyway, just to loosen up those rusty muscles, have your ass in room 10 for my hip-hop class tomorrow morning by seven thirty sharp or I will call you out."

I was surprised how many old people were in the room. I take that back. Older. Korynthia did pretend like she didn't know me, but she embarrassed me anyway.

"Looks like we have a new dancer! Introduce yourself!"

"Hello," I mumbled. "My name is Loretha."

Everybody applauded and yelled out: "Welcome to the club, Loretha!"

Korynthia winked at me. In her orange top and purple leggings she looked like she could be one of those senior models.

There were at least forty people in this room. And all different sizes and shapes, although at least half of them looked pretty damn fit. It also looked like the rainbow coalition in here, which was refreshing. I was standing between a black fella who looked somewhat familiar and a handsome white guy who looked like an old wrestler.

"You know the drill, ladies and gentlemen! Let's warm those muscles up first, and remember, take it slow," Korynthia said, and everybody in the room started swaying to the left and then the right, raising their arms and rotating their ankles and bending their knees and making their fingertips touch the hardwood floor. I was confused but just tried to imitate Korynthia, which was impossible, so I watched everybody else. They all looked like they'd been doing these exercises all their lives. But what *was* clear to me after those first few sways and bends was I should not have worn a thick sweat suit because I was already sweating like a pig and we hadn't even started dancing. I had wanted to hide what I wanted to lose.

Finally, the music started.

And Korynthia started yelling into the microphone that was strapped on her head. With each song she demanded that we move this way and that way. Some folks could and some couldn't but they all moved, including the black guy on my left and the wrestler on my right.

I had forgotten how to move my hips. I was having a hard time proving I had rhythm. I got confused when I tried to get the top of my body and the bottom to do two different things. My body knows how old it is and my mind was telling it you cannot trick nature. But I resented the weak side of my mind telling me what I can and cannot do, so I took a few deep breaths and when I heard one of my old favorites, "Don't You Worry 'Bout a Thing" by Stevie Wonder, my hips and feet got a second wind and they just mimicked what Korynthia was doing. Then my body realized it had a memory and I swirled and flexed and twisted, and before I knew it, I heard Korynthia say, "Good class! See you next week. Stay loose!"

I did not say goodbye to Korynthia, except by making eye contact. She managed to give me a thumbs-up, which I knew I had not earned, but I just winked at her as if to say, *I showed up.*

When I got home, I fell across the bed to relax and congratulated myself for just walking into the class. And while I lay there and dreamed about the moves I was going to master in the next two or three classes, I felt B. B. King nudging my still-socked-and-sneakered feet to let him out.

Our usual dinner would have felt off now that Poochie was gone, so we decided to have Sunday brunch. At the Langham hotel. Under the covered terrace. Where a couple was going to be married under the archway in a matter of hours. Where people were already enjoying the pool and would soon be kicked out. Where, back in the day, movie stars used to hang out and hide out in bungalows. Where I spent the night once when I was mad at Carl for not remembering to tell me he was going on a two-day fishing trip until he was on it. I'd rented a suite, had a massage and a facial, and sat in the steam room melting away my anger. And when I got back to my room there was a bouquet of flowers almost as tall as me waiting with a note asking if I would please forgive him and meet him downstairs on the patio for brunch. The patio where I was now sitting with Lucky, Sadie, and Korynthia.

"Snap out of it," Lucky said.

"I'm out of it," I said.

We were all dressed up. We looked pretty. And we knew it. We were doing this for Poochie, who loved to look fancy whenever she could.

"So," Lucky said. "I haven't seen you huzzies in almost a month and we agreed before we came not to be mushy and sentimental or talk about anything that will depress us, right?"

We all nodded.

"Then let's eat," Lucky said.

And we walked over to the buffet, which looked like the Last Supper. Everybody filled their plates and we were shocked that Lucky beat us back to the table and her plate was not only not full, but the only things on it were cottage cheese, scrambled eggs, a small piece of chicken breast, and a peach that she was already cutting.

"Are you sick?" Sadie asked.

"You did it, didn't you?" Korynthia asked.

I looked at Lucky and knew the answer.

"Yes. A month ago. Just after Poochie."

"Why the hell didn't you tell us?" I asked.

"Yeah," Korynthia said. "What if something had happened and we didn't even know you were in the fucking hospital?"

"I agree," Sadie said. "This was pretty inconsiderate, but we're glad to see you."

"Yes, we are, and I thought it looked like there was less of you," I said.

"Me, too. But I didn't want to say anything," Sadie said.

"So, how do you feel?" I asked.

"Good. I'll tell you all something, though. I don't know what I'd do without Joe. He has been so thoughtful and patient. If I had known this was all I needed to do to get his attention I'd've done it years ago."

"That's not the reason," Ko said.

"Then, what?" Lucky asked, but not in her usual nasty tone. In fact, she actually sounded curious.

"He just wanted to get the woman he married back, and not the size of your body but the size of your heart."

"Oh, shut up," Lucky moaned, with tears falling from her eyes right on top of that pile of disgusting cottage cheese.

"Okay, remember what we said we weren't going to do today? Nothing sentimental!" I said and grabbed for Sadie's napkin because mine had fallen on the floor, but Sadie was using it to wipe her eyes so I just pulled the edge of the tablecloth up to mine, dried them, and stuffed the corner back under the table.

"But these are happy tears. We are proud of you," Sadie said.

"Yes, we are," Ko said. "So how much have you lost?"

"About thirty-six-and-a-half pounds."

Then Lucky started laughing. It was nice to see.

"So, that means a string bikini by summer then, huh?" Ko asked.

"I'll wear it when I go down that slide on the cruise, and finally everybody will know I'm not a whale."

"Stop that right now, Lucky," Sadie said.

"I'm sorry. I'm working on being more positive. Rome wasn't built in a day. And I know that's a cliché, but it's the best I've got."

"Okay, let's eat and say whatever we feel the need to share that's going on in our lives, but make it short because I need to be home by four," I said.

"Hot date?" Ko asked.

"Yes. And they can't talk yet."

"Then, why don't you start, Miss Motor Mouth?" Ko said.

"Hold on!" Lucky said. "I'll go. I have signed up to take a writing class at Pasadena City College."

We all just looked at Lucky like maybe she was losing weight too fast.

"And Joe and I are thinking of selling our house and moving to Panama or Costa Rica next year."

We just kept looking at her like: *Are you fucking serious?*

I took a long sip of my detoxifying apple-cucumber-celery-spinach-cranberry-pomegranate drink, and then stared at my steel-cut oatmeal with no raisins and definitely no brown sugar. I then looked up at Lucky again and realized she was serious.

"Where the hell is Costa Rica again?" I asked. "And what's wrong with Pasadena?"

"Nothing," Lucky said. "Joe and I just feel like we could get us a boat and . . ."

"And what?" Korynthia said, who sounded like she was really pissed. "Walk around in banana leaves and eat coconuts? Do they get Hulu and Netflix down there? Do they have a Whole Foods? How do they feel about mixed marriages in Panama or Costa-fucking-Rica? Have you looked into that? And what about hurricanes? Do you not watch the fucking news, Lucky?"

This was something coming from Korynthia, who'd almost abandoned us for San Diego.

"I think you should do whatever you and Joe want to do," I heard myself say, even though I didn't mean it and I knew Lucky and Joe weren't moving to any Panama or Costa Rica.

"Thank you, Loretha."

"Wait. One more thing," I said, and took the last sip of my detoxifier. "If you move I will kick your ass and never speak to you again. And I will push Joe down the hill so he lands in front of a bicyclist doing forty miles an hour on the outside lane at the Rose Bowl."

"I get it, ladies. You love me and you'll miss me. We have not bought our tickets yet, so please, slow your roll. Ko, why don't you share something uplifting with us?"

"She has to finish that Hawaiian French toast with the rum-battered Kona-coffee whipped cream and pineapple marmalade because she doesn't have diabetes and she teaches a hip-hop class, and a tone-and-body-sculpt class on the side, and she is the only one of us who is having sex," I said.

"Well, that's pretty fucking uplifting," Lucky said and started laughing. It was good to hear her swear, which meant we hadn't completely lost her to the light side.

"Sadie?" I said. "Beam us up while Korynthia eats all the calories she wants and I will finish eating my delicious oatmeal, which would be much better with sugar and raisins."

"I've finally met the right person."

"And?" Korynthia asked, now that she was finished chewing.

"And, she's perfect."

"Well, it's about fucking time!" I said.

"What took you so long?" Lucky asked.

"What's her name? Is she pretty? Is she black? Not that we really care. How old is she? Does she go to your church?" I asked, and then took a breath.

"All your questions will be answered on the cruise," Sadie said, with a smile we never saw when she told us about the minister.

"I say love who you want to love," Ko said. "Speaking of which, I'm in love, too!"

"I didn't say I was in love," Sadie said.

"Well, I am. And I'm going with the flow even though he's younger than I am and . . ."

"How much younger?" Lucky asked.

"He's sixty-five."

"You cradle robber!" Lucky said.

The young waitress, who had been listening to every word, had to cover her mouth as she refilled our water glasses because she was laughing so hard.

"Yes, we're crazy old ladies," I said.

"I hope to be as wild and crazy as you all when I hit fifty," she said, and we gave her high fives.

Chapter 24

I was somewhat relieved when Cinnamon called to tell me the twins were coming down with something and not to come.

"We will pay you anyway," she said.

"And I prefer cash," I said as I pulled into my driveway. I was shocked to see Jalecia's car there. I didn't want to say anything to Cinnamon but heard myself say, "Take care of the little ones, and your mom is parked in my driveway."

"I know. She's been waiting for you for at least an hour. But please don't freak out, Grandma, because I think you might be relieved to hear what she has to say. Really. Love you."

I pulled up beside her and wondered if it was safe to smile despite what Cinnamon had just said. Jalecia got out of the car and I was surprised at how peaceful she looked. I hadn't seen this look on her face in so long I couldn't even remember. Her eyes were clear and her skin looked like she had had a facial or was wearing good makeup. She even had on lip gloss. Her lips looked just like mine: full and shaped like a wide heart. She was wearing the black gauze dress she wore to Carl's celebration of life. The nose ring was gone and her nails were manicured and painted clear. Something *was* going on.

B. B. King started barking from inside the kitchen door as I found myself staring at my daughter.

"Hi, Ma. Don't be scared."

I closed my car door softly.

"I'm not," I said. "I'm just surprised to see you here, but glad to see you. Are you okay? You look good. Better."

"I'm going to be."

I walked over to give her a hug and was nervous and afraid that she might not hug me back, but she did. In fact, she hugged me harder than I ever remember her hugging me.

When she let go, or I should say when we finally let each other go, she stepped back and said, "Maybe you should let B. B. King join us?"

And then she actually smiled.

I walked up the few steps, opened the door, and B. B. King came dashing out, his tail wagging, and he licked my hands and then licked Jalecia's, something I hadn't seen him do in eons.

"Hi there, B.B.," she said, and rubbed his ears like she meant for it to feel good.

"So," I said. "Do you want to come in?"

"No, I'd rather sit here on the steps. I can't stay long."

"You have somewhere you need to be?"

"Yes."

"Where, if you don't mind my asking?"

"I'm going to a treatment program."

This made me sit down on the top step.

"A treatment program for what, Jalecia?"

"A lot of things."

I just sat there because I could tell she had thought about what she needed to say and I wanted to give her enough air to say it.

"Something is wrong with me, Ma. With the way I think. The way I feel. I often feel like I'm drowning. And I've been feeling this way for a long time but too ashamed to tell you or anybody, which is why I think I drink too much even though I don't always like feeling drunk.

But thanks to both of those wonderful and smart doctors you were thoughtful enough to find, what I know now is that I've been depressed for years, which is why it's been so hard for me to control my behavior. I've learned that it would do me a lot of good to take some time to understand it."

"This is so good to hear, Jalecia. So, what more can you do besides what you're already doing?"

"Dr. Gordon, she's the psychiatrist, suggested that a twenty-eight-day inpatient treatment program could help me get properly diagnosed."

"You mean you'd live there for twenty-eight days?"

"Yes."

"But why can't you just go during the day?"

"This place has a whole program to help folks dealing with all kinds of mental health issues learn how to manage them and understand them, and part of that is withdrawing totally from your normal life. I want to know what's going on inside my head that's been making me self-medicate."

"Where is it?"

"All I'm comfortable saying is that it's close to water. And thanks to you, insurance covers almost all of it."

"And you're sure about this?"

"I'm more than sure, Ma. I'm tired of doing and saying hurtful things to you when inside I don't really feel that way. I'm tired of not being a good mother and now grandmother, and I want to stop feeling hopeless and powerless and sad and angry when I shouldn't. I haven't been abused or suffered any major trauma but it feels like I have. The medication they gave me helps, but there's more to it that a pill can't help me solve, and I want to stop this train before I'm totally derailed. I sound like a shrink, don't I?"

And she started laughing. And so did I. We hugged each other and sat there rocking until B. B. King started feeling left out and tried to wiggle his way between us.

We broke apart.

"So, when do you go?"

"Check-in is in three hours."

"Check-in?"

"It's not like *Cuckoo's Nest,* Ma. This is voluntary."

"So, are you driving yourself there? Would you like me to drive you? I can. I don't care how far it is."

"No, I appreciate it, but I don't want you to know where I am until after I finish the twenty-eight days. And I will finish."

"And how does your aunt Peggy feel about this?"

"Not happy."

"Really? I'm surprised to hear that."

"Well, one thing I've already learned is that sometimes people act like they want to help you when what they really like is knowing you need it. Aunt Peggy has some issues of her own that have been ignored, too. But I'm grateful because I might have been dead if it wasn't for her."

"I've been trying to help you, too, Jalecia."

"I know but I didn't want your help because I didn't think I needed it."

"So, what can *I* do to help you?"

"Can I park my car in your garage for a month?"

And she actually started laughing.

I was just happy to see the light in her eyes.

I had forgotten that Kwame's car was in there, but I was not about to bring that up, so I just said, "Absolutely."

"And I might have a small bill for what insurance won't cover for the treatment facility."

"You're worth it, Jalecia. And I'm so proud of you for doing this."

"Thank you, Ma, and I want you to know how sorry I am for all the mean things I've done that have hurt you. When I come back, I hope I will have learned why I did them and how to stop."

"Don't worry about that right now."

"There's my Uber," she said and pointed to the white Impala coming up the street.

She signaled to the driver, who pulled up behind her car as she popped open the trunk. He took two large suitcases out and put them in the Impala. She then handed me the keys.

"Can I visit you?"

"You can but I don't want you to."

"What about phone calls?"

She shook her head.

"You can change your mind, though, can't you?"

"I'm not leaving there until I feel like I have figured out what I need to do to live a healthy life."

And she kissed me on the lips.

And I kissed her back.

"So, you know she's gone," Peggy said when she called me.

"I know," I said.

"She called you?"

"No, she came by."

"Do you know where this place is she's going?"

"Yes," I lied.

"Why didn't she tell me, then?"

"Let me just say this, Peggy. She's somewhere safe. And she's getting the help she probably needed a long time ago."

"She'll be back," was all she said.

"Don't get your hopes up too high."

"Well, she owes me about three hundred dollars."

"She doesn't *owe* you three hundred anything, Peggy. What would've been more ethical was if you'd just admitted that you needed help, but since you tried to make my daughter your dependent, now that she's not, your bank account with me is closed. Goodbye, Peggy."

And I hung up.

But I put five hundred dollars in it anyway. Just because.

"Mama-Lo! It's me! Kwame! I'm coming back! Please call me back at your earliest convenience. Moms is doing much better but she's going to need care and I'm bringing her with me because she deserves to have a better life for the rest of her life and I'm willing to do everything I can to make sure of it. I only have one mom. My bad, you make two. Love you. And hope you're well."

And there were more voicemails.

"Mama-Lo, I forgot to mention that my moms gets social security and Medi-Cal or Medicare—I get them mixed up—but if you know of any of those senior facility places that take it, that would be great."

And:

"Mama-Lo, I know I'm probably getting on your nerves, but I forgot to tell you that because I'll be back in time, I can still take two classes at LACC this summer! I'm psyched! And guess what else? Boone says he wants to come back to L.A. because ain't nothing—I mean—nothing is happening for him in Flint and his girl drop-kicked him to the curb, so he said he's willing to give L.A. another chance. That's it. No more voice messages. I promise! Tell B. B. King I said woof woof!"

I couldn't call him back because I was in the shop and the workers were drilling and hammering and asking me a million questions I couldn't answer, and I couldn't go outside because it was pouring—something it rarely does in Southern California—and the awnings weren't up yet, so I decided to send a text. *Great news! At new shop! Drilling going on. Raining! Glad you're bringing your mama. I know of a good senior facility. Tell me when to start looking for an opening for her. I'm going on a short cruise next month. Are you sure about Boone?*

I decided to buy myself a treadmill. I've only been on it four times, because it was boring and made me feel lonely. I like going to Korynthia's hip-hop class better. She's also threatened to hurt me if I don't start coming to her tone-and-body-sculpt class, so I told her I would after we come back from the cruise. Lord knows I'm dreading it because I don't like the idea of bending and lifting weights and getting down on the floor on my back and then getting back up with a whole lot of folks looking at me when I do something wrong or when I can't do a movement at all. The treadmill is for when I want to sweat in the privacy of my own home.

But I don't want to be old and fat.

And I don't want to end up in a wheelchair.

And when I die, I don't want it to be because of some stupid shit I did to myself. Or because of what I didn't do for myself. And from the looks of things it does not look like we get a do-over.

Chapter 25

It's been hard trying not to worry about Jalecia but it's been three weeks and I was hoping she might have reached out by now, especially since we're scheduled to leave on the cruise soon and I'm worried about whether she's still at that place and if it's helping her. I was hoping she might be feeling good enough to call just to give me a clue how she's doing. I suppose I'd know if she had changed her mind and left because she would've picked up her car. Against my better judgment I decided to call my BFF.

"That was very kind of you to put all that money into my account, Loretha. And not only did I appreciate it, I needed it. Did you get my thank-you card?"

"You're quite welcome, Peggy. And I apologize for being such a bitch that day. I do appreciate everything you've done to help my daughter. I'm not sure if I got your card because I don't check my mail that often, but I'll take a look."

I walked over to Carl's chair, slid the basket close to me, and started sifting through all the envelopes. There were quite a few from Ma, which was a relief that she had decided to start sending them again, and as I flipped through more junk mail than anything, I came across a small yellow envelope that looked like a party invitation.

"Have you heard anything from Jalecia since she went to the treatment place?" she asked, as I slit open the envelope and saw the little card with a colorful bouquet of flowers that said: THANK YOU and inside: BUNCHES AND BUNCHES.

I was touched.

"No. Have you?"

"No. But I wouldn't worry. Not hearing from her is a good sign. I think she's serious, because after she started seeing those doctors she did not miss an appointment. You know you can't call them to get any information, but I'm just glad they're black. I apologize for sounding so negative about Jalecia getting treatment because I was just thinking that she might not want to be bothered with me anymore, but this is why I've also been thinking I could probably use a mental tune-up myself."

"Well, if either of us hears from her, let's just let each other know. How's that?"

"Great. I'll do that."

"Boone bailed, Mama-Lo. And it's a good thing because I don't have time to babysit him."

I had to admit to myself that I was relieved, but I just said, "He just didn't seem suited for Southern California. So, tell me, when will you and your mom be here?"

"Day after tomorrow."

"That's two days from now, Kwame! I thought you were going to give me a heads-up."

"I just did. But not to worry, Mama-Lo, we can stay at a motel."

"No, you will not. I've got two empty bedrooms. Well, one—my new treadmill is in one. But fortunately, it's not being used much.

Wait, what is your mother's name? I've only heard you refer to her as Moms."

"Carolyn. Carolyn Bledsoe."

"How old is your mom? I don't think you ever told me, not that you had any reason to."

"She just made fifty-five, Mama-Lo. But you wouldn't know it looking at her. She's been through a lot."

Fifty-five? I was trying to do the math in my head. How old was Carl back then? But it wasn't really all that important. It was still before me.

"Well, we'll figure this all out, Kwame. So please don't worry. I was going to start looking into it, but I didn't know your timing."

"Are you sure it's okay for us to stay with you? Seems like I'm always imposing; and I don't mean to, but you're all we've got."

We've.

That was so refreshing to hear.

"Don't worry about anything, Kwame. Just tell me what time you're getting in and I'll pick you up."

"No, we can Uber! It's what has kept me from starving in Flint and I can get reinstated in Los Angeles. But thank you so much, Mama-Lo. We get in about nine P.M. We'll call you when we're on our way. I love you."

"I love you, too, Kwame."

When I heard B. B. King barking, I looked in the driveway and saw Lucky sitting in her brand-new white Range Rover. I opened the kitchen door and walked down the steps as she rolled her window down.

"So, is this a late-night life crisis or something?"

She started shaking her head. Then tapped the steering wheel with her palm.

"I have made too many wrong turns," she said, and opened her door and got out. Was that a black bathrobe she was wearing?

"What's going on, Lucky?" I asked, worried about what she was going to say. I gave her a hug. Lucky smelled like mint.

I could hear B. B. King crying but I was not letting him out.

"Have you been smoking?" I asked.

"Yes. I needed something."

"Then maybe I don't want to talk to you since you're under the influence."

"Then don't. But I need to eat something sweet and I need to spend the night."

"For the second time: What the fuck is going on, Lucky?"

"Can you make B.B. shut up? He's getting on my nerves."

I ran up the steps and let him out.

"He lives here and he knows something is wrong, so if he wants to cry he can cry."

"Is that dog ever going to die?" she asked. "I didn't mean that. I'm sorry, B.B."

"See what I mean? That shit gives you Tourette's. You say whatever comes into your head, which is usually something mean-spirited but not what's really in your heart!"

"Do you have to yell, Loretha?"

"What's in here?" I asked, grabbing the In-N-Out bag of what I knew was probably a double cheeseburger and French fries. It fell to the ground and B. B. King snatched the bag and ran with it to the side of the garage. I was in no mood to stop him.

Then Lucky walked over to B.B.'s water dish and threw up in it. B. B. King dashed over and just looked at her as if to ask, *Are you crazy? That's my water dish.* Then he looked at me wondering if I was going to do anything about this.

"Sit," I said to him.

And he sat.

When Lucky stood up she looked at me and said, "I don't want to move to any fucking Costa Rica or Panama. That was all Joe's idea. I told him I'm not leaving my friends and he said he would go without me."

"He didn't mean it."

"Oh, yes he did."

"Come on in."

"I feel sick. My stomach hurts. And I need to drink some water and just lie down, Lo. I fucked up. I should never have smoked that weed. And I'm sorry for doing this to you."

I put my arms around her and walked her into the house and into the guest bedroom, where she sat down on the bed Jalecia had slept in.

"Don't move," I said, and walked back to the kitchen to get a bottle of water from the fridge. I didn't know if I could handle a whole night of Lucky.

"Did you bring anything to sleep in?" I asked, and handed her the bottle, which she drank completely.

"No. I sleep in my underwear, but don't worry, you don't have to look at me. I could use a robe."

"You're wearing a robe."

She looked down as if she was surprised.

"Just get into bed, Lucky."

But she just sat there.

"I'm not sleepy."

"Then go on back home," I said, not really meaning it. "No. Sleep that dope off. Then tomorrow morning talk to your husband, and stand your ground without being a bitch."

Just then I heard my phone ding with a text message. I started to panic thinking it may have been Jalecia, but when I pulled it out of my pocket I was relieved to see it was from Jackson.

Mom, are you still coming in June? We haven't heard back from you in a while and we want to see you! We've moved into a bigger place, which is still small by American standards but we now have an extra room and the girls are saying "Nana" when we show them your picture!

I texted him back and gave him a firmer date I would confirm as soon as I knew when the new shop was going to open.

"I'm finally going to Tokyo!" I said to Lucky and B. B. King.

But Lucky was snoring and B. B. King, who had been lying next to my feet, just looked up at me as if to ask: *Where is Tokyo?*

Lucky was gone when I woke up. I was surprised I didn't hear her leave, or B. B. King whimper or something when she opened the side door. I peeked inside the bedroom and could tell she hadn't even gotten under the covers. I texted her because I didn't feel like talking.

"I hope you came to your senses, Lucky. I thought we were all trying to be more reasonable."

With Lucky gone, I remembered I was supposed to go to the hip-hop class. Lord knows I didn't want Korynthia to curse me out for missing it.

I ate an apple. And half of a whole wheat English muffin that I toasted and spread this stuff called ghee that Jonas told me to buy instead of butter. It tasted like butter but better. I wanted a glass of orange juice so bad I could almost taste it. I didn't have any because I had stopped buying it, but I had yet to figure out what I was supposed to drink instead of it.

Maybe I'll find the answer in one of the million books on diabetes I ordered from Amazon. I think it would be helpful if there was a Diabetics Anonymous where you could meet people struggling with this disease, and we could share tips and not feel so bad if we slipped and had a chocolate chip cookie or a juicy cheeseburger with fries and a vanilla shake.

I had already decided I was not trying to be perfect, but I wanted to prove to myself, Dr. Alexopolous, and my friends—and especially Poochie—that I was finally starting to take this disease, and this third act of my life, seriously.

"Welcome, Loretha!" Korynthia just had to yell, embarrassing the hell out of me. "We've missed you and we've got some new moves, right, ladies and gentlemen?"

And they all screamed: "Yes, we do!"

"But first, let's warm up."

And we warmed up.

And the black guy who occasionally found his way into my row waved at me. He had some good moves and he was friendly, but not overly friendly, which was why I was also friendly to him. But when he eased his way back to my row and stood next to me, I asked where the wrestler was by pointing to the empty spot. When he said he had recently moved to Costa Rica to retire I almost choked.

"Why is everybody moving to Costa Rica?"

"I've been a few times and it's not a bad place to retire. It's beautiful, but I like it here. How have you been? It's Loretha, isn't it?"

"Yes, and to be honest I don't remember you telling me your name."

"I did but you don't remember because you thought I was forgettable."

"That's not true. What is it?"

"Excuse me, James and Ms. Loretha! Are we warmed up? Am I breaking something up?"

I wanted to give her the finger. But instead I said, "I was having a problem and James was kind enough to help me solve it."

"This is how it starts," she said, embarrassing the hell out of me.

I left during the cooldown so I wouldn't have to say goodbye to James.

I wanted to find out if there was any availability at Valley View Assisted Living for Carolyn. Fortunately, I knew the director and I stopped by unannounced, knowing Ma would be in her aerobics class in a different wing. Luckily, there were vacancies. I had tried to convince Ma to get a one-bedroom, but she had said, "I spent my whole life going from room to room. I don't want to walk anywhere but the bathroom." I knew how much Ma's studio cost, and because Carolyn would have to wait at least a year before her Medicaid would take effect in California, I didn't mind paying for her to have a one-bedroom until then. I was just glad I could afford it. Also, considering who Carolyn was, it seemed fitting. And when Jalecia finished her treatment, if she needed help finding a place, I'd do the same for her. Anything to stop her from going back to live with Peggy. If she wants to stay with me until she feels strong enough to live on her own, she can have a key.

Although Kwame had sent me Carolyn's medical records, the director advised me that a California doctor would have to verify them, give her another medical assessment, then provide that one to Valley View. She could move in as soon as the director received them. I was pretty sure Carolyn would be comfortable living here, especially the access to physical therapy and prepared meals, not to mention being around other people, not all of whom were on their deathbeds.

I had let the housekeepers go after Carl passed because I needed something to keep me busy. But I hardly ever cleaned the other two bedrooms, and since I wasn't sure how long Kwame or his mother might need to stay, I called the housekeepers and they were kind enough to help me out on short notice.

The next day, I left the key under the mat and a check for more than what I used to pay them. I also asked if they would like to start coming again on a regular basis and Consuela sent me a text and said of course, that her team of three had missed me and B. B. King.

I spent most of the day at the shop because the painters were almost finished and the new color-stained concrete floors were in; and as soon as I got back from the cruise the new makeup stations and the product stations would be installed. I rehired the two young ladies who had worked at the Los Angeles store, Tanisha and Koi, who were excited when they saw the changes I was making in this new House.

"This place is going to rock!"

"Too bad you couldn't have blown it up like this in L.A."

I'm also going to hire someone to handle the day-to-day operations because I just can't supervise everything anymore. It's not just because I'm too old to do so much, but because I don't want to. This time around I want to have more fun and be more personable. I'm excited about watching how the new House will flourish and the new clientele we're bound to attract. I hired a smart website designer and once we've got everything in its place, I'm hopeful we'll be able to attract more folks who want to be pampered.

I have three interested buyers for the L.A. store and I've explained to all of them that I am in the process of opening a new store, and if they'd be willing to give me another month, we could meet then.

They agreed.

I saw the Uber lights pull in to the driveway and B. B. King almost knocked me down when I opened the front door and headed down the steps. Kwame looked like he'd grown. And when he walked around the black Explorer and held out his hand, his mother gracefully held hers out and Kwame gently pulled her out of the car to a standing position. I could not believe how tiny she looked next to him—a little more than five feet, give or take an inch or two. Her hair was braided in thick tendrils and stopped at her shoulders. From behind her silver-framed glasses I could tell she had been through a lot, but I could still see her beauty. Her blue jeans were a little baggy and so was the floral top under her white denim jacket. We would just try to help keep her spirits high.

After Kwame handed her a cane, she waved at me like I was leaving.

"Hi there, Loretha!" she yelled. "We made it!"

Kwame walked her over to me, bent down, and gave me a big hug. "Hello, Mama-Lo," he said. "This is my mom, Carolyn."

B. B. King edged his way between us.

"Hey, B.B. Looks like you missed me, huh, fella? I missed you, too!"

I walked over to Carolyn and gave her a hug. She must've felt my sincerity because she squeezed me as tight as she could with one arm.

"Welcome to California, Carolyn. Can I help you inside?"

"Oh, no, sweetheart. I can manage with this," and she held up her cane.

As Kwame pulled four or five suitcases from the back of the SUV, I put my arm through Carolyn's and we tiptoed up the stairs.

"Thank you," she said. "Going down is a lot easier. What a beautiful neighborhood you live in. This feels like a dream, you know."

I pushed the front door open and she gasped. I thought maybe she'd seen a mouse or something.

"Is something wrong?"

"No, your home is just beautiful, Loretha. Kwame told me it was, and he said you have a pool in the backyard, too."

"Everybody has pools in Pasadena," I said to make her feel like this was standard. I wanted to say, *Wait until you see San Marino or Valley View, where you're going to be living—they're not so shabby either.*

"Are you hungry? Tired? You want to see where your room is?"

She pressed her hand against her chest.

"My room," she said softly. "I can't believe I'm even here. In California. Thank you, Loretha. I would like to unpack my overnight bag, brush my teeth, and put some drops in my eyes. Just show me where."

And I did.

I gave her the blue bedroom, even though Kwame used to sleep in there, because it was bigger. I had left a lamp on and she just sat down on the bed as if to catch her breath.

"Thank you," she said again. "For everything."

"You're quite welcome."

"Hey there!" Kwame said. "So you really started my car up every now and then, Mama-Lo?"

"I told you I had," even though I wasn't telling the complete truth. When I put Jalecia's car in the garage, I had to move his over to make room but it wouldn't start. So I called AAA, and they gave his a jump and I let it run for hours. But after that, I took to starting it up and letting it run for ten to twenty minutes, which AAA had told me was long enough.

"Thank you," he said.

"Do you need to go somewhere?"

"I do. But just for a few hours. Do you remember my friend Parker?"

"Of course I do."

"I'm going to give him a shout."

I wanted to say *I bet you'll both be doing more than shouting,* but I just said, "You young folks have more energy than the Energizer Bunny."

He walked over and bent down and gave his mother a kiss, and then me. "This used to be my room, I'll have you know, woman!"

"Be safe," Carolyn said, and then leaned over and whispered in my ear. "He told me about Parker. I don't mind him liking boys, but I just wish he could find a black one."

"Kwame!" I shouted. "Just remember that you and your mother have a doctor's appointment tomorrow afternoon and then I want to take her to see the gorgeous place she will hopefully be living in. It's much nicer than here."

"I have to see that to believe it. How far is it from here, Loretha?"

"Fourteen minutes."

She looked relieved.

"I'll be back before daylight," he said, and we heard the door slam.

"I'm sure you're exhausted, Carolyn, so just make yourself at home. If you're hungry I bought some snacks to tide you over until morning, but I admit, I don't have a whole lot of sweets."

"I don't eat anything with sugar," she said to my surprise. "I'm diabetic."

"Me, too!" I said like we had just seen the same movie or something. "Kwame didn't tell me you were diabetic."

"He didn't know until he came home."

"Was it hard?"

"Yes, but I have learned what I can live without."

I squeezed her hand, and she squeezed mine back.

"I also want to thank you for everything you've done for my son, and now me."

"You're quite welcome, Carolyn. He's Carl's son, which makes him my son, too. It's sad to me that Carl never got to know him."

"Wait a minute. Hold on now. What makes you think Carl is Kwame's daddy?"

My stomach dropped.

"Because Kwame told me he was."

"No no no no no! I never told him that. Carl's brother Earl is Kwame's daddy."

"Earl, who died in a car accident twelve years ago?"

"That's him. Back in the day I had a thing going on the side with Earl. I admit after a hard night of partying I woke up one morning and didn't know how Carl had got in my bed, but I was already pregnant. I was pretty low back then, so maybe somebody did see me and Carl that night and just assumed, or maybe I did tell somebody Carl was his daddy. Anything to keep Earl's wife from suspecting, you know what I mean? But I never in a million years thought Carl was going to die and the whole damn family would come out here thinking they was just telling Kwame the truth. I'm sorry."

"Damn."

She couldn't possibly have made this shit up. I felt sorry for her and for Kwame, but when I thought about it, did it really matter that Carl wasn't his real father? No, it did not.

I put my arms around her and we walked to the kitchen. I found some microwave popcorn and grabbed two bottles of sparkling water from the refrigerator, and we sat on the couch until it was all gone.

Chapter 26

I was at Nordstrom Rack in the dressing room trying on the first of six one-piece bathing suits with the hope of finding two or three that might not make me look like a bear, even though I had no intention of getting in the pool. I was pairing them with solid-color wraps when I felt my phone shiver in my purse. I pulled it out and couldn't believe it when I saw a text from JALECIA DRUMMOND, and underneath it the first line said: *Hi Mom. Please check your email.*

As I opened it, my heart was pounding so hard I had to press my palm against it. I sat down on the bench in the bathing suit, took a deep breath, and read the first line twice:

> *Hi Mom. I just want you to know this is one of the smartest things I've ever done in my life. I am learning so much about myself and about depression and coping techniques. They even have a music class and I've been singing and playing the piano even though I can't sing anymore! Anyway, I'm also sending you this email to let you know I have decided to do another twenty-eight-day session because I am sure by then I'll be ready to greet the world with a whole new set of skills. I love you, and will see you in a month. Love, Jalecia. P.S. If I had known*

these kinds of places existed, I would've done this years ago. I hope you are taking your diabetes medication and exercising (which we do a lot of here!). Tell B. B. King and all my aunties I said hi. I already reached out to Cinnamon and can't wait to see my grandbabies. I feel so lucky, and for the first time in years I'm happy to be alive. Love you. Jalecia

I grabbed a wrap, tied it around me, and ran as fast as I could to the ladies' room where I opened a stall and sat down on the toilet and dropped my head into both palms and started crying like a baby until someone said, "Are you all right in there?"

I pulled off too much toilet paper and wiped my eyes and said, "Yes, I'm fine. These are tears of joy and thank you very much for asking."

She tapped on the door three more times as if to say, *Right on!*

I went back to the dressing room and was shocked that everything was just where I'd left it, including my purse. I bought three bathing suits and two cover-ups and thought I looked good in them.

In fact, it felt like I'd lost ten pounds.

Probably because I had.

"What did you buy from my favorite store?" I heard my sister's voice say from behind me. I was tossing my shopping bag on the back seat. She looked pretty and sounded perky for a change.

"Hi, Odessa," I said. "Bathing suits."

"Really? For your pool?"

"No, I'm going on a cruise."

"Where to?"

"Mexico."

She laughed.

"Have you ever been on a cruise?"

"Of course not, Loretha."

"Would you like to go on one?"

"You're not actually asking me, are you?"

"Yes," I heard myself say.

"Are you serious?"

"Yes."

"How many days?"

"Three."

"When?"

"Four days from now."

"Really? How much will it cost?"

"It's free. Except for drinks."

"You know I don't drink."

"Nobody would be forcing you to."

She waved her palm forward and then downward.

"Well, I might have a glass of wine."

I thought I was going to pass out on the hot asphalt.

"Well, a little wine never hurt."

"Will I have my own cabin?"

"No, you'll have to share it with me."

"Are you serious, Loretha?"

"Yes."

"We haven't slept in the same room since we were ten."

"Eleven," I said.

"What made you ask me?"

"Because you're my sister. Isn't that a good enough reason?"

"But you don't like me."

"I love you. Liking you is difficult."

If I wasn't mistaken, it looked like her eyes were tearing up. I couldn't believe I had just asked my sister to go on a cruise with me. I hadn't really thought who I would invite because I'd been so busy with Kwame's mother, the new shop, exercising, reading about diabetes, and learning how to cook and eat. So running into my sister in the parking lot of one of her favorite stores was a happy coincidence. In light of everything that's happened this year, it's about time Odessa and I started treating each other like sisters instead of adversaries. It felt like this was probably the reason Poochie had given me my extra ticket.

"So, do you want to come or not?"

"Was I your last choice?"

"Come on, Odessa. No. You're the only one I've asked. We need to stop this thing between us. Can we, please?"

She looked down at the asphalt and then back at me.

"I've forgotten how to be nice, Loretha."

"Well, it's not hard. So, is that a yes?"

"And all of your girlfriends are going to be on it, too?"

"Yes, including Poochie."

"But I thought she passed away."

"She did, but what's left of her is coming and we're going to officially say goodbye to her. She bought my extra ticket and I believe she'd be happy knowing I was bringing you."

And then Odessa hugged me. I couldn't remember the last time I wanted to hug her.

Until now.

So I did.

We had agreed to meet at the cruise ship, which looked like the *Titanic* to me, but it appeared that I was the first one to arrive. After waiting twenty minutes I decided to go on through security and as soon as I walked out to what was the main deck there was a band greeting me and about forty other folks. When I heard my name being yelled out I saw these wild broads waving at me like they were on a float in a parade. Including Odessa.

I waved back and made my way through the crowd to greet them.

"You're late," Sadie said. She was standing next to a tall blond woman who was nothing to write home about. But Sadie sure did look happy. The woman had her long arm around Sadie's shoulders and walked over to me, shook my hand too hard, and said, "Hi, I'm Callie. So nice to finally meet you."

"Nice to meet you, too, Callie. Welcome to the family!"

Joe walked over and gave me a kiss on the cheek and a thumbs-up, and Lucky smacked him upside the head. Just like old times. There was even less of her than last time I saw her, and she was starting to look younger.

Korynthia then walked toward me holding a man's hand. I knew who this was. "Well, Henry, please meet my other BFF. Loretha, this is Henry."

"Hello, I've heard a lot about you."

Korynthia was right. Henry was handsome and those lips were luscious. His cheekbones looked chiseled and he was tall even though he was a few inches shorter than Ko. He looked like he spent quite a bit of time in the gym, too. His hair was the prettiest silver I'd seen on a man since Carl.

"Stop flirting," Ko said to me, with a deep yes-I'm-in-love smile. She *looked* like she was in love. And she was dressed like it in a long, flowing floral skirt and sleeveless orange top with a sash that wrapped around her small waist about ten times.

I didn't know falling in love was even possible at our age. But between Ko's glow, the look on Sadie's face, and the way Lucky was flirting with her husband like this was their restart, I guessed it was. I was happy for everybody. And with Odessa here, I was just glad to finally feel some love from my sister.

"Okay," Korynthia said. "Well, since we're all here now, Henry has an announcement. Take it away, Henry!"

Henry rubbed his chin.

"Well, when we stop in Ensenada tomorrow, Korynthia and I would really love it if you all would join us for our wedding. It will only take fifteen minutes to make our love official, which will give you all plenty of time to buy us expensive wedding gifts ashore before our big dinner. Will that work for everybody?"

My mouth dropped open.

But I felt my fist fly up in the air. Along with applause.

"Okay," Korynthia said. "Now, how about we all get checked into our staterooms and make our reservations for our spa treatments, and then us ladies will put on our string bikinis and meet up by the pool in a couple of hours?"

"It doesn't take two hours to do any of that stuff, so what are you and Henry going to find to do in your stateroom?"

"Act stately."

She laughed. We all laughed.

Including Odessa, who looked so pretty, soft, like a tall black angel in all white, and I was surprised when she walked over and hugged me, and then whispered in my ear. "Thank you for inviting me. I'm already having fun. I'd forgotten what it felt like."

"Well, I hope you get used to it."

We took the glass elevator up to the eleventh floor, which was where all of our rooms were. I couldn't look down, so I looked at the carpet until the gold doors opened like we were royalty or something. Sadie, who was pulling a carry-on, patted it tenderly, and then smiled at me. We had all been grateful when she had volunteered to keep Poochie's ashes. She had even told us how she talked to Poochie every day, but none of us wanted to hear what she said. We had also decided we would say goodbye to Poochie on our last night, after dinner. I was not looking forward to it.

Our room—or stateroom as it is officially called—was beautiful. It was almost as big and as nice as the resort room Carl and I stayed at in Palm Springs, except the Pacific Ocean was outside this window and below the long balcony.

"Lord have mercy," Odessa said when she stood there looking at the two queen-sized beds with swans made out of soft white towels perched in front of the pillows.

"Which bed do you want, Loretha?"

"If I'm not mistaken, I think they're exactly the same."

"But you should pick the one you want."

"I don't care, Odessa. Fall down on whichever one you want."

And she did. On her back. And she spread her white wings like the swans across the long blue pillowcases. The sheets were so white they looked light blue. We had a honey-colored leather sofa, a round table in front of it, and an orange leather curved chair. I suppose this was for company. Nice artwork. And through the sliding glass doors the Pacific Ocean was out there waiting for Poochie. This was nothing like the souped-up motel room I had when Poochie first started this tradition. This was a stateroom all right. Carl would have loved this.

I fell down on my bed after I made sure the shower was big enough for us to turn around in, and I pulled the blue throw across my chest and arms and closed my eyes.

"This was a good idea," Odessa said. "I mean that your friend Poochie set this up for all of her friends to do."

"Sure was."

"Are you all going to stop this tradition now that she's gone?"

"I don't know."

"I think you should keep doing it and maybe consider adding some new friends. Or sisters. Or daughters. You know what I mean?"

"I do. And I think you might be on to something."

"I'm sorry," she said.

"What are you sorry about, Odessa?"

"For not being a good Christian and not being a good sister."

"Well, I'm sorry for holding you hostage, for wanting you to be more like me, or I should say, wanting you to like me. I didn't know what I did that made it so hard."

"You were happy and I wasn't. You had a husband who loved you and I didn't. You had a child and I didn't. You had a college degree and I didn't. And you were very successful and I wasn't."

"You were successful, too. The problem was comparing our success."

"I'm starting to admit a lot of things to myself."

"Do you still go to church?"

"Not like I used to."

"Why not?"

"Because I was losing a lot of faith in God."

"He's not a magician, Odessa."

"I know but I thought He was."

"And He doesn't judge. We do."

I sat up.

She was crying.

"I don't know what would make you feel all this, Odessa."

"It's because I have not been happy with the choices I've made or haven't made in my life, and if you want to know the truth, I've also been lonely."

"That makes two of us. But I'm trying to learn how to live forward instead of backward."

"How's it going?"

"It's going slow but I'm taking one step at a time."

"I want to be a better sister," she said.

"Then let's both start now," I said.

"I think we already have."

"I do love you, Odessa."

"And I love you, too, Loretha."

And then we were quiet.

"You should give Ma's house to Cinnamon and Jonas because they need it more than me. I actually do like my apartment and it's plenty of room for one person."

I heard her exhale.

"I'm so glad to hear this, Odessa, and they will be, too."

Then I started laughing.

"What's so funny?" she asked.

"Lord, if Ma could see us or be a fly on the wall she would love this."

"Then let's pretend. Hi, Ma!"

"Hi, Ma!"

And we got up and hugged each other, then fell back on our beds and we both fell asleep until we heard a knock on the door that our baggage had arrived. But we knew we had already emptied ours.

I heard a banging on the door and jumped up.

"Who is it?"

"It's us: Korynthia and Henry!"

I ran to the door and opened it.

"Is something wrong?"

"We changed our minds."

"Nooooo. Please don't tell me the wedding is off, you guys."

They both smiled.

"No, this is a done deal," she said pointing to Henry's chest. "We decided we don't want to get married in Ensenada today. We can get hitched right here on the ship anytime. I've been to Ensenada and so has Henry and we'd rather spend the day out on the deck and then go to the club tonight and do a little dancing to celebrate and then sleep in. Are you two good with that?"

I turned to look at Odessa. "If you still want to go to Ensenada, you can."

"I didn't come here to be on dry land. I like this ship."

"And I want to dance," I heard myself say.

"Then we shall dance the night away tonight. And tomorrow we can sleep in, have our treatments, go to a show, and gamble. Then our last evening, well, you know . . ."

And we did.

I had a hot stone massage. I asked Odessa to join me, but she didn't want a stranger to touch her body.

I took the stairs instead of the elevator for six of the eleven floors.

I went to a body-sculpt class with Korynthia and I almost had to crawl out.

I walked around the jogging track with Sadie and Callie for two miles, which was sixteen times around, while Ko and Henry jogged for four miles. Lucky and Joe kicked their feet in the water. It all worked out.

We went to the disco and were surprised we weren't the oldest ones in there. Some guy even told me my silver hair looked beautiful under the lights, and so did I.

We all learned how to twerk.

Except Odessa and Sadie.

We all had too much to drink.

Except Odessa and Sadie.

And what really shocked me was how good the entertainment was. The group was under forty and sang songs I knew the words to. I really enjoyed twerking and suggested that Korynthia add these moves to her hip-hop class. She agreed.

And who was it that hit the jackpot on the one-dollar slots after betting five? Loretha Curry. That would be me. I intend to spend, give, or use every dime of this extra $3,790 on my daughter, my mother, Carolyn, Kwame, and my great-grandbabies. Odessa told me to take her off the list because I had done enough for her.

At breakfast, I did not put any sugar in my coffee but I did put in cream. I was starting to get used to it. And instead of eating French toast or pancakes topped with bananas and hot syrup or waffles with hot syrup or eggs and bacon with hash browns and toast with butter and jelly, I had plain yogurt with berries and whole wheat toast. It was delicious.

For lunch I had a salad with a thousand different vegetables and cooked prawns and then chunks of chicken and oil and vinegar dressing. I did eat a breadstick.

For dinner I had baked chicken. Brown rice. A salad. Steamed vegetables. I passed on the sourdough bread and butter.

I did not give dessert any consideration at all.

I went down that Plexiglas pool slide once I realized I wouldn't get stuck in it.

I sat in the pool.

I did not hide my hips under a cover-up.

I sat there watching everybody doing laps and decided I might take some damn swimming lessons, since I have a damn pool in my backyard. Was sixty-nine too late to learn how to do something new?

As we played miniature golf, I pulled Korynthia aside and said, "And you're sure about getting married, Ko?"

And she said, "Yes, I'm doing it, Loretha. Please don't ask me again about what if it doesn't work out. It will. If it doesn't, fuck it. I tried something new."

As Korynthia and Henry said "I do" in a small chapel and we were all dudded up while Korynthia and Henry wore their exercise clothes, I was just thrilled for them. It also made me wonder if I might ever be kissed again, but what was really weird was that I was even asking myself this question.

On the last evening, the four of us gathered on the top deck. Sadie had her bag with her. The moon was out and there was no breeze even though a staff person had given us a pencil and a piece of string to tie around it so we could see which way the wind was blowing.

"Poochie planned this," I heard myself say.

And when that string moved, instead of feeling scared we all seemed calmer.

Sadie carefully unzipped her bag and pulled out another black nylon zipped bag. She set it slowly on the deck floor and unzipped it. We watched as she pulled out the silver urn and held it in her hand. We all touched it gently with our fingertips.

"So," Sadie said. "Loretha, go ahead, you said you would say goodbye for all of us."

"And remember she said she didn't want us to be mushy or sentimental or sad. This was supposed to celebrate her life," Lucky said.

"Well, would you like to speak?" I asked.

"No, because I can't."

"Then be quiet," Sadie said.

"Do you hear these bitches, Poochie?" Ko asked. "Nothing has changed except you're not here to put them in their places."

And then I said, "Okay. Everybody please shut up."

And the breeze stopped.

"Poochie, we just want you to know how much we loved you and how glad we are that you were our friend and sister. We know you miss us as much as we miss you, but one day we hope to see you again—and don't you owe me five dollars?"

Everybody looked at me, and then the urn, and then started laughing.

"Yeah, and I think you borrowed a book from me, and one day I hope to get it back," Sadie said.

"You don't owe us anything," I said. "But we promise, if you can see or hear us, that we will make you proud with what we do and how we spend the rest of our lives."

Then there was silence.

And Sadie walked over to the edge of the railing, opened the top, and turned the urn upside down until it was empty, which was when we felt another breeze.

Chapter 27

I hadn't seen Ma since Carolyn moved into Valley View. According to Kwame, she apparently does feel like she's living in a fancy hotel. He said she never wants to move, and he has moved into a studio apartment three blocks from his college and is happy knowing his mother's spirits are up and that she's getting the care she needs. He is also thrilled to be an official college student.

"I wish I could've moved all my friends in here," Ma said, as I sat in her gliding chair this time. "But that Carolyn seems nice enough. Too young to be living here. It's too bad we won't get to know each other."

"Why won't you?"

"Because I think I'm coming down with some kind of cancer."

I closed my eyes, then opened them as I looked down at the floor, then I took a deep breath and slowly blew the air out.

Ma was in bed with the chenille bedspread pulled under her chin as if she was cold or had one. She has always been dramatic but this registered as melodrama.

"What would make you say something like that, Ma?"

She slid her hands up and down the right and left sides of her body and said, "Because there are places on my body that are hard that should be soft. Or maybe it's the other way around."

"You don't have cancer, Ma."

"How do you know that? You're no doctor."

"I know that, but the doctors here would've let me know if you had any problems."

"Doctors miss the obvious."

"Ma. Stop it, please?"

And then she started laughing.

"I'm sorry. I'm healthy as a horse. I just wanted to see what it would take to alarm you. Anyway, what are you doing here? You were just here yesterday."

"I wasn't here yesterday, Ma."

She looked at her little calendar on the side table that had four or five stamped envelopes addressed to me next to it.

"Put those in your purse and don't read them until you're on the plane to Tokyo."

"News sure travels fast."

"It's about time you went, though I wish Jackson could come see me before I kick the bucket. Just make sure you send me some pictures for my scrapbook."

I hate when she brings up dying. Like she's looking forward to it.

"So, why haven't you been to see me?"

"Because I've been busy. I'm just about to open the new shop! You want to come?"

"No. I don't really care about makeup. But take a picture for me. Wait a minute. How old are you now, Loretha?"

"Sixty-nine."

"You're old, too. And let me warn you: it's all downhill from here."

"If that's how you see it that's what you get."

"You sound like Oprah. Didn't she cancel her show?"

"She did."

"What in the world is she doing now?"

"She has her own television network."

"Well, that makes sense."

"Has Odessa been by to see you?"

"Of course she has. She told me you took her on a cruise, and I was shocked to hear that considering she was still standing in front of me. I was surprised you didn't throw her overboard. Which made me wonder if maybe she had snuck and had sex with a stranger or something, because she sure has been nice."

That made me chuckle.

"I doubt that, Ma. We're just finally trying to act more like sisters."

"Well, you are sisters. Anyway, Odessa told me she got her lawsuit money. Chump change. Not the hundreds of thousands she was hoping she'd get. Negroes live for settlements."

"That's a racist thing to say, Ma."

"I take it back. Poor folks of every color live for settlements. How's that?"

I stood up. Then bent down and kissed her on the cheek.

"Did you know she quit working here?" Ma asked.

"No. Do you know where she's working?"

"No, I don't, but I kinda miss her nosy ass. Can I ask you a personal question and promise you won't get mad at me?"

"It depends."

She put her glasses on and looked up at me real hard.

"What is wrong with your hair?"

"What's wrong with my hair?"

"It's green," she said.

I got up and walked over to her mirror. She was right. I was so busy rushing to get here I had forgotten to rinse it after I got out of the pool.

"I've been taking swimming lessons."

"You mean to tell me you can't swim?"

"No. I was always too afraid after I almost drowned as a kid."

"Swimming was never much fun to me. It was too monotonous.

And where do you get? Nowhere. I just liked sitting on the edge of the pool, kicking my feet in the water. But anyway, rub some Vaseline all over your silver hair or you'll be looking like a palm tree."

"I usually wear a bathing cap."

"Oh, by the way, I told Carolyn I would teach her how to scrapbook even though I don't know if she brought any pictures with her. So, could you please bring a scrapbook for her but with no flowers on it because she's not big on floral anything, and maybe some writing paper and a Bic because she still has family in Flint she might want to write to, and I assume they can read."

"Stamps? Envelopes?"

"Sure. She's not getting any of mine. Anyway, did I tell you I'm also going to teach Carolyn how to knit?"

"No, you didn't. But you're not that good at knitting, Ma."

"Who cares? She needs to keep her shoulders moving and she can run her mouth, I am not lying."

"But you like her?"

"I like most pleasant Negroes," she said, sitting up in the bed. "She seems lonely, and I'm good company."

"That's very nice of you, Ma."

"I know. Because I'm nice. And please don't tell Odessa I told you about the chump change she got because it'll sound like gossip. She thinks my memory is going but I remember what I want to remember. Now give me a hug and next time, call first."

I had called.

I examined my green hair more closely when I got home. My friends had always made fun of me for not knowing how to swim, and after seeing all of them swimming laps on the cruise, I promised myself I was going to learn. Plus, at one of my appointments, Dr. Alexopolous asked if I had a pool and when I said yes, she told me that swimming was an excellent form of exercise and that the loose skin hanging from my upper arms and the inner tube forming around my waist would disappear if I started swimming.

Bitch.

But it was not as hard as I thought it was going to be. B. B. King loved watching me learn how to time my breathing on top of and underneath the water. I learned how to kick. How to relax and float. And my tall, handsome, sexy, Hawaiian teacher, who was definitely from the Big Island, made me never want to get out of the pool.

In twenty hours, I learned that water was not worth fearing. That waves were meant to ride or swim through. That I needed to learn how long to hold my breath and when to blow air out. But when he asked if I would like to learn how to do the backstroke, I told him no.

I was already looking up.

Ever since I got back from the cruise, B. B. King has not been that excited about getting out of the back seat when we go to the dog park. In fact, he gives me a look of boredom, as if he was asking, *Is this the only park in town?*

I took him to the vet to see if I might have been missing something. Other than increasing his steroids to help minimize the inflammation caused by his arthritis, the doctor said B. B. King was healthy. But he also said B. B. King might be a bit lonely and that dogs have emotions just like us humans.

As soon as we walked out I drove straight to a shelter. When we got inside, there was a lot of barking and crying, but I knew B. B. King was excited because his tail started swaying back and forth like a windshield wiper.

The shelter volunteer looked just like the daughter of that Crocodile Hunter guy and after introducing myself, I said, "This is B. B. King and he needs some company."

She rubbed his head and ears, then flipped her thick pigtails behind her shoulders and said, "Hi there, B. B. King! A wittle lonely, are we?"

B. B. King looked at her as if to say, *What do you think we came in here for? Yes.*

"Does the sex or age matter?" she asked.

"A little younger than B.B. here, but not too frisky. He was fixed a long time ago, so a female would be okay. I don't really care about the breed as long as he or she is not mean."

"Then follow me. B. B. King? How'd you come up with such a cool name for him?"

"He's named after one of my favorite blues singers."

"Oh, that's nice," she said.

It's times like this when I realize how old I am, and things that are common knowledge to me are foreign to young folks. But I don't feel too bad because one day she'll be old, too. If she's lucky.

We walked on the concrete floor down a corridor past sad, bored, and occasionally abused dogs, but at least now they were safe and in clean cages. The volunteer stopped at a cage where there was a white Lab about the size B. B. King used to be, asleep on her little paws. Or at least she was until Mr. King tried to put his snout between a space in the rectangle fence, which was when she jumped up and her tail started wagging and she tried to poke her snout through the space. When I saw Mr. King's tail swishing faster than the speed of light, I said, "We'll take her."

I was buzzed in and could not believe it when the elevator doors opened and there was my sister, looking better than she looked on the cruise.

"Well, hello there, sister," she said, and gave me a bear hug. "What a nice surprise! How are you?"

I was thrilled to still hear the upbeat tone in her voice. I hadn't heard her sound like this in over thirty years. Maybe Ma was telepathic. Maybe Odessa had finally rediscovered sex.

"I'm good, Odessa. Don't you look pretty! How are you and how've you been since the cruise?"

"I've been well, thank you. You don't look so bad yourself, Sis."

I loved hearing her call me *Sis*.

"So what's going on with you, Odessa?"

"Well, first of all, I got my settlement. If that's what it can be called."

"But that's good to hear. Something is better than nothing."

"And I got another job."

"Ma told me you left Valley View. Had enough of Ma?"

"Ma had nothing to do with it."

"So, what kind of work?"

"Well, I drive."

"Drive what?"

"Uber."

"Are you kidding me, Odessa? Aren't you too old? And isn't it dangerous?"

"No, I'm not kidding and I'm not too old and it's not dangerous. In fact, I'm having a lot of fun and I'm meeting the most interesting people, you just would not believe it."

"But aren't you scared?"

"No. I won't go where I think it might be unsafe. And drunks are harmless. I've had to help a few find their cars the night after partying and they always tip the best. The worst that has happened is when they throw up, but Uber pays me to get my car detailed and I just take it to the car wash. Plus, I now have rubber mats."

"And how long do you plan on doing this?"

"Until I don't want to. I'm my own boss. I get paid every single day and I don't have to worry about calling in sick."

"Do you always get this dolled up to drive with Uber?"

"No. I'm not driving tonight. I'm being driven. It's called a date, Sis. Tell you more when there's more to tell."

I heard the babies before I rang the bell, and as soon as Cinnamon opened the door they were both holding on to her long skirt. I hadn't seen her in a long time, and she screamed, "Grandma, what a surprise!"

"Hi there, little cuties," I said, and they let go of her skirt and did that Frankenstein walk over to me and grabbed for my hands. But I was holding a surprise in one of them.

Jonas came out of the kitchen, kissed me on the cheek, and picked up Handsome, who started kicking to be put back down. He wanted to practice walking. Pretty decided to sit down to see what was going to happen next.

"I'm sorry for not calling," I said.

"No apologies necessary," Jonas said. "Is everything okay?"

Cinnamon looked a little worried.

"It's not my mom, is it?"

"No. No news is good news with her, I think."

"So true. So, what brings you over, Grandma? Jonas has made an amazing tofu stir-fry if you'd like to have dinner with us."

"No thanks."

"It's also got ginger, carrots, string beans, and garlic, and a little soy sauce. You won't even know it's good for you."

"I've made some improvements to my diet, but tofu isn't one of them. Not to change the subject, but I was just wondering how soon you all might want to move into your new home?"

I pulled the key ring out from behind my back and held it up, dangling the three keys in the air.

They started screaming and jumping up and down and I was being hugged and kissed on both cheeks. Handsome started rocking his body from side to side and Pretty looked confused, but then realized how happy everybody else was so she just started clapping and singing her favorite song in a language even I understood.

"So," Dr. Alexopolous said with a smile, something I couldn't remember seeing her do in all the years I'd been coming to see her. "You finally listened to me, I see."

I can't believe how much I used to not like her. She is much nicer and the frown she used to wear is gone. Like maybe she'd had a little Botox. Her hair is thicker and I can tell it is a wig! Money well spent. She smiled at me again, and I wanted to take back all my mean thoughts, but it was too late so in my head I just asked God to forgive me.

"So, what's the verdict?"

"Whatever you've been doing, keep doing it. Your A1C has dropped to a manageable number. And you've lost a little over twenty pounds since we saw you three months ago. You should give yourself a high five."

I gave her one instead.

"So, what have you changed?"

"I've been eating healthy and I've been exercising."

"I knew that, but I just wanted to hear you say it. I'm so pleased to see you're making these changes, Mrs. Curry."

"You can call me Loretha."

She leaned forward on her elbows, wove her fingers together, and looked me in the eye.

"Please know that I'm not trying to sound like that doctor on the TV show, but I just have to tell you that if you can view these changes as permanent and not as a temporary fix, you'll probably be adding years to your life. Healthier years."

That landed.

"I'm going to try," I said.

Dr. Alexopolous then leaned back in her chair, but this time she crossed her arms and looked at me with curiosity and empathy.

"So tell me, Loretha. How is your daughter?"

"I think she's doing better."

"You mean you don't know? She didn't see either of the doctors?"

"Oh, yes. She definitely did. She's been at a twenty-eight-day treatment place and she opted to stay for another twenty-eight. She should be home soon."

"And will home be with you?"

"I'm not sure what she's going to want to do, but my door is open."

She stood up and held out her hand.

I shook it.

And she patted mine.

"She took the right step. Life has a way of working out when we work at it. Stay the course and I'll see you in three months. Before you know it, you'll be America's first Top Senior Model!"

And she laughed.

And so did I.

Chapter 28

"So, what's this all about?" Lucky asked, looking at the dishes I spent hours making spread around the table on a lazy Susan.

"It's called dinner," I said.

"It's really pretty. It doesn't look like anything we've ever eaten here. I know you didn't make all of this, Lo," Sadie said.

"I did. And, Lucky, you can eat everything on this table."

"I know exactly what it is," Korynthia said. "It's called a healthy meal and we should all just shut up for a minute and thank Loretha for taking the time to make all these beautiful dishes, then ask her to explain what the hell it is. And even if we don't like it when we taste it, we should just all pretend like it's delicious and eat it anyway, okay, Lo?"

I threw a dish towel at her, but missed on purpose.

"First of all, I would like to say: get used to this if you plan on eating here ever again. All of these mouthwatering dishes are from my diabetes cookbooks. Which I hope doesn't spoil them for you, but too bad. Now I want to announce that the new House of Beauty and Glamour will have its grand opening in a few weeks and your invitations are under your plates."

And of course everybody just had to lift their plates up, but when I cleared my throat they slid them back.

"Could you just tell us what the hell each one of these is, so I can decide what I want to take home?"

I knew Lucky was going to be difficult, even though she's been trying her best to lose the bitch that's still huddling in a little corner somewhere deep inside her.

"Okay. This is called chipotle grilled pork tenderloin with strawberry-avocado salsa. And this is spicy brown rice. That's spinach and onion couscous. Those are salmon fishcakes. And the salad is spinach, feta, and goat cheese. As you can see, there is no bread, and I will never do this shit again if you keep giving me grief. I spent all afternoon preparing this meal for you huzzies to impress you. So, somebody please bless the food and then let's eat up."

"Wait a minute," Korynthia said. "Who is that cute little dog B. B. King has his arms around like she or he is his baby?"

"That's Billie Holiday. She's a rescue dog. And apparently B.B. thinks he's her stepfather. She has perked him up like a double shot of espresso."

Both dogs looked at us as soon as they heard their names.

"Hi, B.B.!"

"Hi, Billie!"

"What is it with you naming dogs after our most beloved and revered singers, Loretha? What ever happened to Butch and Sparky and Princess?" Lucky asked.

"I'm honoring their memory."

"But they're dogs," Lucky said. "Wait. I take that back. I'm trying to get used to not being negative. So please forgive me, bitches."

"You know, I've been thinking," I said.

"Not again," Lucky said, but then crossed her lips and said, "By all means, let's hear it."

Everybody threw their dinner napkins at her. Lucky threw them back with a smile.

"Let's bury calling each other bitches. We aren't bitches. We're lifelong girlfriends. Deal?"

"Deal," the chorus said.

"Now, can we bless the food since some of it might need to be microwaved if we keep jabbering? How about you, big mouth?"

Of course I pointed to Lucky.

All of us closed our eyes and bowed our heads. But then we looked up because B.B. and Billie were snoring.

"B. B. King, wake up!" Sadie yelled and tried not to laugh.

He lifted his head and looked around like he didn't know where he was. But he then dropped his head and closed his eyes and we heard nothing.

"Okay," Lucky said, as we bowed our heads again. "Lord, thank you for letting Loretha prepare what looks like an interesting meal that I hope is good, and please bless this food and our lifelong friendship. And even though we will always get on each other's nerves, you know it's all out of love. Please say hi to Poochie for us and let her know she will always have a seat at our table and in our hearts. We hope you continue to guide us and keep us healthy and safe and strong. Amen."

"Anything else you want to add?" Korynthia asked Sadie.

"I loved every word of it," Sadie said.

"Why am I not surprised?" Lucky asked.

"Okay, let's eat," I said. "And thank you, Lucky."

She rolled her eyes at everybody else and looked at me and said, "You're quite welcome, Lo."

And we ate.

And every bowl and plate on the table was empty. Of course, I had made extra of everything and stashed it in the back of the second shelf of the fridge for tomorrow because I knew they would eat it all since it was delicious. If only I'd known how tasty healthy could be, I would've been eating like this years ago.

"Next time don't be so damn stingy with the portions," Ko said.

"And give me the name of those cookbooks. I'm sure Joe would appreciate a meal like this, too."

We just smiled at her.

Lucky then took a deep breath.

"I would like to say that having gastric bypass surgery was the smartest thing I've ever done. I've decided not to beat myself up anymore for allowing myself to become obese. I feel lucky to be alive. I'm not trying to get all mushy, but losing Poochie has helped me appreciate the fact that I have choices and it's not too late to make healthier ones. And I know I can be a bitch, and I probably always will be, but I want to be a nicer bitch. And I hope you bitches—my bad: ladies—will keep on loving me anyway. Also, Joe and I have decided to stay put. We are thinking of turning the guesthouse, which he's not living in anymore, into one of those Airbnb- or VRBO-type places, which is exactly what we're going to be renting when we go to Panama, Costa Rica, Kenya, where we might go on safari even though I'm scared of big animals. All I know is right now is the best time of our lives and Joe and I have decided to milk it. But it'll be low-fat."

"Wait a minute," I said. "What about the reefer?"

"I still take a hit every now and then, but it helps me balance."

"Balance what?" Sadie asked.

"My equilibrium."

"You've got to be kidding," I said.

"Sometimes I do lose my balance. And marijuana helps."

"Whatever works," Korynthia said. "But we'll be able to tell if you're stoned, so watch your step."

We all just applauded and laughed at the same time, which woke up B.B. and Billie so I walked over and let them out the side door.

When I came back, Sadie waved her hand for Korynthia to go.

"Well, ladies, I'm not turning my house into any Airbnb or VRBO. My wonderful new husband, Henry, is handy, on a whole lot of levels I might add, and he is fixing up the house to bring it up to the twenty-first century. So all of my grandchildren and great-grandchildren, including Bird's little ones, will soon be able to come spend some weekends and the summer—but not the whole damn summer—with their grandma and their new grandpa. And, Loretha, FYI, I am going to be working at the House when it opens because selling real estate is not fun. I love the new House. It's classy as hell and I think it was a blessing the old one got robbed. Anyway, Henry and I will be doing some traveling and might be joining Joe and Lucky from time to time, so let me know if I get vacation pay! So, there you have it."

"You're hired," I said.

"You don't think I'm too old?"

"It's my shop. And I'm old. And what the hell does being old have to do with anything? We're not dead yet."

All eyes turned to Sadie.

"So, I would like to acknowledge how grateful I am that you all mostly kept to yourselves what you thought you knew about my sexuality. I was afraid to admit it to myself for fear that I would be punished by the Lord, but over the past years so many people have come out, including people in the clergy, who after all are human. I know that too well after making a fool of myself with one of them. When Callie and I met at my new church, she comforted me and I allowed myself to accept her comfort, which turned into love. I have to say how happy I am to have friends like you all who have not ever given up on me. And I am proud to let you know that I am now one happily married lesbian and even though we eloped we intend to have another ceremony just for us girls. Plus, I want gifts. I am also happy to have returned to the Pasadena library system where I will oversee the reading program. I know it's a cliché, but age ain't nothing but a number. I'm owning it. As much as I own my love for you all."

We all applauded.

"Well now, I've told you about my grand opening, but I am also thrilled to announce that I have sold the L.A. store to two beautiful young black college graduates. Oh. And I look forward to taking another cruise next year, but can we please go somewhere more exotic, like the Caribbean?"

Everybody nodded.

"So, I have to ask you all," I said. "With so many changes happening, do you ladies still want to keep having these dinners once a month?"

They all looked at me as if I was crazy.

"But what if we have nothing to report?"

"That will never happen," Ko said.

"These dinners give me life. This is where we know it's okay to feel what we feel and say it without worrying about being judged," Lucky said.

"Well, that's not true," I said. "But who better than each other to judge each other?"

Everybody nodded.

"Poochie would agree if she was still with us," Lucky said in a soft voice.

"She is still with us," Sadie said.

And we all nodded again with a smile.

"Okay," I said, and clapped my hands. "I would just like to put this out here right now. I do not need or want a birthday party this year."

Everybody looked at one another as if they had something to tell me and were fighting over who was going to do it.

"We decided in Vegas that we were done with celebrating your birthday," Lucky said. "You aren't as special as you think you are—well, maybe you were to Carl—but we all agreed that we should just have one big bash in Vegas for all our birthdays, on an agreed-upon date we'll all vote on."

I was thrilled.

With that we knew we were full. But as my besties started clearing the table, the doorbell rang. Everybody froze.

But no one more than me.

I looked out at the driveway and did not see a car, so it wasn't

Kwame. I couldn't imagine who might be ringing my doorbell at nine thirty at night.

Everybody looked at the front door. I was shocked when I saw a short Afro through the clear part of the stained glass. When I opened the door, there was my daughter, smiling, looking strong and beautiful. B. B. King and Billie Holiday rushed up behind her, wagging their tails.

She hugged me like she hadn't seen me in years.

"Hi, Ma."

"Hi," I said with a little trepidation.

"Welcome home, Jalecia!" everybody behind me screamed.

"Well, are you going to just make your daughter stand out on the front porch?" Lucky said.

"Come on in here, baby!" Ko yelled, and just as I was reaching out to take Jalecia by the hands to gently pull her into my arms, Korynthia brushed right past me and yanked her inside.

"You look five years younger, sweetie. Maybe I should go where you've been," Lucky said and then realized maybe she'd said the wrong thing. "I take that back. I'm sorry."

"It's all good. Hi, Aunties!" Jalecia said and started smiling like she hadn't seen them in years. Everybody ran over and hugged her, and I just stood there watching the joy on my daughter's face and I knew something good had happened to her.

Chapter 29

I insisted that everybody leave the dirty dishes and kitchen to me. They understood and were out the front door in less than ten minutes flat.

I closed the door and when I turned around, Jalecia was in the kitchen looking over the mess.

"Did they eat everything?" Jalecia asked.

And then laughed.

"Maybe they did. Maybe they didn't."

Then we wrapped our arms around each other again, as tight as we could.

She pressed her forehead against mine and whispered, "I'm sorry, Ma."

I backed away and looked her in the eyes. "You don't have anything to be sorry about, Jalecia. Didn't you learn that in there?"

"Yes."

"Then why are you apologizing for something that isn't your fault?"

"How do you know that, Ma?"

"Because I read up on mental illnesses."

"You did? What did you learn?"

"That sometimes how you feel and how you think make you do things you don't really want to do. And it's not your fault."

"Were you sitting in on some of my sessions or what?"

"Your aunt Peggy told me some things about your father, and her."

"Really?"

"She told me that you didn't drink because you liked getting drunk."

"Yes, I did." And she started laughing. "What I didn't like was not remembering what I did when I was drunk and being hungover all the time. But the worst was that I was a mean drunk. You more than anybody got the brunt of that anger, Ma."

"I'm not worrying about that."

"I know. But you didn't deserve it. You're a good mother and I feel very lucky you didn't kick me to the curb. I met a lot of people there whose parents won't have anything to do with them."

"Some folks do run out of patience. And I can't lie and say you didn't test me. But I don't know how you give up on your own child, I don't care how old they are."

"Well, I don't know all about that. I heard some horror stories in there."

"So, you obviously got a lot out of going through this treatment program, then?"

"Yes, I did, Ma. Look at me."

And I did.

She looked confident. Like she had been through something and had come out on the other side.

"I'm happy to tell you I believe you have your daughter back, and these were probably the most fruitful fifty-six days of my whole adult life."

I backed away and looked into her eyes. She meant what she had just said. There was a light inside them that'd been missing for years.

"I know this might sound corny, Ma, but honestly, for years I felt like I've been lost at sea and I couldn't figure out how to get back to shore. I forgot who I was before this disease, this depression, took over my mind and my heart and started robbing me of my best self. And the only way I knew how to shut it down was with eighty proof. But, of course, that didn't work."

"So, do you feel like you've got it cured now?"

"Depression isn't curable, Ma. But what I learned is that it can be managed. I've been suffering from it for years but just didn't know it. Now that I do, I know I don't need to be ashamed to say I suffer from it. That, in and of itself, is a very big deal. I didn't tell you the name of the treatment center because I didn't want you to try to check up on me, but anyway, they have the best psychiatrists and psychologists to assess you and help you understand why you feel the way you do. They give you hope and confidence, something I haven't felt in years. We had these workshops all day that explained so much and we even had to keep a journal every night and write down our thoughts and feelings. I cried a lot. I even had to interview myself, Ma. And I asked myself some hard-ass—I'm sorry—some very hard questions that I couldn't answer. But I'm starting to."

"Like what, if it's not too personal?"

"Like why I was so jealous of my younger brother when he hadn't done anything to me."

"And what was your answer?"

"I wanted all the attention and I thought he was stealing it."

"He did steal some of it, but he was the new kid on the block and he didn't know he was robbing you of anything."

"I get it now, and one day in the very near future I want to apologize to him, too."

"Well, I'm going to Tokyo real soon and if you'd like to go with me you can tell him face-to-face."

"I wish I could, but I can't."

"Why not?"

"Because I'm hoping to be able to live in sort of a safe house, where

I can still get the kind of support I need and they help you find work or maybe even go back to school."

"Really?"

"Really. But insurance won't cover all of it."

I just gave her a look as if to say, *Do you really think there's an amount too high to help save your life?*

"Thank you, Ma."

"So how long would you live there?"

"Three months is what they recommend. But I can come and go. It's not like being in jail or a hospital."

"Well, it sounds healthy, so you don't have to explain anything else. But you know what? We can FaceTime Jackson if you're up to it."

"What time is it over there now?"

"I just know it's tomorrow. But let me think."

My heart was pounding because I couldn't believe what Jalecia had just said. That she wanted to call her brother was a very good sign. I looked at the spot where I always put my phone, but it wasn't there.

"What are you looking for, Ma?"

"My cellphone."

"Did you get my message telling you I was on my way?"

"No! You know what? I think I left it in the car. I'll go get it."

"No. I'll go."

I watched her walk out the side door. It didn't feel like she was really here and I was still looking at the door when she came back in, holding my phone in the air, and said, "It's dead. So, there you go."

She handed it to me and I just set it in my lap.

"Ma, you know what? You look good. As soon as you opened the door I could tell you've lost quite a few pounds. What have you been doing?"

"Eating better. Exercising. Dancing. Swimming."

I really liked the sound of that after I said it, especially because it was true. I was glad she noticed.

"Well, we ate good because each house had a chef. And we had to exercise every single day."

"You lived in a house?"

She nodded.

She was busy scrolling and clicking her cellphone and I heard her say, "It's nine forty here and it's one forty tomorrow afternoon there."

"What kind of house?"

"A big beautiful house. I had my own room. We had a TV. It wasn't like Jack Nicholson or Nurse Ratched, if that's what you're thinking."

That would never have entered my mind until she just said it.

"Does Jackson have a normal job or is that a stupid question, Ma?"

"He works for a tech company. Does all of their photography."

"He always was creative."

"So were you, Jalecia. You were pretty good on the piano."

"So, how old are his twins?"

"They're almost two and a half. They speak Japanese and English, not well yet, but they can say *okay* and *Nana* and *peekaboo*. I'm just waiting for them to get cuter."

She started laughing and so did I. We weren't laughing at the fact that the babies weren't cute, but because we could finally laugh together.

"What about Aiko?"

"She's a stay-at-home mom."

"Why do so many women these days want to stay home? I never wanted to do that. But there goes that negativity. Stop. If she wants to stay home with her babies, that's her choice. And speaking of babies, I can't wait to see my grands."

"They are cuties. I have babysat them from time to time and even been bitten by Handsome."

"I hope I get to babysit them soon."

"I'm sure you will. So, did anybody read what you wrote in your journal?"

"No. Thank God. It was just meant for us to be honest with ourselves. I still like to do it, and may do it forever. In fact, I'm going to buy myself a few new journals."

"Let me."

"But you don't know what my favorite colors are anymore?"

"Purple. Yellow. And emerald green, if I remember correctly."

"Good memory, Ma. Maybe we can pick them out together. And thank you. Again."

"You're welcome. Did you make any friends while you were there?"

"I wouldn't say I made friends. There were people who were being treated for all kinds of disorders, not just depression, and some of them were staying as long as six months. I was screened the first two weeks in order for the doctors to figure out if I might be bipolar, but I'm not. I met quite a few folks who were, though. Once I was diagnosed and prescribed the right medication, I started feeling a little better and then I was feeling a lot better. That was why I wanted to stay for that extra session, because I wanted to make sure the medication would still work. But anyway, I don't think I want to talk about this any more tonight. I'd like to call my brother, and then could I take a hot shower and lie down? I can't believe I'm really here. I feel so blessed."

This was a lot to take in, and I heard myself say: "This is all great to hear, Jalecia. But you know what, are you hungry?"

"Yes. I'm starving."

"Then would you rather we call Jackson tomorrow? Or, even the day after that? Give yourself a chance to unwind. And eat?"

"You know you might be right, Ma. I'm tired. I was nervous about seeing you, and seeing my aunties was a wonderful surprise. I think I would like to be rested and more poised when I talk to my brother. I don't want to freak him out."

"I don't think you'll freak him out. Well, maybe a little, but in a good way. I'm feeling a little tired myself, but I'm so happy to see you. I feel like I'm re-meeting the daughter I used to know, and I like her. Love her."

She hugged me again. And I took out all my hidden dishes from the fridge and made her a plate. She didn't even question what it was, but she did say, after she finished it all, that this was the kind of healthy meal they ate where she'd been.

"I'll do the dishes," she said.

"No, you won't. Would you like some hot tea or does that make you feel like an old lady?"

"I would love some hot tea. It's what I've been drinking every night for two months, instead of vodka."

"And, where are your bags?"

"Still on the front porch. I only have one. I'm traveling light."

As soon as B. B. King and Billie Holiday heard the front door open they struggled to get up and beelined to it.

She brought her black duffel inside and stood there for a minute.

"Okay to put it in my old room?"

I just gave her a look.

She took it in and when she came out I set her tea down on the coffee table in front of the couch and she sat down. I sat in Carl's chair. B.B. and Billie were back on their bed, heads sideways, his front leg and paw already resting on her, and their eyes were slowly closing.

"Ma?"

"Yes."

"There were people in there with me who had gone as long as twenty years before they were ever diagnosed. You have no idea how good it feels when you find out what's been making you think in ways that you don't want to. I am grateful to you for finding the right doctors for me, and if I hadn't gone to that place by the ocean, I was probably going to die. I knew it. And most of the folks in there with me knew it about themselves, too."

I took a slow sip of my tea.

All of a sudden B. B. King started snoring and Jalecia looked back by the kitchen door.

"So who is B. B. King's little friend?"

"That's Billie Holiday."

"Of course she is."

And then she looked at me.

"Can I ask you something, Ma?"

"Of course."

"Do you still miss Carl?"

"Of course I still miss him. But the longing for him is less, probably because I know he's never coming back."

"You know, I'm going to be forty-two this year."

"You're telling me like I don't know?"

She chuckled. "Well, I learned more about myself writing in my journal than I ever realized, and I was just wondering about you, Ma."

"What about me?"

"I mean you're sixty-nine years old, and I was just wondering what kinds of things you've come to realize after being alive all these years?"

"Wow," was all I could say. "Honestly?"

"Honestly."

"Well, no one has ever asked me anything quite like this before."

"I didn't mean to put you on the spot. I just want to know what you've learned. How it feels to be old. Or older. If you've come to any conclusions. Are you still hopeful? What do you regret? What is it you want to do with the rest of your life? Would you ever get married again? Simple stuff like that. No pressure. I'm going to get some more tea. Do you want more?"

I just shook my head no.

"So, this is what happens when you start to feel clearheaded, then, huh?"

"To be honest, I've always wondered, but I never thought to ask you. And what I did learn was there's never going to be a total clearing."

That was a lot of questions. But it's not like I hadn't thought about all of this stuff before. And now my daughter wanted me to tell her what I usually kept to myself?

I took a long sip of my tea, pressed the button on the recliner until I was almost looking at the ceiling. I didn't say anything after I heard the microwave beep and Jalecia came back with her steaming hot tea and sat back down on the sofa. She just crossed her legs, and waited, as if I was about to give her a sneak preview into the future, of what she might expect, which was impossible because I could only speak from my experience, not hers. After a few minutes, I wiped the corners of my eyes and took a deep breath.

"Well, for starters, a lot has happened inside me since I lost Carl. I realized that nothing can ever be the way it was. And why should it? I've made a lot of mistakes, but there's no sense beating myself up about it. I've learned from some of them, but maybe not enough of them. But that's okay. There's also a reason why it's called the past. I have learned that it's not too late to start taking better care of myself. I am grateful for having you and Jackson, and for having good friends. I don't have a whole lot of regrets because I've done what I wanted to do the way I wanted to do it. So, to answer your question, I don't feel old. What I do feel is grateful to be alive and in relatively good health. Which is why I'm doing everything I can to slide into home so I leave gold dust behind me."

I couldn't believe I just said that.

But I did.

And I meant it.

And I suppose I needed to say it.

And I suppose my daughter already knew what I was going to say but she just wanted to hear me say it.

I didn't even notice Jalecia had gotten up from the sofa when she walked over, pulled the lever down on the chair, and then pulled me up to a standing position to give me a hard high five. Then we squeezed each other like mother and daughter.

In the morning I woke up in a panic. Even though I was happy to see my daughter and grateful for everything she had said and everything we talked about, my heart was beating so hard I could almost hear it. I lifted the duvet up and slid out of bed in slow motion as I stepped over my slippers, quietly opened my bedroom door, and walked down the hall to her old room. I took a deep breath and slowly opened the door wide enough to see the shape of her feet under the light blue duvet.

I was in the pool when I heard a familiar deep voice say, "Ma, what are you doing out there in the pool this early?"

Jalecia, who was barefoot and still in her pajamas, had turned my phone to face me and there was Jackson wrapped in a black kimono. For some reason he looked Japanese. Although his hair was black and curly, his skin was almond, like his daddy's. I stayed in the water to hide my bosom.

"How are you?" I asked, motioning Jalecia for my towel, which she refused to toss.

"Who's holding the phone, Ma?"

And Jalecia turned it around to face her.

"Hi, Jackson. I'm your long-lost sister, Jalecia, remember me?"

"Hello, sister! I've been hoping to find you, but you found me so now neither of us are lost. You are still beautiful. Like our mom. How are you?"

Jalecia was already crying.

"Give her a second, Jackson! Can't wait to see you all in a few weeks!"

"We'll be waiting for you!"

"Where's Aiko and the twins? Probably sleeping. I forget it's tomorrow night there," I said.

"They're actually in the country with Aiko's mother so I have peace and quiet for the next twelve hours. Jalecia? Are you still there? It's okay, Sis. Really."

Jalecia finished drying her eyes and turned the camera so they could see each other.

"Jackson, I just want you to know how sorry I am for how cruel I was to you all those years when we were growing up. Can you forgive me?"

"What are you talking about? I don't remember you being mean to me. I just remember you were a brat."

"She was a brat!" I yelled as I grabbed my towel and slung it over my shoulders because I didn't want my son to see my breasts.

"Ma, what are you doing in the pool this early?"

"I have to do my laps and it's how I get my day going."

"Good for you! So, tell me how've you been, Jalecia? Can you come with Mom? It would be so nice to see you in person. The twins would love to meet you and so would Aiko. We live in a small apartment, but we'd make sure you're comfortable. This way we could finally have a long overdue family reunion! How's that sound?"

Jalecia looked at me, but Jackson couldn't see her face. She was crying again.

"Hello? Come on. This would be so nice; and Aiko and I were thinking of coming over for Thanksgiving since it's not exactly a holiday here. Akina and Akari would love coming to America! Gobble! Gobble! Say yes. We need this. I need to see you both. I mean what are you doing that's stopping you from flying a mere twelve hours to see your brother and his family?"

"You know what, bro. I would love to sit next to Ma on that plane but I have had some serious health issues and I've made a commitment to doing everything I can to stay on track. I'll tell you this much, I'm just so happy to see your handsome face and to know you're doing well. You sound happy and content, and I will look forward to seeing you and your family for Thanksgiving. How's that sound?"

"That sounds like you're doing what's smart. Okay, big sis. It isn't life threatening, is it?"

"Not as long as I do what I need to do."

"I understand. Could you text me your number so I can FaceTime you? I want you to meet the twins and Aiko!"

"Absolutely. Ma said they are so cute!"

"Yes, they are! Okay, they'll be home from the country in the morning so I'm going to get a solid night's sleep, but thank you for reaching out, Sis. You have made my night. And, Ma, do a few laps for me. See you soon! Love you! And hugs to you both."

And the screen went blank.

Jalecia sat down on the edge of the pool, pulled her pajama bottoms up, and put her feet on the top step.

"I told you it would be okay, didn't I?"

She nodded and smiled.

"It's nice that he doesn't remember the ugly stuff," she said.

"You remember what hurts, but some of us learn how to forgive and some stuff is worth forgetting. So, why don't you come on and get in! I keep this pool at eighty, otherwise I'd never get in here."

"I can't swim and I don't have a bathing suit, but I'll just pull my pajama bottoms up a little higher and stand here and watch you."

"You had swimming lessons when you were a kid, Jalecia."

"And that's the last time I swam because I didn't like to open my eyes."

"Would you like to learn how now? Because if you do, I know a really good swim teacher."

"Maybe. But it's not a high priority, Ma."

I got out.

"Ma! Well, look at you! So, this is what swimming and eating right can do for you? What size are you now?"

"Would you believe a twelve?"

She nodded.

Of course, I was just kidding because this swimsuit was a fourteen. But I still held out my hand and gently pulled my daughter out of the shallow end.

Chapter 30

Kwame hung ten giant gold, silver, and white pearl balloons from the awning in front of the new House of Beauty and Glamour. He also blocked a parking space and put the neon yellow sign there that I had professionally made which read:

GRAND RE-OPENING!

THE NEW LOCATION OF
THE HOUSE OF BEAUTY AND GLAMOUR
Wine/Refreshments
3–5 P.M.
20% Discount on Everything!

I wish I could get rid of the *glamour* part of the name because I don't like it anymore. Plus, glamour is so subjective—a word Korynthia has been using lately that I have discovered applies to a lot of things—but it's now a "brand," which means it's too late to change it after all these years. But then again, I decided that everybody who works here should dress to live up to it.

I looked at the clock.

It was two fifteen. I went back to my office to change into my real clothes in case someone showed up early.

John Legend was singing "Live It Up" on the playlist Kwame had made.

Perfect.

When I returned, I realized I was dressed to the nines, if I did say so myself. And since hips don't lie, mine were still a little too curvy to wear that tight white dress Korynthia had bought me as a store-opening gift, thinking I could "rock it." But you have to know what not to wear. Which was precisely why I had on a red pantsuit with a white silk tee and ruby earrings. I was praying these three-inch silver pumps wouldn't hurt because they were as high as I could go.

The caterers had made a very cool display of finger foods. I slid a triangle turkey sandwich from the tray and put the entire thing in my mouth. On a separate table was sparkling water, tea, and that espresso maker you just use pods for because who needed a mess? I was going to have a bartender but that seemed a little over the top, so I decided to just have wine and use those throwaway clear glasses I got from Target.

Which was why Jalecia wasn't coming.

"Take pictures and if you need me to help in the store while you're in Tokyo I'll be more than happy to, but only on condition that I can get a free makeover."

I promised her.

Fatima, one of my new makeup artists, had already done me up and sprayed my face to set my makeup. I felt pretty.

Kwame and Parker had left about forty-five minutes ago to pick up his mama and Ma, who only agreed to come when she found out Carolyn was coming. Kwame drove my Volvo to pick them up so their wheelchairs would fit. The good news was Kwame had also agreed to house- and dogsit when I finally board that plane to Tokyo next week.

As soon as I heard Nat King Cole singing "Unforgettable," I also heard the chime and saw Kwame and Parker pushing Carolyn and Ma through the front door. Ma was decked out in her silver wig and a red suit and those fake pearls she loved better than the real ones I had given her years ago. She had on gold ballerina slip-ons—I couldn't imagine where she got them. Carolyn looked like she had gained a few needed pounds and she looked nice in her red dress and slip-ons just like Ma's. There was a whole lotta red going on in the House this afternoon.

Before I could say hello, Ma started popping her fingers and said, "Lord, I love me some Nat King Cole!"

"Hello there, foxy ladies!" I said loudly, even though they were the first to arrive.

"We're not deaf, Loretha! But this sure is a classy place you got here. Better than that other ugly one. I like it except this floor looks like a candy apple. But to each his own."

"Hello, Loretha. This place looks like something you see in a magazine. Very classy. And thank you for inviting me."

"You're welcome, Carolyn, and I hope you enjoy yourself this afternoon. You both look lovely."

"We know it," Ma said, as she wheeled herself over to the rack where all the paisley robes were.

"Do these come in petite? You know I've shrunk."

"Yes, they do."

"They are pretty," Carolyn said, rolling next to her, but she acted as if she was afraid to touch them.

"I'll get you one for your birthday," Ma said to her.

"But my birthday was two months ago."

"Then I'll buy it today and you can wait and wear it next year. I just hope I get the family discount. Where is everybody? I thought this shindig started at three?"

"It does, Ma."

"Well, it's almost two thirty."

I walked over and gave them both a kiss on the cheek.

"Do you have any place where we can sit without taking up all this space with our Mercedes-Benzes?"

"Hold on a minute, Geraldine," Carolyn said to Ma. I hadn't heard anybody call her by her real name since I was a kid. "See those nice leather recliners over in that room with the floors that look just like my gray kitty I used to have?"

"Those are for makeovers," I said.

"What kind of makeovers?" Ma asked.

"I have two wonderful makeup artists who just put a little something extra on your face to make you look prettier."

They looked at each other.

"Then we want to sit in those chairs. Come on, Carolyn, get your lazy behind up. You know you can make it over there. You've been doing real good."

They both stood up and locked their wheelchairs, then locked arms and walked over toward the beauty room.

"Watch your step now, mademoiselles!" Kwame said.

They both just waved their hands in the air and the two makeup artists, Fatima and Lucia, who had been waiting in our relaxation room in the back, came from behind the curtains and introduced themselves.

Fatima, who could be Lupita Nyong'o's twin, had a shaved head and was six feet tall. She always wore African beads and went barefoot.

"Are you from Africa?" Ma asked her.

"I believe we all are," she said. "But yes, I'm from Senegal."

"And I'm Cuban," Lucia said.

"You don't look Mexican," Carolyn said.

"She's from Cuba, Carolyn. Where Castro was a dictator."

"Oh, where the folks came on boats and went to Miami."

"So what look are you two seeking?"

"I'm seeking sexy and seventy," Ma said, though I was trying to pretend like I wasn't listening.

"I just want to feel like I'm out on a date," Carolyn said.

"I'm your date, honey!" Ma said and started laughing. "How long will this take, because we want to look good by the time the guests get here."

"It depends on how beautiful you want to look," Fatima said and touched Ma's cheeks. "You have beautiful cheekbones, ma'am."

"Why thank you. And take as long as you need because we might get you some new customers if you do us justice!"

"How much will this cost?" Carolyn asked.

"Don't worry about it," Ma said. "My credit is good here."

"Okay, ladies, I'm going to put these paper cloths across your chests so we don't get any makeup on your beautiful dresses, then we're going to lean the chairs back and we just want you to close your eyes and relax."

"I love this already," Ma said.

"I feel like we're in a movie," Carolyn said.

"Then roll 'em," Ma said and closed her eyes.

Like clockwork, at two forty-five my girls arrived dressed to kill. All except Sadie, who had her wife call to tell us she had laryngitis and wouldn't be able to make it. But Sadie was never that keen on makeup or getting gussied up anyway, so it was okay. And Lucky, who was now about fifty pounds lighter, wore a belted purple dress that hung on her like a beautiful drape. I was so proud of her. She had told me that of course Joe was not coming and Ko had told me Henry, who had been a big help, opted to leave this day for the ladies, but it was really because the NBA playoffs were on and he had invited his boys over.

We turned the door chime off because people were coming in like everything was free or something. I couldn't believe it when I saw Peggy walk in. She looked good. Like she had turned to Jesus or something. She walked straight over to me and said, "Hello, Loretha.

Thank you for inviting me. Congratulations on your new place, even though I never saw the other one. You look good in that red. Can I give you a hug?"

And I hugged her without answering and whispered in her ear, "Thank you for everything you did for my daughter. And I'm sorry for being so ungrateful."

She pushed me away and then whispered in my ear, "You had a right not to trust me, but I was going through a hard time myself and Jalecia made me feel like I was finally responsible for somebody. But we're here now and she's good, so it's all good, okay?"

And then we stepped away and looked at each other and smiled.

"If you would like to pick out something you might like, anything, just bring it to the counter. And thank you for coming."

"Can I get one of those girls to put some makeup on me?"

There was a line forming but I said, "Yes. I'll see to it that you get cuts."

"Thank you, Loretha," she said and walked over and took a seat. When I saw the various ages and ethnicities waiting, it was clear that adding makeup artists was a damn good idea.

I started waving when I saw Cinnamon—who had left Jonas and the babies at home, thank you, Jesus—and she was dressed like she was going on an audition. But right behind her was Odessa, who, unless I was seeing things, had a man by her side. I could not believe it when right behind them was my fine swim teacher. I suspected every woman in the place—white, black, Latino, and Asian—would be drooling over him, since he was now the tallest and sexiest of the four men here. I hoped Kwame wouldn't lay eyes on him with Parker around!

Odessa walked over to me and said, "Sis, I would like you to meet a good friend of mine. Derrick, this, of course, is my twin sister, Loretha. I told you it would be a classy beauty supply shop, didn't I?"

He was good-looking and looked like he used to box, but he took my hand and kissed it and said, "This is very nice indeed. Odessa has also told me so many wonderful things about you, I'm glad to finally meet you."

Finally?

"I've heard a lot about you, too, Derrick, and hope the three of us can have dinner sometime in the near future."

"You can count on it," he said, and Odessa was smiling from inside, which I had not ever seen before.

Cinnamon gave me a kiss and whispered in my ear: "He's the handyman who has apparently come in very handy. And by the way, Grandma, Ma has come by to see us and she looks and sounds so good. Just so you know, I'm not getting an audition on *The Voice* because my singing isn't up to snuff, but I'm not quitting because I like working there. This is just beautiful, and now, let me find something I can't afford."

What an opening. And what a crowd. People were buying all kinds of hair and makeup and skincare products, even jewelry. The food and drinks were being devoured. The music was pitch perfect and folks were complimenting how refreshing it was to come to a beauty supply so organized that you didn't have to hunt for things.

Everybody kept asking Korynthia if she was a senior model and she lied and said yes, which prompted her to remind me and Lucky that we'd better be in hip-hop class tomorrow. But I told her I couldn't make it because I was going to be at my favorite spa getting a hot stone massage, a pedicure, and an age-defying facial to celebrate my opening.

She gave me a thumbs-up.

Moments later, in walked Serenity and Roxie, the two young women I had sold the L.A. House to. They had the same look children have on Christmas morning when they look under the tree at all the gifts. They clearly were not expecting the store to look this way, which made me feel good. They waved and walked through the crowd, and I clapped my hands loudly and shouted to everyone:

"Excuse me, everybody! Attention please! I want you all to meet the new owners of the L.A. House of Beauty: Serenity and Roxie!"

Everybody applauded.

The two girls smiled.

"Thank you, Mrs. Curry!" Serenity said to me as we walked toward the makeup. "We are completely and unequivocally dumbfounded! We can't imagine what it's going to take for us to get our house in the same zone as this. It is just so cool. The floors alone! But we can afford concrete!"

"Don't you young ladies worry. You're going to be just fine."

"We brought you a gift!"

And Roxie stuck her hand inside the large fuchsia shopping bag she carried and whipped out what looked like a pie.

"It's sweet potato. We made it! For you! And we hope you like it!"

"Why thank you. I will do my best, but not until later as I'm a little stuffed."

"Then you can set this one out because we made two! The other one's in the bag for you to take home!"

I hugged them both. "Thank you. Now please look around, mingle, and don't even think about paying for anything."

And off they went.

Peggy gently squeezed my shoulder. "What a nice crowd. Look at all the folks with bags. I'll definitely be back, Loretha. Also, I would really like to visit Jalecia. And you sometimes."

"That would be just fine," I said. "I'm sure Jalecia would love to see you. You're still family."

"Look at us," Ma said, making her way over with Carolyn. "Tell me we're not sexy!"

"And we know it," Carolyn said.

"I'm not ready to go yet, Carolyn. You think I went through all

Chapter 31

Of course I overpacked.

I needed to buy things for the twins after Jackson tried to weigh them so I could figure out what U.S. size to buy even though he and Aiko insisted it wasn't necessary. Of course it was necessary. I wanted them to know that this black woman they did not know had come bearing gifts and hugs and hopefully tickles. And if I get to meet their other grandmother, maybe Aiko will be able to tell them I'm the same as her.

I was excited and nervous about being gone for six days and really wished I could stay longer. I didn't want my grandbabies to forget me, which was why I'd already decided I'm not going to go another year without seeing them.

I said goodbye to Jalecia and gave her my sweet potato pie to share with the people in the house where she's living.

"Hug my brother for me, Ma, and please FaceTime me if we can figure out the right time difference."

"I will. And you're good?"

"I am very good. I spent the night with my grandbabies."

"What? I thought you couldn't . . ."

"Ma, I tried to explain that it's not a jail. Anyway, they are just hilarious and so cute and they even slept with me."

"I'm looking forward to sleeping next to mine, too!" I said, trying not to cry.

But I did.

And she hugged me.

And I hugged her back.

Odessa insisted on driving me to the airport.

She was an hour early.

"You don't want me to order you as my Uber?"

"Come on, Loretha."

After she opened the trunk and picked up one of my three bags, I grabbed her by the arm.

"Wait a minute. I don't want to feel like a customer!"

She just laughed, put the other two in the trunk, and I could tell she was about to open the back door for me, but I got in the front seat.

"So," she said. "Before you ask, I'll just tell you. I am not in love, but I am loving his company."

"Who are you talking about?"

"Don't play that silly game with me, Loretha. His name is Derrick. You might want to remember it."

And she started laughing.

"So, what's it like?"

"What's what like?"

"The sex."

"I prefer it."

And then we both started laughing, which we seem to be getting used to.

"I hope you get to have it again one day, Lo. Carl would want you to, we all agree."

"Who is *we*?"

"Ma, all your girlfriends, and your daughter."

"Did you all get together and talk about my sex life without me?"

"Maybe."

"Anyway, I'll just say this: you've come full circle and it makes me very happy. Now step on it! We only have until tomorrow to get to the airport since you got here yesterday."

And we started laughing again.

"I hope you enjoy seeing my nephew. And I hope those little ones are growing into their looks."

"Watch yourself now, O. They are cuter than we were at this age."

And with that we were quiet for a few minutes.

"I'm also happy Jalecia is doing so well. You know I knew depression was her issue all along."

"And how would you know that, Odessa?"

"Because she's not the only one in the family who's been struggling with it."

I turned to look at her. "You?"

"Yes, me. I wasn't born mean, Lo. But it was the reason why my husband left me. Little did I know. And not to sound like a hypocrite but it was the reason I turned my life over to God. Anyway, back then there was no name for my moods and when I was finally diagnosed, it wasn't something you just told everybody. So I didn't. It's only been the past nine or ten months that I finally found the right doctor and was prescribed the right medication."

"Why didn't you at least tell me, Odessa?"

"Because I didn't want you to feel sorry for me."

"Sorry?"

"Or be angry at me."

I squeezed her thigh.

"I think we're all finally trying to set sail, Odessa; and it feels like the wind is blowing in our favor."

And we didn't say another word until she pulled up in front of Japan Airlines and I insisted that the skycap take all the bags out and carry them inside.

My sister and I hugged each other hard.

And kissed each other on both cheeks.

"Have a safe trip," she said. "And when you come back I hope you can say something in Japanese."

It is tomorrow morning in Tokyo.

Of course, the flight attendants are all Japanese and their skin is dewy, their lips are red, and they're all pretty and short. I want to see how they reach to help you with carry-ons, but I won't be staring. Yes I will. I was still five-seven when I had my last physical and I've been wondering when I was going to start shrinking. This plane feels like I'm in one of those space movies where everything looks like it's in the future. I could be on my way to the moon.

I do not have a carry-on and am asleep before we take off.

When I wake up, I don't know where I am. I press the Call button. I eat the savory teriyaki beef I ordered along with a cup of hot water and lemon, something I would never drink at home but I might start. Dessert? No thank you, but thank you. I am now wide awake, but most people here in business class have their black eye masks on. I have no idea when I should try to go back to sleep since it'll be afternoon when I get to Tokyo. But I would love a cup of coffee so I order one, and it is much better than Starbucks.

I am excited and anxious, but I don't want to watch a movie on the iPad that Kwame loaded for me. I remember Ma's instructions to read whatever surprising things she had put in her yellow, pink, and three blue envelopes. I am prepared for anything.

I open the yellow one: it is an expired 20 percent off coupon for Bed Bath & Beyond. I just shake my head.

The pink one, which she had handwritten, says: *You still have room for love.*

What?

The first blue one is a picture of a gorgeous and sexy seventy-year-old model, Maye Musk, that says: *I am what I make up.* I didn't get it.

The second blue one: *Don't apologize for living. Have some damn fun.*

The last blue one is a fortune from a fortune cookie that looks like she's had for years: *Listen to your mom.*

That woman.

In the days leading up to my trip, I'd been making a list of everything I would love to be able to do and see in the short time I'm in Tokyo, even though Jackson told me he had quite a few must-see-and-dos. I had to remind him that technically I was only going to have five days of daylight hours there. There were things I wish I could see that I won't be able to, like those plum and peach blossoms, because I had missed spring and read that in Japan the seasons are like clockwork. So, I narrowed it down to this:

1. Ginza. The famous shopping area where they close the streets to traffic on Sunday, even though I have a problem with crowds.
2. Mt. Fuji.
3. That Meiji Shrine, which everybody who has ever been there swears is a must-see. According to the descriptions, they say it will feel like a mystical forest, but so long as it doesn't make me feel like Judy Garland in *The Wizard of Oz*, I'll be okay. I should put this on the bottom of my list because most shrines scare me, especially the ones in New York City.
4. Hot springs. No. I forgot. We have one in Palm Springs, which is only a two-hour drive. And it's not cheap.

5. The NTT Docomo Yoyogi Building. One of the tallest skyscrapers that looks like the Empire State Building, which I have not seen in almost thirty years.
6. The statue of that dog Hachikō, so I can show the picture to B. B. King and Billie Holiday when I get home!
7. Ride that bullet train. But not that Hello Kitty one. If at all possible. I just want to know what it feels like to go two hundred miles an hour on a track. But you couldn't pay me to do this on Amtrak.
8. Disneyland. If I just have to, but this is where you take your grandchildren, especially when they can't really talk that much.
9. Walk up and down the busy and quiet streets, but especially Shinjuku Gyo-en, the beautiful and serene Japanese garden right in the middle of the city.
10. I would love to see an American movie with Japanese subtitles. Jackson said in Japan they do not walk out of the theater until the very last credit to show respect to everyone who helped make the film. He said when he saw *Black Panther,* it took almost three hours before they were able to leave.

This would be enough for about fifteen days, but I will not be heartbroken if I only get to do or see three or four of them. I came here to spend time with my son and his family even though he's the one who told me to make a list of everything I wanted to see.

But he is on the top of this list.

Jackson does not have a car because he said they were unnecessary, which was why I begged him not to bother coming to meet me. It's over an hour's drive but he told me not to take a taxi because it was "cost prohibitive." I told him I didn't care but I was not getting on any bus with three bags, so when I found out they had Uber, I took it, which was a van that I had to share with four other people. It only cost about a million U.S. dollars to get to their apartment in Jiyūgaoka, which, according to Google, is an "upscale and trendy neighborhood." I was more curious where the ghetto might be in Tokyo. And if they had one, I wanted to see it.

We passed Disneyland.

When we got closer to the actual city, I spotted what looked like the Empire State Building crammed between a million other skyscrapers that were even taller. For a minute I thought that maybe I was heading into Manhattan, but I knew it was Tokyo because I was too tired, and for me it was still yesterday.

Tokyo is no doubt beautiful. But I knew that before I came. I had googled everywhere I didn't really care if I ever saw. And when the Uber van finally stopped in front of my son's two-level apartment, there was my tall chocolate son standing close to the curb with his arms crossed next to a yellow gingko tree. My friends in the van said goodbye in their native languages and waved to Jackson, who waved back and said something in Japanese. He helped the driver set my bags on the sidewalk.

Then he stared at me a few long seconds, kissed me on both cheeks, and hugged me like he hadn't seen me in a hundred years.

"Hello, Ma," he said, and sounded like he did before his voice changed. "You look prettier in person than you do on FaceTime! Was your trip okay?"

"Do I look like I'm alive?" I asked, and pushed him with all the love in my tired hips. And then I hugged him again like I hadn't seen him in a hundred years.

"So this is home," I said.

"For now."

"What?"

"I'll tell you later."

He grabbed the two big pieces of luggage and, as I picked up the other one, he got a stern look on his face and said, "Absolutely not. I'll come back and get it. It's safe right there."

So I walked up the stairs. When he pushed open the door, he took his shoes off and I did, too, and put them right next to two pairs of Hello Kitty tennis shoes and a pair of cool orange sneakers I knew had to be Aiko's.

"Welcome to Tokyo!" I heard and when I looked up another level of stairs, standing there were the twins who already looked to be about three feet, with long black hair, and their mother who was even prettier in person. By the time I got to the top step I realized the twins looked just like Aiko. I felt bad for thinking they weren't that cute, but we all grow into our looks. I was nothing to scream about when I was their age.

"Hello, Nana!" they said simultaneously and in perfect English.

When I got to the top landing I was crushed by hugs around my hips and upper arms and I just said, "Hello, daughter and granddaughters!"

"Finally, I get to meet my other mother in person!"

"Maybe you and Jackson should get married again while I'm here and I'll give him away!"

She laughed. And I hugged her while the girls took me by the hands and led me up more stairs.

What a crib, as the young folks say. It looked like an ad for a magazine, except I couldn't help but notice that every piece of furniture was low, which was why when I went to sit down I got a catch in my back. And over the next few days I would wonder if Jackson got tired of ducking under the doorways or if he ever missed. When they took me down the hall to my room, the bed was on the floor. Everything was low. But I liked it.

"Ma," Jackson said, ducking his head in the doorway. "Do you need to lie down for a bit? If so, I can close the door so the girls won't bother you."

But it was too late, they had run around him, hopped on my bed, patted it, and said "sweep," which was exactly what we did. For an hour. When I opened my eyes they were staring at me. "Heyyo, Nana," they said at the same time, and then pulled me out of bed.

"Wait!" I said, and they stopped dead in their tracks.

"Nana brought something for you."

"Legos?"

"Nikes?"

I just shook my head while laughing because for some stupid reason I wasn't expecting them to even know what these things were! I know they're bilingual, but Lord have mercy!

I walked over and got the bag with all of the things I'd bought and took the girls out into whatever room this was, which was when I heard Jackson say something to Aiko in Japanese. She said something back to him in Japanese, then turned to me.

"Jackson wondered if it would be okay to take you out for dinner, but I said I would much prefer to prepare a traditional Japanese meal on your first night. How does that sound, Ma?"

She just called me *Ma*. I loved it.

"I would love to taste your cooking, sweetie."

"Sweetie!" the girls said simultaneously. "Sweetie!"

"I can help."

"You can't because I won't let you. Would you like some hot tea or sake?"

"Tea," Jackson said.

"How long have you been speaking Japanese, Jackson?"

"I had to learn when I got my first job here. I took a crash course, but when everybody else is speaking it, you catch on faster. I love this language."

I gave him a thumbs-up, and the girls did the same.

They had already opened the luggage and started pulling out all the stuff I shouldn't have bought them and squealing. They ran over and hugged me like they might not ever see me again and then grabbed me by the hand and pulled me upstairs where the kitchen and dining room were. Things are different in Japan.

And while the girls played, Aiko told me about her family and I told her about mine.

She told me why she fell in love with my son.

And he told me why he fell in love with her.

She prepared something amazing that I'd never tasted in a Japanese restaurant in America before.

"So, you have your tourist list then?" Jackson asked.

"I do."

"Throw it away. We know the best spots for tourists."

"What about black people?"

"We aw bwack!" the girls said at the same time.

"And Japanese," they said.

I was tired again, and after I was given a tutorial on how to turn on the shower, I realized I should've asked how to flush the toilet, which looked like a rectangular computer screen on top of the tank. I just pressed a few controls and was surprised when the seat started heating up. In fact, I actually jumped up and started laughing because I remembered growing up when Ma used to accuse me of being hot in the ass. I thought I had gotten it back!

In the morning, Aiko took the girls to what I assumed was preschool. Jackson said, "Since we don't have you for long, I would first like to take you to Shinjuku Gy-oen, because there we can talk and we may not have this kind of peace for the rest of your short visit, okay?"

And so we did.

I thought I was in an enchanted Japanese forest full of lush beautiful trees and flowers and ponds.

Jackson said, "Can you sit on the grass okay, Ma?"

I just looked at him.

"Do I look handicapped?"

"No. In fact, you look quite healthy."

And then he reached inside his backpack and took out a kind of black tarp like I'd seen other people doing. He spread it out on the grass and we sat down and just looked at the pond and the trees. High above the trees I saw the Empire State Building again.

"So," he said. "I have some good news."

"I'm all ears."

"I'm coming home."

"What do you mean you're coming home? I thought you were happily married, Jackson."

"I am. We are. And Aiko's mom is coming, too. Can't leave her here or she'd be all alone."

I could not wipe the smile off my face.

"Are you serious? You mean you're coming home to live?"

He smiled.

"I love Japan. But I have been away from my family long enough. I want the girls to grow up in America. Pasadena. I miss you and I want to get to know Jalecia and see Grandma and all of my pretend aunties again. I just want to live in a more diverse country. By the look on your face I know I've shocked you."

I nodded yes.

"And this is definitely for sure?"

He nodded yes.

Then I started clapping.

"How soon?"

"Spring. So we'll have to miss this Thanksgiving but I hope you won't be too disappointed since we'll be back for good."

"I was not expecting you to tell me anything like this, Jackson. But gobble gobble!"

And instead of a hug, I gave him a hard high five!

For the next four days we did #1, #2, #6, #7, and #9, and thank God we did not have to do Disneyland.

On my last day, I met Aiko's mother, who spoke very little English. She is sixty-five but looks fifty. Her skin looks like gold satin. Maybe she should bring some of this water with her when she moves to Pasadena.

With all this good news, as much as I enjoyed seeing my son and my daughter-in-law and my grandchildren, I was ready to go home.

Not because I was bored. I was exhausted. And one thing had become clear: I'm too old to jet set.

I also want to sleep in my big bed with the thick mattress and my fluffy duvet.

I want to eat American food.

I want to be able to read the signs.

I want to see some black people. Some Mexican people. Some Chinese people. Some white people.

I want to see some tall people.

And there are too many people in Tokyo.

Too many cars.

And again: Tokyo is beautiful. But so is Pasadena.

And knowing that my son and his family will soon be living in America, next time *I'll* play tour guide. And I'll even take Akina and Akari to the real Disneyland.

Chapter 32

Everybody who could drive offered to pick me up. But I didn't want to talk since it was two o'clock in the morning, so, of course, I Ubered home. At the rate I'm going, I may never drive again.

At first B. B. King and Billie Holiday pretended like they didn't recognize me when I walked in the front door. But then they decided it wasn't worth being nasty just because I went on vacation and realized it would be in everybody's best interest if they had an attitude adjustment, which was why B.B. almost knocked poor Billie against the oven to get over to me first. I couldn't tell if the sound he was making was joy or "where the hell have you been and you could've told us you were going on vacation," but apparently they decided they were grateful I was back and licked both of my hands.

When I heard Kwame come out of Jalecia's room, he looked a year older. "Mama-Lo," he said, and wrapped his long arms around me. "Welcome home! But I wish you would've let me pick you up! Jackson said you had a great time, but you didn't get a chance to do as much as you wanted to."

"I did plenty. Even went on a train that did two hundred miles an hour."

"Get out. That is so unnecessary. This is just one reason why I'm afraid of foreign countries," he said.

I did not say another word.

I was just glad to be home.

I forgot to buy souvenirs.

When Jalecia asked, "Ma, you didn't bring back one thing to prove you even went to Tokyo?"

"Well, yes," I said.

"Then where is it?"

"Well, Jackson is bringing his adorable little girls and wife and his mother-in-law back home next spring for good. And I'm sure he'll bring a few souvenirs. How's that?"

"Seriously, Ma? Jackson is really coming back home?"

"Yes, he is. Just like the rest of us."

When I walked into Korynthia's hip-hop class, I thought I was seeing things. First of all, Henry was here. So were Lucky and Joe. I knew none of them had an ounce of rhythm, but I gave them credit for coming. There were a lot of new bodies and I looked around but didn't see my dancing buddy James, who usually beat me here. I was not only disappointed, but also a little worried.

"Okay, everybody, let's warm these bodies up!" Ko said and pressed Play. I wasn't sure who this singer was, but my arms started swaying the way they were supposed to. Lucky, who had on black leggings with a flared skirt over them, waved to me, but Joe, who was in sweats and a baggy sweatshirt, was totally engrossed, like he meant business.

I waved back to Lucky and gave her a thumbs-up.

"Do I get a thumbs-up, too, Miss Loretha?" I heard James ask, and when I turned to my left he looked a tad more handsome today than I remembered in the week I'd been gone.

I gave him a thumbs-up.

"We missed you," he said.

"We?"

"Me."

"Really?"

"Really," he said. "Heard you went to Tokyo."

And when we heard what everybody knew were the first few beats to "My Prerogative" by Bobby Brown, James and I started rocking our hips back and forth.

"I did."

"If you don't mind my asking, was it for business or pleasure?"

"Why?" I asked, but not snarky, as Korynthia would say.

"Curious minds would just like to know."

"Pleasure."

"Did you have fun?"

"James and Loretha, if you would prefer to have a tête-à-tête instead of making your hips go around the world, would you mind taking it out into the hallway?"

We tried not to laugh and moved a little farther apart so we would not be tempted to have another tête-à-tête, and after swaying and swirling and reaching and rocking to the beat of "Get Ur Freak On" by Miss Missy Elliott, Korynthia finally said, "Okay, let's cool it down." And when we saw her slowly swaying her hips back and forth and then heard her singing into the microphone along with Tina: "Left a good job in the city, working for the man every night and day, and I never lost one minute of sleepin'," James and I were already oscillating because everybody in here knew this was Korynthia's favorite mix. Then she said, "Okay everybody, let's take it nice and easy now. Tina's gonna finish cooling you off, and all you fellas in here don't take these lyrics personally because it's the beat that's important, so here we go now: 'All the men come in these places, and the men are all the same. . . .'"

"Great class, everybody!" Korynthia yelled and ruined the entire mood. "Have a great day! Live life like you mean it!"

I looked over at James.

And he was looking at me.

I smiled at him.

And he smiled back.

I picked my towel up and he picked his up, too.

I wiped my face.

And he wiped his, too.

"Have you cooled down already?" I asked.

And he said, "No."

"So, James. Can I ask you something?"

"Anything, as long as it's personal."

"Would you like to have a cup of coffee with me?"

He smiled at me again.

"Absolutely. You must've been reading my mind."

ACKNOWLEDGMENTS

Although you write alone, there are people whose support, confidence, and faith in the story you're telling are always floating in the room. They are my always and forever smart and intuitive agents, Molly Friedrich and Lucy Carson, and my patient, thoughtful, and brilliant editor, Hilary Teeman, who helped me navigate my way in the telling of this story. I am also grateful to my BFFs since forever, Valari and Gilda, for my not having to explain why I "couldn't talk" or "couldn't go", and last but not least, my son, Solomon, who continues to make me proud and feel even more blessed, for his unwavering support, love, and pride in his Mama (but especially for his purple sweet potato, almond milk, and ginger smoothies).

And we rock on.

ABOUT THE AUTHOR

TERRY MCMILLAN is the #1 *New York Times* bestselling author of *Waiting to Exhale, How Stella Got Her Groove Back, A Day Late and a Dollar Short,* and *The Interruption of Everything,* and the editor of *Breaking Ice: An Anthology of Contemporary African-American Fiction.* Each of McMillan's nine previous novels was a *New York Times* bestseller, and four have been made into movies: *Waiting to Exhale, How Stella Got Her Groove Back, Disappearing Acts,* and *A Day Late and a Dollar Short.* She lives in California.

TERRYMCMILLAN.COM

TWITTER: @MSTERRYMCMILLAN

ABOUT THE TYPE

This book was set in Albertina, a typeface created by Dutch calligrapher and designer Chris Brand (1921–98). Brand's original drawings, based on calligraphic principles, were modified considerably to conform to the technological limitations of typesetting in the early 1960s. The development of digital technology later allowed Frank E. Blokland (b. 1959) of the Dutch Type Library to restore the typeface to its creator's original intentions.

FREE PUBLIC LIBRARY UNION, NEW JERSEY
3 9549 00544 2554